LOVE IS NEVER EASY

<u>*Other novels by P.L. Hampton*</u>

Picking Chrysanthemum

LOVE IS NEVER EASY

A Love Story

P. L. Hampton

iUniverse, Inc.
New York Lincoln Shanghai

Love is Never Easy
A Love Story

iUniverse books may be ordered through booksellers or by contacting:

iUniverse
2021 Pine Lake Road, Suite 100
Lincoln, NE 68512
www.iuniverse.com
1-800-Authors (1-800-288-4677)

ISBN-13: 978-0-595-35724-6 (pbk)
ISBN-13: 978-0-595-80201-2 (ebk)
ISBN-10: 0-595-35724-5 (pbk)
ISBN-10: 0-595-80201-X (ebk)

Printed in the United States of America

This novel is dedicated to my Mom and Pops, Patricia and Preston Hampton. I want to thank the two of you for all the time, effort, and patience both of you devoted towards my growth as a man and human being.

Contents

Acknowledgments

Once again I have to thank my wife, Tonya. You are my muse. Your insightful thoughts and suggestion always bring out the best in me. I hope I have risen to the challenge. Also, I would like to thank my father, who contributed a great deal to this book with his helpful insight as well. Pops, your suggestions were priceless. Mom, I love you for your infinite wisdom. I have to thank my editor Joanne Shepard. Joanne, you were vital to the shaping and molding of this novel. I must also thank the ladies of H.I.P.S. book club and my book club Impressions, particularly Felicia Brown, for supporting me and making me understand the importance of "keeping it real."

Of course, I cannot forget my boys across the nation in various locales like Seattle, Los Angeles, San Francisco, Anchorage, Columbus, Atlanta, Chicago, Minneapolis, Cincinnati, Oakland, Houston, New York, Phoenix and Mount Pleasant, Michigan.

I want to thank Blanche Richardson at Marcus Books in Oakland for her words of advice, "Stop talking about writing a book and write a book." I've taken your advice and have not looked back since.

I want to give special thanks to Ms. Charlene Lacro-Nelson, my mathematics teacher at Rainier Beach High in Seattle. If it was not for her guidance, belief in me, and constant vigilance I doubt I would have seen the importance of investing in my future.

Lastly, I want to thank the countless individuals who have truly supported me in this endeavor. I feel fortunate to have met each one of you as I journey down this road called life. I want to say thank you to; Steve, John and Tracy, Kenny and Amber, EJ, Naomi "Lou-Lou", Clareen, Dana, Miquel, Stephen and Shawn, Melanie and Dewayne, Yvonne Moore and last but definitely not least my good friends Byron and Twanya Hill.

Looking For Love in All the Wrong Places

Ivy

My name is Ivy Martin.

I am a thirty-six year old single black female born and raised in Minnesota. There are not many black folks up here in "The Great White North." Yet there definitely are more of us than people think. I have never been married and I have no kids. Of course, I would love to be married and have kids at this point in my life but I refuse to just settle for any ole' body. I want Mr. Right not Mr. Second Best, and I am fully content on being single until I find such a man. I admit I get lonely at times, but I have plenty of girlfriends to keep me company. Of course, they cannot take the place of a man but I don't need a man to make me feel good about myself. I'm looking for a man to compliment me—not complete me. I deserve to be treated like a queen. I won't settle for nothing less.

I will admit that I do yearn to have children. There are times I can hear my biological clock ticking. I'm thirty-six years old. I don't want to be too old to enjoy certain things with my child. I also don't want to take my child to school and my son or daughter has to constantly explain to his or her friends that I am their mother and not their grandmother. I have considered adopting, but I have always dreamed of raising a child of my own in a traditional home, one with a mother and a father. Despite national statistics and magazine articles proclaiming the sorry state of romance for black women, I refuse to believe the hype that states it is difficult or next to impossible for me as a black woman to enjoy my life with a wonderful black man. Although, I readily admit life does get lonely for a single black woman—particularly in Minnesota.

I grew up on Minneapolis' Southside. I am the product of two hard working parents—Russell and Erma Martin. I have two sisters, Teresa and Cynthia. I am the oldest. I went to De La Salle High where upon graduation I went to Howard University and then on to Howard Law School in Washington D.C. After law school I returned home to Minneapolis, so I could be close to my family. I joined a regional law firm, Grimble & Kline, where I was made associate and placed on the partner track.

Before going to Howard my world consisted primarily of Minneapolis. There were the occasional trips to Iowa to watch the Drake relays as well as the annual trip to Wisconsin Dells but that was about it. Of course, I cannot forget the family trips to Chicago for the Taste and Lord knows I will never forget the sole trip we took to Disneyland. However, I do not consider being cooped up in the back of a station wagon with my two sistahs for thirty-six hours a good-time. Besides that I never really saw too much of the world outside of Minneapolis until I attended Howard.

Going off to college as well as being a lawyer at Grimble & Kline changed my perspective of the world outside of the Twin Cities. I saw people and places I had only imagined. However, the only problem with my job was that on many occasions I was too busy conducting business to truly enjoy the sights of a specific city. Having to see a city through taxicab windows and from restaurant tables while negotiating with opposing counsel is not exactly my idea of fun. Still, what I did see broadened my horizons on life and people in general. If I were really intrigued by a city, my girlfriends and I would spend a weekend there to really get the flavor of the place. In that regards my job has done wonders for me. Nevertheless, my job is also a curse when it comes to romance.

Many men find my job intimidating. For starters let me say, it is not like the pool of eligible black men in Minnesota is large to begin with. The fact many black men are behind bars, gay or interracially dating has made the pickings even slimmer. Not to mention, my profession and pay makes finding a good man even harder. It is not like I am boojie or high maintenance and need a man who is making at least as much money as I am to be happy. It is not like that at all. I consider myself to be down to earth. I don't think I am better than anyone else. I've dated just about as many blue-collar brothas as I have professionals. I have even dated men still living at home with their mamas. Despite that, men still feel threatened when they see a successful black woman with her own car, her own house, and her own money.

So, where does that leave me?

Mainly with the wannabes who grew up in suburbia and only date me so they can say they dated at least one sistah in their life. Or I'm left with those brothas, so, stuck on themselves that they think they are God's gift to women. In the legal profession you run across plenty of brothas like that. You know those brothas whose egos have expanded well beyond their shoe size. These brothas have reached some level of success in their lives and believe they're above all "those other niggas" as one brotha put it to me. They're always talking about their jobs, their cars and who they know. When they find a woman who has a mind of her own and does not readily agree with them, they feel threatened. Usually in the end, these fools go out and add a white girl to their trophy case to go along with the nice car and the big house. I know that may sound harsh but it is true.

Sadly enough, I run into plenty of these types of men. There are also the brothas who use the excuses that black women are nothing more than gold diggers, too lazy, too high maintenance or too outspoken as a reason to sleep with the first hoochie mama, white or black, that walks their way.

Brothas kill me…. They are always complaining about sistahs being nothing more than gold diggers looking for a man to take care of them. Yet, when they meet an independent woman who has a mind of her own, their main complaint becomes, "You don't need me."

And men have the nerve to say women don't know what we want!

I've done the club scene. I've heard all the pathetic lines that any one man can give. From what's your sign? To do you have any kids? I even had one brotha tell me he was a drug dealer as if I was supposed to be impressed. Any woman who falls for a line like that should not be allowed to procreate. As if the lines guys give are not bad enough, I want to know what is up with the pimp daddy outfits brothas wear nowadays. I mean these cat daddies come up in the clubs with these hot pink, yellow and turquoise suits with matching brims and alligator shoes thinking they are killing it…. What is that?

For the brothas who dare to dress this way, I think you might have a better chance of getting a lady if you bought a new wardrobe and left the pimp daddy clothes at home or more appropriately saved them for Halloween.

Now, after striking out at the club I tried my hand at online dating in hopes of meeting a decent brotha. I was a little leery to the prospect of sitting in front of my computer chatting with someone who possibly turned out to be a psychopath but I figured, "What the hell!" It couldn't be any worse than if I had taken some of the fools I had met in the club home. At first chatting online was fun and mysterious. It was sort of like playing a game of "guess who?" The only problem with online dating was I continuously met men who outright lied about themselves or who turned out to be married. Online a person can pretend to be anybody.

Of course, there was the occasional freak in the crowd who emailed me a picture of them-self buttnaked. These guys I usually ceased cyber chatting with after a close inspection of the goods. There was one brotha I had to meet after inspecting his photograph. His name was Curtis. Let's just say, if Curtis were a value meal at Mickey Ds he would definitely be a super size. I initially agreed to go out on a date with Curtis because I was curious to know if he was really packing as his picture suggested…. Needless to say, his photograph was not digitally enhanced. For a while there, Curtis played the role of maintenance man. Whenever I was in the need, he would drag that monster over and make sure all my body parts functioned properly. However, even the monster in between Curtis' legs could not make up for the fact we had nothing in common. So, we hooked up a few times before I got tired of him and stopped calling. Good sex without something of substance behind it can only last for so long. Sex simply unto itself does not equate to love.

After a while, I gave up on the online dating thing. I found the real love affair I was cultivating was the one with my computer. All too often, I found myself rushing home so I could frantically check my email. I was spending so much time in front of my computer; I began to neglect other facets of my life. When I realized this, I let the idea of "computer love" fall to the wayside. Besides, in a city like Minneapolis the pickings are too slim to have any success at meeting a black man online. For a black woman, such as myself, online dating is best attempted in a larger city preferably with a larger African American population.

Hell! I even went as far as trying those three minute dating services where you pay a fee to go to a bar and sit around with a bunch of other women while a group of men is given three minutes to circulate from one woman to the next. I tried it once and will never do it again. First of all three minutes is never enough time to make a personal connection. Second of all, I felt like I was apart of an assembly line. Then to top it all off there were no black men. In the end I felt used. The whole experience felt like the dating service had taken advantage of my loneliness in order to turn a profit.

My friends use to tell me to go to church if I wanted to find a good man. Yet, I don't feel comfortable using the Lord's house as a pick up joint. I've attended churches where everybody is more concerned with who is there than the pastor's sermon. Besides, due to my job it's hard for me to make it into church on a regular basis. I know that is a poor excuse for not getting my butt up on Sunday's but it's the truth.

Despite all of this, I still love black men. Sometimes, I wonder if black men love us—black women. I mean the way we are portrayed in music videos makes me question a black man's commitment to black women. It is sad when I think about it, but black men has helped in perpetuating the stereotype of black women being Jezebels—nothing more than hussies chasing the dollars and full of lust.

Still, I don't know what I would do without my black men. There is just something about my brothas. Something about them speaks to my soul. I guess since brothas make me feel this way it should not be any surprise to me that women of other ethnic groups find black men attractive too. For me a brotha is the epitome of manhood—masculinity, strength and beauty all rolled up into one.

Nevertheless, I'm curious to know when did dating a black woman go out of style? Was there a memo circulated and I simply missed it?

Lately, I have considered dating outside my race. It isn't as if that is something unheard of in Minnesota. I've seen plenty of sistahs with white men. Not too long ago, I went out to dinner with an attorney by the name of Derrick who happens to be white. Dinner was pleasant and the conversation was good. However, I did not feel comfortable. I often felt as if I had to watch what I said. It was almost as if I didn't want to come off sounding too black. I didn't feel free to cut loose and be myself. It felt almost as if I was interviewing for a job. I guess that was due to my own insecurity. The date ended amicably with us going our separate ways. Derrick called a few times afterwards, but I never returned his calls. I don't know why. Call me a dreamer, I guess. I just felt like I should've been able to meet a half way decent brotha out here. Of course, it could have been my strict criteria when it came to men as to why I was alone in the first place.

My mom and I are close. In fact she is one of my closest friends. Whenever I tell her about my dating woes, she always claims that I am being too picky or I'm just too damn fickle. Yet, I realize my mother grew up in a time when women conformed in order to be appealing to a man. I try to tell her it is a new day and age, and women don't have to compromise themselves in order to get a man. Whenever, I tell her this she always throws it back in my face by telling me, "Where has this new age woman gotten you?" She usually answers her own question for me with a resounding, "Alone."

I can't help but wonder at times if she is right. I mean look at the predicament I found myself in before I met Thaddeus—alone and spending a helluva a lot of money on batteries for my toys…if you know what I mean. I needed to find myself a man real soon. I hate to say that, but it was the truth. I was beginning to think I had to move to a city with a higher black population in order to find a level headed brotha secure within himself and the things he wanted out of life in order to take advantage of what I had to offer.

I started to wonder if I did not meet such a man did that mean I had to settle? I was starting to believe that was the case.

Then I met Thaddeus.

Erin

I'm Erin McCormick.

I am twenty-nine years old. I was born and raised in Denver, Colorado—the Cherry Creek neighborhood. It is an upper middle class neighborhood in Denver complete with upscale boutiques, manicured lawns and expensive cars. My father is a pediatrician and my mother is a gynecologist. They met at the University of Colorado School of Medicine. After a year of courtship they were married. Two years after they were married I was born. I am the only proof of Jonathan McCormick and Sharon Walls' union. When I reached the ripe age of four my parents divorced. So from the age of four on, my life was divided into two. I had two beds, two wardrobes, and two sets of parents. I spent the school year with my mother and my summers and the occasional holiday with my father. My mother remarried my stepfather, Steven, and gave birth to my younger brother, Lawrence, and my little sister, Hannah. My father remarried my stepmother, Carolyn, who had two grown sons of her own, Chance and Martin.

Up until graduation from high school, I pretty much lived a sheltered life. I did not branch out far from my little clique of friends or our typical hangouts. Yet, following high school I was ready to spread my wings. So, I decided to attend the University of Minnesota. Its distance was far enough away from Colorado where I didn't have to worry about my mother and father sticking their noses into my business. Yet, it was close enough to where I could easily go home when life became a little too hectic.

To celebrate my newfound freedom, I managed to talk my father into buying me a one-way plane ticket to Paris as a graduation present. I had heard stories of people backpacking through Europe during the summer so I wanted to do the same. To say the least, it was one of the most exuberant and liberating experiences of my life. I learned so much about life, other people and cultures—not to mention what I learned about myself. Meeting the countless cute European guys only enhanced the experience. I doubt I would have experienced anything even remotely similar to my time in Europe if I had stayed at home and worked a summer job like the majority of my friends. That summer I became a woman.

I had the typical college experience while at the University of Minnesota. Like all freshmen I partied way too much. Then spent, basically, the rest of my time in college trying to make up for all the partying I did my freshman year. My sophomore year I joined a sorority, Delta Gamma. I am a DG girl. I moved into the sorority house and continued my partying ways, but I managed to keep it to respectable levels. Most of the guys I dated in college were spoiled "frat brats," who grew up in Minnetonka, Eden Prairie or Edina—posh Minneapolis suburbs. It was not until my junior year did I commit myself solely to one guy. That was the year I met Brian. It was not like I was a slut in college, sleeping around. I just saw no need for a boyfriend when I could have so much more fun dating.

Brian and I met in a marketing class. I took the class because it was required for my major, Marketing, and he was fulfilling an elective requirement. I had seen Brian once or twice about campus, but that was about it. I knew he was in a fraternity, however I did not have a clue as to which one. So, I simply admired him from a far. However our mutual class together provided me with a setting where it was a bit easier to initiate small talk, especially when Brian and I were placed in the same group tasked with developing a marketing strategy for a fictitious product. Eventually discussions about school became more intimate and romance soon blossomed.

Like many of the "frat brats" I use to date, Brian was from a well-to-do family. Yet unlike many of the typical guys from privileged backgrounds, Brian seemed to be somewhat grounded in reality. Like all relationships, our relationship started out in harmonious bliss. We suffered from the usual symptoms such as the warm fuzzes whenever we saw each other. Everything between us seemed to go great. Even my parents met Brian and fell in love with him. Unfortunately, euphoria wears off over time and the real Brian began to emerge. The real Brian came with quirky little flaws and plenty of insecurity.

Soon after my senior year, the honeymoon period ended for Brian and I. I graduated from the U of M and began working at a local advertising agency. Brian on the other hand, still had a year of school left before earning his degree. In the beginning Brian was good at concealing his jealousy. Yet, over time his persistent questions about my job revealed how much he did not trust me. If I happened to mention a guy I worked with, Brian would ask me twenty questions about our relationship before flying off the handle and proclaiming, "He wants to get in your pants!"

The fact my job called on me to travel at times on production shoots only intensified Brian's jealousy. During these business trips Brian became increasingly more insistent that I was cheating on him. I confess there was some fraternizing, even flirting, between employees at our firm and on occasion you would hear of two people getting together but that was the extent of it. Even I was guilty of some innocent flirting, yet nothing more. Still, it did not seem to matter how hard I tried to convince Brian I was not involved with someone else—he adamantly believed I was.

After a while I got tired of it. I could not go out with my girlfriends without him calling me the next morning and putting me through an inquisition. He always suspected I was having some secret rendezvous with another man. It also did not help that he did not trust nor like my friends, Belinda and Stacy. Brian could not stand Belinda, who had been my best friend since college. We met through Delta Gamma. She is a sorority sister. I met Stacy from my job at the ad agency. When I begin working there, Stacy was a temp. She later left for a permanent job at another advertising firm in town. So as you can see it did not matter what I did or whom I hung out with because in Brian's eyes I was always up to something.

After a while I couldn't stand his persistent phone calls asking me, "Who were you with?" and "Where did you go?" so I ended it. Yet like the song goes, "breaking up is hard to do." Despite the fact I had called it quits, we still saw each other. He claimed he would work on his jealousy and I would wilt like a flower and take him back. He would bite his tongue for a month or two, before reverting back to his old self and I would once again proclaim it was over.

This on-again-off-again relationship lasted five years. Of course, I did not help our relationship along by dating David, a guy who worked at my job, during one of our many break-ups. Still, every time I dated someone else I always seemed to find myself right back in Brian's arms. It was not as if Brian did it for me. It was more like I became used to the fact that Brian was always there—a constant in my life. All the other guys I dated during our ins and outs just didn't keep my interest. Either they lacked personality, or they cared less about what I had to say and more about what *was* in my pants. Although Brian was not my knight in shinning armor, I was at least familiar with him and I knew his habits and tendencies. Taking the time to figure these things out in someone else frightened me. So, I simply stuck with Brian…Old Faithful.

At the time I met Thaddeus, Brian and I were once again trying to work things out.

Thaddeus

I'm Thaddeus Brown.

My friends growing up on Chicago's Southside use to call me "T-Money." The name was bestowed upon me by one of Southside Chicago's greatest blacktop basketball legends, Floyd "Superfly" Banks. Floyd was dubbed "Superfly" not only for the way he handled the rock on the basketball court but also for the skillful manner in which he handled the ladies. I can recall the day when Superlfy gave me the name "T-Money" like it was yesterday.

It was a hot summer day and everybody in the neighborhood had gathered at Rainbow Park to play basketball. I was playing a pick up game while Superfly and his friends waited along the sidelines to play the winner. I remember overhearing Superfly tell his friends my jumper was like money—every time the ball left my fingertips a brotha was sure to get paid. To prove it, Superfly bet anybody brave enough that I would not miss a shot. I was stunned Superfly even recognized my ball handling skills. See, Superfly was older than me. He was highly respected in the hood by ball players and hustlers alike. So for such a comment to come out of Floyd "Superfly" Banks' mouth was considered the utmost of compliments. Although, I admit Superfly did not win every bet. He did make more money than he lost that day. From that day on I was known around the neighborhood as "T-Money."

As a kid growing up, basketball was my passion. I loved basketball. On the basketball court all my troubles, all my worries, disappeared. Basketball was my escape. It kept me out of trouble and away from the lure of gangs. Everywhere I went I had a basketball in my hands. Sometimes I would get the ball taken away from me by the older kids in the neighborhood as I walked to the playground. Still, that did not stop me. They could not kill my dream of making it big in the NBA. Over time, I perfected my jumper until it became a thing of beauty. As soon as I pulled up for a jump shot and the ball left my hands, everybody knew they would hear nothing but the sweet sound of the net snapping as the ball glided effortlessly through it. When I hoisted up a shot very rarely was there the need to rebound. Like Floyd "Superfly" Banks use to say, my jumper was like money.

Not only did I demoralize opponents with my jump shot, but I also use to send plenty of fools to the emergency ward knocked knee or with busted ankles trying to keep up with my wicked crossover dribble. I could break anybody down. No one in the Chi possessed the ball handling skills I was blessed with.

I played the two spot, shooting guard, for Kenwood Academy High in Hyde Park on Chicago's Southside. I was a young, skinny, kid with plenty of raw talent and a lot of promise. I was one of Chicago's premier prep athletes. I had not only college but also pro scouts coming to see me play. I was highly recruited by most of the big name colleges in the nation. Mind you, this was before jumping straight from high school to the pros was in vogue. I had visions of being the first high school basketball star since Darrell Dawkins, "Chocolate Thunder" himself, to go pro straight out of high school. This was way before Kevin Garnett, Kobe Bryant and LeBron James. This was no pipe dream. It was very much a possibility for me. Then I blew out my knee in the second to last game of my senior year.

I remember that day vividly. My team had cleared the rebound and we were running a fast break. A teammate passed me the ball and I sprinted towards the hoop. There was no one near me. I was alone. It was just the hoop, the basketball, and me. I had intentions of doing a thunderous dunk that would have drove the crowd wild. It was going to solidify my place as the next up and coming NBA superstar. Yet as I planted my right foot to take flight, I heard something pop. Instead of soaring in the air I ended up on the floor in pain.

I blew out my knee—for no apparent reason whatsoever my knee decided to give out. Damn near every ligament in my right knee was torn to shreds. After that, the NBA was a long shot. I was devastated. Gone in a split second were the dreams of flashy cars, women and enough money to support a small third world nation. Yet beneath the despair, I believed once I rehabilitated my knee I would at least have a shot at the NBA…. Obviously that didn't happen, but the idea that could be a possibility kept me going.

The countless basketball scholarships to nationally renowned college basketball programs like Michigan, North Carolina, UCLA and Duke dried up the moment my knee gave away. Suddenly the only schools willing to take a chance on me were junior colleges. I knew even if I proved I could play at the junior college level my chances of breaking into the NBA were slim. So with a reconstructed knee, I switched my focus from basketball to academics. I still had visions of playing in the NBA, yet I realized I needed to have a back up plan just in case things did not work out as planned.

My grades upon graduating from Kenwood Academy were not the best. Since I thought I was on my way to the pros I was rather laxadazacle about studying and doing my homework in high school. On top of my low grade point average, my S.A.T. scores were downright lousy. So, that further whittled down my choice of colleges I could attend. In the end, I decided to attend

Clark Atlanta University—a historical black college—in Atlanta, Georgia. I got
a partial basketball scholarship that handled some of my college expenses,
which was better than nothing at all. Financial aid and work-study took care of
my remaining tuition.

During my time at Clark, I was one of the top five scorers in the Southern
Intercollegiate Athletic Conference. My junior and senior year, I was *the* top
scorer in the conference. I had a few pro scouts come and watch me play, but it
was nothing major. They tried to fill my head with garbage about how I could
make it in the NBA as a free agent. There was some truth behind it, yet I knew
by entering the league as a free agent my chances of ever making a pro basketball team were next to impossible. Some scouts suggested I go to the CBA, but
I was not hearing that. Just like anything else, the NBA is about politics. I knew
while I languished on the bench waiting for my chance, some kid drafted in the
first or second round would get all the playing time. In turn, I would sit on the
bench awaiting my chance. I just did not have the patience to sit around and
bide my time. Many of my friends and family thought I was crazy because even
a bench warmer in the NBA makes six figures, but I was not feeling that. I did
not want to go to the NBA and sit the bench just so I could say I played in the
league. I wanted to actually be on the floor playing, not getting splinters in my
behind because I sat the bench.

I managed to graduate from Clark Atlanta University with honors. I was
awarded a BA in economics. Although I had proven I had game, I also proved
that I was not some dumb jock. I could have gone to the NBA and sat the
bench or played overseas. There was a team in Frankfurt, Germany, Athens,
Greece, and Madrid, Spain, trying to recruit me. Still, such possibilities did not
excite me. I had heard how lonely it could get playing ball abroad away from
family and friends, unable to speak the language or understand the culture. Of
course, I had images of being an international playa, putting my mack down
on all the honeys in Europe but I opted to go to grad school instead. To tell you
the truth, I wanted to stay close to home…close to my mom. So grudgingly, I
let go of my childhood dreams of playing professional basketball and settled
for being just another neighborhood playground legend. It was hard to do but
I had to face reality.

I am what you might call a mama's boy. I was raised in a single-parent
home. My mother, Mabel Brown, pretty much raised my brother, James, my
sister, Althea, and I on her own. I'm the baby of the bunch. Mama occasionally
got help from relatives but overall it was pretty much a one-woman show, my
father—Raymond Brown—passed away when I was two. One evening while

on his way home from work, my father was hit by a bus…. He died instantly. Many of my relatives and father's friends tell me I'm the spitting image of my dad. I often look at old photos of my father and see a slight resemblance. Regardless of our similar features, it pains me that I never had the opportunity to know the man. James and even Althea, at least have fleeting memories of our father. Unfortunately for me…I don't.

My mother never remarried following my father's death. She chose instead to live the life of a spinster. I could always hear the heartache in Mama's voice whenever she spoke of my father. It was often hard for her to even look at old photographs of him. On occasions I would often over hear my mother in her bedroom crying at night. It was not until I got older did I understand my mother suffered from a severe broken heart. As a child I use to pray for God to bring my father back so I could meet him and my mother could be happy again. Sadly, those prayers were never answered.

As a young man growing up I yearned for the positive influence a male could have on a young boy's life. In my father's absence I often gravitated to older boys in the neighborhood like Floyd "Superfly" Banks and others to show me what it meant to be a man. To a young, impressionable, mind such as mine this could be detrimental, especially growing up on Chicago's Southside. There were some pretty shady dudes who use to call my neighborhood home. For example one of Althea's boyfriends named Sammy Ward, I completely idolized. The only problem was Sammy Ward was not a good role model to imitate.

Sammy Ward, everybody called him "Stretch," was one of the toughest brothas on the Southside of Chicago. Stretch was a stone cold thug. You name it Sammy Ward did it. He was a stick-up kid, burglary; you name it…Stretch did it. Stretch was one of those brothas that demanded respect. For a brief period I wanted to be just like him. Stretch was feared and respected. As a child growing up it was hard for me to decipher the difference between the two. Nonetheless, the effect Stretch had on people when he came around was a sight to see. Fortunately for Althea, Mama found out about Stretch's rep and put an end to that romance. Eventually, someone who thought he was bigger and badder put an end to Sammy Ward's life.

Still, none of the guys I emulated could live up to the bigger than life image I had painted of my father. Mind you, my mother was not a pushover. Mama stayed on our behinds, day in and day out. I owe a lot to my mother. I truly believe if it were not for her keeping a vigilant watch over us—James, Althea, and I would have fallen prey to the lure of the streets like a lot of kids in our neighborhood. In Chicago temptation lurks around every corner—some good but the majority of it bad. Without question I dabbled in the occasional mischief children often got themselves into, but that was it. In most cases a good whopping quickly put James, Althea, and I back in our place. We knew before we went outside to play our homework and chores had to be done. And when those streetlights came on, our butts had better been in the house. Despite my mother's heavy hand, there is only so much a woman can teach a boy about being a man.

Since the picture of my father was incomplete in my mind, I looked towards my family to fill in the blanks when it came to developing an image of my father. My father's friend, Melvin, use to always remind me of my father's loyalty to his friends by continuously telling me the story of how my dad came to his rescue when his car broke down during a severe snowstorm. On occasion even Mama parted with a tale or two. She spoke affectionately of how my father had no money to take her out dancing so he would push all the furniture in the living room against the walls, light a candle, put on a record, and dance with her while we slept. Even James and Althea vaguely remember days spent with our father in the park. I have no such memories to fondly hark back on. I have no memory or mental image of my dad. At times I felt as if God had cheated me out of knowing my father.

Over time the countless stories my father's friends, uncles and aunts spun became the foundation for what I would later on in life use to measure my worth as a man against. From their stories I managed to piece together an image of my dad being this hard working, loving man, loyal to family and friends. The many jovial pictures I had seen and the numerous stories told to me helped solidify this portrait. I got the impression from everyone that my dad was a good man. In a lot of regards, I've tried my best to measure up to my father. However, I often feel I have fallen short. Sometimes I wondered if the fact I was trying to measure myself up against a ghost had anything to do with my feeling of inadequacy.

Regardless, while attending Clark I met my ex-wife Stephanie. Stephanie was also from Chicago…Evanston to be exact. I did not know her before attending Clark. Stephanie claims she had seen me play basketball during the high school basketball tournaments. Of course, I would not have recognized her in a sea of faces. Besides, back then I paid little attention to girls. Basketball was my girlfriend. I ate, slept and breathed basketball. Of course, I had a few girlfriends in high school but they could not compete with my love affair for basketball.

After graduating from Clark, Stephanie and I returned home to Chicago. As I stated earlier, I decided to attend graduate school so I took the necessary tests and enrolled in Northwestern's Kellogg School of Business while Stephanie worked full-time. I worked a part-time job as a waiter to supplement the income I received as a teacher's assistant. Times back then were rough. Sometimes we had to decide on whether to keep the lights on or eat. Yet, going through such hard times only made us appreciate the good times.

Upon completion of my master's degree I landed a job at Dyson & Rhodes, one of the most prestigious consulting firms in the country. The only problem was the job was in Minneapolis and not in Chicago as I had hoped. I wanted to stay in Chicago, but this was an opportunity I did not want to pass up. It took some effort on my part to coax Stephanie into moving to Minneapolis, but in the end she agreed to join me. So I packed up all my belongings and headed to Minnesota.

Now, I had heard from all my boys who occasionally visited Minneapolis or lived there at one time or another that Minnesota was a "black man's paradise." The reason being, a brotha had no problem hooking up with a white girl in Minnesota. From some of the stories my friends told me. I would have thought white women were treating black men like kings in Minnesota. Many of the brothas I grew up with who claimed to be pimps told me they never had a problem locking down some fine ass, corn-fed, white girl from Minnesota. I could have cared less about white women at the time. Besides, I was bringing Stephanie with me. Even though I had dabbled in vanilla occasionally, I preferred the sweet taste of chocolate.

Once Stephanie and I had settled in, I realized life in Minneapolis was not that bad. Money at the time was not a problem and we were able to afford a lot of things in Minnesota that would have cost us an arm and a leg in Chicago. Stephanie and I were able to buy a nice home in a decent neighborhood in the city and afford a brand new car for both of us. That is unheard of in Chicago. Still, there were certain things about Chicago I missed. Although, Minneapolis allowed me to enjoy some of the comforts in life that might have taken some time for me to acquire in Chicago, Minneapolis definitely lacked the flavor one finds in The Chi. Minneapolis did not have places that could compare to Harold's Chicken or Giordano's pizza. Arnellia's in St. Paul came close, however, it still lacked the flavor of the juke joints back home.

Also, Chicago has a much more diverse nightlife than Minneapolis. A person can listen to jazz, reggae, blues, R&B, funk, salsa, house and even enjoy the stepper's sets. Chicago's nightlife is so eclectic. Other than New York, I seriously doubt there is any other place in America that can compare. Minneapolis, on the other hand, is more homogeneous. Minneapolis caters more to the country-western, pop, or top 40 crowd. There may be one or two clubs in the city that played R&B, mixed in with Hip Hop on certain nights, but that was about it. There were a few bars in the Cities that played live jazz. However, if a person was in the mood for real reggae, there is only really one place to find it—The Blue Nile. Otherwise, the possibility of an individual hearing some good reggae or dancehall music depends a lot on whether they are in the right place at the right time. So, obviously moving to Minneapolis from Chicago had its drawbacks.

While I'm talking about the transition of moving from Chicago to Minneapolis, another thing about Minnesota that blew my mind was Minnesotans love affair with winter. I guess I should've expected as much since winter lasts anywhere from four to five months out of the year in the Upper Midwest. Still, sitting on a frozen lake, freezing my ass off fishing is not my idea of fun. If a person in Minnesota is not ice fishing during the winter, then they're out riding their snowmobiles. These people even have parades and festivals in the dead of winter that requires a person to be outside. Now it gets cold in Chicago, but it is down right frigid in Minneapolis. Regardless of the weather, people still bundle up their kids in snow pants and big heavy down coats and go to these outdoor functions. Back home in The Chi, everybody I know in my neighborhood is in the house during winter…where it is warm!

In spite of Minneapolis' lack of nightlife and the long winters, my job kept me busy. So, I rarely had time to partake in partying or ice fishing. Despite my extensive travel schedule, my relationship with Stephanie was great. My constant travel was hard on our relationship but we managed. Besides, we knew it was only temporary. I did not plan on being a consultant all my life. Plus, Stephanie was able to find a good paying job and we decided to make our relationship legitimate following the birth of my son Thaddeus Jr.—who we refer to as Little T. Looking back now, I wonder if Stephanie and I rushed into marriage simply because of the birth of our son.

Originally, I had only planned on living in Minnesota a couple of years. I was willing to stretch my commitment out maybe three years at the most. Yet the way things were going, I would've possibly stretched that out to five years before putting in a request for a transfer to the firm's Chicago office.

Regardless of my plans, everything came to a screeching halt the day I got laid off.

When the economy took a turn for the worst, it took me down with it. With companies cutting back on expenses, consulting fees dried up. Leaving consultants such as myself out in the cold. To maintain costs, Dyson & Rhodes started laying people off. Unfortunately, I was one of the unlucky few who were shown the door. It was around this time when the situation between Stephanie and I got rocky. Other than unemployment benefits we had to basically depend solely on Stephanie's income to support us, and to put it mildly her salary did not cut it. As can be expected this put undue stress on our marriage, which manifested itself into heated arguments. After thirteen months of an endless job search I was able to land a job at Midwestern Federal, a local bank, as an independent contractor yet at lower pay. Nevertheless, by the time I had accepted the job at Midwestern Federal, Stephanie and my relationship had deteriorated beyond repair. The end came when I stopped at the neighborhood supermarket after playing basketball one Saturday afternoon and found Stephanie in the car exchanging kisses with a mutual friend of ours, Cedric. Despite her infidelity I tried my best to move on and make the marriage work at least for our son's sake. Still, after numerous attempts at reconciling—including visits to a marriage counselor—Stephanie and I called it quits.

I admit I was no saint. At times I was too preoccupied with kicking it with the fellas than spending time with Stephanie, especially after Little T was born. I had a hard time adjusting to life with a child. No longer did Stephanie and I enjoy the freedom we had enjoyed when it was just the two of us. Life became more regulated. It also did not help Stephanie suffered from postpartum to the point the doctor put her on medication. It took me some time but I realized my life had to be a little more structured whether I liked it or not.

Plus, I was not the most faithful man to Stephanie. I occasionally messed with other women on the side while we dated in college. I admit I took her through hell. Yet, she stuck with me. What can I say? I was young and immature. It was due to my past infidelities as to why I tried so hard to make our marriage work. Despite my scandalous behavior in college, I took my wedding vows seriously and remained true to Stephanie while married. It was not until I discovered Stephanie with Cedric did it become painfully obvious to me our marriage had reached its end and I sought comfort in another woman. By that time, I had lost all hope of the two of us ever reconciling. It was very stupid of me, I know. I thank God, Stephanie did not find out about my affair until after the divorce papers were finalized.

Regardless of our trials and tribulations, I always believed Stephanie and I could work things out. When we couldn't I really took it to heart. I viewed my inability to save our marriage as an indictment on my ability to be a man. I saw myself as a failure. After our divorce I fell into a severe bout of depression.

I readily admit it to anyone who asks me to this day...I still love Stephanie. Although the love I feel for her now is different. How could I not have some feelings for Stephanie? Despite the bad times, we had plenty of good times. Stephanie is after all the mother of my son and that holds a very dear place in my heart. However, as a couple, Stephanie and I just did not work. Just because I loved her it did not necessarily mean Stephanie and I were destined to be together. Believe me, it took me a lot of heartache and time to come to that realization.

Now until I could get back on my feet I briefly moved in with my boy, Darius. In hindsight, moving in with Darius was not a wise decision. Darius was my boy from Clark that happened to get a job in Minneapolis after graduating. He was a brotha from Oakland, who had seen *The Mack* maybe one too many times as a kid growing up. He was into nothing more than macking women out of their panties or getting them for their money. If it did not involve one or the other, Darius had nothing to do with them. If you let Darius tell it, he held a doctorate in pimpology instead of a BA in political science.

Darius always claimed to have learned about pimping from his uncle, a self-professed pimp, who ran hoes from Anchorage to Tijuana. Darius was the type of brotha that mainly messed with white women but if a sistah happened to listen to his game and bite, he would reel her ass in too. Nevertheless, Darius was in love with white women and would do anything to get one...even if it meant answering swinger ads. Darius was notorious for answering such ads stating, "Wife seeks first sexual encounter with well hung black male. Must be willing to let husband watch."

Whenever I questioned him as to why he would take the chance of playing Russian roulette with his life, he typically would reply, "If some white dude wants to sit back and watch me have sex with his wife that's cool with me." So it goes without saying, Darius landing a job as a stockbroker in Minneapolis was like letting the fox into the hen house. A city like Minneapolis, notorious for interracial dating, was nothing more than a fertile breeding ground for Darius.

Now, moving in with Darius was not the best move for me while I struggled to pick myself up after the divorce because it denied any chance of Stephanie and I ever getting back together. The main reason being Stephanie hated Darius. The second reason being Stephanie's girlfriend, Chanel, lived in the same apartment complex. Chanel had taken it upon herself to inform Stephanie of every little thing that went on in Darius' apartment while I lived there.

I will not profess to have been innocent while living with Darius. To be quite frank, I was an outright dawg. Since he was a bachelor, Darius' apartment was filled with temptation. If the abundance of alcohol in the apartment did not drown my sorrows, than the numerous women did. And I partook in both. The best way to pick up a man's self esteem and help him get over a woman is another woman. So believe me when I tell you, the drinks were flowing and the ladies came and went in sufficient enough numbers to cloud my judgment. I feel ashamed to say I needed sex to restore my delicate ego, but I was going through hell at the time. My marriage had failed. I know it sounds shallow but when everything else was going wrong in my life my sexual conquests gave me something to feel good about...at least temporarily.

My other friend, I hung out with on a regular basis was a brotha by the name of Marcus Gowens. Marcus was a newly wed. Marcus was born and raised in the Twin Cities, and had graduated from the University of Minnesota. In college Marcus had aspirations of being one of those politically conscious rappers. He was apart of a rap group called the Hard Knots and went by the moniker, Wordsmyth. However, their brand of conscious rap did not catch on with record label execs because of the growing popularity of gangsta rap at the time. So Marcus went on to the University of Minnesota's Law school were he felt he could best serve his community as a lawyer. Immediately following law school, Marcus started his own practice.

In his words Marcus refused to take part in what he called "corporate share-cropping." If someone questioned him as to why he chose to start his own law firm instead of working for a big law firm he would proudly reply, "To defend the record number of brothas and sistahs society is locking away behind bars."

If you cannot tell from that comment, Marcus is very pro-black.

I met Marcus in kind of half hazard way through Darius at a party and we have been boys ever since.

Although Marcus is an attorney, he still takes every opportunity he can to spit his rhymes at local cafes and jazz clubs. I call him a coffee shop revolutionary. One of those guys sitting in a coffee shop talking about revolution while sipping a latte. I've seen Marcus recite his poetry a few times, and I will be the first to admit the boy is nice. However, the one thing I cherish the most about Marcus other than his uplifting poetry is that he is the sensible one out of Darius and I. He always tends to keep a brotha grounded. The entire time I was trying to re-live my bachelor days, Marcus was steady in my ear trying to get me to think reasonable about what I was doing. Marcus is the polar opposite of Darius. While Darius is a self-professed pimpologist, Marcus is a happily married, socially conscious, artiste cat. Of course, that explains why the two of them have such a hard time getting along.

Marcus' wife, Lisa, is a lawyer as well. Since it is hard to depend on Marcus' clients to pay on a timely basis, Lisa works in a corporate law firm where income is more reliable. Lisa is what Darius likes to call a boojie, hyphenated, woman. Instead of taking Marcus' last name, Lisa went for the hyphenation…Lisa Coffield-Gowens. Don't get me wrong; there is nothing wrong with it. With all due respect Lisa is good people. The only knock I have on Lisa is that she runs Marcus ragged. The sad thing about it is that he lets her. Marcus claims he is only doing right by his woman and brothas need to just mind their own business. If that is what makes him happy then who am I to argue. However, let the truth be told, Lisa wears the pants in Marcus' household and she makes no bones about it.

After living with Darius for close to two months, I realized the lifestyle Darius led was not for me. I liked my life drama free. Darius on the other hand always seemed to be surrounded by drama. I was too old for that. So, I moved out and got a place of my own. It was a nice condominium in downtown Minneapolis on the Mississippi River. I did not want to be a playa like Darius. Nor did I want to be hemmed up by a woman like Marcus. I was in search of the Holy Grail. I wanted that special blend of a woman who allowed me my freedom, but whom I enjoyed being around. The type of woman, who was secure enough in herself and our relationship to let a brotha hangout with the fellas. Yet, she was the type of woman a man looked forward to spending time with.

The only problem with a woman like that is that they are hard—if not impossible—to find. Not to mention, the dating game has changed so much since I was in my twenties. Brothas today has to buy a woman everything under the sun to prove their love and devotion. I've heard stories of men damn near having to whip it out on the dance floor in order to satisfy the size requirements of a potential lover. It sounds hard to believe, but I've heard worst.

In the past, I did not have any problems catching a lady. However, at the age of thirty-four the task was a little bit more difficult and required a bit more finesse. Most of the quality women who were abundant back in the day were suddenly scarce. In my tireless search for that one special woman I visited churches, bars, jazz clubs and sports bars. It seemed like every woman I met had a sob story to tell. If they did not have a "down on their luck" story, then they were rushing a brotha into some form of commitment. Some women I met were just plum crazy.

Although the women I was dating were not of exceptional quality, I doubt I would have recognized a good woman even if she were right under my nose. At the time I was simply going through the motions—doing what a newly single man was suppose to do even if my heart was not in it. I was still suffering from an emotional hangover. In many regards I was bitter. I was very guarded when it came to giving another woman my heart. There was only one woman I dated before Ivy and Erin whom I had considered a relationship with...Trina. Although, everything between us started off good things turned sour real fast.

I met Trina at one of Marcus and Lisa's church potlucks. Marcus and Lisa were not devout Christians, however, they did see a necessity in fellowship. Marcus had been nagging me about attending church with him and Lisa, so when he informed me their church was putting on a potluck I figured that was as good a time as any to get a healthy dose of the Lord, especially while I filled my belly. It was at the potluck I met Trina. At the time Trina was new to the Twin Cities. She had moved there from Gary, Indiana.

Trina ran a good game on me in the beginning, but in the end it became clear to me she was nothing more than a hood rat. The signs were there. I just think I chose to ignore them. Such as the time I went to the liquor store and I asked her if she wanted something to drink and she told me a forty ounce of Old English. At first I thought she was joking, but I quickly realized she was serious. Now understand, this was coming from a woman who was not only supposed to be sanctified but refined. I expected to hear something like wine come out of her mouth not malt liquor. Another hint that Trina was not what she seemed to be came when she told me she was saved and did not believe in pre-marital sex. Needless to say, we were knocking boots within the first week we met.

Of course, the kicker came after I complained for about a month about how much I wanted a DVD player and Trina unexpectedly shows up at my door one night with a DVD player along with a DVD disc still in the deck. To make matters worse the serial number was scratched out. Now it did not take someone with exceptional intelligence to figure out how Trina came about the DVD player. It also became painfully obvious to me I had to get rid of Trina. When I broke off the relationship Trina demanded the DVD player back, which I had no problem doing. I was kind of nervous about having stolen property in my home anyway.

I guess I did not move fast enough in getting Trina's DVD player back to her because I came home one evening to find not only the DVD player missing, but pretty much everything else in my condo. Not only did Trina help herself to the DVD player, but she also helped herself to my stereo, my TV, my couch, my pots and pans, and the sheets right off my bed. How nasty can you get? Stealing someone's dirty sheets?

Of course, I did not have any proof Trina did it other than the last time I had spoken to her she told me, "Since you're taking your time in returning the DVD player to me, I might have to get somebody to get it for me." In the end I could do nothing more than chalk it up as a lesson learned.

That brings me to Ivy and Erin. After Trina, I really was not in the mood to be dealing with any more women. In fact, I had pretty much cut dating out of my life. When I met Erin and Ivy, I was still living in Minneapolis working for Midwestern Federal and still very much apprehensive about women period.

Chances Are

Ivy—Looking for Mr. Goodbar

I met Thaddeus through Lisa. Lisa is married to Thaddeus' friend Marcus. I made Lisa's acquaintance when she started working at Grimble & Kline. At the time of Lisa's hiring there was only one black attorney at Grimble & Kline…me. Due to the fact we were the only two black attorneys at the firm, Lisa and I naturally gravitated to one another and eventually became the best of friends. It amazed me how the two of us was born and raised in Minneapolis, yet never met nor heard about each other. The Twin Cities' black community is rather small, so I find it remarkable when I meet someone black close to my age I know nothing about. I had seen Lisa at a few Minnesota bar association functions but that was about the extent of it. I had assumed Lisa to be another transplant from out of state like most of the black attorneys in Minnesota.

Lisa had been at Grimble & Kline maybe six months before she invited me to a Bid Wiz party her husband's friend, Darius, was hosting at his apartment complex. At the time Lisa invited me, I was stressed out over an approaching trial not to mention my review for partner was fast approaching. I was well aware the partners were scrutinizing my every move. Still, Lisa managed to talk me into going to the card party in hopes of getting me to unwind.

I rode with Lisa and her husband, Marcus, to the card party because I did not want to get lost. I was terrible when it came to directions. Even though I was from the Twin Cities, I had a hard time finding places. The night of the Bid Wiz party was the first time I met Lisa's husband, Marcus. Marcus was a baby face brotha who appeared to be non-threatening. He seemed to be a truly sweet man. Marcus' boy, Darius, on the other hand was a dog and he made no bones about it. As soon as I walked into the party, Darius was all up in my face his mack. Don't get me wrong, Darius was a fine brotha but ,, demeanor immediately turned me off. At the time I was ...ui a man, but I was not looking for somebody like Darius. Besides, Lisa had already given me the low down on Darius and his preference for white women before we arrived. I figured he had invited the numerous white women at the party. I quickly learned Darius had no shame in his game. To rid ourselves of Darius' company, Lisa and I let Marcus converse with his boy while we mingled elsewhere.

Now some men just emanate sex appeal. It's as if it seeps out of their pores like syrup. To behold such a man is intoxicating. To be in such a man's presence for far too long will leave a woman drunk with desire. Such is the case with Thaddeus. Not only is the brotha fine, but most important of all the man is sexy. Thaddeus possesses an animal magnetism that is hard to resist. It is a basic primal attraction—dare I say lust that instantly drew me to him. In my opinion a sexy man wins out everyday over a man who is just good-looking. Good-looking men can only be looked at for so long, before the cute face and tight butt get played out. Without that added umph to go along with the cute face a brotha gets boring very fast. Believe me, Thaddeus had that umph and a whole lot more.

Now, I noticed Thaddeus the moment he walked into the party. It was hard not to notice the man. It was not because Thaddeus is just that fine. The real reason was because Thaddeus was a new face in the crowd. A new black face in Minneapolis did not go un-noticed, particularly a black male. Like I stated earlier, the pool of eligible single black men in Minnesota is extremely small. So a new face in the crowd sticks out like a sore thumb.

Now Thaddeus wasn't pretty boy fine nor did he possess the athletic, jock, type build. Thaddeus was simply fine. He was that tall drink of water on a hot summer day. Thaddeus reminded me of a deep dark chocolate Hershey's bar strolling into the party that night and I was yearning for a bite. Now, judging by countless other women's attention Thaddeus commanded simply by entering the room, I knew I was not the only woman who wanted to sample that chocolate.

I watched as Thaddeus said "hi" to a few individuals as he made his entrance. However, it became clear to me by the way he embraced Marcus and that asshole Darius—I had already drawn my own conclusions about Darius—that they were friends. Seeing that Thaddeus knew Marcus, I knew that was my opportunity to meet him. The way competition was amongst women for single men, I refused to simply admire Thaddeus from afar all night long.

And judging by the number of women eyeballing him, I knew I had to get up close and personal with Thaddeus Brown early. At the time Lisa was conversing with one of her girlfriends. I can't recall the girl's name for I forgot it immediately after Lisa introduced us.

"What girl?" Lisa snapped. She was obviously annoyed by my elbow jabbing her in the ribs.

"Who is that with Marcus?" I asked.

Lisa looked over to where Marcus and Darius were standing and smiled. "That's Marcus' boy Thaddeus. He's from Chicago. He used to be a consultant for Dyson & Rhodes. Marcus told me he's doing contractual work for Midwestern Federal now."

"Is that right?" I sized Thaddeus up.

Lisa noticed my sudden interest in Thaddeus. It wasn't as if I was hiding it. Lisa immediately felt the need to warn me. "Let me just warn you before you get all worked up over the brotha that he has baby mama drama."

Now, I usually do not get involved with men that have kids. That was an unwritten rule of mine. A man with kids generally meant there would always be drama between that man and the baby's mama. Further more, I've always had a problem of sharing—particularly my man. Of course, my reluctance to date a man with children could've been another reason why I was alone. Judging by the number of black men, young and old, with kids nowadays that significantly narrowed down the field of eligible African American men I could consider as potential mates. However when it came to Thaddeus, I overlooked the fact he had a child for some reason.

"How old is the kid?" I watched Thaddeus' every move.

"I think he is either four or five," Lisa stated. I quickly had to stop staring for Thaddeus and Marcus glanced over in our direction.

When I was sure their attention had been redirected, I returned my gaze to Thaddeus' tall chocolate frame. "What about the mama?"

For a woman, the whereabouts and status of the baby's mama is an all-important question. I've always believed there had to be an ample amount time between the separation of the baby's mama and the man in order for the man to have severed any emotional ties. However, the fact Thaddeus and his previous significant other had a child together meant there was a lasting physical connection forcing the two of them to keep in touch.

"Thaddeus and Stephanie have been divorced for over a year and a half now."

"Divorced?" I stated.

"Yeah. From what Marcus tells me, he caught his wife cheating on him."

Thaddeus and Marcus began to walk over in our direction. "Chill girl, here they come," I insisted. I could see Lisa out of the corner of my eye staring at me like I was crazy.

I didn't blame her. Here I was a thirty-six year old woman, acting like a teenager. I couldn't help it. Thaddeus had me feeling giddy.

"You ready girl!" Marcus shouted to Lisa, while they made their way towards us. "Darius said he is ready to get this thing started."

"I'm ready if you are baby," Lisa piped.

"Well, then lets take these fools money," Marcus proclaimed. "By the way Ivy, this is my boy Thaddeus. Thaddeus this is Ivy. Ivy is one of Lisa's co-workers." It was quite smooth how Marcus just slid right into our introduction.

"So are you a lawyer too?" Thaddeus questioned.

It was obvious he had been briefed. I kept telling myself to keep my cool before telling him, "Yes, I am."

"What type of law do you practice?"

Suddenly at that moment I blanked out. I couldn't believe it. I had totally blanked out. I had become so hypnotized by the shimmer of his baldhead and those luscious brown lips; I had totally missed the question. If it were not for Lisa, I probably would have stood there with a blank expression on my face the entire night.

"Excuse me?" I could see Lisa out of the corner of my eye trying not to laugh. Her attempt to suppress her laughter made me breakdown into a kool-aid grin of my own. I could not help it. I wanted Thaddeus and I could feel my body singing his name. I only worried he would open his mouth and say something stupid—totally ruining everything.

"I said what type of law do you practice?" Thaddeus repeated, this time smirking. I remember at the time, I could not help but imagine what it would be like kissing his dark brown lips.

"I'm in litigation. I'm a trial lawyer." I attempted to regain my composure.

"Well, I brought my boy over here because he doesn't have a Wiz partner for the tournament. I was wondering Ivy if you wouldn't mind helping him out since you don't have a partner either?" interceded Marcus.

"That is of course if you know how to play Bid Wiz. I'm kind of leery of brothas and sistahs from Minnesota claiming they know how to play Wiz," Thaddeus interjected.

"What do you mean brothas and sistahs from Minnesota? Where are you from?" I played it off like I didn't know.

"The Chi!" Thaddeus exclaimed with pride.

"Well, I don't know who you have been dealing with, but we do got soul up here in the Minnie-apple."

"Tell 'im girl." Lisa slapped me five.

"Now, we may not know all the prison games you brothas play down there in Chicago but up here we know how to throw down on some Wiz," I stated.

"Alright, alright…I guess I'm going to have to find out." Thaddeus smiled.

Thaddeus then looked over at Marcus and said, "I've barely known the girl for five minutes and she's already talking mess. I like that. It reminds me of home." He turned and looked me in the eyes. I knew at that moment I had him. All I had to do was play my cards right, figuratively and literally.

"Well, we're going to go over and put or names in the hat and see who we draw. You guys want us to put your names in the hat too?" asked Marcus.

"Yeah, why don't you do that," Thaddeus declared. "I'm going to fix myself a drink, so I can get in the mood."

"Up here in Minneapolis we're always in the mood," I teased as he walked pass me.

"There you go," Thaddeus replied.

Lisa waited until Marcus had made his way over to where Darius stood putting names in a baseball cap and Thaddeus went into the kitchen to fix himself a drink before whispering, "He's yours for the taking girl." I couldn't resist a smirk.

The entire evening was charged with a sexual energy that made it hard for the two of us to concentrate on cards. The sly glances across the table and well-placed innuendos in our conversation did not help me focus. People accused us of talking across the table, which was true. The only problem was Thaddeus and I was not talking about cards. Nevertheless, I managed to dedicate enough of my attention to the game that we made it to the finals.

In the finals we played Darius and another one of Thaddeus and Marcus' friends, Rob. Now, Darius and Rob were big time shit talkers. They talked cash money every chance they got. That did nothing but piss me off and make me eager to beat them. I'm not big on talking mess but believe me when I tell you; Thaddeus did enough shit talking to make up for the both of us. On top of Darius and Rob's mouth Thaddeus and I had to endure a couple of bad hands at the onset of the game, which only made Darius and Rob talk even more. We were set twice and more than a hundred points behind. Fortunately for us, Darius and Rob did not know how to bid their hand or we would have definitely lost. At that point our physical attraction for each other took a backseat to winning the pot and shutting Darius and Rob up for good. Thaddeus and I were able to run a Boston and pick up the subsequent hands, which set Darius and Rob back too far to ever recover. Winning the two hundred-dollar kitty was nice, but what was even more gratifying was watching Darius sit there dumbfounded. I had only known Darius for a short while, but I already disliked him. Over time I would detest him.

By the time Thaddeus and I finished our last hand it was late. Pretty much everybody had left, except Lisa, Marcus and a few stragglers. Two stragglers were white women, so, I figured they were waiting for Darius and Rob. The only reason why Marcus and Lisa were still hanging around was because they were my ride home. Despite it being late, Thaddeus proposed we go out and eat—sort of like a victory dinner. Lisa and Marcus were tired and wanted to go home and get some rest. I was not ready for the night to end. I was having fun. It had been a long time since I had gone out and had so much fun. So when Thaddeus inquired as to whether I wanted to get something to eat, I jumped at the opportunity. So, Thaddeus informed Lisa and Marcus that he would drive me home.

We said our good-byes to Lisa and Marcus and went in search of a place to grab a bite to eat. At first Thaddeus had a craving for breakfast but we had trouble finding a late night restaurant. When searching for a restaurant became too much of a hassle we decided to settle on pizza. Thaddeus claimed to know of a pizzeria in the Warehouse District that stayed open pretty late, so that is where we went. I could've cared less if we ate pizza or an early morning breakfast just as long as I enjoyed it with him.

I was quite surprised to find the pizzeria so crowded so late at night. Thaddeus said it was usually that way on Fridays and Saturdays after people left the nightclubs and bars in the Warehouse District. It had been a while since I had been clubbing, so I wouldn't have known.

We sat there, talking over pizza and soda pop for the better part of the night. We must've scratched the surface on every topic possible. I bored Thaddeus with talk about my family, my job and the case I was trying on Monday morning that was giving me fits. Thaddeus talked about his job, his son, and his failed marriage. I found Thaddeus warm and personable. He did not come off aloof like of the men I had dated. His frankness was a breath of fresh air. I had gotten tired of so many brothas sugar coating the truth or lying. Needless to say, Thaddeus and I became so engrossed in each other we lost track of time. We did not leave the pizzeria until 3:30 in the morning. We must have talked for two hours. By the time we reached my townhouse in Eden Prairie it was five minutes past four. Once at my townhouse I invited him in and we talked for maybe another half an hour.

It was late and I could tell he was drowsy. Instead of letting him drive back into the Cities exhausted, I invited him to stay the night on my couch until he felt rested enough to make the trip back into Minneapolis. Thaddeus was thankful and made his home on my sofa. After we determined he was going to stay, I went into my bedroom to put on my pajamas and grabbed Thaddeus a pillow for the night. When I returned I was delighted to find Thaddeus standing in my living room shirtless. I couldn't help but imagine what he looked like naked. It was obvious Thaddeus took care of himself. For someone who was thirty-four, Thaddeus was in far better shape than many twenty-four year old men I knew. I tried not to stare as I handed him the pillow. I did not want him to get the wrong idea. With the exception of Curtis, it had been quiet some time since I had a half-naked man standing in my living room.

I think Thaddeus caught me looking by the smirk on his face as I handed him the pillow. As he took the pillow from me, he drew me in close to him and gave me a soft, supple, kiss. Although he caught me off guard, I did not resist. I had been yearning to taste those juicy lips of his all night. Thaddeus' lips were ever so sweet. The feel of his lips against mine set my body afire. Thaddeus' tongue parted my lips and danced a tantalizing tango with mine. I could feel an inferno being kindled inside of me. Like I said...it had been a while since I had been with a man. Although I wanted Thaddeus, I did not want our first night together to turn into a freak-show. If this was a budding relationship worth nurturing, I wanted it to start out on the right foot. Despite that, I could not suppress the childish grin that swept over my face, nor resist giving him a seductive switch of my hips when I pulled away and hurried off to my room.

Now, most men would have taken that as an invitation to follow me into the bedroom. There had been plenty of nights, I had to fight off men whom had gotten the wrong idea and conveniently forgotten the meaning of the word "no." Thaddeus simply seemed to take the innocent smile and sashaying of my hips in stride before wishing me a "good night."

I woke up the next morning fully expecting Thaddeus to be gone. The older I got the more I realized the men I brought home did not like to stick around. That didn't bother me. For the older I got the less I wanted them to hang around. It seemed like every man I brought to my home either made up some lame excuse, so they could sneak out in the morning or I had to kick them out because they made themselves comfortable. Curtis was notorious for overstaying his welcome. So, when I came into the living room to find the couch empty and the blankets folded in a neat stack it did not surprise me. Although, I had expected as much I was disappointed Thaddeus did not at least say good-bye. It became clear to me as I moseyed over to my patio door to look out upon a new day as to why Thaddeus had not told me he was leaving. That was because he was still there. I was somewhat taken aback to find him sitting outside on my patio furniture.

Now mind you, it was the middle of January. It was still bitterly cold outside. Even as Thaddeus sat outside there was still snow on the ground from the last snowstorm. Fearing the bitter cold yet desiring to join him, I tightened the belt on my robe and walked outside.

I remember walking outside into the blustery cold. I mean I had on pajamas, a full-length bathrobe along with a pair of slippers and I was freezing. I knew Thaddeus was cold sitting there with only a T-shirt, jeans and socks on. I could not help but think this man was crazy to sit outside barely clothed during winter.

"Good morning." I took a seat in the patio chair next to him.

"And a good morning to you." Thaddeus smiled. "Did you sleep well?"

"Yes, I did," I replied. I really wanted to say I would have slept a helluva lot better if he had joined me in bed, but I resisted. "You're going to catch pneumonia sitting out here with hardly any clothes on."

"I know, but it's just so peaceful out here. The peace and quiet helps me clear my head, you know," he explained. "It reminds me of when I use to lock myself in my room so I could get away from my brother and sister. It was the only way I could get a peace of mind. Since I was the youngest, they use to always tease me. So any time I could get to myself was special." Thaddeus smirked as if he was reliving a fond childhood memory.

"When I locked that bedroom door it was the only place I could be alone. I use to sit there sometimes for hours staring out the window thinking. I think my mom knew I needed that time to myself because she refused to let James or Althea disturb me."

"What would you think about when you stared out the window?"

"Everything."

"So, what are you thinking about now? If you don't mind me asking?" I pried. I couldn't help myself. I was being nosey.

Thaddeus looked at me and smiled. "I was thinking about how hungry I am."

Thaddeus' response was an obvious deflection of the question. It did not bother me. Although, Thaddeus and I had talked the night before I did not expect for him to open up and express his deepest feeling to me just yet. The brief peek we had given each other the night before into our personal lives sufficed for the moment. Besides, we had only known each other barely twenty-four hours.

"Come on, let's get inside and warm up to a cup of hot chocolate. And if you're good, I just might cook you breakfast," I said. I took his hand and lead him into my townhouse.

Thaddeus grinned. "Just tell me what I have to do?"

I usually don't cook for a man I hardly know, but Thaddeus did not strike me to be just any ole man. He touched me in a special way. I guess if I had to point to one thing about Thaddeus that really drew me to him, it had to be that he came off as being sincere. I don't know if it was the way we conversed or if it was just the vibe that seemed to flow through us when we were together. I really couldn't put my finger on it. He did not seem to pretend to be someone or something he was not. With Thaddeus it was basically what you saw was what you got and I liked that. Besides, I didn't think Thaddeus would be too hungry since we had eaten pizza only a few hours earlier.

I was wrong.

The sound of his fork clanking against the plate told me differently. He wolfed down the pancakes I had cooked for him. After breakfast, he put on his shirt and shoes and told me he had to go. It seems Thaddeus had promised his son he would spend Sunday afternoon with him.

I didn't get upset. I understood.

Before he departed, Thaddeus apologized for the unexpected kiss the night before. I assured him it was not a big deal. Deep down, I silently hoped there would be more kisses to come. Of course, I kept that thought to myself. Thaddeus left by giving me a hug. Unlike other men who had came by my house I really did not wish to see him go. Yet, I knew it was far too early for the two of us to spend an entire day snuggled up in my bedroom.

After Thaddeus left I lounged around my townhouse for a while. I watched a little television, all the while dreading the fact I had to prep for trial on Monday. Even though I had a big case Monday morning, I found it hard to concentrate. I often caught myself daydreaming. I imagined what it would be like going out on a date with Thaddeus, the two of us enjoying candlelight dinners together, spending hours upon hours simply talking the night away as well as nights filled with his firm chest pressed up next to mine. I could not help but bristle with excitement at the possibility of my fantasies becoming reality. It was a far cry from the occasional nights of sex with a guy who simply sufficed.

Lisa called later that afternoon. She was curious to know what happened after we left the Bid Wiz party. Of course, I gave her all of the juicy details. I knew I could trust Lisa to keep a secret. We were attorneys—half of our job was keeping secrets. I thought about asking Lisa for Thaddeus' phone number since him and I had conveniently forgotten to exchange telephone numbers before he left. However, I knew if I called him it might appear as if I was desperate. That was not the type of signal I wanted to send. Yet, I did want to see him again. Of course, I was assuming Thaddeus wished to see me as well. Thaddeus could have not given me his phone number for a reason.

So, there I was Sunday afternoon wondering what to do next. Is he going to call me? Should I call him? What do I say if he does call? Is he really interested in me? I must've asked myself those questions a thousand times. Unfortunately in my case, I was forced to continuously ask myself these questions until I bumped into Thaddeus again or I swallowed my pride and begged Lisa for Thaddeus' phone number.

Erin—How About Over A Cosmopolitan?

When I decided to meet Belinda and Stacy after work for happy hour, I had no intentions of meeting anybody. Yet, it always seems like when I don't want to meet someone, somebody tends to fall right into my lap. Also for the record, I did not intend to become apart of some love triangle. I went to the bar, so I could unwind and vent. I was stressed out. One of my advertising firm's biggest clients hated all my proposals for their new ad campaign, and was threatening to take their business elsewhere unless they saw something to their likening soon. Not only was I running out of time, but I was also running out of ideas. On top of that, my latest attempt at reconciling with Brian was not going so well. Then as if to make matters more complicated, Thaddeus walks into my life.

As usual our local watering hole was crowded with the usual after work happy hour crowd. It took me awhile to find Belinda and Stacy amongst the aqua blue lights and crush of people at the bar, but I eventually found them. Upon my arrival, I noticed Belinda entertaining one potential male suitor while Stacy appeared preoccupied with another. I managed to squeeze my way up to the bar between them and order myself a Cosmopolitan. It didn't take long for Stacy to rid herself of her companion and join me for a drink.

"What happened?" I said. I watched as the gentleman walked away.

"Nothing, I simply told him my friend was here," replied Stacy.

"Oh, I didn't know it was that easy to blow a guy off nowadays." I caught a glimpse of the guy as he disappeared into the crowd. "He definitely was a hottie," I added.

"Yeah, I'll give him that." Stacy took a sip of her Mai Tai. "He has been trying to get me to go out with him for the longest. The only problem is…I work with him. You know how I feel about dating guys I work with…that is a definite no-no."

"Since I have gone down that road before, I can totally understand where you are coming from," I assured her. I turned my attention to Belinda. "What's their story?" I asked. Whomever the guy was Belinda was preoccupied with he was definitely commanding a great deal of her attention.

"I don't know. He was here when we walked in. You know Belinda; she spotted him the second she walked through the door. He's just her type." Stacy rolled her eyes.

Stacy and Belinda couldn't have been any more different. Belinda was from Minneapolis, while Stacy was from a small town in Outstate Minnesota called

Monticello. Just as Belinda displayed sophistication, Stacy was about as Plain Jane as they came. Belinda was very opinionated and open-minded while Stacy, on the other hand, was very conservative and closed-minded. Stacy's experiences in life did not extend beyond Monticello, Minnesota, and the Twin Cities. Belinda and I found ourselves many of times trying to convince her the things she heard of or witnessed on television were not always true depictions of life. I can sympathize with Stacy somewhat since there was a time I was just liker her...naïve.

Growing up in private schools provided me with a sheltered life. I did not have much interaction with people of different ethnic or economic backgrounds until I journeyed off to college. I was in for a rude awakening when I arrived at the University of Minnesota. Although I learned a lot about other people and their culture, my freshman year of college was by and large a culture shock for me.

Anyhow, the rolling of Stacy's eyes was a sign of her disgust towards the type of guy Belinda was talking to. See, Stacy's ideal man was white. While Belinda who dated all types of guys, preferred black. The gentleman Belinda was talking with just so happened to be black, which is what warranted the rolling of Stacy's eyes.

I glanced over Belinda's shoulder to check the guy out. He was exactly Belinda's type—tall, dark and handsome. He had the body of a jock or ex-jock. I will admit he was a good-looking man. I must not have been too discreet in my observation of him for he caught me peeking and gave me a sly little wink. I gave him a polite smile before returning to my Cosmo. I did not want to give him the impression that if all else failed with Belinda, he had an open invitation with me.

"At least he's good looking," I told Stacy in Belinda's defense.

"That is a matter of opinion," Stacy snapped. "He claims to be waiting for a friend," she remarked. There was a hint of cynicism in Stacy's voice. No one wanted to admit coming to a bar alone. People who did always claimed to be waiting for a friend.

That is when Thaddeus walked up to the guy and proved that he was indeed waiting for someone. I really did not pay much attention to Thaddeus at first. I mean I did notice he was attractive, yet it was not like he was the only attractive guy in the bar. Thaddeus simply came over and interrupted Belinda's conversation with a brief remark to his friend and that was it. It was at that point that Belinda decided to come up for air and introduce us to her companion. His name was Darius. He in turn introduced everyone to Thaddeus. After the initial introductions, Darius and Thaddeus briefly whispered amongst themselves. I can only imagine what was being said judging by the immediate attention Thaddeus suddenly directed in my direction.

Thaddeus and Darius went back and forth a bit before Thaddeus professed, "Only under the cover of night," to Darius as he made his way over to the bar. I can only imagine what he was referring to.

Thaddeus motioned to the bartender. "I'll have one of those," he said pointing at my martini. "In fact make it two. It looks as if the lady is about done with hers." The bartender nodded his head and went about making our drinks.

"Thank you," I told him.

"Don't mention it. Does your friend want a drink?" Thaddeus asked, motioning towards Stacy. Stacy had conveniently found her co-worker again and chosen to ignore us.

"I don't know? If she does let him get it for her," I proclaimed. I thought it was rude of Stacy to turn her back on us once she saw Thaddeus make himself comfortable at the bar next to me.

The bartender returned with our Cosmos and Thaddeus willingly paid. He handed me my glass and slightly raised his glass as if to say cheers. He took a sip before releasing a deep sigh. It was like the liquor had taken a heavy burden off his shoulders. Since we were stuck with each other, I didn't see any harm in striking up a conversation. Besides, I was curious to know what had invoked such a sigh of relief.

"You sound as if your day was just as rough as mine."

"Rough, is not the word," spouted Thaddeus.

"Tough day at the office I suppose."

"I wish. Nah, I'm having some baby mama drama." Not until I met Thaddeus had I ever heard of or even knew what the term "baby mama drama" meant.

My lack of understanding must have shown on my face for he smiled and quickly translated for me. "I'm having some problems with my son's mother."

"Oh, I see," I replied. I tried to sneak a peek at his hand to see if I noticed a ring. There was no ring. However that didn't necessarily mean he was not married. I have met plenty of married men in a bar who had stuck their wedding bands in their pockets as soon as they walked out of the house. Regardless of a ring or not, I always made it a practice to ask a man about his marital status.

"So you're married?"

"Nope, I've been divorced now for a year and a half."

It is always nice to get a guy's response to this question for the record. As plenty of women know…men do have a tendency to lie. Not to be unfair to Thaddeus, but many married men claim to be either separated or divorced when they are at the bar. However, it's comical on how many marriages suddenly reconcile after a guy gets what he wants from a woman. It was a lesson I learned the hard way during one of my many break-ups with Brian.

"Sorry to hear that?" I told him.

"It's no big deal, we got married for all the wrong reasons," Thaddeus answered.

"How long have you been divorced again?" I had heard him correctly the first time. I simply like to repeat the question because plenty of men are too stupid to remember what they told you the first time. It was my way of testing them.

"A year and a half," Thaddeus repeated. He passed the first test. Either Thaddeus was telling the truth or he had played this game before. If he had given me a different answer than the one he had provided earlier, our conversation would have ceased right there.

"That is not very long," I added. Of course, I have heard of couples that were married for shorter periods of time.

"Like I said, we got married for all the wrong reasons," Thaddeus reiterated. He polished off his Cosmopolitan and ordered another.

"I know this is being nosey, but why do you have a problem with your ex-wife?" I knew asking such a question was kind of forward of me, but I could not resist.

I mean…here I was a total stranger, Thaddeus might have known me for maybe five minutes, and I was already asking him to divulge personal information to me. Maybe it was the alcohol. I don't know. To me it just seemed like asking that question at the time flowed with the natural progression of the conversation. Yet, by the look on Thaddeus' face my question was not well received.

"I'm sorry, I really shouldn't have asked you such a question." I apologized profusely in order to head off a scene. Thaddeus simply stood there as if he was contemplating on whether to tell me off or walk away.

Eventually he took a sip of his newly arrived martini and said, "There's no need to apologize." After hearing him say that I silently thanked God, he did not curse me out right there in the middle of the bar. "If you really want to know, I disagree with how often I can see my son. My ex-wife refuses to be flexible with me. Sometimes my job causes me to work long hours and instead of her working with me to allow me to see my son on other days that may be out of the parenting agreement, my ex-wife just does not let me see him at all."

"Why would she do such a thing?" I asked. "She is only hurting your son."

"She doesn't want me around. She's got a new boyfriend, so that may have something to do with it. Regardless, I never do her wrong when it comes to child support. So, I don't understand why she has to treat me this way when it comes to seeing my son? Not once! Not once, have I been late in paying child support."

"So, what are you going to do?"

"I have no choice, but to see him on the days the parenting agreement allows for me to see him," Thaddeus stated. He quickly finished off his second martini.

"You really love your son don't you?"

"He's my heart."

"That's good to hear." I smiled.

After that I very wisely got off the subject of his son and ex-wife and on a much safer topic such as work. Of course, I complained to him about my troubles at work before he told me about his job. I was shocked to learn Thaddeus was once a consultant with Dyson & Rhodes, one of the most prestigious consulting firms in the nation. In all honesty, Thaddeus did not strike me as the type of person to work for such a conservative firm as Dyson & Rhodes. I also discovered from our conversation that Thaddeus was currently performing contractual work for Midwestern Federal. I got the feeling life was hectic enough for him without the additional stress of his ex-wife.

Thaddeus and I talked for some time. The more we conversed the more I found myself intrigued by him. Not only was he good-looking, but also intelligent. That is a rare quality to find in a man at a bar. Most guys I meet at the bar acted like horny Neanderthals. They usually try to feed me as many drinks as possible in hopes I said "yes" when I should have said "no." Thaddeus on the other hand, seemed to be more interested in conversation than a one-night stand. The two of us probably would have talked all night if it were not for Belinda. Since she met Stacy at the bar and Stacy had left some time ago it was my duty to take her home, which only made sense since Belinda and I were roommates.

The night ended with Thaddeus giving me his business card. He suggested we get together and have lunch. I promised I would give him a call to set up a date knowing full well I did not intend to. It was the customary line I fed men when I did not want it to appear like I was blowing them off. If I were not trying to mend my relationship with Brian at the time, I might have taken Thaddeus up on his offer. I found him quite alluring. A part of me wanted to call Thaddeus. However, I knew that was counterproductive to Brian and I patching things up between us. Besides, I misplaced Thaddeus' business card, which negated any urge I may have had to call him in the future.

A few weeks after that night at the bar I realized my plans of reconciling with Brian were once again going nowhere. Whether subconsciously or consciously, my mind drifted to thoughts of Thaddeus. Thaddeus had made it painfully obvious to me that I did not need to settle for a guy like Brian. He had given me proof there was at least one man who made me feel alive. I know that is weird to say about him especially after meeting him only once and in a bar at that, but Thaddeus made me feel like it was okay to be me. I felt like he accepted me for me. In the make believe world in my head, I wanted to believe Thaddeus liked me for me and not because he believed he could change me into something I was not like Brian. So as can be expected I ended my relationship with Brian…again.

Of course, I know people may think I suffered from "jungle fever" but that was not the case. I admit I grew up in a household where it was pretty much assumed I would fall in love and marry someone who looked like and came from a similar background as mine. Of course, my parents professed they would have loved me no matter what type of person I fell in love with. Nevertheless, there was always that underlying expectation the person I feel in love with would be white. So yes, I did have a natural curiosity to know what it would be like to be with someone different than me. Yet, I experimented dating guys from different ethnic backgrounds in college. So, I had satisfied that curiosity.

Thaddeus was more than just a novelty to me. I was able to see beyond his outward appearance. That night at the bar, I believed I had caught a glimpse of a man I wanted to know better. Yet, since I lost his business card I was unable to take advantage of Thaddeus' offer of lunch.

After that evening at the bar, Belinda began dating Thaddeus' friend—Darius. Occasionally, Darius would come by the apartment and I would inquire about Thaddeus. I don't know why? I think I wanted to know if Thaddeus was still available. I can honestly say meeting Thaddeus ruined me ever getting back together with Brian. I found myself constantly discussing Thaddeus to Belinda. No matter how hard I tried, I simply could not get Thaddeus off my mind. He had really made an impression on me. However, it took a little over five months before I was able to act on my feelings.

Thaddeus—When It Rains It Pours

Now, there are times when a man can't get a woman to look his way…let alone speak to him. Then there are times when women are ringing a man's phone off the hook, driving him crazy. As with all things in life—even women—it is either feast or famine. Never is a man privileged to choose from a consistent group of women. Since meeting Ivy and Erin within two days time in the same week, Erin on Friday and Ivy on Saturday, I realized I might be enjoying a period when the women I had to chose from was plentiful.

I've never dated a white woman before. I've slept with plenty, but never dated. Dating requires some sort of commitment and public display of affection. There are specific activities a couple tends to do which require some show of public affection. To be quiet honest, I was not ready to openly be seen with a white woman. Now, sleeping with a woman requires nothing more than a telephone in order to make the booty call, maybe a little something to drink, and if you insisted a bed. Most important of all, it is done in the privacy of someone's home, motel, or car. Regardless of where it is done, most of the time it is done away from prying eyes. I had yet to reach the point of someone like Darius, who did not give a damn what people thought about him when they saw him out with a white woman. I admire that quality in him. I myself feel self-conscious about meeting a white woman, even if she is a co-worker, somewhere outside of work. In relation to history it has not been that long ago when black men were lynched for just looking a white woman's way.

Anyway, what did dating a white woman say about me?

C'mon, I was a brotha who looked up to such black icons as W.E.B. DuBois, Stokely Carmichael, Malcolm X, Patrice Lumumba and Angela Davis just to name a few. Didn't dating a white woman negate my blackness? To black women it was the equivalent of treason.

In my household growing up, there was no such thing as black and white. It was always us and them. It was always spoken of in a confrontational context, sort of like good versus evil. There was never any need to clarify who "them" were. When you heard somebody say "them people"—you knew who they were referring to. Throughout my adult life I have tried to take the blinders off and open up my mind and eyes to the world surrounding me, yet I still find it hard to shake the stigmatism I grew up with. No matter how hard I try, I often find myself breaking white people down into their camp and black people into theirs'.

Regardless, I've still had my share of white women. However, I have never loved them. For so long my heart belonged to black women. Besides, there is nothing in the world that will ruin your chances with a black woman more than a white woman. Sistahs might let you slide with a Latino or even an Asian babe, but if you step out with a white woman on your arm it is within a man's best interest to make sure that white girl is fine as hell because the word will get out fast. Believe me, once a man is spotted with a white babe he might as well hang it up for he will surely fall from a black woman's graces. So, the white woman a brotha steps out with better be bad cause it is damn near impossible for a brotha to get back with a black woman after that. And if a brotha does happen to make amends for his indiscretion, you can best believe a brotha is gonna to hear about "that white bitch" for the rest of his life.

With that said, you could understand why I didn't think too much about Erin after that Friday night at the bar. Besides, I can never tell with white women. It's hard for me to gauge if they are truly genuine in their interest or seeking to fulfill some life long fantasy of being with a black man. Or even worst fulfilling some dare, their girlfriends might've put them up to. Most of the time I've found white women usually just have some itch about black men they needed scratched. Afterwards, they usually return to their boyfriends or husbands with their curiosity satisfied. Usually the encounter becomes a cute story for white women to tell their girlfriends over a cup of cappuccino.

I figured giving Erin my business card was enough to let her know I was interested, and if we saw each other again after that night it was cool with me. How serious she took my offer, I don't know nor did I really care. Besides, giving Erin anything more than my business card would have attracted undue attention, which might have been bad for the both of us. I did not want some sistah, who happened to be at the bar having drinks that Friday night to think I was trying to push up on Erin and take her home. Believe me, it only takes one sistah to have seen me talking to Erin that evening and I would have been the talk of every black beauty salon in Minneapolis for a week and that is regardless if Erin was an attractive white woman or not.

Still, I want to make it clear. I noticed Erin the moment I made my way over to where Darius and Erin's friend, Belinda, were standing. It was hard not to notice her. Erin is an attractive woman. Maybe a little too nosey for my tastes but she is still good looking. Erin possesses a look that reminds me of Sharon Stone. She has long sandy blonde hair highlighted with platinum blonde streaks splashed throughout. Erin has the bluest eyes I have ever seen. They were absolutely hypnotizing. She wore a beige pants suit that hugged her athletic physique in such a way that was not only sexy but also classy. The combination was alluring.

Now the whispering Erin overheard after Darius and Belinda made their initial introductions was nothing more than Darius telling me, "You might want to get up on that dawg. I caught her checking me out earlier." He then nodded in Erin's direction.

"You can best believe if this doesn't pan out right here," Darius was referring to Belinda, "I just might have to kick a little game her way."

I promptly looked over in Erin's direction; she caught me checking her out. I didn't care. "I told you I like dark meat. I am a legs and thighs man. I could care less for the wings and breast of a chicken. You can keep the white meat," I reminded him. Darius just smiled.

"Where's Marcus?" I asked.

"Where do you think? At home! Lisa has got that negro's drawls buried in the backyard somewhere. I talked to him earlier today and he said he would catch up with us tomorrow at the Bid Wiz party.... You're coming right?"

"Yeah, I'll be there."

"Cool.... In the interim why don't you go over there and entertain ole' girl for me while I put a bug in her girl's ear." I must've given Darius a cross look for he quickly reminded me. "Ah don't act like you wouldn't hit that if the offer was extended." He had a point.

I could not help but smile and say, "Only under the cover of night, my brotha. Only under the cover of night," as I walked over towards the bar.

Other than the personal questions, I found Erin quite charming. In fact I found her charm and wit quite refreshing. I had taken her for a dumb blonde with a pretty face but not much upstairs. Contrary to what I believed, she had a brain and was very apt at using it. The number of topics we discussed that evening were numerous. We talked about so many different things I can't recall half of them. What I do remember, however, was how opinionated she was and how she did not shy away from expressing herself. I find that to be an attractive quality in a woman. Don't ask me why, I just do. I find women who can speak their minds, sexy.

Still like I said, I did not think much about Erin after Friday night. The reason being the whole bar scene, people usually come to bars with the intentions of picking someone up. There is nothing wrong with that. I myself just was not into the bar scene. Besides, the way diseases are circulated amongst people nowadays; the risk is not worth a brief moment of pleasure.

Regardless, I gave Erin my business card. I did not want her to think I was only about the booty, even if that was my intentions. The invitation to lunch signified I was interested, but it was not too forward. It leaves the decision to call or in Erin's case to email me up to her. This is what I like to call game. It makes the woman feel as if she is in control of the situation, but in reality she is the one whose buttons are being pushed. Since I did not hear from Erin after that night, I did not think twice about her. If things are not meant to be, then they are simply not meant to be. Dating is nothing more than a mating ritual based on chance. Kind of like a game of roulette or better yet craps. Sometimes you roll a seven or an eleven and sometimes you crap out. It all depends on Lady Luck.

Darius hooked up with Erin's roommate, Belinda, and he informed me Erin was constantly going in and out of a relationship with an old boyfriend. He claimed she occasionally asked about me. I never really understood why she would ask Darius about me if she had a man. Yet, I never understand half the things women do. Regardless, meeting Ivy Saturday night—the very next day—at Darius' Bid Wiz party pushed Erin to the back of my mind.

That Saturday, I arrived at Darius' Bid Wiz party fashionably late. I was not worried about Darius starting the card party without me. Darius never did anything on time. He always ran on CP time. When I arrived to find everyone drinking and mingling, it was obvious Darius was holding true to form. I stepped into the party surveying the scene. Although, Darius' parties tend to draw the same crowd every time, every once and a while a new face would grace the party. I gazed around the party searching for that one woman worthy of my undivided attention that evening. Before I could thoroughly scope the place out, I noticed Darius and Marcus conversing across the room. I made my way over to where my friends stood saying my "hellos" to acquaintances as I passed them by. When I finally reached Darius and Marcus, I could over hear Marcus discussing the aesthetics of one of the female guest's behind.

"You might want to keep your voice down a little before Lisa hears you," I forewarned. I caught both Darius and Marcus by surprise. I must of scared Marcus half to death. He looked as if he was about to piss in his pants. Yet, when they realized it was me they relaxed and gave me a pound and a firm hug before asking my opinion of the female in question.

"Yo T, what do you think? Does Monica have a tail on her or what?" Marcus posed the question to me.

As I looked across the room to examine the derriere in question, Monica's, I spotted Ivy. Ivy stood there simply talking with Lisa. There were three reasons why Ivy stood out at a party like Darius'. One, the pool of eligible black women in Minneapolis is small. So a new face like Ivy's immediately stood out. Two, like I stated, Darius' parties always seemed to attract the same people time and time again. From time to time there may be a new face in the crowd, but usually it was the same people who came to Darius' last party. That brings me to my third reason. Although new faces occasionally appeared at Darius' parties, they were pretty much ignored because they usually were not fine.... Ivy was fine.

Ivy wore a very colorful dress that immediately caught my eye. Ivy's dress rested seductively above her knees, showing just the right amount thigh to tease a brotha. The way that dress hugged Ivy's curves I could not help but fantasize about the beauty it may have concealed. Ivy's hair hung just above her shoulders in a well-kept bob. It was obvious by the way her smooth caramel skin glowed and her tight physique that she was a woman who took care of herself. The only problem with that was determining if she did it for her own personal benefit or to attract a man. If Ivy did it for her own benefit that was good for it meant she would most likely maintain that figure after tying a man down. If Ivy was simply staying in shape to attract a man that usually meant bad news for she was more than likely to stop working out and blow up like a house as soon as she was able to get a man to say, "I do." Some men dig "healthy" women but I'm more into the athletic type and Ivy fit the bill.

Now I stated the obvious when it came to Monica's behind, or onion as brothas like to refer to them as. "Yeah, she's got a tail on her but it is not tight. That ass has too much junk in the trunk. Monica has a butt that will fall to her knees when she takes those tight jeans off."

"I don't know what you're talking about? That behind is right!" Darius protested.

"Tell me about it." Marcus gave him a pound.

"Darius, what would you know about that anyway? You don't mess with nothing but white girls. Half the women you mess with don't even have an ass," I exclaimed.

Marcus laughed. "He's got a point there."

"Whatever! The two of you might want to start looking at these white girls because they're starting to grow asses on them," Darius professed.

I made sure the conversation did not deviate from the subject of women. "Enough about Monica. I want to know who is the new face over there with Lisa?" Both Marcus and Darius directed their attention towards Ivy.

"Ah man to hell with her! That broad is stuck up!" Darius exclaimed. Darius was easy to read. I presumed he had made a play on Ivy and gotten shot down.

"Son please, Darius is upset because Ivy played him off." Marcus confirmed my hunch. "I tried to tell Darius, he should slow down. He can't be rushing sistahs like he does these white girls out here, but he does not listen. He only knows one speed—hard and fast."

"I figured as much," I said. "Still that does not answer my question. Who is she?"

"That is Ivy Martin, she works with Lisa at Grimble & Kline."

"What's the low down on her?" I quickly sized her up.

"I really can't tell you my man. I just met her tonight myself. I can tell you, she is looking for a Wiz partner and from the looks of it she is still looking for one," Marcus proclaimed. He accompanied his comment with a devilish grin. "If you want I can make it happen?" Marcus' grin turned into a full-fledged smile.

"Make it happen," I insisted.

"I don't know now. Ivy ain't one of these women you and Darius are use to messing around with. This is a woman of sophistication and substance. She needs to be approached by a brotha with superior game," Marcus joked.

"Come on now playa? What's my name?" I gave Marcus a sly grin.

"Oh yeah, I forgot who I was talking to. This is my boy T or Sweet T as the ladies like to call him." Marcus smiled.

"You're damn right." I quickly acknowledged his keen sense of observation.

"I apologize brotha. I thought I was still talking to Darius' mixed up ass." A chorus of laughter circulated amongst Marcus and I.

"You fools laugh all you want," Darius interrupted. "I guarantee you that if you take your sorry ass over there you're going to get your feelings hurt."

"Don't hate baby, jealousy is a terrible thing," I teased.

"To hell with you guys," Darius responded. He promptly gave us both the finger. "I'm going over here and get this card party started."

As Darius got the Bid Wiz tournament going, Marcus and I made our way over towards Lisa and Ivy. Marcus informed Lisa that Darius was about to start the card party before smoothly introducing me to Ivy. I must admit his delivery was flawless. Up close, Ivy was even more stunning than from a distance. It was evident she had a body to die for. Ivy wore a coral color lipstick that made her lips absolutely delectable. Of course when I went to make myself a drink after it was confirmed we were Wiz partners, I made sure to pay close attention to her backside. Like I told Darius at the bar the night before, I like the dark meat. I assure you Ivy did not disappoint.

The legs and thighs on this woman were firm and shapely. Those two muscular mounds of flesh resting majestically at the base of her back sent shivers up my spine just looking at them. Those cheeks protruded out from her backside with firmness and strength. It was like the period in an exclamation point, firm and always making a statement. It was a beautiful thing. It was not like so many behinds I had encountered lately, spreading all over the place once I got them out of their pants like runny ink.

Other than the fact she was fine, what I liked the most about Ivy was her laid back attitude. Ivy did not come off as pretentious or stuck-up. Ivy was very much down to earth. I barely knew the woman and she was already cracking jokes. For a lady of her caliber, a lawyer and a damn good-looking one, that was rare. Most women I knew who had it going on, usually acted sadiddy as if they were above talking shit. To say the least, we hit it off right away.

It was obvious there was chemistry between us. It was equally apparent by how determined Ivy became when it came time to play Darius in the championship round of the card tournament that she did not like Darius. It did not surprise me. A person either liked Darius or they hated Darius. Darius' arrogant behavior turned plenty of people off. By the way Ivy celebrated after we set Darius and Rob to win the pot, it was obvious which camp she fell into. Now I know this may sound corny, but after winning the tournament I did not want the night to end. I was having a good time and I really wanted to get to know Ivy better…talk to her in a more one on one setting. So that is why I suggested we go out to eat.

I knew Marcus and Lisa were not up for it. I had spotted Marcus dozing off while Ivy and I played our last hand of Wiz. Since Marcus had informed me Ivy rode with him and Lisa that meant if Ivy was interested in grabbing a bite to eat she would be forced to ride with me. Thus, giving us the chance to be one on one minus the distractions. I know it was a gamble but I figured it was a chance I had to take if I wanted to get to know Ivy beyond a few hands of cards. Fortunately for me, Ivy wanted to grab a late night snack as well, which played right into my hands. As I had suspected Marcus and Lisa had decided to call it a night.

I decided I wanted to eat somewhere intimate, but not overly private. I did not want to give her the impression it was a date. Instead, I wanted to keep it light and informal. So after a brief moment of indecision on where the two of us could go and maintain the same kind of vibe we were enjoying, I recommended we eat at a pizzeria in the Warehouse district in downtown Minneapolis called Pizza Lucé. The atmosphere in the pizza parlor was laid back and cozy. We made ourselves comfortable in a booth and talked. I wanted to preserve the rapport Ivy and I had established at Darius' card party. I've learned over time the more relaxed the setting the more at ease your date will feel.

Ivy and I sat in the pizza parlor conversing for some time. We were so engrossed in one another we lost track of time. Not until the pizzeria started to clear out did we realize the time. It was three thirty in the morning when we left the pizza joint. Although it was late, I refused to let the night end just yet. I was really enjoying Ivy's company. So, I was pleased to drive her to her townhouse in Eden Prairie. It gave us more time to talk. However, I did dread my return trip back into The Cities.

Now, I want to set the record straight. I had no intentions of staying the night at Ivy's place. Although I was not looking forward to the drive back into Minneapolis, I had not secretly plotted to spend the night at Ivy's townhouse. When Ivy suggested I sleep on her couch rather than allowing me to drive back home at four thirty in the morning the first thing that crossed my mind was not getting the booty. I am not going to say it did not cross my mind. However, it was not *the* first thing on my mind. Truthfully, I was exhausted. I simply wanted to go to sleep. Besides, over the course of the night it became obvious to me Ivy was a woman who was not searching for a one-night-stand. I respected that. She was the type of woman that demanded a man's respect before allowing a friendship to turn into a relationship.

Plus, if we had sex that night all the respect I had for Ivy would have been thrown out the window. Any man will profess that if a woman sleeps with him on the first date, she automatically falls into the hoe category. It does not matter if a woman usually behaves this way or not. It does not matter what happens from that moment on—a woman will be stereotyped as a hoe.

So, it goes without saying. If something sexual was going to take place between us I wanted it to be when the two of us felt the timing was right. Despite this fact, I could not resist giving Ivy a kiss when she brought me a pillow. Her lips had been beckoning for me to indulge them all evening. At that particular moment I could not resist. When our lips parted and Ivy pulled away I could tell our kiss had made a lasting impression. The kool-aid grin that spread from ear to ear said it all.

The next morning I awoke to thoughts of my son, Little T. Usually when I get in such an introspective mood I like to find a place where I can be alone. In my solitude I tend to constantly work over a problem in my mind. As a kid growing up my mom use to tell me I think too much. She called me a worry-wart. As a child I would lock myself in the bedroom I shared with my brother and stare out the window at the stars and make believe I was an astronaut exploring the universe. It was during these periods of seclusion I felt closest to my father. When I sat there all alone he no longer seemed to feel like a distant stranger to me. He became more than just a name. Other than basketball, astronomy was the only subject in school that interested me. I always seemed to find my father when I gazed out amongst the stars.

Although, Ivy's patio was not the room I grew up in as a child it seemed inviting enough. I may have sat there maybe a half an hour before Ivy braved the cold and came outside and joined me. Whenever I get in such a mood I usually want to be left alone, however, I found Ivy's company comforting. Still, I did not share with her my inner most thoughts. I guess you can say that is Stephanie's curse she so graciously bestowed upon me. Since my divorce, I had become very cynical when it came to my feelings. Like all spurned lovers, I built a wall around my heart. No doubt, this posed a problem when it came to building a fulfilling and lasting relationship with another woman. Still, it saved me the heartache.

Ivy fixed me breakfast that morning and I humbly thanked her. Since I only had Little T for the day, I wasted no time getting dressed and leaving. I had only so much time with Little T before my time was up and Stephanie demanded I have him home. Ivy seemed to understand. She did not cop an attitude or trip like some of the women I dated.

Little T and I spent most of Sunday afternoon hanging out at the Children's Science Museum before heading back to my place to relax and play video games. Even though I was content with spending time with Little T, I could not help but think about Ivy. I contemplated calling her several times. The only problem was I forgot to get her phone number. Of course, if I really wanted to call Ivy, I knew I could simply get her phone number from Lisa. Nevertheless, I did not want to go that route. So I decided to sit back and wait until I could get it from her personally.

How that was going to happen, who knew?

Yet, what I did know was that Ivy was the first woman I had felt totally comfortable with in a long time and I didn't want to let her or that feeling slip away. Ivy and I just clicked. Of course, I realized I was basing my opinion on one night. Anyone could pretend to be someone they were not for twenty-four hours. Besides, I had been down this road before. I knew everything was not always what it seemed to be and people over time changed. So, I approached

my budding feelings towards Ivy with caution. Still, regardless of my apprehension I could not stop thinking about her.

Even though we had a good time, I did not want to assume it was cool to
call Ivy at home. For all I knew, Ivy's boyfriend could have been out of town.
Women can be just as scandalous as men. Even if that was not the case, I still
had a dilemma when it came to seeing Ivy again. After mauling this problem
over for a while I recalled Ivy telling me she had to be in court on Monday. I
suddenly had an idea. It probably was not the best idea but it was the best idea
this desperate man could come up with at the time.

Why Do Fools Fall In Love?

Ivy—R.E.S.P.E.C.T.

The entire day Sunday and even into Monday I found myself thinking about Thaddeus. This was not good for I had a court case I needed to prepare for. Nevertheless, I could not stop thinking about Thaddeus. Thaddeus is right—we just clicked. When Thaddeus and I met it did not feel as if we were two strangers meeting for the first time. Instead, it felt like we were two old friends getting reacquainted. Now, if you think I was having a hard time focusing before the trial on Monday—try to imagine how I felt when I saw Thaddeus sitting in the courtroom. Up until the moment I noticed Thaddeus sitting there amongst the few faces in the gallery, I had been doing an excellent job of arguing my case. My motions were being granted and it appeared opposing counsel was fighting an uphill battle when it came to swaying the judge in his favor. However, after I spotted Thaddeus sitting amongst the crowd I became flustered. I found myself constantly referring to my notes. By the time court adjourned Thaddeus had disappeared.

I was furious. Not at Thaddeus, but with myself. I had let Thaddeus get to me. Worst of all, I let Thaddeus see he had an affect on me. And to top it all off, he witnessed this in the courtroom—the one place in the world where I needed to exhibit confidence. That *was* not good. Most men tend to act a fool, once they discover the mere sight of them makes a woman weak in the knees. Although, Thaddeus did not strike me as that type of brotha I could not be for certain. I had only known the man barely forty-eight hours. There was no telling what type of person would emerge once Thaddeus felt comfortable enough around me to let his guard down.

Even though I had not slept with Thaddeus, I was beginning to believe things between us had started out a little too intense. His unexpected visit at the courthouse showed me the man was resourceful. So taking that into consideration, I decided to slow things down a bit. I wanted to navigate myself back into the driver's seat. If Thaddeus and I were going to progress towards something a little more serious, I thought it was best we got to know each other beyond one night and develop a mutual respect for one another.

Upon leaving the courthouse, I arrived at Grimble & Kline to find my admin, Judy, rattling off my numerous messages and missed calls as soon as I got off the elevator. It was not until Judy said, "A gentleman by the name of Thaddeus Brown called," did I pay close attention. "He did not want to leave a message with me, so I put him through to your voicemail."

It was not until I noticed the peculiar look on Judy's face did I realize I had rushed into my office and picked up the phone's receiver at the mention of Thaddeus' name. I did my best to regain my composure by telling her, "Thank you," and instructing her to shut the door behind her on the way out. When I was certain Judy was gone, I skipped over all the irrelevant work related voice messages until I reached Thaddeus'.

"Ivy." I just loved the way he said my name. "I hope I did not startle you this afternoon by showing up at the courthouse. I was in the area, so, I thought I would drop by and see you in action."

I knew that was a lie. I didn't know one person who visited the county courthouse—especially someone black—unless they had a ticket to pay or show up in court. Most of the black people I knew tried to avoid the courthouse like the plague.

"Anyway, I was hoping…" Thaddeus continued, "when you were done tonight, maybe you would like to meet me somewhere for dinner. I have to work late tonight, so, I thought maybe somewhere downtown would work. Give me a call at work when you get this message. My number is 612-555-8921. I'll be waiting for your call." I saved the message realizing this may be my one chance to redeem myself for the way I acted in the courtroom earlier as well as retake control of the situation.

At first, I thought about not calling Thaddeus at all. Instead, wait to see how long it took for him to call me. I eventually gave up on that idea because there was a remote possibility Thaddeus might not call back at all. In such a case I would feel like a fool. Feeling like a fool once again was not my intentions. I wanted to keep Thaddeus guessing but I did not want him to get away. So, before I returned his phone call I devised a plan as to how I would play our conversation. Like I said, I wanted him to know I was interested but I did not want Thaddeus to think he didn't have to put forth any effort to get me. Once a man feels he's got a woman wrapped around his finger, he tends to stop doing the little things that are so important to a woman. Things like pulling out a woman's chair or opening the door for her. I may be an independent woman but I still enjoy being treated like a lady.

I called Thaddeus back as planned and after a brief discussion we agreed to meet at a small jazz café located along the Mississippi river called Sophia. It was a small quaint place that played live jazz and served good food. I had been there once before, so I was familiar with the restaurant. However, the way Thaddeus spoke of the place I got the impression he was a regular there. I could not help but assume this was maybe the place he took all his little girl-friends. The one thing I intended to make clear to Thaddeus from jump was that I was not one of those women chasing him all over town. Nor did I expect to be treated that way.

I met Thaddeus at the café around eight. I had to prepare for the following day in court, so I recommended a late dinner. When I walked in I noticed him sitting at the bar nursing a drink. Thaddeus appeared to have company. The thought of turning around and leaving crossed my mind for I was just too exhausted to play games, not to mention too damn old. Thaddeus would have never seen me or even known I was there. Instead, I decided to use this as an opportunity to see if Thaddeus treated me like his date or like some friend happening to join him at the bar. It would let me know just how interested Thaddeus was in me.

"Hey you?" I said. I took a seat next to Thaddeus at the bar, opposite his other female companion.

"Hey! How you doing?" he exclaimed. Thaddeus gave me a hug and flashed me a warm smile.

"I'm doing great. I hope I'm not interrupting anything here," I said. The comment was in reference to the woman sitting so close to him, she damn near was sitting in his lap.

"Nah, not at all. Saundra this is Ivy. Ivy this is Saundra. Saundra is a co-worker of mine down at Midwestern Federal. I told her about you, so she decided to come down here and meet you for yourself," Thaddeus explained.

"How you do?" stated Saundra. Saundra gave me a phony smile accompanied by a weak handshake.

I immediately knew what Saundra's game was about the second she opened her mouth. Saundra was nothing more than a sistah, who had been trying to get with Thaddeus under the pretense of friendship but in actuality wanted to be much more. She was only there to check out the competition.

"Fine, thank you." I returned Saundra's phony smile with one of my own.

"Well T, I better get going. It's getting late and I have a few errands I have to run before I turn in for the night." Saundra smiled.

"Drive safely," Thaddeus replied.

"I intend to. It was a pleasure meeting you Ivy." Saundra put on her coat.

"It was nice meeting you too." I was all to glad to see Saundra go.

When I was certain Saundra was gone I looked over at Thaddeus and smirked, "T, huh?"

Thaddeus gave me a sly grin. "T what?" He knew what I was referring to, yet he chose to play dumb.

"She called you T."

"All my friends call me T," answered Thaddeus. He gave me a shit-eating grin. Saundra wanted to be his friend all right, I thought.

I suddenly had to catch myself. I had known this man two days and there I was questioning him in regards to his relationship with a co-worker. That was not the way I intended to start the evening. The last thing I wanted was for Thaddeus to think I was sweating him. I forced myself to step back and play it cool.

So I looked over at him and asked, "Well when will I be privileged enough to call you T?"

Thaddeus glanced at me coyly and smiled. "When I get to know you better." The negro thought he was cute with that sly remark.

Thaddeus had reserved us a table, so we did not sit at the bar long before being seated. Our conversation quickly went from nicknames and co-workers to his surprise visit at the courthouse. Although I found the gesture heart warming, I never had a man so eager to see me he brought his behind down to the courthouse. I politely explained to Thaddeus how it would be wise he fore-warned a sistah before making his next visit. He understood and apologized for making me feel uncomfortable. I accepted his apology and told him to forget it.

Dinner was delicious but the company I had chosen to keep that evening was even more delectable. Seeing and talking to Thaddeus was relaxing. It felt natural. Thaddeus had a knack of making me feel special without having to do anything out of the ordinary. Just like Saturday night, Thaddeus and I got lost in one another. I don't know what it was about Thaddeus that allowed me to feel totally uninhibited, and let down my guard. Those two nights with him I felt like I was the most beautiful woman in the world.

When I finally noticed the time it was ten thirty, well pass my bedtime on a weeknight especially when I had to appear in court the following morning. I like to be well rested when I appear in court. Despite it being past my curfew and the dead of winter, I accepted an invitation from Thaddeus to take a walk along the Mississippi.

A winter breeze blew in off the Mississippi from the southwest. The gentle blow of the wind caused the night air to feel bitterly cold. Yet, I did not mind. I had dressed appropriately for the weather. The trees that lined the banks of the river had yet to develop the necessary foliage to shield us from the breeze, but Thaddeus and I did not seem to mind. Despite the biting cold, it was still a very beautiful evening. The beauty of the snow and the frozen Mississippi gave the impression I had stepped into a winter wonderland. Spring and fall are the most beautiful times of the year in the Twin Cities, however, at times winter do have its moments. As we walked along the river Thaddeus reached out for my hand and I gladly placed my hand in his.

The lights of Minneapolis' skyline reflected off the ice-laden Mississippi, displaying a dazzling array of colors. Despite the weather, the stroll along the riverbank was quite romantic. I think I saw Minneapolis in a totally different light that evening. We did very little talking. We simply walked. I think meaningless conversation would have ruined the mood.

After our walk, Thaddeus escorted me to my car. An awkward moment of silence developed between us as we said our good-byes. The inclination for a goodnight kiss was strong, however, I was determined to rebuff Thaddeus if he tried. I wanted Thaddeus to appreciate the feel of my lips next to his. The only way to do that was to make Thaddeus hunger for them. However, this time he resisted the urge as well. I sensed he wanted to kiss me, but he appeared to restrain himself. I could not figure it out.

Instead of kissing me, Thaddeus told me, "I would like to see you again."

All I could manage was, "Me too."

"So then, where do we go from here? I mean do I give you my number and wait for you to call me or do you allow me to get yours?" I couldn't help but smile. Thaddeus thought he was slick by easing his way into asking me for my phone number.

"I think you deserve the right to call me." I smirked. I tore some paper away from the gas bill envelope I had stuffed into my purse that morning and wrote down my phone number.

I remember the anticipation that filled me when Thaddeus asked for my phone number. I could not help but contemplate maybe Thaddeus was the one. At the ripe age of thirty-six it is a rarity for a black woman to find a brotha who was not broke, had a job, did not have a police record and above all else was attracted to black women. I am not exaggerating.

I remember before we departed that night Thaddeus telling me, "I'll call you," while I handed him my phone number.

Now whenever a woman gives a man her phone number, she runs the risk of having handed the number over to a lunatic or someone even worst a bug-a-boo—a person who constantly calls and annoys you. Thaddeus turned out to be neither. In fact he was pretty apt at piquing my interest. It took Thaddeus two whole days before he called me. It was just long enough to drive me crazy. The man had me wondering if he intended to call me at all. Thaddeus had me second-guessing myself to the point I wondered if I had given him an incorrect phone number. Can you believe that? This man had me believing I did not know my own damn phone number.

During the two days I did not hear from Thaddeus I considered asking Lisa for his number. Although I wanted to, my pride would not let me. I decided to save that option in case of an emergency. I guess Thaddeus knew what he was doing. He had basically done to me what I had intended to do to him…keep him guessing. If that was his mission Thaddeus was successful. When Thaddeus finally did call, he left a message at work inviting me over to his place for dinner and a relaxing evening spent watching a movie. There was no way I was going to turn down a free meal. Besides, I was curious to know if this brotha truly knew how to cook. To me there is nothing sexier, than a man that can throw down in the kitchen.

I called Thaddeus back and confirmed our dinner date. I looked forward to seeing him and unwinding at his place. At the time, the lawsuit I was trying was dragging on longer than I had expected and it was really starting to wear on my nerves. The fact Thaddeus lived in a condominium downtown along the Mississippi made the offer even more inviting since it negated my long commute out to the burbs.

When I arrived at Thaddeus' condo I was greeted by the sounds of Miles Davis and the tantalizing smell of dinner. Thaddeus demanded I make myself at home as he prepared our plates of chicken smothered in mushroom gravy with wild rice and broccoli. I will be the first to admit the brotha can cook. After dinner Thaddeus and I planted ourselves in front of the TV with the intentions of relaxing to a movie.

I recall sitting on the couch complaining about work and how stressed out I was when Thaddeus informed me, "I can help relive your stress."

I replied, "Yeah, I bet you can," with a grin.

"No, seriously, I can," stated Thaddeus. Thaddeus proceeded to grab my feet and place them in his lap. What came next was a foot massage like none other. The man got some lotion and kneaded my feet and massaged my toes. Of course, one thing led to another. However, I did not allow for us to get carried away and let the foot massage take us to the bedroom. Although, we had got ourselves worked up that evening, I was not ready to sleep with Thaddeus just yet.

Thaddeus and I went on teasing each other like this for close to two months. During this time period, we spent virtually every day together. We went to the movies together. We went to dinner and dancing at the local clubs. Sometimes we danced the night away to Ska and Reggae music. I was never really into Latin music until I met Thaddeus. It was during one of these late night excursions I learned Thaddeus was an excellent meringue dancer. The man never ceased to amaze me.

The two of us often double dated with Lisa and Marcus or my girl Gloria and her husband, Harold. Of course, that depended upon Harold and Gloria's ability to find a babysitter. A couple of weekends we broke with our typical routine and visited Thaddeus' family in Chicago. His family was very open and warm. I felt very much at home around them. His sister, Althea and I hit it off right away. In fact the second time Thaddeus and I went to Chicago, Althea and I spent an entire day together—shopping, eating, and just partaking in girl talk.

Although, it was hard at times to refrain from sex during this time period we somehow managed. Usually, I was the one practicing as well as enforcing the restraint. A few times Thaddeus seemed frustrated by my insistence to wait but deep down I was certain he knew why I wanted to wait. When it happened I wanted it to mean something.

Despite our trips to Chicago, our favorite thing to do was to sit around his condo with a good bottle of wine and listen to music. It was wonderful how both of us were connoisseurs of music. We would sit around and listen to Miles Davis, John Coltrane, Wynton Marsalis, maybe even Stevie Wonder or India Arie. Thaddeus absolutely loved India Aire. He wore India Arie's song, "Good Man" out. He often played it over, and over, and over until I forced him to stop. *Songs in the Key of Life* by Stevie Wonder was by far our favorite album. Both of us loved sitting up at night playing that album and reminiscing. I recollect those evenings the most. Although they were the simplest of dates, they were also the most intimate. On those nights it was just the two of us, and the music.

Still, after two months the level of sexual tension between us was pretty high. Thaddeus and I had gone as far as some heavy duty petting here and there but abstained from doing "the do." I knew my explanation of needing time to make sure we built a strong foundation on which to base our relationship on was wearing thin with him. Hell, my excuse for abstaining from sex was losing traction even with me. By the time March rolled around, my body was aching and I was ready to explode. And that is exactly what happened one beautiful evening.

I can recall the day vividly. It was a Thursday. Springtime blossoms had begun to bloom early, already setting the landscape ablaze in floral pastels. Other than fall, spring is the most beautiful time of the year in the Twin Cities. The only problem is that it's extremely short and sandwiched in between a bitterly cold winter and a hellishly humid summer.

I finished work that day and gone directly to Thaddeus' condo. Up to this point, I had been spending a lot of time at Thaddeus' place. I found his condo's proximity to my job convenient when it came to those evenings I did not want to be bothered with rush hour traffic or the weather. The ease of simply leaving work and being at Thaddeus' apartment in ten minutes was wonderful. I never told Thaddeus this, but I'm quite sure he figured out I had began to keep a set of clothes in my car in case I unexpectedly stayed the night. Over time that became pretty frequent.

Anyway, back to that evening. Like I said, it was a gorgeous evening. It was a usually warm day for March in the Twin Cities. It was such a nice day Thaddeus and I chose to eat dinner outside on the balcony. Once the sun had dipped below the horizon, we fell into our regular routine of cuddling on the couch in front of the television. This particular evening however we decided to enjoy a bowl of chocolate pudding while we watched TV. Thaddeus had found out I loved chocolate pudding, so he made it often when he knew I was coming over. As we sat in front of the TV that evening, Thaddeus decided to be a clown and smear pudding onto my cheeks and lips.

"What was that for?" I tried licking the pudding off my face.

Thaddeus stared at me and replied, "So, I can do this." Thaddeus then proceeded to kiss the pudding from my lips.

That was all it took. Before I knew it clothes were flying off and Thaddeus had smeared a chocolate pudding trail down my chest. Thaddeus licked and kissed at the pudding trail down to my breast. His kisses lingered upon my flesh like the morning dew—searing my skin with desire. The way he took his time slowly suckling the pudding from my nipples sent heat waves coursing through my body. The warm embrace of his tongue and soft lips upon my skin sent shivers down my spine. I reeled in the gratification. Thaddeus created another pudding trail leading from my chest down to my navel. He eagerly lapped at the trail all the way down to the fertile delta that rested in between my legs. Thaddeus hastily smeared pudding along the erotic regions of my inner thighs until he reached the ticklish spot behind my knees. His lips and tongue embraced my calf and foot stopping momentarily to show each individual toe special attention.

By the time Thaddeus had worked his way up my other leg, licking and kissing, a raging inferno was burning inside of me. When his tongue danced at my moistened furrow at the juncture where my thighs met, my body beneath the waist seemed to wither and melt away in ecstasy. His tongue tickled the node at the crest of my moist valley causing my body to shudder with pleasure. His oral lovemaking caused my toes to curl. It was hard for me to stay put as his tongue electrified my body by titillating my spot. The whole affair had become too much for me to bear. Even as I wiggled off the couch and onto the floor, Thaddeus kept up his pursuit—his tongue never giving up its assault. It was if he intended to taste every part of me. Thaddeus' ravenous appetite sent a wave of love flowing through me until I couldn't take it any more. In convulsive fits of pleasure my body bucked and quivered as each muscle in my body stiffened as I screamed out in ecstasy.

Judging by the expression on Thaddeus' face, I could tell he was full of himself from how I reacted to his oral lovemaking. He licked his glistening lips as if to savor every drop of me. Not wanting to be out done, I decided it was my turn to make him squirm.

Once I was able to gain control of my faculties I grabbed the bowl of chocolate pudding and gently placed my hands in it until my palms had a thin layer of chocolate pudding covering them. As Thaddeus sat there staring at me I caressed his manhood, gently massaging the pudding upon it until a thin sheet of chocolate pudding coated it. His sighs of satisfaction let me know he found pleasure in my touch.

When I felt Thaddeus had grown antsy from anticipation, I slowly engulfed as much of him as possible into my mouth. Thaddeus released a groan of delight as I went to work. As my mouth and tongue danced a rhythmic tango, I could feel Thaddeus' body becoming tense from the mounting pleasure building within him. Just when I was certain he was ready to explode...I stopped.

"What are you doing?" Thaddeus questioned. Anxiety was written all over his face. I could not help but smile at the power I wielded over him at that moment. Thaddeus would have done anything I said just as long as it meant he could reach his climax.

"I want you," I cooed. Thaddeus' eyes grew as big as saucers.

"Wait, a minute. I'll be right back." Thaddeus rushed off.

"Where are you gong?"

"To get protection."

"Hurry up," I said. I was frustrated and raring to go.

Although I was on the pill, I was glad Thaddeus was considerate enough to suggest protection. Despite the possibility of contracting HIV most men still are skittish about wearing a condom. With so many brothas living secret lives, a sistah couldn't take a chance. I did not think Thaddeus was bisexual, however, nowadays a woman could never tell. There are plenty of black women out there who thought the same of their significant other but found out the hard way.

Thaddeus rushed back prepared for lovemaking. By that point my body was screaming out his name. There was no denying it…I wanted him. I wanted him in the worse way. I wanted him to reach into the deepest recesses of my body and feel my hunger.

I mounted Thaddeus, slowly easing myself down on top of him. It had been a long time, so there was no need to rush. I wanted to relish every inch of him. My body burned with desire as each inch of him nestled itself inside my womb. It is impossible to forget the feeling of a man inside of you. I only hoped my proceeding performance was beyond good because I wanted Thaddeus to be whipped by the time I was done with him.

A wave of pleasure swept over me as I felt our pelvic regions touch. After nights of imagining my pillow as my lover, it felt good to feel a real man beneath me. In the beginning I started off slow. I wanted to allow the both of us to settle into a rhythm we both felt comfortable with. Once we had established a sustainable groove, I slowly quickened the tempo until we were rocking back and forth at a feverish pace. I had every intention in the world of leaving a lasting impression on Thaddeus. I wanted him to go to work the next day thinking about me. As our pace quickened we both found it hard to withstand the passion consuming us. We could do nothing more than give in to it and explode into uncontrollable fits of satisfaction. I was spent. I wilted right there on top of him in a heap of sweat.

Thaddeus and I must have lay there on his living room floor for maybe ten minutes. Neither one of us moved or said a word. We were nothing more than, an entangled mass of flesh, drenched from head to toe. When I finally eased my head up off of Thaddeus' chest to look down into his eyes, I could not help but smile.

"That was good," I panted.

"Tell me about it," Thaddeus sighed. "However, no one said it had to end." Thaddeus was still inside of me and I could feel him once again beginning to grow.

It had been a long time since I had sex with a man all night long. I think we must have christened virtually every room in Thaddeus' condominium. I probably got maybe two hours of sleep that night. The two of us were dangerous together. It was if we were trying to kill each other. I damn near blacked out a couple of times. I think I was trying to make up for lost time. I was literally exhausted the next morning but it was one of those "good tired." It was the type of tired when you are utterly exhausted but you're smiling from ear to ear. I was sprung and there was no denying it…. I never knew pudding could be such an aphrodisiac.

The following two months I practically lived at Thaddeus' condo. I rarely saw my townhouse. I might have gone to my townhouse maybe twice a week and that was mainly to pick up the mail. After a while, I no longer kept a bag of clothes in the car. Instead, I kept them in the closet. Thaddeus had allotted me some closet space. I know we had only known each other for five months but I felt things had progressed far enough where I felt comfortable spending a significant amount of time with Thaddeus. To be quite frank, I envisioned Thaddeus and I being together for a long time. I even dared to envision marriage.

My parents loved him. My girlfriend Gloria and her husband Harold thought we made a cute couple. Thaddeus even gave me every indication things were headed in the right direction when he introduced me to his son, Little T. That was a big step for him not to mention for me. Thaddeus had always told me he never introduced his son to any woman he was dating unless it was serious. Thaddeus also informed me that up until he met me, he had not found a woman worthy of meeting his son. Of course, I was honored but also a little hesitant about meeting his son. Yet, after talking my concerns over with Gloria, Lisa and my mother I realized I did not need to feel pressured to play Little T's mama when he already had one. When I accepted that fact, I was able to feel relaxed in meeting Thaddeus' son.

Despite my family and friends approval, after a while I began to sense things between Thaddeus and I starting to change. There were no overtly obvious signs that presented themselves to me—it was just a woman's intuition. For example, Thaddeus started cutting back on cooking and eventually he stopped cooking completely. I did not expect Thaddeus to always cook; yet, I did not expect to become his maid neither. On top of that, less time was spent cuddling whenever we relaxed in front of the TV. I tried to keep telling myself that maybe I was making something out of nothing but I could not shake the feeling I was getting. It started becoming more apparent that something was wrong when we would argue over really petty things such as me not rinsing my plate or the fact I hogged the covers at night. Thaddeus and I had our disagreements in the past but never on the level or frequency they were beginning to occur. I asked Thaddeus on several occasions if there was something bothering him, yet he always told me "no." I knew he was lying. Still, I did not know what to do or say to make him open up.

Then one evening while we were driving to meet Lisa and Marcus for dinner, Thaddeus dropped a bomb on me. "I think we need some time apart."

Erin—Time To Move On

For close to six months, I admired Thaddeus from afar. I had originally assumed I had lost Thaddeus' business card. However, one afternoon after aerobics class I was pleasantly surprised to find Thaddeus' card buried at the bottom of my gym bag. I was simply cleaning out my gym bag and there it was at the bottom of the bag. How it got there…I did not know nor did I care. I was simply glad to have it in my possession once again.

I must have debated on whether I should call Thaddeus for over an hour. I did not know what to say or if he even would remember me. After all it had been almost six months since Thaddeus and I had met at the bar. The solution to my dilemma came to me in the form of Thaddeus' email address printed at the bottom of his business card. I figured at least email would save me the humiliation I might receive if I called him and he did not remember me. Also, if he was not interested in seeing me, all Thaddeus had to do was simply not reply to the email. I would be disappointed, but at least that way it saved me the embarrassment of having him tell me to get lost after it took me so long to get up the nerve to call him. Of course, there still was the possibility of me having to call him if the email address on the business card was no good.

So for the better part of a day, I sat hunched over my computer writing and rewriting an email I hoped conveyed the message that I wanted to see him without sounding too desperate. It took me some time but I managed to craft a three sentence email basically reminding him who I was, apologizing for taking so long to take him up on his offer of lunch, and proposing we get together sometime soon for Cosmopolitans. I know that last part sounded a little corny but I figured if he did not have a clue as to who I was or the place and time we met the reference to Cosmopolitans would possibly jog his memory. I think I spent just as much time re-reading the email as I did writing it. Finally, after much deliberation I clicked send.

The anticipation of Thaddeus' response made me a nervous wreck. I repetitively checked my email throughout the day to see if he replied. Although, he did not respond to my email as fast as I would have hoped I was pleasantly surprised to see Thaddeus' reply sitting in my email inbox. I was also pleased to read that he remembered me. I wondered if he had to talk to his buddy, Darius, in order to jog his memory. Thaddeus had agreed to take me up on my offer of Cosmopolitans and suggested we get together some place for drinks. He conveniently ended his email with his home phone number.

The rest of the day I acted rather flighty about the whole thing. Belinda had to calm me down before I called Thaddeus to set up a place and time for us to meet. I don't know why I was so excited to see him. Thaddeus and I had not seen each other since our brief encounter at the bar. Yet, here I was eager to meet a man I hardly knew and only met for one night…a little over five months ago.

I called Thaddeus and set up a time and place for us to meet the following week. I wanted to stay close to home, so I suggested a small—quaint—pub in St. Paul called Billy's. It was on Grand Avenue close to my apartment. Thaddeus seemed okay with my selection and assured me he would meet me there at the agreed upon time of six o'clock. Just in case he got tied up I gave him my home and cell phone numbers.

Thursday of the following week I left work early in hopes of getting home and changing into something a little more casual before hooking up with Thaddeus. However, rush hour traffic across the Mississippi into St. Paul forced me to head directly to Billy's if I intended to make it there on time. It did not occur to me until I stepped into the bar and did not see Thaddeus that I should've suggested we meet somewhere in downtown Minneapolis since we both worked downtown. It would have allowed for us to avoid rush hour traffic. Since I barely made it to Billy's on time and I had left work early I was certain Thaddeus was going to be late.

When Thaddeus finally arrived it was a quarter to seven and I was already nursing my second drink. Fortunately for him, I had decided I would give him until seven o'clock before giving up and heading home. Unlike our first encounter I noticed Thaddeus immediately. It was not as if there was an over abundance of black men in the bar. I waved to Thaddeus just in case he may have forgotten what I looked like. He gave me a warm smile as he made his way over to the table.

Thaddeus was very apologetic for being late. "I'm sorry I'm late. I got caught in traffic and then on top of that, I passed this place twice before I realized this was it."

"I'm the one who should be apologizing. I should have suggested we meet somewhere in downtown Minneapolis to avoid traffic," I confessed.

"Don't worry about it, maybe next time. So how are you doing? Long time no see," Thaddeus commented. He took off his jacket and got comfortable. I could not help but sense he was just a tad bit nervous but that seemed to ease once he had something to drink.

Thaddeus' conversation and company was wonderful. Our conversation was lively and intriguing just like it was the night at the bar. It was nothing beyond the typical dinner date dialogue—the usual getting to know you kind of stuff. The elusive or at times direct questions pertaining to a person's relationship status, hobbies, as well as the customary small talk. I told Thaddeus about my on-again and off-again relationship with Brian making sure to stress that our current status was off. Thaddeus assured me he was single but eluded to the fact that he had been dating somebody, but it was no longer serious. I took that for what it was worth. I contemplated asking him if it was his ex-wife, but decided to leave well enough alone. I saw no need to pry unless things between us grew to the point were I needed clarification. I had made that mistake before and did not intend to make the same mistake if I could help it. Besides, every time I had asked Thaddeus' friend Darius about his love life, Darius always informed me that Thaddeus was still in search of Missus Right. That worked well for me because I was looking for Mister Right.

Thaddeus has a certain quality about him that puts a person at ease. However, I think I may have gotten a little too comfortable judging by the expression on Thaddeus' face the moment I whipped out my pack of cigarettes and proceeded to light a cigarette.

Thaddeus quickly asked me in a subdued tone, "You smoke?" Now, I am strictly a social smoker. I only smoke when I'm out with the girls or at a bar having drinks. If I wanted to I could easily quit. It's just that I've grown accustom to having a cigarette when I have a drink.

"If you want me to put it away I can?" I said. I did not want to paint this unflattering picture of myself as some kind of chain smoker inhaling five packs a day.

"Nah, if that's your thing go right ahead."

I took maybe two or three drags on the cigarette, before sitting it in the ashtray and letting it burn itself out. Although Thaddeus had told me he had no problem with me smoking, I could tell it did not sit well with him. Other than the cigarettes the evening seemed to have gone well. We hugged and exchanged phone numbers at the end of the night with the promise to stay in touch.

That was a Friday.

By Sunday I was bouncing off the walls. I could not understand why Thaddeus had not called me. I could not help but believe the incident with the cigarettes had totally turned him off. I consulted Belinda and Stacy to get their opinion on what should be my next move and got some varying advice. Belinda recommended I stop fretting about the ordeal with the cigarettes and simply call Thaddeus. Stacy on the other hand recommended I give up chasing a black guy because they're irresponsible and think about giving Brian a call.

I ignored Stacy's advice.

I agonized whether or not to call Thaddeus for two days. Finally on Tuesday, I gave in to temptation and called him. See, I'm the type of person who feels I should get what I want and at that point I wanted some kind of relationship with Thaddeus. It did not matter to me if it was nothing more than friendship. I wanted to make Thaddeus apart of my life in some fashion. I attribute such an attitude to growing up in an environment where my parents attempted to compensate for me growing up in a broken home by giving me whatever my heart desired. Certainly that is not how life works, and I understand that but at that moment—at that particular time—I wanted Thaddeus. I found him to be such an engaging and genuine guy; I simply wanted some kind of link to him. So I called him.

I did not want to take the chance Thaddeus did not call me because he was not as unattached as he let on, so I called him at work. Thaddeus seemed surprised to hear from me. I jokingly gave him a hard time for his inability to call. Thaddeus explained to me how he intended to call but got busy. I forgave him, however, not without giving him a hard time on how he should never let it happen again. Other than the initial awkwardness, the dialogue between Thaddeus and I was great. I found it really easy to talk to him. If we had not been at work, I think we could have talked forever. These back and forth phone conversations at work went on for about a week. I think Thaddeus and I talked to each other at least once a day. There was a desirable comfort level that developed between us. At times, I often found myself eagerly awaiting his call. Although, we spoke daily I felt as if the telephone was becoming an obstruction. It was convenient and it allowed neither one of us to put forth the effort to see each other. I could not help but grow impatient trying to figure out when Thaddeus was going to ask me out. I am the type of person that likes to feel like things are progressing along. If I don't get the feeling things are moving forward I get frustrated. After a while I realized that if I wanted to see Thaddeus again it was going to be up to me to initiate it.

So, during one of our many phone conversations I nonchalantly asked him, "So, am I ever going to see you again? Or are you going to continue to avoid me?"

"I'm not avoiding you. What gives you that impression?"

"The fact I have not seen you since we had drinks at Billy's on Grand."

"That was not that long ago," professed Thaddeus.

"That was almost two weeks ago," I proclaimed.

"Okay, when do you want to see me?" came Thaddeus' reply.

I had hoped he would set himself up. It made it easy for me to suggest a time for us to get together. "How about Friday? There's a movie I've been dying to see."

There was a slight hitch in Thaddeus' voice before he replied, "I see no problem with us doing that."

That slight pause in his voice made me second-guess him. I knew Thaddeus had told me he was dating other people yet I could not help but wonder if there was something more to his dating than he was telling me. "Thaddeus, is there something you're not telling me?"

"What do you mean?"

"I sensed some hesitation on your part when I asked you to join me for a movie Friday night."

"I was simply trying to remember if I had my son, Little T, on Friday or Saturday...that's all."

Although his excuse sounded legitimate, I needed reassurance. "Thaddeus, do you have a girlfriend?"

"I told you, I'm not seeing no one seriously."

"Then what is it? Is it because I'm white?" I questioned.

"Not at all. The fact you're white has nothing to do with it. How can you ask me such a question? I hung out with you in public in St. Paul didn't I?"

"Yeah." He had a point.

"Then why would you ask me such a crazy question like that? That is like me asking you have you ever been with a brotha before or are you fulfilling some secret fantasy of being with a black man? Is that the case?"

"No." Thaddeus is very skilled at turning the tables on a person.

"Okay. I said I would go to the movies with you. Why are you tripping? Are we going to the movies on Friday or what?" he inquired. It sounded almost as if he was challenging me.

"Friday it is," I said. I could not help but feel stupid for even questioning him.

I had no intentions of making Thaddeus and my relationship one based on color, so I felt stupid bringing up the subject of race. Yet, I had lived around Belinda long enough to have seen her run into her fair share of black men who wanted to date her but were reluctant to be seen in public with her because she was white. Even though Thaddeus had assured me that was not the case—I still could not help but feel unsure if he would show up Friday night.

"Then Friday it is," Thaddeus chimed, before saying good-bye.

Thaddeus and I agreed upon a movie theater close to my apartment. I thought maybe after the movie we could come back to my place and relax. I made sure to leave the cigarettes at home this time. I did not want to repeat the mistake I made the first time around. To my delight Thaddeus showed up. Thaddeus picked me up and we rode in his car to the cinema. The evening was going fine until I stood in the foyer of the movie theater waiting for Thaddeus to buy our popcorn and soda pop and I noticed four black women glaring at me. Belinda had warned me of the possible headaches I might run into when dating a black guy. Not heeding Belinda's warning of looking the other way in such situations, I instinctively looked over in their direction.

Wrong move.

These women's ice-cold stares quickly turned into verbal threats. I tried to ignore them in hopes of avoiding a scene but it was too late. A chorus of "white bitch," and "She knows, she better look away. Just because she's with a brotha doesn't mean shit," spewed from their mouths.

I tried to act like I did not hear them, yet that was hard to do for their voices grew louder with each insult. I felt extremely uncomfortable. I was certain the situation was bound to escalate when one of the black women became extremely loud and appeared to be heading in my direction. I figured the best thing for me to do was find Thaddeus before an altercation ensued. I may have been able to protect myself against one of them but not four.

Unable to believe how petty these women were acting, I unconsciously rolled my eyes and gave them a disgusted shake of my head before rushing off to find Thaddeus. Of course, that gesture was followed by taunts of "Fuck you bitch," and threats of "Why don't you bring your white ass over here and do that," as well as "We'll be waiting for you after the movie is over bitch." Although I was bothered by the entire incident, I did not say anything to Thaddeus. It was best I kept it to myself. I still questioned Thaddeus' feelings towards being seen with me and I did not want him to feel subconscious by telling him about those women. They obvious lacked class and did not warrant any more attention than the little I gave them.

I had managed to put the episode in the foyer behind me. I refused to let some jealous women ruin my evening. In fact, Thaddeus and I managed to enjoy ourselves. Unfortunately that lasted until we were midway through the movie and Thaddeus excused himself to go to the bathroom. When he returned Thaddeus was in a panic telling me we had to leave. I did not understand why. When I asked him for an explanation all he could say was that there was something wrong with his son. Sensing it was urgent; I felt I had no choice but to go. Not until we were in the car and half way to my house did Thaddeus discover that the emergency was a false alarm. He apologized profusely for causing us to miss the remainder of the movie. I told him to forget it. I assured him we could rent it on DVD. Besides, the movie wasn't that good. I suggested we go to my apartment and relax. The entire evening had been an experience I much rather chose to forget.

When Thaddeus and I arrived at my apartment I was surprised to find Belinda home. Before I had left to the movies, Belinda had assured me she would be gone when I returned. She had a date with Darius. By the look on her face when Thaddeus and I walked in I sensed her date with Darius had been cancelled. Of course, Belinda was curious to know why we were home early, so I explained to her Thaddeus' false alarm pertaining to his son. Since neither one of us was having the best of evenings I thought a bottle of Merlot would liven things up.

We drunk and talked for a while before Belinda turned in for the night. It was close to eleven o'clock when Belinda went to bed finally leaving Thaddeus and I alone. By that time, the liquor had loosened both of us up and we were feeling a little frisky. It was difficult trying to keep our hands off each other. It did not take long before we found ourselves making out before Thaddeus pried himself away professing he had to go.

Thaddeus explained to me his ex-wife was planning to drop his son off at his place in the morning and it was imperative that he be there when she arrived. I understood, so I reluctantly let him go. However, I thought I would give Thaddeus a little something to think about before he left. I quickly unzipped his pants and gave him an oral treat. I could tell from the way Thaddeus took his time leaving, he really enjoyed my going away present. I readily admit that evening only made me want him more. However, Thaddeus assured me he only had his son during the day next Saturday so we had plenty of time to get together and finish were we left off.

It definitely gave the two of us something to look forward to.

Thaddeus—Trying To Keep Things In Perspective

I had gotten myself into a real predicament when it came to Erin and Ivy. I guess I wandered into the situation with both women not fully aware of the consequences. My whole attitude was since we were just dating no harm was being done. I never figured things to get serious because deep down I knew I was not looking for another full-blown relationship. In the beginning with Ivy, I thought a relationship was what I wanted but I quickly realized I mentally was not ready. I still had some emotional scars leftover from my divorce that needed time to heal. It was this emotional baggage, which I carried around I fear contributed to me being a little more than hesitant when it came to committing myself to another woman.

Earlier I said another woman could take a man's mind off of a woman. The only problem with that statement is another woman cannot make a man forget about that particular woman. In Ivy's case, she was the victim of my inability to realize this fact sooner rather than later. Despite the way I felt about Ivy, I always found myself comparing her to Stephanie. That was not fair to Ivy. At least with Erin, I hinted to her I was not seeking to get tied down by making it clear I still intended to see other women. Nevertheless, I think I could have definitely handled the situation with Ivy a lot better.

I really was into Ivy. I liked everything about her. I liked her style—her whole persona. I mean everything about Ivy seemed to mesh with me perfectly. She was exactly what I was looking for in a woman. Yet, something inside of me was having a hard time letting me move on beyond Stephanie. I know that is wild for me to say, especially after all of the headaches Stephanie had put me through. But I found it hard to trust another woman with my heart due to the pain I suffered at the hands of Stephanie. If I had only met Ivy earlier, life would have been so much simpler.

During the week I tended to play basketball with the fellas, Darius and Marcus, at the downtown Minneapolis YMCA during lunch. The Monday following meeting Ivy at Darius' card party I decided to skip my regular lunchtime basketball game in hopes of catching Ivy in action down at the courthouse. I assumed sitting inconspicuously amongst the many faces in the courtroom gallery would be harmless. I sincerely doubted Ivy would even notice me.

I was wrong.

When Ivy caught a glimpse of me sitting in the gallery, I debated on whether I should stay or leave. I suddenly detected a sense of nervousness on her part. At that point I decided it was best I left.

Wishing to make up for my surprise visit at the courthouse, I decided to call Ivy and invite her to dinner at a small jazz café along the Mississippi river called Sophia. To my surprise she accepted my invitation. Contrary to what I told Ivy over dinner that evening, I had not told Saundra everything about our weekend. I did inform Saundra that I sneaked into the courthouse to see Ivy. She quickly informed me that was not a wise move. Saundra recommended I ask Ivy out to dinner, so I could explain my unexpected visit to the courthouse and assure her I was not a stalker.

I figured Ivy would arrive at Sophia's late. So, I invited Saundra to join me mainly to keep me company. Saundra had been busting her ass on a project for me and I felt I owed her at least dinner and a drink to show my gratitude. Besides, I was not certain Ivy was even going to show up. Now, Ivy's hunch about Saundra wanting to be more than just friends was accurate. Saundra had been flirting with me ever since I arrived at Midwestern Federal. It was not as if Saundra was a bad looking woman. However, I dated a co-worker before and it turned into a bad experience. So from that point on, I adopted a stringent policy of not dating co-workers. In my opinion inter-office romances seemed to always blow up in people's face.

Soon after Saundra left the bar, Ivy and I fell right back into the same ole familiar groove we had established Saturday night at the pizzeria. As expected dinner was lovely and the conversation was lively. When I asked Ivy to take a walk with me along the river I knew it was getting late, but I did not want the night to end. Although it was cold outside, the snow and the full moon made for a beautiful evening along the riverbank. The moon shined bright that night, so I thought a walk would cap the evening off nicely. The only sound that seemed to break the tranquility of the evening was the sound of the trees swaying in the breeze. The red neon sign of the old Golden Medal Flour mill next to my condominium complex, Stone Arch, reflected off the sheet of ice covering the Mississippi as it glowed bright. The sign was remnant of a by gone era in Minneapolis when the grain industry reigned. The neon green lights and green trusses of the Hennepin Bridge gave one the illusion the bridge glowed against the backdrop of the moonlit night. It was romantic.

After our stroll along the banks of the river, I escorted Ivy back to her car. I wanted to give her a good night kiss but decided against it. I did not want her to think that was all I wanted from her. For the first time since my divorce I believed it just might be possible for me to fall in love again. This was an awakening for me. I had sworn to never give my heart to another woman again. Yet, there I was contemplating a relationship with Ivy.

I remember talking to Marcus and Darius about Ivy that following evening. Both of them had some reservations about my budding relationship with Ivy. While Marcus' concerns pertained more to the possibility Ivy and I may have been moving too fast. Darius was concerned with another friend falling into the clutches of a woman. Although their concerns were valid, I assured Darius and Marcus they had nothing to worry about. In my mind I had everything under control. My strategy was to take things slow and see where they led.

I waited a few days before calling Ivy. I knew she was busy. Besides, I did not want to give her the impression I was sprung. If I had called immediately the next day it would seem like I was anxious to see her. I couldn't have that. I figured the time spent not talking to each other would give us both enough time to evaluate the situation and decide if we wanted to pursue our interests further. Nonetheless, I called Ivy and invited her over to my place for dinner. I had seen how Ivy carried herself in public, so I wanted to see how she behaved in a little more intimate setting.

It was a frigid day. That January was extremely cold. I think the mercury hovered close to zero most of the week. I thought it was a perfect evening to enjoy a delicious meal and delve a little deeper beyond the superficial level. I got the impression Ivy felt the same. Following dinner we settled down in front of the TV with a nice bottle of wine to cap off what had been a very pleasant evening. As we saw more of each other over the weeks we spent many evenings following dinner cuddled up in front of the television

Now, the episode with the chocolate pudding that un-seasonally warm March night was totally spontaneous. I did not plan that. However, Ivy's desire to wait had worn my patience thin. Not to mention, I had grown tired of using manual means to satisfy myself. Nevertheless, sooner or later judging by the amount of time we spent together something was bound to happen. Now, I've always considered making love an art form. The blending of mind, body and soul to form with luck an incredible and hopefully climatic event. Making love reminds me of a painting. Each time a painter starts a painting he or she attempts to elicit a feeling—an emotion—shared by both the painter and the individual viewing the painting. If a connection is made between the painter and the observer a masterpiece is born. If the painting does not stimulate the observer's senses then the artist has created garbage. The same can be said for making love. If there is a connection then you hopefully have a masterpiece. If not…then you have nothing more than sex, empty and hollow. Ivy and I made a connection—a very passionate one. I recall looking into Ivy's eyes that night after making love and wondering if she was the woman who would make me believe in love again.

When I look back on that night it is not difficult for me to understand why I developed such a strong bond with Ivy. From the beginning every thing between Ivy and I seemed right. It also helped that Ivy was a beautiful woman. Her caramel frame is picturesque. Whenever we made love, it was like our bodies communicated to each other in a language totally foreign yet completely understood. It's hard to explain. It was if our bodies knew inherently the language of love.

One day at Ivy's townhouse following that eventful night, I was helping Ivy install a shoe rack in her bedroom closet when I stumbled across a pair of fire engine red stilettos in her closet. Ivy tried to assure me the shoes were a holdover from her club hopping days. I really could have cared less. What intrigued me the most about those shoes was the idea of seeing Ivy's long, lean, legs in those high-heel pumps. It took a little coaxing, but I managed to get Ivy to model the shoes for me. Initially Ivy was hesitant but she caved in to my persistent begging. Once she put those red pumps on—it was over. The sight of Ivy in those red stilettos instantly aroused me. We made love right there on the floor of her bedroom. Our bodies just communicated with one another like that…. We never held back.

On occasions following that afternoon, Ivy would don those fire engine red pumps and prance around my condo hoping to get my attention. It always worked. Whenever I saw her in those stilettos I could not control myself. The sight of those long, sleek, mocha brown legs sprouting up out of those pumps made me want her.

Now, I had known Ivy was living out of the trunk of her car for sometime. She was at my condo almost every day, yet she always had a change of clothes. There was no other way she could have a change of clothes unless she had planned ahead and brought a change of clothes with her. After a while I got tired of Ivy living out of her car and simply told her she could keep a couple of outfits at my condo. At first, Ivy's constant presence at my condominium did not faze me. In fact, I enjoyed having her around. Then one day while searching for my shaving cream I stumbled across a box of Tampax tampons in the cabinet under the bathroom sink. In an instant all of that changed.

I can recall standing there staring at that box of tampons trying to figure out how in the hell I had gotten to the point where female toiletries were occupying space in my condo. To find a box of tampons under my bathroom sink pretty much meant my ass was locked down. I was once again involved in a full-blown relationship. As I surveyed the rest of the bathroom I quickly noticed Ivy had her own toothbrush and face cloth. I don't know what happened but it appeared I had been so blinded by love I neglected to pay attention to my surroundings. I walked into my bedroom in a daze. I glanced into the dresser drawer I allowed Ivy to keep a few of her belongings in and suddenly realized Ivy had moved in a month's worth of underwear. I opened the bedroom closet to find Ivy's clothing occupied a quarter of my closet space. When I informed Ivy she could keep a change of clothes at my place, I had envisioned maybe one or two outfits, not six.

I sat there on the edge of my bed in bewilderment. I tried to figure out what happened to my mantra of taking things slow. Judging from the box of tampons, her toothbrush, underwear and clothes that slogan had got thrown out the window. Ivy had moved in. Believe me, I enjoyed Ivy's company. However, the idea of having her living with me was not what I had envisioned.

Was I over reacting to something as mundane as a box of tampons?

Maybe.

It was not as if I did not see this coming. All the signs pointed towards Ivy moving in. Still for some reason I missed the clues. Or could it have been I was so frightened to fall in love again I chose to ignore all the signs?

Regardless of the reason, I was once again in a monogamous relationship and whether I wanted to admit it or not that box of Tampax was a neon sign affirming the fact. I had promised myself after Stephanie I would take my time and enjoy the single life before jumping back into a relationship. However, it appeared to me that the nights of making love and warm discussions in front of the television had clouded my judgment. The fact I was once again in a serious relationship, brought on an extreme panic attack. The whole idea of being locked down to solely one woman scared the shit out of me.

Suddenly, I felt like I was being smothered.

Of course when Ivy and I started dating, I had assumed plenty of time had transpired between my relationship with Stephanie and dating Ivy for me to have recovered from the heartache. Obviously, I was wrong. There still were some lingering issues I needed to resolve. As usual I convened the fellas, Darius and Marcus, and discussed the matter with them. After a lengthy discussion both of them unanimously agreed I should create some space between Ivy and I.

Of course, that was easier said than done.

There is no easy way for a person to tell someone they care about that they need some time to themselves. It is even harder when the problem creating the need for space does not dwell within your relationship with your significant other but within you. Understanding what needed to be done made me irritable and withdrawn. What else could one expect when I realized I had to do something I really did not want to do. Yet, if I continued to act like nothing was wrong and lead Ivy on that was not fair to her. I know I could've picked a more opportune time to tell Ivy how I was feeling than in the car on our way to dinner with Marcus and Lisa, but I question if there ever is a perfect time to deliver bad news. We never made our dinner date with Marcus and Lisa that night. Instead, we returned to my condo where I spent the remainder of the night trying to explain to Ivy why I needed to be alone.

In the beginning, it seemed no matter how hard I tried to convince her how I was feeling Ivy just did not believe me. There was no doubt in her mind I was sleeping with another woman. It did not matter how many times I explained to her these were personal issues I needed to resolve. Ivy simply did not believe me. I realized it was hard for her to understand I suffered from hang-ups created from my failed marriage to Stephanie. I think the fact that my wounds were emotional and not physical, planted the seeds of doubt in her mind. So after a night of talking and tears, Ivy gathered her belongings and walked out of my condo the following morning.

Despite breaking it off with Ivy, we stayed in touch. The only difference was that we did not converse every day. We went out a couple of times within those two weeks before I began seeing Erin. We mainly talked a lot during these little rendezvous. Yet, one time we ended up having sex. Having sex during our hiatus was unwise, yet it was hard to simply go cold turkey. I know the fact we slept together gave mixed signals but it was difficult for me to abruptly cut off my feelings for Ivy despite my insistence of needing some time to myself.

Regardless of our inability to keep our relationship strictly plutonic during this period, I began to believe Ivy understood the need for me to achieve total closure when it came to Stephanie. The more I explained to her where I was coming from, the more I began to feel Ivy believed me. Of course, I totally ruined everything I built with Ivy when I replied to Erin's email and went out with Erin roughly two weeks after I supposedly told Ivy I needed time alone.

I know it looks shady and believe me when I explain my side of the story to sistahs willing to listen they call me every name in the book. I've been called everything from low down dirty dog to sell out.

Should I have accepted Erin's invitation for drinks after work?

Nope. Yet in retrospect, I repeatedly tried to convince myself that meeting Erin for drinks was nothing more than two adults getting together for cocktails, nothing more—nothing less. I did not want to admit to myself that I was attracted to her.

Was I fooling myself?

Yep.

I was attracted to Erin. There was no denying it. I wanted to believe I was not attracted to her. I tried to persuade myself we were only getting together for drinks and nothing else. I told myself if drinks and a little small talk led us to sleeping together than that was cool. Yet, I refused to contemplate anything else beyond a one-night stand. Erin was not the first white woman I found attractive. She was, however, the first white woman where the attraction went beyond being strictly physical. I had met plenty of white women who stimulated me physically. However, I never stuck around long enough to see if there was anything of substance to our relationship beyond the bedroom. Yet, there I was meeting Erin at a pub in St. Paul. Not my typical modus operandi when it came to hooking up with white women. A typical date with a white woman for me was to meet them at a bar, maybe have a drink or two then follow the woman to her place or the nearest motel. In hit and run instances such as that I never let a woman know where I lived. There are just way too many crazy women out here nowadays.

See, when it came to dealing with white women I was capable of handling trysts in the dark. In those situations it was nothing more than sex—simply two bodies going bump in the night. However with Erin, I found myself attracted to more than what resided in between her legs.

Being attracted to Erin really made me self-conscious.

What did dating a white woman mean?

What did it say about me?

Did it mean I no longer found black women attractive, or that they no longer satisfied my needs? Or even something worse like I had been so deeply scared by my divorce that I sought out a type of woman that was the exact opposite of my ex-wife? Or was it due to the prevalence of interracial dating in Minnesota?

Was it a case of "when in Rome, do as the Romans do?"

I know interracial dating is nothing new and in this day and age it is not uncommon. People are openly dating and loving outside of their own ethnic group. Yet, my reply to such assertions is that "we've only scratched the surface of race in this country." Race in this country is a touchy subject. No matter how much people want to make believe it is not. Color is the indicator we use to differentiate ourselves and whether we admit it or not, the sight of a black man and white woman together evokes certain emotions—certain feelings.

Look, I was raised on the Southside of Chicago. I use to call the corners between 83rd and 87th Street along Stoney Island Avenue home. Also, I lived for several years in southwest Atlanta. Both areas could be classified without a doubt as the black parts of town. Sometimes I could literally go days without seeing a white person unless I passed them on the expressway. I did not have to deal with them at work. Growing up and living in the "black parts" of town had meaning. On Chicago's Southside and in southwest Atlanta, being black was a matter of pride. It was the common factor that bonded people in the neighborhood together.

I guess what I'm trying to say, is that being black means something to me.

So the fact I questioned my blackness when it came to dating Erin was relevant. How else could I explain halting a budding relationship with a very beautiful, well-rounded, black woman such as Ivy only to turn around and entertain an invitation from Erin…a white woman? It was not as if my issues pertaining to Stephanie had just disappeared over night.

My mother raised me to believe a black man was made for a black woman. Mama constantly told me no love is greater than a black man's love for a black woman and visa versa. I would become furious whenever I saw a sistah with a white man, yet there I was considering a relationship with a white woman. I was suddenly a hypocrite and I hated myself for it.

Anyhow, I met Erin at the small pub in St. Paul as planned. I am not familiar with St. Paul. In comparison to Minneapolis, I typically refer to St. Paul as the "other city." I rarely went to St. Paul unless I had to take care of business or frequent a couple of jazz clubs with Marcus or one of the numerous clubs along Rice Street. Needless to say, my lack of knowledge of St. Paul and rush hour traffic made me extremely late. Honestly, I was quite surprised to see Erin still there when I arrived. She had greeted me with a frantic wave of her hand. I remember silently wishing she did not do that for it drew attention to us.

I was somewhat nervous at first. I constantly wondered if someone I knew would walk in and see me with Erin. After a while my nerves managed to ease. Still, I worried about someone who knew Ivy walking in and catching me sitting there with Erin…. Fortunately that did not happen. Dinner and conversation was nice. The only thing that turned me off about Erin, was the fact she smoked. I hated kissing a woman that smoked. Their mouth always smelled and tasted like an ashtray. Other than that, the evening was relaxing. We promised to get together again soon.

Now, there were two reasons why I did not call Erin that weekend. One is because I knew Erin was trouble. I figured if I just believed our date was nothing more than a night out on the town with an acquaintance, temptation would be avoided. The second and most important reason why I avoided calling Erin that weekend was due to the sudden concern I had for my son's well being. From talking with Little T I learned Stephanie's new boyfriend, Willard—whom I despised—was putting his hands on her. I had met the brotha a couple of times when I went by the house to pick-up Little T. I occasionally saw him out at the clubs. Whenever I saw Willard at the nightclubs, he was always snuggled up next to some woman trying to lay his mack down. This was while he was supposedly dating Stephanie. Of course, I did not see what Stephanie saw in the brotha, but hey, that was none of my business. If it was true, the fact Stephanie dated a man who laid his hands on her disappointed me. Yet, what could I do? Stephanie was a grown woman. She could do whatever the hell she wanted to do. Still, that was not the Stephanie I knew.

My mother raised me to never put my hands on a woman unless she was threatening my life. So, there was a part of me that wanted to kick Willard's ass simply for being in my opinion—a weak excuse for a man. However, I had to remind myself that Stephanie and I were no longer together and what Stephanie did was Stephanie's business.

What was my business was the environment, which Stephanie raised my son in. If Willard was indeed laying his hands on her I had to let my displeasure of Little T living in such an environment be known. I have never hit a woman. No matter how mad Stephanie may have made me at times, I never hit her. Even when I caught her with Cedric I did not strike her. So, I could not let another man influence my son into believing beating up a woman was acceptable.

When I dropped Little T off Sunday night, I made it very clear to Stephanie how I felt about Little T living in a home where domestic violence was tolerated. As expected there was some bickering back and forth, Stephanie even accused me of being jealous. Maybe I was? Who knows? Regardless of my personal feelings, that was beside the point. I really did not care how much Stephanie ranted and raved just as long as my point concerning Little T came across loud and clear.

One good thing did come out of the whole ordeal; I was able to take my mind off Ivy and Erin for the weekend. I did not talk to either one of them that entire weekend. Monday, however, was a different story. My dilemma pertaining to both Erin and Ivy resurfaced on Monday when Ivy called to see how I was doing and why I neglected to call her over the weekend. Then Erin called on Tuesday. This talking to Ivy and Erin went on for a couple of weeks. I would talk to one and then the other virtually every day. It was a juggling act I felt I had under control as long as I kept Erin at arms length. Then Erin cornered me into taking her to the movies and everything changed.

The subject of going to the movies caught me totally off guard.

Erin was right; the hesitation she heard in my voice was due to my uncertainty of being seen with her in public. Being seen with Erin in public forced me out of my comfort zone. I was comfortable being with a white woman in the dark. There was no need for talk in such situations. However going out on dates in public, I've always felt left interracial couples open to racial and cultural minefields. When I say interracial minefields, I'm referring to the innocent slip of the tongue that may be taken offensively by one's date. Of course, that is not to mention the surprised glares from strangers interracial couples receive occasionally whenever they are out. I noticed the glares even when I was out talking business with female colleagues from work whom were white. On top of that, I was still kind of seeing Ivy. Although we had supposedly broken up, there was still the possibility someone who knew Ivy would see me out with Erin.

Despite my indecision, Erin had boxed me into a corner. I couldn't rightfully tell her that I would not go out with her simply because I had reservations about openly dating a white woman. Just the thought of me saying such a thing made me feel like a bigot. So I agreed to go to the movies. I silently hoped she would pick a theater out of the way so I could rest assured no one I knew would see the two of us together. I was relieved when Erin told me the movie was playing at Har Mar theater in Falcon Heights, a northern suburb of St. Paul. Everyone I knew lived in Minneapolis or a Minneapolis suburb, so, I figured I was safe…. I should've not counted my blessings too soon.

I insisted we saw a late show. I wanted to slim down the chances I would bump into somebody that knew Ivy or me even further. I picked Erin up at her apartment late. I wanted to arrive at the theater late. That way when we walked in it would be dark and nobody would be able to see us. Everything had worked out as I planned until about half way through the movie when I had to use the bathroom. I recall standing at the urinal in the bathroom when Marcus walks in. Not thinking I instinctively said, "What's up Marcus?" As soon as his name escaped my mouth, I knew I was in trouble.

"What the hell are you doing here?" I screamed. My predicament suddenly came into focus.

"What do you think I'm doing here," Marcus said. He pulled up to the urinal next to me. "If I would've known you and Ivy were coming to the movies I would have suggested we double date. I could've saved some gas."

"I'm not here with Ivy," I sighed. I quickly zipped up my pants. I had to try to figure out how I was going to get myself out of a jam.

Marcus gave me a perplexed look. "Don't tell me you're here with that white girl you told me about?"

"Yep, that's why you got to go."

"I got to go! You must have lost your mind. I paid twenty-five dollars to see this movie and that is what I intend to do," Marcus exclaimed. Marcus zipped up his pants and walked over to the sink to wash his hands.

"Come on Marcus, I can't have Lisa seeing me with Erin. You know she would tell Ivy as soon as you guys got home," I pleaded.

"I'm sorry T, but that sounds like a personal problem to me. Besides if I try to get Lisa out of here now, she's going to think I'm up to something and I can do without the drama. I would like to help your cause you're my boy and all, but my hands are tied. Anyway, you should know better than to be messing around with a white girl. If I didn't know any better, I would think you were hanging around Darius a little bit too much. Some of him is rubbing off on you."

"Yeah, whatever. I can't believe you would do me like this," I said dejected.

"Do you like what?"

"Like this!" I shouted.

"Man, call me tomorrow. You're tripping. And don't forget to wash your nasty ass hands!" Marcus shouted, walking out the bathroom.

"Yeah, later."

I stayed in the bathroom trying to formulate a plan to rescue my ass from my dilemma. I couldn't just stay and let Lisa see me with Erin. Not only would Lisa tell Ivy, but every other sistah in Minneapolis willing to listen. Every sistah would know I was into white girls by the time the sun came up. That's when I came up with the idea of telling Erin that Stephanie called while I was in the restroom. When I returned to the movie theater I forced Erin into leaving by telling her something was wrong with Little T.

It took a little more effort than I had expected to get Erin out of the theater, yet, she did eventually play along. About half way to Erin's apartment, I faked like I was calling Stephanie back on my cell phone and learned Little T's emergency was a false alarm. In actuality, I called Darius who talked shit to me the entire time. I didn't keep him on the phone long for I could hear he had company in the background.

I felt more relaxed once we got to Erin's apartment. At least there I knew there wouldn't be anybody there who knew Ivy. We drank wine and watched TV for a while with Belinda, whose date with Darius was unexpectedly cancelled. Obviously Belinda did not know about Darius' other plans. Once it got late Belinda went to bed leaving Erin and I alone. It must have been the alcohol for as soon as Belinda left the room things between Erin and I got freaky. If I was not expecting Little T over at my place early the next morning, I might have stayed the night.

I don't know if it was the alcohol talking or the fact I got caught up in the moment…. Whatever it was, I told Erin I only had Little T during the day the following weekend. I assured her, we could finish up where we left off the following Saturday.

I would regret telling Erin that little piece of information because it would come back to haunt me.

Friends

Ivy—A Man Is Never Satisfied

When Thaddeus told me he needed to take a break I was devastated. I couldn't understand why? I thought everything was going good. Of course, things had gone a little flat in our relationship but I was certain we could work through whatever issues were bothering him. In no way did I assume Thaddeus' "little problem" would lead to us breaking up. I thought we would eventually talk things over and move on. Never did I think we would break up. I kept asking myself over and over again, "What did I do wrong? What did I say that might have changed things?"

What hurt me the most was the fact I was starting to think that maybe Thaddeus was "the one." I definitely found myself falling in love with the man. That is why when Thaddeus stated, "I think we need some time apart," it felt as if he had kicked me in the stomach.

Initially, I thought it was another woman but after a while I let go of my insecurities. At some point I decided to have an open mind about the entire situation. It was difficult at first, but I tried my damnedest to understand where Thaddeus was coming from. I was falling in love with the man and I wanted for us to get beyond this brief hang-up. Although Thaddeus and I were no longer a couple, I still came around…just not as frequently. I had a vested interest in this man. I was not going to just let five months go to waste, so some other woman could easily step in and take my place. That was not going to happen! So I gave him his space but stayed in the background. However, all that changed the Friday night Lisa called.

I was at home that evening reviewing a brief, making notes to myself as well as to my paralegal whom was scheduled to prep the client for court Monday morning. I should have known by the way the phone rang it wasn't good. First of all it was eleven o'clock at night. Secondly, it just seemed to ring with a sense of urgency. Still, I ignored my gut feeling and picked up the phone before checking the caller ID. Privately, I hoped it was Thaddeus possibly making a booty call. I was desperately in need of some company and searching for any reason what so ever to put the legal brief down. Of course, I intended to play hard to get at first only to eventually give in to his pleas to come over…. I too had needs that needed to be met.

I did not expect to pick up the phone and hear Lisa's voice.

"Hello," I said. I attempted to sound drowsy, if it had been Thaddeus that would have been my excuse to play hard to get before succumbing to his begging.

"Ivy? What's up girl it's Lisa…. Are you asleep?"

"Nah, I'm just sitting up here reviewing this legal brief."

"Girl, you work way too damn much. If you don't make partner then nobody in that damn firm deserves to. Isn't your review coming up?"

"Yeah, the Friday after next. I never understood why you were not on the partner track?"

"Girl, I don't have the patience to play the political games those old farts like to play. Besides, I want to have a life so staff attorney suits me just fine."

"I hear ya."

"Anyway, as much as I wish I had called to talk about work…I didn't."

"I was starting to wonder."

"Nah girl, I called to tell you about Thaddeus." As soon as she said Thaddeus' name I instantly assumed he was hurt or in dire need of my assistance.

"Why what's wrong?" I asked, concerned.

I could hear Marcus in the background interrupting Lisa before she cut him off. "Shut up! Your boy is wrong! And it is my business! Ivy is my girl! You just need to mind *your* business!"

"Girl what is going on?" I panicked.

"Girl, you are not still messing with that buster are you?"

"Who?"

"Thaddeus?" Lisa insisted. She acted as if I was supposed to know just who, she was referring to when she used the term "buster."

"No, I told you we decided to take a break." Thaddeus was the one who actually made that decision but she did not need to know all of my business. "Why?"

"Because, I just saw that negro at the movies with a white girl." My heart dropped like a rock.

"Excuse me?" I hoped I had misheard her.

"You heard me girl—a stone cold white girl! She had blonde hair, blue eyes and a flat ass! The whole nine!" Marcus interrupted again. "So, what if it was dark I saw her!" Lisa shouted. "Marcus, why don't you just shut up? Ivy are you still there?"

"Yeah, I'm here," I said, somberly.

"I swear, I thought Thaddeus was different than all these other trifling brothas up here in Minnesota. I'm sorry I even introduced you to that sorry ass brotha."

"Don't be…it's not your fault. Besides, like I said we're taking a break from each other. So, if he goes and decides he wants to see someone else that's his prerogative," I replied. I tried not to sound fazed.

"I hear ya girl. I just thought you should know."

"I appreciate it. I'm not trying to be rude, but I got to get back to this case. There are a few things I want to nail down before Monday morning."

"I hear ya. I'll call you tomorrow," Lisa assured me.

I wanted to tell her don't call but that was not what came out of my mouth. "Okay…. I'll talk to you tomorrow."

"Bye."

"Bye."

I wished I had never picked up the phone.

I had a hard time trying to continue on with my work after hanging up the phone. After a while I simply stopped trying.

That was a long, restless, night for me. I drifted in and out of sleep continuously. I guess the thing that bothered me the most was not the fact that Thaddeus was with another woman nor the fact the woman was white, it would have hurt regardless of the woman's ethnicity. The real pain for me came from the fact that I had believed Thaddeus. I started to truly believe Thaddeus needed time in order to get Stephanie out of his system. I couldn't believe I actually bought that bullshit. I actually believed him. I had gotten so wrapped up in him that I lost sight of the world around me. There is a lot of truth in the phrase, "Love is blind."

Saturday morning I did nothing. I had intended on going to the gym then into the office to tie up some loose ends. Instead, I put on my robe got myself a bowl of cereal and planted my butt right back in the bed where I stayed most of the day. I didn't answer the phone nor did I pick up any legal briefs to review. At that moment in time, I really could've cared less about work. I simply sat in bed and psychoanalyzed myself as if I was the one to blame for not being able to hold on to Thaddeus Brown. I tried to convince myself that Lisa was lying or joking. Yet that fantasy evaporated when I asked myself what would Lisa have to gain by lying to me or by playing a cruel, inhumane, joke. I think I laid in bed until about three that afternoon. Occasionally, I got up to check the caller ID after someone called—a few times I noticed Thaddeus' number. I promptly erased his phone number from the caller ID log. It was not until late that afternoon that I felt in the mood to answer my phone. I assumed it was Lisa calling me back as she had promised, however, if it was Thaddeus I was prepared to quickly hang up. It was neither; instead it was my girlfriend Gloria.

"Hello," I said, somberly into the phone.

"Hey girl it's me."

"Gloria?"

"Who else? How many people do you know who always says 'it's me' when they call?"

"Well, two…maybe three," I said before she cut me off.

"Never mind…. What are you doing tonight?" Gloria demanded.

"I think I'm going to stay home tonight."

"Nah girl, we got to go out. These kids have driven me completely crazy today. You should have seen them cutting up at the mall today. I told Harold he was going to have to stay home with their little bad asses tonight because I was going out. So, you best believe you're not staying in the house tonight. We're going to get done up, put on something nice and tight and get our butts out on the town."

"I don't know Gloria. I kind of just wanna stay home."

"Girl, it's nice and hot outside. You got all winter to sit in the house. You got to get out and enjoy a Minnesota summer when you can."

"Maybe some other night."

There was a pause on the other end before Gloria finally got the hint. "Okay, what is wrong with you?"

"Nothing, I'm just not in the mood," I professed.

"Yeah right. I know any other time I say let's go out; you're the first one out the door. What's going on?" I sat there silent for a moment wondering if I should update Gloria with the latest piece of gossip, when she figured it out for herself.

"Does this have to do with Thaddeus?" I said nothing. "What did he do?" She took my silence as a yes.

"Lisa saw him at the movies last night with another woman."

"Shut up!"

"Yep! And to top it all off, it was a white girl."

"Oh hell no! The negro was prancing around town with some white broad? He needs a break—please! It sounds more like to me the negro needs something broke! Where I'm from we don't play that! If you want we can jump that negro and the white girl! I'm down!"

Gloria was always down. That stemmed from her Detroit upbringing. To be a vice president at a local biotech firm, making six figures, Gloria at times was the epitome of ghetto. Gloria was not a big girl nor was she small by any measure of the word. Nevertheless, I have witnessed Gloria on a couple of occasions drop a dude who got a little too free with his hands in the club.

"Nah, there is no need for that."

"That does it! You're definitely going out tonight."

"Come on now Gloria, I'm not in the mood."

"Well, you better get in the mood because I'll be there to pick you up at nine thirty, so put on something sexy. Besides, it's not everyday I'm able to get away from these rugrats of mine so be ready. You hear me?"

"Yeah," I sighed. When Gloria had made up her mind, there is nothing you can do to change it. Even if I had said no, I knew she would be over at my house at nine thirty sharp regardless.

"Also, call Lisa and tell her to come too." Gloria paused for a minute. "You know what? It might be better if I call Lisa. In the state of mind you're in, I know you will probably forget. What's her number?"

"612-555-6845," I replied.

"Got it! I'll be there at nine thirty so be ready!" The phone suddenly went dead. Gloria had hung up without saying good-bye. I reluctantly got out of bed and headed over to the closet to see what I might wear that evening. Although, it was six hours before Gloria would arrive, I thought rummaging through my closet for something to wear would give me something to do rather than sitting in bed sulking.

Gloria was there promptly at nine thirty. She suggested we go to a local club that catered to the older crowd on Saturdays called Quest. The club played old school music on Saturday nights. Gloria informed me on our way to Quest that Lisa would meet us there.

Lisa was already there when we arrived. She had a table, which was good since it meant we did not have to hang around the bar like barflies. Gloria and I sat down and made ourselves comfortable while soaking in the ambiance and feeling sorry for the sad state of affairs for a single black woman in Minnesota.

"Woo girl! There is a whole lot of ugly going on up in here!" Gloria proclaimed, surveying the room.

"You're right about that," Lisa cosigned. "However, there are two cuties over there by the bar." Gloria and I peered over at the bar to see the two guys Lisa was referring to.

"Yeah, I saw them when I walked in but they look like they still got their mama's breast milk on their breath. I just came here to dance not get my freak on. Those two young bucks are trying to get them some and I really don't feel like hurting anybody's poor little feelings tonight," Gloria stated.

"I'll tell you one thing about young brothas, they definitely got stamina. Their only problem is they haven't mastered the skills of totally pleasing a woman," I interceded.

"What are you referring to?" questioned Lisa.

"You know what I'm talking about." I raised my eyebrows as if to give Lisa a hint.

"What the hell does this mean?" Lisa in turn raised her eyebrows back at me.

"Damn, do I have to spell it out," I said in disgust.

"Girl, will you just spell it out!" Gloria begged.

"A lot of these young brothas don't put it in their mouth," I said, exasperated.

"It?" Lisa looked over at Gloria for help.

"Come on Lisa stop acting dumb," I told her.

"*It* could mean anything," Lisa interjected. "People are into some really kinky stuff nowadays."

"I'm talking about your stuff, okay," I conceded.

"Ivy, why are you acting sadiddy? Girl, you're with us. You're not at work around all those white folks. We all know you're a hoe. Besides, I am quite sure we have all heard the word 'pussy' before," Gloria stated.

"Do you always have to be so vulgar?" I asked.

"I like to get straight to the point. I don't have time to dilly dally around the subject," Gloria stated.

"Well, just because the two of you have heard the word "pussy" before does not mean I want the rest of the club to hear me say it," I protested.

Gloria looked around the club. "I am quite sure the people in here have heard the word "pussy" before too. If they haven't, then it is time they did. Hell, I'm surprised they still make brothas that don't go downtown? I thought them type of brothas went out of style in the eighties," Gloria exclaimed.

"Oh yeah, girl they're still around. I dated this young brotha a couple of times and when I suggested he do a little snacking, he told me he don't do that," I replied.

"So, what did you do? I bet he gave you that bullshit line, 'If you do me first then I'll do you.'" Gloria lowered her voice to sound like a man's, which caused Lisa and I to erupt into laughter.

"You know it!" Lisa laughed, exchanging a high five with Gloria.

"That is exactly what he said," I assured them. "However, I was not in the mood for playing games so I sent his ass packing and never called him back."

When the laughter subsided. "Speaking of men," Gloria said turning her attention back to me. That was exactly the reason why I did not want to go out that night. I wanted to forget about Thaddeus for a couple of hours I did not want to be reminded of him.

"Please, can we not go there," I sighed. Despite my deep hope, the evening did not turn into a counseling session I knew it would. Fortunately, right when I said that the waitress came over to the table so we could order our drinks. Yet, even she was only a brief reprieve from Gloria's interrogation.

"So Lisa, Ivy tells me you caught Thaddeus out last night creeping with some white hoe?"

"Yeah, and he knew he was busted too because the negro tried to creep out of the movie theater before the movie was even over."

"Come on please. I do not want to hear this," I insisted.

"Fine, but I'll tell you one thing, a man is never satisfied," Gloria proclaimed. At that time the waitress returned with our drinks. Gloria took a sip of her margarita before going on. "A man can have all the money in the world and he still wants more. He could have a woman at home giving him all the loving he can stand and he still wants to sneak out and try to find him some more. I don't get it. When is enough, *enough*?"

"Who knows girl! A man believes a woman is suppose to work, clean, take care of the kids and be a super freak all at the same time. And if you so happen to tell a man you're tired he will whine about how deprived he is," Lisa interjected.

"You're right about that. Take Harold for example," Gloria rambled. "The man never gets his fill. I love that man to death but I'll give that negro some and the next thing I know he comes a knocking again, trying to double dip. I give him some twice a week and he wants it three. If I give it to him three times a week, he wants it five. If I were to give it to him five times a week, he would want it twice a day.

"A man is never satisfied. Sometimes, I can't get in the house without him rubbing my butt and talking about how he wants to wax that ass. Sometimes, while I'm undressing he's got his hand in between my legs like he's digging for gold. I often wonder if he thinks my stuff is going to get up and runaway or something. Whatever happened to getting a woman in the mood? You know a little Isley Brothers. Hell, I would even settle for whining ass Keith Sweat."

"Girl, tell me about it," Lisa chimed in. "I don't know what it is about a woman's privates that will cause a man to forsake life, limb, God and family."

"It's that pussy power, girl," Gloria interjected.

"I don't see what's so special about it. I mean have you ever put a mirror down there and looked at yourself. I mean it looks all right but there is nothing special about it," Lisa added.

"I don't know about you girl, but my cootie cat is fine," Gloria exclaimed. She reached over and slapped me five. A chorus of chuckles rose from the table.

"I tell you," Lisa continued, "If Marcus isn't complaining about how he isn't getting enough he's begging me to put it in my mouth. Do you know he had the nerve to try and stick it in my butt." I winced at the thought. It was obvious by the course of the conversation the drinks were loosening everybody up.

"I don't have no problem with giving my man head, in fact I enjoy it. Now, what I do have a problem with is someone trying to stick their stuff up my behind. Let me tell you it is not one of the most pleasurable experiences in the world," Gloria assured us.

"T.M.I.! That is way too much information for me!" I shouted.

"You've had anal sex before girl," Lisa said in surprise.

"Yeah, it was a little present I gave Harold. He had been begging me and begging me to do it for the longest. So, one night I got up enough nerve to let him try it. Girl, I thought I was going to split right down the middle. My eyes got to watering, my legs went numb and it felt like somebody had set my ass on fire," Gloria insisted.

"Damn Gloria, I would have never guessed," I said in shock.

"Don't sound surprised. I try to please my man. When are you women going to understand you got to feed your man if you don't want him to stray?" Gloria proclaimed.

"I hear ya and all, but I don't know about doing all that just to keep my man around," Lisa replied.

"Regardless, after doing it I told Harold never again. I think the whole novelty of it must've worn off anyway because he has not asked me about it since," Gloria added.

"If you ask me, I think a guy doing it to a woman in the butt has some homosexual tendencies," I exclaimed. Both Gloria and Lisa started cracking up.

"I'm serious! What makes my behind any different than some dude's behind! You might want to watch Harold, he sounds like he might be on the Down Low if you ask me! Harold might not be asking you for it no more because he is getting it somewhere else!"

"She got a point there," Lisa said, laughing.

"Shit! I'll cut 'em! I'll cut his thing right off. Anyway, I think it is more of a curiosity thing with most men," Gloria stated. "Once they do it they usually loose interest. However, some brothas say it is a much tighter fit."

"It sounds like to me some of these women out here might need to start doing some calisthenics to tighten their shit up! Because I'll be damn if I let somebody run up in my behind because he thinks it is a tighter fit!" I exclaimed.

"While ya bullshiting, some sistahs like it in the boo-tay!" Lisa laughed.

"Oh Lord!" I could not believe my ears.

"Ya girl!" Lisa exclaimed, "Negros and booty holes is just like brothas and white girls…they're full of shit."

"Can we not go there?" I really was not in the mood to entertain such a topic.

"So, you're saying brothas with white girls is nothing more than jungle fever? Two people exploring their curiosity, just like brothas and anal sex," Gloria commented.

"Exactly! Particularly these trifling brothas up here in Minnesota! Brothas are too stupid to realize most of these white women are with them because they are successful and have money. And if the negro doesn't have no money, he's traipsing around town with some white trash or fat ass white heifer. If they were to happen to go broke or get down on their luck that white girl would leave them in a heartbeat.

"And then whom do you think they come running to? A sistah that's who! These white women out here are just as underhanded and if not more so, gold diggers than any black woman I know!" Lisa exclaimed.

"At least a sistah is willing to tell a brotha up front, what her game is all about," Gloria added.

"That's right! These white women make a brotha think they love them, then turn around after a year or two and divorce them for everything they got!" Lisa proclaimed.

"I think it is nothing more than black men's pre-conceived idea of success…. For example look at these professional athletes and brothas who so called made it. Most of them walk around here with these Barbie dolls on their arm. Our young men grow up seeing this believing once they make it they got to go out and get themselves a white girl to make the picture complete…. Or another brotha."

"Tell me about it. It's down right scary being a single black woman nowadays. Brothas are just being plain greedy! Trying to have it all. Sleeping with men and women. Trying to have it both ways. I don't care what anybody says, God did not intend for a man to be with another man! It just aint right!" I proclaimed.

"Tell it girl! Tell it!" Gloria raised her hand as if she was testifying.

"Don't you know the fastest growing segment of the population contracting HIV in this country is black women…. Now that is scary. If our black men are not abandoning us for white women then they're killing us off," Lisa stated.

"Yet, we're still here supporting—sometimes taking care of—their black asses. Isn't that sick and twisted," I interjected. I doubted this bothered Gloria and Lisa as much as it did me. They had already managed to tie down a half-way decent man.

Gloria shook her head in disgust. "Hmm…Just hearing the two of you talk makes me glad I got a man."

"Count your blessings," I informed her. "Because more and more I am starting to think I'm being a little too narrow minded in my criteria of a man. I'm starting to think long and hard about dating white guys," I proclaimed.

"What!" Gloria looked at me in shock.

"Yeah. Why not? Maybe I have not given dating a white guy a fair chance," I said in my defense.

"I don't know about laying up next to a white boy," Gloria professed.

"Why not? How long am I suppose to wait for a "good" black man? Gloria you have the luxury of saying that because you have a man," I stated.

"I aint mad at ya, girl. I just don't know if I could do it," Gloria insisted.

"In my opinion, brothas have made it clear they have choices in whom they date. Why can't black women? Hell, brothas damn near trample over sistahs to get to the nearest white woman.

"Why do black women have to feel beholden to black men if they are not beholden to us? Should I continue ignoring a decent white guy in order to keep dealing with knucklehead brothas who want to play games?"

"Ivy's got a point," Lisa chimed.

"Whatever. To be honest with you, I'm tired of talking about it. If brothas want to be with white women or other men then to hell with them! It's a tired subject!" I continued.

"Sistahs need to stop feeling sorry for ourselves just because some of these idiots don't recognize a good thing even if it slapped them in the face! We need to start loving ourselves as women! The way some of our sistahs carry themselves just to get a man's attention is a shame! Now, I don't want to talk about white girls, dudes on the DL or Thaddeus anymore tonight!" I announced.

"No one said anything about Thaddeus," Lisa countered. Lisa was right. No one had mentioned Thaddeus.

"Oh that's my song!" Gloria exclaimed. The Labelles' "Lady Marmalade" pumped through the speakers. The margarita definitely was beginning to work its magic. "No one sings this song like Patti," she exclaimed. "You know girl, I wont say anything else about white women, brothas or Thaddeus except this…you're going to have to cut the brotha off. No more phone calls, no more conjugal visits. If Thaddeus wants some space between him and you then you give it to him—*for real!*"

"You're right about that girl." Lisa added her two cents as she bobbed her head and sung along with the chorus, "Hey Sister, Go Sister, Soul Sister, Go Sister."

"I don't know about you two, but I'm about to grab me one of those young bucks over there at the bar and dance," Gloria exclaimed. As Gloria sashayed her way over towards the bar I could not help but admit to myself she was right.

Erin—I Prefer Love

Although I did not want Thaddeus to leave Friday night, I'm glad he did. I did not want us to get carried away under the pretense of alcohol. Alcohol tends to cloud one's judgment and make for an awkward situation in the morning. Besides, if Thaddeus and I were to become intimate I wanted it to be because we wanted it to happen that way not because we were too tipsy to keep our libidos under control. Still, I readily admit I found myself taken by him. Thaddeus possessed a charm and wit, I found hard to resist. To simply be in his presence or hear his voice seemed to put a smile on my face. Yet, I did not want to appear as if I was crowding him. That is why I restrained myself from calling him Saturday morning and telling him—despite the incident with the women in the foyer of the movie theater—how I enjoyed myself Friday night. I did not want him to feel like I was smothering him.

I think that was the problem with Brian and I. Although we had taken our time before becoming intimate, we had not taken enough time to become friends. Regardless of what I knew was best…I hoped Thaddeus would soon see me as a romantic interest as well. I was assured there was indeed hope when Thaddeus called Saturday afternoon to let me know he planned on hanging out with his friends that evening, which in my opinion was a start. He definitely did not have to make me aware of his plans for the night.

Belinda could tell I was falling for Thaddeus. Like it was not obvious by the way I beamed whenever he called. "Let me guess? That was Thaddeus, Mister Dreamboat himself." Belinda teased.

"Yes." I smiled.

"I can always tell when you are talking to him because you light up like a Christmas tree. You really like him don't you?"

"I don't know what it is about him Belinda? I just can't stop thinking about him and believe me when I tell you they're not bad thoughts." I could not help but giggle like some schoolgirl experiencing her first crush.

"So, is he coming over?" Belinda sought to know.

"No, he was calling to let me know he was going to hang out with his friends tonight and that he'll probably call me later on tonight or Sunday morning." Once again I couldn't keep from smiling.

"Well, I guess that tells me Darius has plans for the evening." Belinda paused for a moment before screaming, "Girls night out!"

"Sounds good to me."

"How about The Wild Onion? It's close, so if we get too drunk we can easily stumble back home. Not to mention it's Saturday and we should get plenty of entertainment from the sorry guys there trying to work their pick-up lines."

The Wild Onion was notorious for being a meat market on Friday and Saturday nights. Usually when we went on a Friday or Saturday, we spent most of the time cracking up at the losers working the crowd with the same pathetic line until they found a woman desperate enough to take the bait.

"Sounds good, I'll call Stacy and let her know."

Belinda grimaced at the thought of Stacy joining us. "Do you have to invite her all the time? Sometimes Stacy can be such a kill joy."

"Why not? Stacy is our friend."

"No. Stacy is *your* friend and since you're inviting her you're baby sitting her," Belinda insisted. I knew it was Stacy's ignorance that was the source of Belinda's dislike for her. At times even I questioned what it was I saw in Stacy. However, I did not share in Belinda's attitude towards her.

Stacy came by around ten and since it was such a beautiful evening we decided to walk to the Wild Onion. As expected the place was packed with its usual Saturday night crowd of college students and middle age men looking to boost their egos by scoring with a girl barely above the legal drinking age. The crowd as promised presented us with plenty of laughs for a delightful evening.

We parked ourselves at the bar and engaged in a little girl talk while we smoked before getting in a few laughs at the expense of a few of the bar's patrons. Everything was going great until I noticed a good-looking guy standing at the bar with a cute butt.

"That guy sure does have a nice ass," I said. I did not think twice about the comment after I said it nor did I realize what I said would lead the night spiraling, precipitously, downhill.

Stacy turned to see whom I was talking about. "I was starting to get worried about you there for a minute."

"What do you mean?" I said. I took a sip of my drink.

"You know this whole black thing." As soon as the words came out of Stacy's mouth I could see Belinda roll her eyes. The guy I stated as to having a cute butt was white.

"Well, if you're curious to know Thaddeus has a very cute butt too," I quipped. Belinda could not help but smirk knowing I said it just to spite her. At the time Stacy's comment really struck a chord with me. I truly believed if she were a true friend, she would not try to tear me down.

"I just don't know what you and Belinda see in black guys. I could definitely see myself with one of those hot Latin lovers or maybe even an Asian guy, but a black guy never. Just the sight of white women with black guys annoys me. I would much rather see a white woman with an A-Rab than a black guy."

"See, why I told you not to bring her along," Belinda interrupted. Belinda was pissed.

"Not now Belinda," I replied, before laying into Stacy. "You know Stacy you might want to stop believing every freaking thing you see and hear on TV."

"Don't get mad at me," Stacy protested. "They do it to themselves. They're the ones talking all that broken English. What do they call it…Ebonics? Whatever happened to plain old English? It is the chosen language of this country. And what is it with all those funny names they name their kids. Whatever happened to simple names like John and Paul? What type of names are Travon and Raekwon?

"They wear all those baggie clothes that show their underwear. They're always calling their women 'bitches' and 'hoes.' Every black guy calls his friend 'my nigga.' I mean what is up with that? If you or I was to say that, we would probably get our butts kicked." Stacy had a valid point.

"Stacy you're right, there are some black people who may act that way but not all of them. However, you can't make such sweeping judgments about all black people. You can't lump a group of people into one category from what you see in music videos. That is just like if a black person said all white people were rednecks. We know that is not true."

"You're just wasting your breath," Belinda interjected. "Just let it go. She will never understand."

"I just don't get what it is the two of you see in them," Stacy replied. Sometimes it was futile to argue with Stacy, so I did as Belinda suggested and let it go. Yet, just when I thought the evening could not get any worse…it did.

"Oh, there's Marty and John," Stacy exclaimed. I looked up just in time to see Marty and John walk in. They immediately noticed us sitting at the bar. Just in case they didn't see us, Stacy made sure they did by frantically waving them over.

"What the hell are they doing here?" Belinda asked. The Wild Onion was not one of Marty and John's regular haunts.

"I invited them," Stacy blurted out.

"You did what!" I exclaimed. I could not believe Stacy would do such a thing.

"I asked them to come join us," Stacy reiterated.

"Without asking me?" I inquired.

"I don't see what is the big deal?" Stacy stated.

The big deal was that Martin or Marty Knoll and John Ostagaard were Brian's best friends. Stacy had the hots for Marty. However, unless he was drunk and had struck out with every girl in the bar—Marty never gave Stacy the time of day. Whenever Stacy was not around Marty always talked about her like she was a bumpkin. Yet, she never listened to me. Of course, Stacy invited him to the Wild Onion that night in hopes of getting something started between them. However, I was sure Marty came as an emissary for Brian in an attempt to find out what I was up to.

"I can't believe you," I hissed. I watched as Marty and John made their way over to where we sat.

"What?" Stacy replied. Stacy played as if she did not hear me.

"Hey! How are you guys doing?" Marty shouted. He tried to act surprised to see us. "What brings you guys here?" Marty's shit-eating grin did little in hiding his true intentions.

"Just out having a few drinks amongst friends. If you don't mind we kind of want to keep it that way," Belinda replied. Belinda did not care for Marty or John and did not hide it.

"Oh, okay we can go someplace else," retorted Marty.

"No, never mind Belinda, stay here and drink with us. There is a chair open right here next to me." Stacy patted the stool next to her.

"That's all right I much rather stand," Marty replied.

"I'll take it," John said. John plopped his fat ass down on the stool much to Stacy's dismay.

"So Erin, how are you doing?" Marty asked. Marty wasted not time in getting right to the point.

"I'm doing great Marty and you? What are you guys doing here? I thought you guys usually hangout at Grandma's pub near the university."

"We thought we would try out someplace different tonight. Besides, we haven't seen you around lately so we were kind of worried about you." I knew when Marty said "we" he was referring to him and Brian—not him and John.

"No need to worry Marty. You can let Brian know I'm doing fine without him."

"Who said anything about Brian," Marty proclaimed.

"You didn't have to say anything about Brian, I just know that is who you are referring to when you say 'we.'" At that moment I wished I had simply stayed home.

"Whatever…. So, where is your new boyfriend?"

"What new boyfriend? What are you talking about?"

In all honesty, I truly did not understand what Marty was getting at. "You know the black guy." I shot a cold glare at Stacy, who quickly looked away. I should have known in order to get Marty to come to The Wild Onion, Stacy told Marty about Thaddeus.

"For your information, Thaddeus is my friend."

"Oh, is that right? We were starting to believe you had been hanging around Belinda a little too long." Marty, John and Stacy chuckled.

"And what do you mean by that!" Belinda snapped.

"Come on Belinda, everybody knows you prefer the brothers," John added.

"You know what, I'll tell you why I 'prefer the brothers.'" Belinda stared Marty and John down. "They treat me with respect. They don't treat me like I was a piece of meat. They don't come to a bar to get me drunk off my rocker in hopes that will be the only way they can get me in bed. Nor do black guys come to a bar and harass me about the things in life I do or do not like. They like to dance and do other things than get drunk and most importantly they accept me for who I am. They're not all about themselves," Belinda said sternly.

"I thought you liked black guys because they had some good fried chicken," Marty interjected. He was able to manage another round of chuckles from Stacy and John.

"Believe me Marty, if you're going to believe in stereotypes then you better believe in them all because I don't date black guys to eat fried chicken. I date them because of that other little myth. You know the one about the size of their dicks…. Of course, pencil dick assholes such as yourself would not know anything about that.

"Now if you will excuse me, I'm going to go enjoy my drink someplace else. Erin come and get me when you're ready to go," Belinda seethed, before storming off.

By that time I was furious. "What the fuck is your problem? Do you practice at being a prick or is that something that comes naturally to you? I do not appreciate you talking to my friend like that! I mean did you come here with the intentions of harassing us?"

"Erin you know that is not the case." Marty suddenly became defensive.

"Well, you sure as hell could have fooled me. You know Marty, I thought you were a smart guy, a bright guy, but I see you're nothing more than an idiot. You know what else? I like Thaddeus, I like him a lot, and the fact that he is black does not bother me. In fact it would not bother me if he were white, black, brown, purple, green or yellow. Do you know why Marty? Do you know? It is because I prefer love. I choose love and whatever color it may come in.

"Maybe, if you and people like you." I gazed in Stacy's direction. "Start thinking outside of the little box you have let people place you in, you might be able to find true love. Now, if you don't mind I'm going to go find my friend." When I was done I stormed off in search of Belinda.

When I found Belinda, we both were very eager to leave.

Thaddeus—The Difference Between White Women and Black Women From a Black Male's Point of View

I should have stayed at Erin's apartment that Friday night. Stephanie called me early Saturday morning to inform me she was flying to Chicago to see her parents and she was taking Little T with her. Stephanie promised me, she would make the weekend up to me by giving me one of the holidays Little T was suppose to spend with her.

What could I do?

When I violated the parenting agreement Stephanie's lawyer usually threatened to drag my black ass back into court. When she violated the agreement my lawyer simply tells me there isn't much I can do. I didn't understand it. I was a good father. I paid my child support on time and I tried hard to be an active participant in my son's life. It annoyed the hell out of me how Stephanie pretty much got to dictate the terms of the relationship I shared with my son. It is because of this pared relationship with Little T, why I believe I have a complex when it comes to being a father. My idea of what a father should be was loosely based upon the stories I heard people tell me about my dad, and I was not living up to those stories.

Since I grew up in a household where there was no male role model to show me the ropes on how to be a man, the stories of my father's strict discipline and compassion became the guidelines by which I judged as well as measured myself. Of course, trying to measure up to stories that may have been embellished upon or totally false was foolish. It was even more dangerous for me to compare myself to a ghost. However, I was somewhat forced into this make believe image of what a man should be because I never had much of a male figure around to compare or contrast myself against. Like I said, I had my older brother James and maybe one or two of his friends whom I may have thought were cool while growing up but none of them carried the same kind of mystique or aura as one's father. I often found myself envious of other children with dads growing up. It was this same feeling I desperately wanted to avoid my son from experiencing as a child. However for me to do that I needed to be an active participant in my son's life and that was hard to do with Stephanie constantly jerking me around.

Since Little T was not going to be spending the day with me, I decided to relax instead of going to the watch the Twins play the White Sox. My son and I went to at least one Twins/White Sox baseball game religiously every year. It was an annual ritual of ours. Of course, there would be other games later on in the season. Still, I kind of had my heart set on that particular game. I guess I was in the mood for stale beer, over cooked hot dogs and a good game of baseball. Since I suddenly had nothing to do, I decided to call Darius and see what he had planned for the day.

Darius picked up the phone on the first ring, "Hello."

"What's up?"

"Ah nothing, just laying here in bed." I looked over at the clock to see it read a quarter to twelve.

"Good looking out for a brotha last night," I said, in reference to his help with Erin.

"No doubt. Who were you trying to kill off?"

"I was not trying to kill off nobody. I was trying to work myself out of a jam. That's why I had to call you in for back up. I had gone to the movies with Erin when Marcus and Lisa showed up. I had to high tail it out of there."

"Whaaat? Did they see you?"

"I saw Marcus but not Lisa. Besides, we got out of there before the movie was over."

"Right, right…. So did you hit it?"

"Nah, just some hardcore freaking."

"I hear that. You know that girl wants to be on your squad. Ever since the night you met her, she has been asking me about you. You might want to put a little more work in on that one. Erin's got a good job and she's fine as hell. She could turn out to be a cash cow. If you hit it right."

"Ah, I don't know."

"What do you mean you don't know? Did you hear what I said, that hoe is a cash cow," Darius reiterated.

"I heard you the first time," I informed him.

"Nigga don't *talk* about pimping…*be* a pimp. You got to drain these hoes for their cash just like they would drain you."

"Whatever."

"Well, if you're uncertain about her you might want to cut her loose so I can give her a few tryouts for my team." Darius had no scruples. It didn't matter to him if he was sleeping with her roommate.

"Listen to you. What's up with her roommate, Belinda? She claimed you cancelled on her at the last minute last night?" I reminded him.

"I had to T, Belinda's catching feelings man. She's coming around here acting like she's my lady. You know I can't have that. Besides, I had this young white freak over here last night. The broad was scared she was too young for me. You know I had to let that hoe know I was blowing backs out before she could grow pubic hair. The female was up in my in apartment screaming and hollering. I had that young girl begging for mercy." Darius could not help sounding crude.

"She still there?"

"Nah, I kicked her ass out this morning. She was trying to stick around and play housewife. I think she started catching feelings. I had to tell her if she wasn't cooking or cleaning she had to get the hell out. Besides, I'm suppose to have lunch with this gray girl, Raquel, and I couldn't have her lingering around the pad." That explained why he picked up the phone so fast.

"That's a new name."

"Ah, she's this bisexual chick I met the other night at the club. I think she's a stripper."

"Bisexual huh?"

"Yeah. Don't tell me I got to school you on bisexual babes?" Darius proclaimed.

"I guess you're going to have to school me brotha because I don't understand why dating a bisexual babe is all that. How do you even know she is bisexual anyway?"

"She told me. Don't you know that with a bisexual babe you don't ever have to worry about women because she will always bring them home to you? And the beauty of it is, it isn't as if you're cheating on her because she's enjoying them too."

"Man, you've got problems. You might want to think about seeking professional help. So, I take it you're busy this afternoon?"

"I don't know. I called Raquel about an hour ago but she has not returned my call, so I'm about to give her the boot. You know me, I don't chase down no females. Why what's up?"

"I thought about coming over to your place and watching the Twins play the White Sox."

"That sounds cool. I can call this broad and tell her to forget it."

"You got any brew?"

"You know me playa. I keep only the good stuff. No beer in my cupboard. Now if you want some Crown, Hennessey, Grey Goose or Belvedere I got it. However, you're going to have to bring the juice for the Goose and the Belve. If you want beer you're going to have to bring it yourself."

"I guess I'll go to the liquor store and get a case of beer."

"Cool, you do that. I'm going to call Marcus and tell him to get his narrow ass over here too. He needs to give his lips a rest from kissing Lisa's behind."

"The game starts at one, so I'll see you in about an hour."

"Cool."

"Cool."

By the time I got dressed and went to the liquor store, the baseball game was already in the third inning. When I arrived at Darius' apartment Marcus was already there, which was good because I wanted to find out if Lisa suspected anything the night before at the movies.

"What's the score?" I shouted. I walked into the apartment and placed the beer in the refrigerator.

"Five to two. Chicago is leading in the top of the third!" Darius shouted.

"Is the Chi putting a hurting on 'em?" I teased. Marcus was a big Twins fan.

"Shut up and bring me a beer. Besides, when was the last time the White Sox won a World Series?" Marcus shouted.

"Whatever…. You know the Twinkies can't hang with the Chi," I boasted, handing him a cold one. He immediately popped the top and began downing the beer.

After watching the Twins strikeout to close out the third I asked Marcus, "So, did Lisa know that was me last night at the movies?"

"I don't think so?" Marcus replied. Marcus did not sound too confident.

"You don't think so? What do you mean you don't think so? What the hell is that? That is either a yes or no question." I paused a moment before realizing. "You told her didn't you? You told her it was me didn't you?" Marcus tried to act as if he had suddenly gone deaf.

"Judging by how quiet he has gotten, I would suspect that means 'yes,'" Darius answered. Darius got up off the couch to make himself a drink.

"Damn Marcus, how could you? I can't believe you! You're supposed to be my boy!" I exclaimed. That was it! I knew my name was mud. By the end of the day most of the sistahs in Minneapolis would know. From that day on, I knew if any sistah spoke my name it would be with contempt in their voice.

"I am your boy but Lisa is my wife. Besides, you guys made so much noise leaving, she couldn't help but figure out it was you with that white girl. Why are you sweating if Lisa knows anyway? You're not with Ivy anymore."

"How could she have known it was me Marcus—unless you told her? It was dark. Besides, that does not mean I want my game with Ivy to be totally blown out of the water."

"You should have thought about that before you went prancing about town with that white girl."

"You know you need to take that thong off and stop acting like a bitch," exclaimed Darius, sitting back down.

"Fuck you Darius." Marcus proceeded to give Darius the finger.

"So, what are you going to do T?" Darius asked. Darius sipped on his fresh drink in between insulting Marcus and questioning me.

"I don't know?" I said in disgust. "My game with Ivy even if I wanted to go back is shot, thanks to pussy whipped over there."

"That's right I'm whipped and loving it," proclaimed Marcus.

"Shut up, you've already done enough damage for one day," Darius demanded, sticking a cigarette in his mouth.

"Come on, do you have to do that?" Marcus complained. Marcus and I were non-smokers, so we hated it when Darius lighted one up.

"Last time I checked, this was my muthafuckin' house. If you don't like it you can get out." Marcus simply huffed and returned his attention back to the television. "So T, what are you gonna do? Are you going to see ole girl again or what?"

"Who?" I was not sure if Darius meant Erin or Ivy.

"Erin," Darius said. He exhaled a plume of smoke, which quickly dispersed itself throughout the room.

"I don't know."

"What's the problem?" Darius asked. Marcus suddenly tried to act as if he was more interested in the game than our conversation.

"I don't know. I feel funny dating a white chick. I feel as if everyone is looking at me. I mean how do you deal with it?" I asked. I had never dated a white woman before so I was looking for some insight into how I might be able to cope.

"You know, I use to be just like you…insecure. But I realized I was not going to let someone else keep me from being happy. If the type of woman that makes me happy is white so be it." Marcus damn near choked when he heard Darius say that.

"Negro please, you like white women because they're stupid enough to put up with your shit!" exclaimed Marcus.

"I'm not going to lie. I got it bad for white girls. Yet, I do not think you should be the one to talk. You fell in love with the first piece of ass you got." Darius and Marcus always seem to wind up going at it.

"Yeah, if you think so," Marcus replied. I felt it was my duty to come to Marcus' defense since I had known Darius a lot longer than Marcus. I knew the true reason why Darius had an affinity for white women had nothing to do with the fact they brought him extreme joy.

"You know Darius, if my memory serves me correctly you really didn't start showing a interest in white women until you caught your girl, Jacqueline McCray, going down on your roommate in college," I interrupted.

Marcus' eyes got as big as saucers at hearing that piece of information. "Ha!" Marcus yelled.

"Ain't nobody talking about Jacqueline McCray," exclaimed Darius. Just the mention of Jacqueline McCray had made Darius agitated. She definitely was a sore spot with Darius. At one point in time, Darius had contemplated marrying the woman.

"Just like a typical brotha. You get slighted by one sistah, so you turn your back on all black women," Marcus stated.

"Go to hell Marcus! You don't know shit!" Darius exclaimed.

Darius quickly changed the subject from Jacqueline McCray back to my current dilemma. "Look, I'm serious T. When I first started dating white women I would see sistahs giving a brotha dirty looks and swaying their heads back and forth like their heads were on a swivel. That was until one day there was this one chicken head hating on me from the sidelines at this restaurant. I mean she was dogging a brotha out. I tell you she almost had me running for cover.

"I eventually got tired of it, so I walked over to her table and said, 'Check it out? If I was to bounce this white babe right here, right now, and get with you…what would you be able to do for me?' You know what she said."

"No what?" I said.

"She said, 'Do for you? It is more like what can you do for me?' You know what I did?"

"Nah, what?" I replied.

"I stared her dead in the eyes and said, 'That is exactly why I'm not with your dumb ass.' With a black woman it is always about her. A brotha can't even get to know a sistah before she is begging him to buy her a drink or talking about how she needs help with her rent or wondering if his health plan will cover her and her badass kids. And you know what? It isn't like I would not do that for a woman, but god damn can I at least get to know her name first?"

I had to agree with him there. "I feel you on that one."

Marcus even agreed. "I have to give you that one," he stated.

"When a broad approaches me like that I always ask her, 'What do you have to offer me, other than some pussy?'" Darius smiled. He put his hand out for me to give him some dap and I gladly gave it to him.

"You know something else," Darius was on a roll, "sistahs don't take care of themselves like these white women do. I see white women in the gym working out or outside jogging. Doing whatever it takes to remain healthy and in shape. Very rarely, do I see a black woman in the gym. They much rather blow up, instead of take care of their bodies. The cold part about it is that sistahs act like brothas should just be cool with it."

"Wait a minute now, I have to disagree with you on that," Marcus interjected. "Every black woman can't look like Halle Berry or Angela Bassett. Black women come in all different shapes and sizes and each shape and size has its own unique beauty."

"That is true," I agreed.

"That maybe is true. Still, why can't they stay the size they were when a brotha met them? Why after they lock a brotha down, they got to start blowing up? Stop taking care of themselves? Obesity is not cute! Being overweight leads to diabetes and heart problems. Diabetes is one of the fastest growing diseases among black women."

"He's got a point," I told Marcus. Marcus did not have a reply.

"See, sistahs need to stop hating on these white broads and figure out what it is they're doing to attract so many brothas," Darius exclaimed.

"Darius, you're lost!" Marcus shouted. "A brotha enslaved to the belief that white women are the standard by which beauty is judged. Why can't you see brotha that the black woman is the epitome of beauty? From the way a black woman wears her hair to her style and dress. Black women don't just glow brotha, they radiate. Black women set the trend all other women attempt to duplicate. White women are the ones injecting collagen in their lips to make them fuller and having operations so their pancake asses don't blend in with their backs.

"It is white women who go to the tanning salon, so their skin can resemble that honeydew brown our sistahs have naturally. All these characteristics are traits only found in one woman—a woman of African descent.

"So, I can't see how the two of you can even date white women. Especially, when you have these beautiful wonders of nature out here looking for black men. To tell you the truth, I don't trust white people. White people are just too phony and sneaky for me. They smile in your face while they stab you in the back. If the revolution was to go down today, I bet your white girlfriend would turn your ass over to the Klan in a heartbeat. In my opinion I think they're all closet racist," proclaimed Marcus.

"Oh shut the hell up Marcus! Are you trying to sit there and tell me that you have never thought some white woman you happened to see was fine?"

"Nope," Marcus replied with pride.

"You're a muthafuckin' liar!" Darius shouted.

"Think what you want," stated Marcus.

"Have you ever called a white dude or white woman a cracker behind their back or under your breath?" Darius asked.

"Yeah, so what?" Marcus replied.

"Well, what does that make you? Are you not a closet racist too?" exclaimed Darius.

"That's different. I have over four hundred years of oppression to justify my hatred," Marcus informed Darius.

"That's bullshit. When it pertains to you, you're justified. You know, before you open your mouth you need to think about what you're saying!" Darius yelled. Darius conveniently waved off Marcus' comment.

"Whatever…. I call them crackers because I can not trust them!" declared Marcus.

"Yeah, whatever," Darius snapped. "You know what a sistah's problem is?" Darius got back to the point he was trying to make. "Sistahs stress a brotha out. White women don't do that. They let a brotha relax and get situated after a hard day's work instead of hitting him over the head with petty shit as soon as he walks in the door. A sistah bombards a brotha as soon as a man's key hits the lock. Not only that, they're always bumping heads with a brotha over every little damn thing. It's like they're in constant competition with a man for who is going to wear the title of man of the house. I can seriously be without the headache. If you want an example of a brotha beat down by his wife look no further than Marcus." Once again Marcus gave Darius the finger.

"I hear what you're saying, but not all sistahs are like that." Everything Darius was saying was not exactly true.

"Thank you, Thaddeus," interjected Marcus.

"Maybe not, but I can tell you these white women out here are more willing to please a man than most black women."

I knew what Darius was referring to but I played dumb. "What are you talking about?"

"I'm talking about sex. A white girl will suck your dick no questions asked. There is none of that negotiating like there is with a sistah, where it feels like your balls have been taken hostage and you're trying to negotiate their release. And if a brotha does get a sistah to go down on him, nine times out of ten she may give him one or two good licks before she comes up for air and then expects a brotha to go down on her.

"With a white babe there is none of that. A white babe will usually give a brotha a blowjob with no questions asked. She will suck your dick until she gets lockjaw. Why, because to them it is simply a part of sex. It isn't anything that gets bestowed upon a man like a reward. To a sistah giving head is like adding the whip cream and cherry on top of a banana split. To a white babe the whip cream and cherry is already included." Darius was obviously amused by his analogy.

After he said that I couldn't help but think how quickly Erin went down on me in comparison to Ivy. In fact, I had a hard time remembering when was the last time Ivy gave me head. After giving it some thought getting head once in five months from Ivy and once in one day with Erin did not do good in refuting Darius' argument.

"You know what," Darius added, "If I get head on a regular basis I have no qualms about going down on the woman giving it. Of course, that is if she has her stuff all trimmed up and ready to go."

"That is the only beef I have with sistahs, they do not keep their stuff tidy down there. I usually got to tell them to clean that kitchen up and that is something I think they would like to keep neat just in case someone might want to take a trip downtown. Its like a brotha has to go on safari through the bush to find it," I exclaimed.

"Believe me when I tell you my brotha, that is not a problem specifically reserved for sistahs," Darius interceded.

"Thaddeus please, I'm quite sure there has been plenty of times you had your head in a face full of fur. Besides, some people like it hairy. I personally like to see some pubic hair. If you ask me, it looks weird to see a grown woman's stuff clean-shaven like some little girl's coochie. It makes me feel funny to even look at it.

"And Darius all that crap your talking about is nothing more than unadulterated bullshit. You are not doing anything more than perpetuating stereotypes about our sistahs!" Marcus proclaimed.

"Whatever you want to call it that's fine with me. However, while you're over there fantasizing about getting a blowjob, I'm getting my nutts slobbered on all night—every night." Darius smiled.

"I don't need to fantasize," Marcus assured him.

"Well, at least I don't have to wait until Christmas every year to get a little head," Darius shot back. Marcus simply sat there in silence.

"It's like I said, white women are just freaky like that. They're not uptight about sex like black babes. They breakout toys, do threesomes and all that kinky shit. They even let you plug the dookie-chute."

"The what?" I exclaimed. I wanted to make sure I heard Darius right.

"You heard me, I said plug the dookie-chute."

"Oh, that's nasty!" I exclaimed.

"You're making me sick." Marcus set his beer down as if he was going to throw up.

"Come on now. Why brothas act like they are not curious about having anal sex with their woman. Hell, there ain't no shame in my game." Darius took a drag from his cigarette.

"That's your problem, you have no shame," Marcus murmured.

"Look, it's just like a few years ago when every brotha claimed he did not eat pussy. Nowadays you can't find a brotha that does not brag about giving some babe a good tongue-lashing. Hell, you've got singers singing about going down on some female. So, don't you fools act like you have never tried to sneak in through the back door? You know the 'oops' it slipped routine. The only problem is I bet when you tried, your girl's butt cheeks clenched up so tight even if your dick was made out of titanium it was not going to get pass them."

"You're right about that," Marcus said. Marcus shook his head as if he was experiencing a flashback. "I tried one time with Lisa, she looked at me as if I had lost my god damn mind. I remember her telling me, 'Just because shit comes out does not mean shit goes in.'" All of us could not help but burst out in laughter.

"See, even Marcus has tried it," Darius said in his defense.

"Despite, all that you've been saying," Marcus interceded. "There is nothing like black love. It is filled with so much passion and caring." Both Darius and I stared at Marcus in bewilderment.

"You might want to get in touch with your feminine side when the fellas aren't around. Also, are you saying that can't be achieved with someone who is not black?" Darius countered.

"Why is it when a brotha shows some sense of love and caring he has to be feminine? That is part of our problem right now. We refuse to try and relate to our women.

"Why can't black men be real and tell it like it is? We want someone to have our back, to love and to have someone to care for just as much as anybody else.

There is nothing wrong with it. It doesn't make us any less of a man. In my opinion there is nothing like seeing a black man and a black woman in love.

"And to answer your question, I'm not saying that this same kind of feeling cannot be achieved with someone else it's just that there is something special about seeing a black man and a black woman together."

"There is only something special about it because we act like it is a rarity. What about love? What about two people being in love? Very rarely do you hear of two people regardless of color being married longer than five years. Besides, have you ever gone out with a woman who was not black?" Darius inquired.

"Yeah, a Puerto Rican babe. I use to call her my Spanish Fly." Marcus smiled. Marcus was obviously full of himself. "I didn't get the same vibe with her that I got when I was with a black woman."

"That is sad to hear. Most Puerto Rican babes I know is fine as hell," I interrupted.

"Regardless, let's just say everything Darius said about black women is true," Marcus continued.

"I don't know about that. There were plenty of sistahs in college who would drop down on their knees at the drop of a hat," I interceded once again.

"Let's just say Thaddeus, that it's true for the sake of Darius' argument," Marcus argued. "So, what if a sistah may believe giving head is something reserved for that one special man in their lives, instead of every man they meet. And so what if a black woman does not find a man having sex with her in the butt pleasurable.

"How would you feel if your woman flipped your ass over and ran up in you? I would assume you would not like it too much, and if you did you might want to re-examine who you're calling feminine. So, what if a black woman feels this way? What is wrong with that?"

"What's wrong with it is that a brotha isn't going to wait until Hell freezes over to have a sistah give him a blow job! And for your information, I have never had anything other a few fingers up my behind," Darius replied. Marcus was suddenly speechless.

"You've let a woman stick her fingers up your butt?" I exclaimed.

"Yeah, every once and a while. I've found that it intensifies the sex," Darius explained.

"Damn! I know that must be uncomfortable as hell! If you ask me that sounds borderline gay to me! There isn't that much difference between a finger, a dick or a dildo," I proclaimed.

"Tell me about it!" Marcus exclaimed.

"Ah here we go," Darius protested.

"Come on now Darius? If one of us had said something like that to you, you're telling me you would not have looked at us strange?" I professed.

"Nope. See for you sexually inept brothas a man's prostate gland is the male version of a woman's G-spot." Darius was a smug son-of-a-bitch when he thought he knew something.

"And if my memory serves me correctly. The only way to get to a man's prostate gland is through his ass," I bated Darius.

"Yep," Darius replied.

"So, you're telling me you would not look at Marcus or I funny if we told you we like women to stick their fingers up our ass!" I proclaimed.

"Nope." Darius tried to suppress a smile.

"Negro please! Hell, I'm a little concerned that you're going to turn around and tell us you like puffing on tube steak." I could not resist agitating Darius further by taking his admission one step further.

"Come on now, T? You know me!" remarked Darius.

"I don't know dawg! A lot of brothas nowadays are coming out of the closet. A brotha can't be too sure nowadays. Brothas need to know your status. Like I said there isn't too much difference between a finger and another man's dick other than width and length.

"Besides, I know that female's fingers had to have smelled like shit for a week because we know you don't wash your ass," I stated. At this point Marcus was laughing uncontrollably.

"So what if it did stink? That is in no way, shape, or form a reflection upon me." Darius tried to fight back his laughter. At this point I was on the floor dying of laughter.

"And believe me, there is a very big difference between a finger and some-one's dick. You fools should not knock the finger technique until you try it." Darius snickered.

"That's nasty!" I exclaimed.

When the laughter died down and the jokes passed, Darius looked over at me. "All jokes aside, what are you going to do about these females?"

"That's a good question. To be perfectly honest with you I don't know," I told him. "I enjoy spending time with both of them. I've made it clear to both of them I'm not ready for a serious relationship, so I don't see the harm in dat-ing them both. It isn't as if I'm leading them on."

"Hold on T. Now, I know your divorce with Stephanie has kind of made you hesitant to jump back in the water again when it comes to commitment. I also know to you this looks like nothing more than dating. But to these women it's going to look like you're trying to have your cake and eat it too," Marcus proclaimed.

"How's that? I've been on the up and up with the both of Erin and Ivy."

"That doesn't matter," Marcus reminded me. "There is no woman in the world, whether she is black or white, that likes to share. It doesn't matter if you mean no harm. These women are going to start seeing it as if you're using your failed marriage as an excuse to play games."

"He's got a point." Darius stamped his cigarette out in the ashtray.

"So, what are you guys trying to say? Are you saying I should let one of them or maybe both of them go?"

Marcus looked me straight in the eyes and said, "What you do is your business playa. All I'm trying to say is that if a woman thinks you're trying to have your cake and eat it too, then you're in trouble."

This is Me

Thaddeus—Trying To Keep It Undercover

Looking back, I should have heeded Marcus' warning. Instead, I ignored him. I believed that as long as I continually told Ivy and Erin the truth there was no way I could get myself into trouble.

I couldn't have been more wrong.

When I realized I had a problem on my hands it was too late. Lisa had told Ivy about the incident at the movie theater. Ivy could not have made it any more apparent to me that she knew about Erin than by ignoring my phone calls. It did not take a genius to know that my relationship with Ivy was on the ropes. It was going to take some major ass kissing by me to get back in good with Ivy.

That Saturday I hung out with Darius and Marcus. After the Twins/White Sox baseball game, we went out to a sports bar and then a club. Even Marcus managed to make a night of it. Marcus claimed Lisa was out with the girls, so he had no commitments to keep for the evening. I could only imagine whom Lisa and "the girls" were talking about. I tried calling Ivy several times Sunday but after constantly getting her voicemail I gave up trying to reach her.

I figured it was best I let things die down for a couple of days before trying to call her again. By then I figured she would be a little more receptive towards me. At that time I could explain to her my side of the story. Erin called later in the day and explained to me how her Saturday night out with her friends was terrible. Erin did not go into great detail as to why she had such a horrible time, and I did not pry. I assumed it was none of my business. Our conversation was brief before I hinted I had work I needed to tend to before Monday. I really didn't have any work to do. I just didn't feel like talking.

Monday morning I had concluded I was just going to lay low for a while and avoid Erin until I could straighten things out with Ivy. That plan worked fine until Erin called me that afternoon. It appeared a friend of Erin's had rented a boat and was planning on having a party on Lake Minnetonka, the upcoming Friday night. Erin and Belinda thought it would be nice if Darius and I joined them.

"Please Thaddeus, you have to come. Darius said he was not going to go unless you came," I remember her saying.

"I don't know. I have to talk it over with Darius. The fellas were supposed to go out Friday night." I was already preparing my lie just in case Darius was not down with the boat ride either. "If Darius don't mind spending the fellas night out on a boat, then I'm game."

"Come on please, Thaddeus? It would mean so much to me," Erin begged.

"I have to talk to Darius first," I reiterated.

"I understand. If you can talk Darius into going if he sounds skeptical," Erin pleaded.

"Yeah, whatever," I sighed.

It was then after setting me up with the party on Lake Minnetonka, Erin dropped a bomb on me. "My father will be in town Wednesday thru Friday for a pediatrics convention at the Convention Center. He plans on staying Saturday and leaving out of town on Sunday. I know you're probably busy with work during the week and we might be at the party on Friday, so he suggested that we get together for dinner on Saturday."

"What do you mean by 'we'?" I did not see why "we" had to have dinner with Erin's father.

"He wants to meet you," Erin answered.

I could not believe my ears. Erin wanted me to meet her father. That was big. I really did not think we were at that stage in our relationship where I should be meeting her father. Meeting a woman's parents was not a regular everyday event. I recall my mind racing to come up with an excuse that would rescue my behind from meeting Erin's dad.

"I have Little T on Saturday," I said in haste.

I was certain I had wiggled my way out of dinner. I figured if her dad wanted to meet me, he would have to catch me another time…. That was if I was still seeing his daughter.

"I thought you said you only had your son for the day. We can easily arrange to have a late dinner around seven or eight o'clock. My father really wants to meet you." I was pissed. I had forgotten I had told Erin I had Little T only for the day Saturday.

Just as I was contemplating another lie Erin confronted me. "Look Thaddeus, you don't have to go. I know you may feel awkward meeting my father, and I totally understand. It was just that he has heard me talk about you and he really wants to meet you." I could tell by the sound of her voice, Erin was hurt by my hesitancy to give her a definitive answer.

"Look Erin, I thought we were just kicking it. You know dating. Nothing serious. Meeting your dad tells me that you are taking this a little more serious than just mere dating. I'm sure I've already explained to you my reluctance to getting serious…. We're still getting to know each other. Besides…" I brought my voice down to a whisper so my co-workers in the neighboring cubicles could not hear me, "does your father know I'm black?"

"Yes, he knows you're black. It isn't like I can hide that fact from him. He would recognize it the minute you walked into the room. Look, if you don't feel comfortable with meeting my father that is okay. I understand. I can have dinner with him and we can get together afterwards. I don't want you to go if you are going to feel uncomfortable."

After giving it some thought I grudgingly told Erin, "All right, I'll go." I regretted telling her that, the second the words came out of my mouth.

"Thank you Thaddeus. You don't know how much this means to me."

"Yeah, yeah, yeah…don't mention it. I got work to do, so I'll talk to you later." I was disgusted.

"All right. I'll call you later…. Bye."

"Yeah later." I hung up the phone. As soon as I placed the receiver in the cradle a voice inside my head screamed, 'sucka!'

Upon hanging up the phone with Erin, I immediately called Darius. Darius' assistant answered his line and informed me he was busy. When she asked me if I wanted to leave him a message, I informed her I would rather be placed on hold. This was an emergency. I could not explain my dilemma to an answering machine.

It took Darius a minute before he picked up. "This is Darius Thomas," he said, properly into the phone. If you did not know Darius, you would've swore he was white.

"Man, I'm in trouble," I said.

Darius hesitated for a moment before saying, "T?"

"Yeah."

"Brotha you need to identify yourself," Darius stated. I could hear the door to his office shut in the background.

"My bad."

"It's cool. What's up?"

"I just got off the phone with Erin."

"She talk to you about that party Friday on Lake Minnetonka?" Darius asked.

"Yeah, I told her I had to talk to you first," I informed him.

"That is the same thing I told Belinda."

"Are we going to go or not?" I posed the question to him.

"I thought about it, and I don't see why not? We can get free food and drink. Belinda told me the boat ride should be over by ten thirty or eleven. By that time we could leave them behind and hit the club."

"That's cool and all, but we're going to be trapped on a boat with them for two hours. It isn't as if we can get in the car and leave when the party gets dead. And you know at parties like these all people want to do is get drunk and talk about work."

"You got a point there. So then what do you want to do?" Darius redirected the question right back at me.

"I can't call it."

"I say we go and get drunk at somebody else's expense. Afterwards we kick them females to the curb and bounce to some place else."

"Sounds cool with me. But I have not told you the worst of it."

"What else is going on?" Darius questioned.

"Erin asked me to have dinner with her and her pops on Saturday."

"Whaaat! Are you serious?"

"I kid you not."

"What did you say?"

"What could I say, she had cornered me," I stated.

"You told her you would go?" Darius was astonished.

"Yep."

"Oh dawg, you fucked up." Darius could do nothing but laugh. "Next thing you know, she is going to be dragging you to jewelry stores pricing rings."

"Nah, hell no! I made it clear to her that we are friends," I assured him.

"Yeah right. That is what came out of your mouth, but your actions are telling her something else," Darius chided.

"You're right. What should I do?"

"Call her back and tell her you're not going to go to dinner with her and her pops. Tell her it aint that type of party with you and her."

"But I already told her I would go."

"So. Just tell her you're not going."

I thought about it for a second before telling Darius, "Yeah. You're right. That's what I'm going to do."

"Good, now I've got to let you go. Some of us got to work," Darius teased.

"I here ya. I'll holla at you later," I told him.

"Later."

"Later."

Although I knew what I needed to do, I couldn't bring myself to call Erin and cancel right after I had agreed to go to dinner with her and her father. I decided I would wait until later to call her and tell her I didn't feel comfortable having dinner with her dad.

Now the only problem with that plan was that I procrastinated for so long that before I knew it, it was Friday. By that time it was virtually too late. When Darius picked me up for the boat party, he asked if I had talked to Erin about dinner with her father. When I told him "no" he simply shook his head in disbelief. He didn't say anything else about it…. He did not have to. I knew exactly what Darius was thinking. He didn't need to say a word.

Darius and I met Erin and Belinda at the dock on Lake Minnetonka. Lake Minnetonka was a ritzy area populated with million dollar homes. The houses around the lake housed some of the Twin Cities richest residents. Erin and Belinda had brought their friend Stacy along for the boat ride. Since Erin and Belinda were coming from St. Paul and Darius and I was coming from Minneapolis, we decided it was best if we drove in separate cars and met up at the dock instead of all of us trying to pile into one car. Judging by the throng of people that had gathered at the dock to board the boat there was only one other brotha attending the party besides Darius and I. I've learned over time this meant it was going to be a long night.

After everyone filed on to the boat and the boat pulled out onto the lake, Erin did her best to introduce me to as many people as possible. Personally, I hate attending work related functions. Although that may not have been the host's intentions it quickly became clear to me as Erin introduced me to those in attendance, most of the people worked with Belinda. I always feel uncomfortable at work related functions. I feel as if I can't be myself. I have to be cognizant of everything I say and do. I get the perception people view me and judge me simply by what they see. Of course, I really could careless what people thought of me. Yet, during these types of functions I preferred to be somewhere else where people did not make judgments based on my appearance.

After the initial introduction most pretentious people, white and black, find themselves at a lost for words for a brotha with earrings, wearing baggy jeans and boots. I love watching the shock on their faces when I tell them I am a graduate of Northwestern's Kellogg School of Business. People's whole perception of me change. I know people base their initial opinions about a person on their appearance. However, it pains me how people can't simply accept people for who they are. I don't think people have a clue as to how mentally taxing and on an even deeper level, how hurtful it is to constantly battle people's stereotypes day in and day out.

Unlike me, Darius views events like the boat cruise where the majority of the partygoers are white as work. He does his best non-threatening "Uncle Tom" persona and works the crowd. Every individual there other than me, Belinda and Erin becomes a potential client. So, Darius immediately begins conversing with anybody who would listen. I have a hard time being phony like that. Although I was certain with some of the ladies, Darius was talking about more than mutual funds and stock portfolios.

Darius later confirmed my suspicions when he found me out on the deck and informed me, "This one gray girl said she wants to do me."

I remember looking over at Darius in shock. "You're lying."

"Nope, I'm dead serious. I was just shooting a little game her way and out of the clear blue she said she wanted to have sex."

"Who?" I asked.

"The one right there," Darius said. Darius turned to wave at a raspberry blonde staggering out of the cabin. By the looks of it the woman was pretty drunk. I was quite sure, Darius was not the first person she made such a proposition to that evening. Of course, that did not bother Darius.

"What about Belinda?" I questioned.

"What about her?"

"This boat is not that big. It is not as if you can sneak off without Belinda noticing you were gone?"

"True that.... True that. What about the bathroom?" I can tell by the way Darius asked the question that he had seriously contemplated it. Darius was scandalous.

All I could say was, "Darius, you got problems. Do you hear me, you got some serious problems," and chuckled.

At that point Belinda interrupted our conversation. "Are you done handing out business cards?" Belinda inquired. Belinda wrapped her arms around Darius.

Darius gave me a sly smirk and strolled off with Belinda away from the raspberry blonde. Belinda was not a bad looking woman. She had long, flowing, auburn hair and she appeared to take good care of herself. The fact she was a manager was a plus. It always amazed me at how a brotha like Darius managed to snag women, albeit white, who appeared to have their act together and seemed to be out of his league.

I admit I was not as social as Darius when it came to mingling with the crowd that Friday night. I either hung around Erin or stuck close to the bar. I figured if I got semi-drunk it would help me deal with the dead crowd. It was not as if I could pass the time dancing. They had some music playing in the cabin of the boat, but it was techno. Techno music is not my thing. Now if they played some house music it would be a different story. One couple, that appeared to have way too much to drink, was in the cabin making complete fools of themselves.

The night was not all bad. I did meet one guy by the name of Travis. He was a cool white dude. I recognized him from playing hoop at the downtown YMCA. Travis seemed to be having about as much fun as I was at the party and had chosen to get drunk to help himself cope with the evening as well. Travis had been forced to come by his girlfriend just as Erin had pressured me into tagging along. Outside of Darius, Travis was about the coolest dude on the boat.

When I questioned Travis as to why he was not having a good time his response to me was, "Too many of the people on this boat are plastic." I could not help but agree with him.

I had attempted to talk to the other brotha—Darius and I spotted boarding the boat earlier. When I approached him with the universal head nod and "What's up?" I received a frigid, "What's up?" accompanied with a cold handshake. I quickly deducted the brotha probably had something to lose by breaking character. More than likely he was there with people from work. If that was the case, it was too his advantage to remain in character rather than being perceived as being too black by colleagues. Of course, I could've been wrong about the brotha. That could've just been his personality. Nowadays there is no standard behavior for black people since we have infiltrated every facet of society.

I can't explain how relieved I was when the two-hour cruise was over. I was ready to go home but Erin, Belinda, and Stacy managed to talk Darius and I into going to a restaurant on the lake. We thought we would go and have a few drinks, before heading home. Darius and Belinda already had their booty call hooked up for later, so that killed the idea of ditching the females and heading to the club. Erin had hinted to me about us getting together later after the boat ride. I simply wanted to go home and go to bed. I assumed that was why Erin and Belinda suggested the restaurant. It gave Erin more time to try and convince me to go home with her. Looking back, we should have did all of us a favor and gone home after the boat ride.

By the time we found a restaurant that everybody could agree upon we were pretty tipsy. Erin's friend, Stacy, was really drunk. The five of us got a booth and immediately ordered a pitcher of beer. At first the conversation amongst us was cool, nothing more than small talk. Then Stacy opened her mouth.

"I'm losing my tan," Stacy shouted. She spoke to no one in particular. "I might need to go to the tanning salon."

"Why would you do that? Why don't you go sit out in the sun and get it back?" I asked.

"Because, I would burn a lot easier than if I was already tanned," Stacy professed. She talked down to me like I was stupid. I considered saying something to her about it but decided to bite my tongue.

"I don't understand?" I said.

"If someone white is going somewhere like Florida or the Caribbean, it is best that we go to a tanning salon first so we don't burn when we get there," Belinda interjected. "However, I don't see what Stacy is talking about has to do with that."

"For real! I did not know that," I replied. "Did you?" I asked Darius.

"Nah, I never heard of anything like that," Darius remarked.

"Duh...I wouldn't think you would. You guys are black," Stacy stated. By this time I was really getting tired of Stacy's flippant comments. She had been making little snide remarks all night. I was beginning to think she had a problem with me.

I could not help but counter her snide remark with one of my own. "I guess, I would not have to worry about getting a tan since I have a natural one."

"You don't tan?" Stacy slurred. "I mean your complexion doesn't get darker."

"Yeah, I get darker if I'm out in the sun," I stated.

"But you don't get dark like a monkey.... Do you?" Stacy asked.

I was shocked. I wanted to believe I misheard her. So, I asked Stacy for clarification. "I don't understand. What do you mean 'dark like a monkey?'" Of course, by this time the entire table had become silent.

I think everybody but Stacy realized what she said could be taken as offensive. I could also tell that Darius was waiting to see if she would correct herself or be stupid enough to answer my question. Unfortunately for Darius and I, Stacy was stupid enough to try and answer the question.

"You know, dark like a gorilla. You know black-black." With that one statement, Stacy confirmed all my suspicions about her. She was ignorant, borderline stupid, and yes...prejudice.

It did not surprise me.

In Minnesota, people tend to hide behind what they like to call "Minnesota Nice." I learned early on they were hiding behind ignorance. Most of the people in the Twin Cities come from these small, rural, farming towns in Iowa, Wisconsin, North and South Dakota. Outside of the images these people see on television many rural Minnesotans have very little contact with people whom look different than them unless they move to the Cities. So in the Twin Cities there are many people like Stacy who tend to act colorblind but generally believe the stereotypical images of the different ethnic groups they see on TV.

My first reaction was to curse Stacy out, but I quickly realized I did not need to match her ignorance with my own. It was what everybody expected. So, I bit my tongue. Judging by the rage on Darius' face, the look of shock on Erin and Belinda's face and by how quiet the two booths next to ours had become, I knew everybody anticipated my reaction.

I simply looked over at Darius and asked, "Ya ready to go?"

"Hell yeah! Let's get the fuck out of here before I catch a case! Lord, knows I can't have that because I need my job!" Darius shouted. Darius stared at Stacy.

"God damnit Stacy!" Belinda screamed. By this time Darius and I had proceeded to the door. "Darius, she's drunk!" Belinda shouted. Darius kept stepping.

As Darius and I walked out the door I could hear Stacy yell, "What did I say?"

Erin quickly responded, "Stacy, you're such a idiot!"

Darius and I had made it to the car and were about to pull off when Erin rushed outside. She knocked on the passenger side window and I reluctantly rolled it down. "Thaddeus please don't go. Stacy is drunk. She doesn't know what she's saying."

"I think Stacy knows exactly what she is saying."

"Come on Thaddeus. Please come on back inside so we can leave together."

"Nah, I've had about as much as I can stand for one night."

"Well then maybe I'll come by later." Erin was not going to give up easily.

"No need for that, I'll be asleep."

"Are you sure?" Erin caressed my cheek.

"Yeah, I'm sure," I assured her. After what just happened in the restaurant I was not in the mood for no sweet talk.

"I'll call you tomorrow then, okay?"

"Whatever," I stated. Erin gave me a goodnight kiss and whispered, "Don't go to sleep."

"Tell Belinda to forget it too," Darius yelled. Erin started back towards the restaurant dejected.

By the time I got home Erin had already left two messages on my voicemail. As I was getting ready for bed the phone rang again. The number on caller ID told me it was Erin. I would not have been surprised if she was calling from outside my apartment building. Erin was not going to give up. So, I simply turned off my ringer and went to bed.

Saturday morning I called Darius, and we tripped out on the night before. We couldn't believe how ignorant Erin and Belinda's friend, Stacy, could be. Although I had neglected to answer Erin's calls, Darius did get with Belinda after all. After talk of Friday night, the conversation invariably switched to the dilemma I faced that evening with Erin and her father.

"Are you going to call and cancel dinner with her pops?" asked Darius.

"I don't know? After last night, it sure has crossed my mind. If I hear another person say something in reference to black folks and gorillas, they're liable to catch a beat down," I replied. Darius couldn't help but laugh. I was not joking.

"So, I take it that means you're not going to go?"

"Nah, I'm going to go but you can expect me to be a little touchy after last night."

"Just remember he's her dad, so, don't beat'em down too bad if he jumps out of line." Both of us chuckled. Even though we were able to make light of the situation that took place the night before, it still bothered me.

I could not talk to Darius for too long for I had to pick up Little T. If I were one minute late Stephanie would not let me hear the end of it. So, it was imperative that I picked him up at our agreed upon time.

I was five minutes late to pick up Little T, but surprisingly Stephanie did not greet me with her usual profanity-laced tirade. In fact, I did not see her. She simply sent Little T out to the car. I took Little T to his tee-ball game. When it was over we went out for pizza. After pizza we went back to my place, so he could change out of his dirty baseball uniform and into some clean clothes. It was a nice day outside so I thought it would be a good idea we got out of the house and enjoyed the weather. I figured we would maybe walk along the river and possibly play a little catch depending on his mood. While he changed clothes I noticed several bruises on his shoulders and arms. I should have known something was up by the way he tried to quickly explain how he had gotten them.

"I fell playing tee-ball," he rushed to explain.

Although the bruises seemed fresh, I did not recall Little T taking a tumble at the game that afternoon. I guessed it happened at practice. Kids are not specific on exactly how an accident occurs. Looking back now, I realize I should have asked more questions. I doubt it would have changed anything. It's just that being his father; I should've investigated into those bruises a little bit more in depth.

Before Little T and I headed out, Erin called wanting to confirm we were still on for dinner. She feared the incidents of the night before might have changed my mind about meeting her father. I assured her I still intended to meet them for dinner. There was a sigh of relief in her voice. Erin informed me, we would be eating at Capital Grille, an expensive steakhouse in downtown Minneapolis. Erin also asked me to dress semi-casual. That was just what I did not want to hear. It sounded more like I was heading off to a job interview instead of dinner. It was not a good sign of things to come.

After dropping Little T off back at Stephanie's, I came back to my condo and dressed for dinner. I drove to Capital Grille seeking to be prompt. I did not want to be early nor did I want to be late. I did not want to prolong the dinner date any longer than necessary by being early. I also did not want the dinner to get started off on the wrong foot by being late. So, I met Erin and her father, Mr. McCormick, promptly at six o'clock.

In the beginning, things seemed to be going well. Mr. McCormick did not seem to be this stuffy white dude I had pictured him to be. Nonetheless, I could sense he was somewhat reserved in the beginning. I think my appearance threw him for a loop judging by his passing comment about guy's wearing earrings. However, after a line of questioning lead to me inevitably telling him I graduated from Northwestern's Kellogg School of Business and worked for Dyson & Rhodes, our conversation seemed to come a little easier. I could easily see when I mentioned Dyson & Rhodes, Mr. McCormick viewed me in a different light.

Still, I could sense the atmosphere turn sour when I mentioned my son. Mr. McCormick did not think I caught it, but I saw the wayward glance he shot at Erin when I spoke of Little T. And if I didn't catch it, Erin's proclamation of "What?" in response to her father's glare only confirmed her father's stare.

Mr. McCormick responded to Erin's question by saying, "Oh, I was just amazed by how much you look like your mother." I knew that was bullshit. Nevertheless, I did not let on like I knew there was a problem.

When dinner arrived I briefly excused myself from the table, so I could wash my hands. When I returned Erin was visibly upset. Erin and her father was doing their best to act as if nothing had transpired in my absence. Mr. McCormick tried to be convincing, but he was a terrible actor. I acted as if I didn't sense anything was wrong. However, the lack of conversation during dinner between the two of them laid claim to the mood change. I guess talk of Little T had put a damper on things. In all honesty, I really could've cared less. After the previous night, I just wanted to eat my meal and head back home.

After dinner, Erin walked me to my car. She informed me; since it was her father's last night in town she wanted to spend the remainder of the evening with him. That was cool with me. I totally understood. Besides, I really was not in the mood to entertain anyone. The night before still had me in a foul mood. Erin informed me she would call me later, yet, I told her not to bother. I made some lame comment about how she should enjoy her father while he was in town. I doubt Erin would have been pleasant company anyway because she still seemed upset by whatever had transpired while I was in the bathroom. Erin gave me a kiss on the cheek before going her separate way.

When I got home, I got undressed and instinctively thought about Ivy. I don't know why. I missed her. As I milled about the condo I could not help but feel like she took a part of me with her when she had moved out. I thought about the seductive way Ivy's hips swayed when she walked. They always seemed to call out to me. I missed her smile. Ivy's smile always seemed to brighten my day. I missed the nights we laid in bed and talked until the sun came up. Sometimes we would go out on the balcony and watch as the sun inched its way across the sky turning night into day. Times like those we always wondered why it seemed like time were passing us by. I missed Ivy. There was no denying it.

I figured I had let Ivy cool off long enough. I had tried calling her at work that week, but only got her assistant who would put me directly through to her voicemail. Ivy, still, refused to take my calls. I knew I was wasting my time contemplating calling her at that hour of the night, but I was not ready to give up hope just yet.

When Ivy's voicemail picked up, I left her another message to go along with the hundred other messages I had left her since I saw Marcus and Lisa at the movie theater. "Ivy, what's up? How long are we going to play this game? Will you just call me? Please. We need to talk. At least let me tell my side of the story? I want to hear from you."

With that said, I hung up the phone and went to bed.

Ivy—Love's Roller Coaster

I woke up Sunday morning after going out with Gloria and Lisa physically and emotionally drained. I had no intentions of getting out of bed. I must of laid in bed for an hour and a half simply staring at the ceiling. It was hard for me to sleep in bed alone. It was an adjustment I did not think should've been so hard for me to make. I had pretty much been sleeping by myself for years before Thaddeus Brown came waltzing into my life. Yet, there I was acting as if Thaddeus had always been a fixture in bed next to me.

As I laid there, I could not help but think about the prickly sensation I received upon my fingertips whenever I ran my hand over Thaddeus' bald-head. Nor the countless nights we would dance until our feet were sore. Or how Thaddeus looked at me in a crowded room and made me feel like there was no one else there but me. The evenings we walked along the Mississippi and Thaddeus pointed out such constellations as the Big Dipper and Orion to me amongst the endless array of stars. There were the numerous evenings I lay in bed and watched the sun creep over his face, accentuating his cheekbones and highlighting his beautiful brown lips as it began to descend beyond the horizon.

Sometimes when he slept his lips would part ever so slightly to reveal the small chip on his bottom front tooth and a slight gap between his two upper front teeth. It was Thaddeus' flaws, which caused me to fall in love with him. I guess you can say it was his imperfections that made Thaddeus utterly perfect to me. Yet, there was someone else now enjoying those long evening walks and evenings of lovemaking. Another woman was admiring the beauty in his chipped tooth…Someone else had captured the love I once thought was mine.

I missed Thaddeus. I missed him dearly.

When I went to my closet to put on my robe, I could not help but notice my red stilettos sitting on top of my shoe rack. Thaddeus use to refer to them as my "fuck-me-pumps." We enjoyed many wild evenings together whenever I wore those shoes. No matter what I did—everything seemed to remind me of Thaddeus.

I eventually made it downstairs that morning and ate breakfast. I tried to review a legal brief to occupy my mind, however, I could not stop thinking about Thaddeus. Before I knew it, I was listening to Stevie Wonder songs and crying. I really can't tell you why. I don't know if it was because I felt sorry for myself, or the fact Thaddeus was seeing someone else that hurt me more. I guess it was a combination of both. I had to get out of that house. I knew if I stayed in that townhouse I was going to go crazy. I did not want to go over to Gloria's or Lisa's because I knew it would only be a repeat of what I heard the night before. There was only one place I knew I could go where I would find a sympathetic ear that would listen and a shoulder to lean on…my parent's house. My mother would not judge me…she would simply listen.

When I pulled up into the driveway of my parent's house in South Minneapolis I was pleasantly surprised to find my sister, Teresa's, car parked in the front. As always my dad was outside feverishly tinkering on one of the many antique cars he had parked in the driveway while my brother-in-law, Bernard—Teresa's husband—looked on. My father collected old cars and fixed them up. Or as my mother would say he collected junk and turned it into more junk.

"Hey Dad," I shouted as I walked up the driveway. My dad peered out from behind the hood of the car.

"Hey, baby!" my father exclaimed. He walked out from the front of the old car to give me a hug and a kiss, something I desperately needed at the time.

"Hey Bernard." I greeted Bernard with a huge hug as well.

"What's up Ivy?"

I could see my nephews, Jason and Jermaine, playing in the backyard so I called out to them. "Hey you guys!"

They stopped for a brief moment to shout, "Hi Auntie Ivy." I started to feel better already.

"So, what are the two of you doing with this old piece of junk?" I asked Bernard.

My dad cut his eyes at me. "This is a classic. You were conceived in the backseat of a 'piece of junk' just like this." He was pretty sensitive when it came to his cars.

"Oh daddy, you know I was just kidding. Where are Mama and Teresa?" I inquired.

"They're in the house," Bernard replied.

"Well, I guess I'll go on inside and see what they're up to and let you men get back to whatever it is you were doing," I said, walking inside.

As soon as I stepped in the house, my nose was treated to a cornucopia of smells made to please the senses. I could smell, fried chicken, candy yams and most important of all mustard greens. Unfortunately, I did not live close enough to my parents to have the luxury of enjoying a meal such as this every Sunday. Mama always cooked a huge Sunday dinner after church.

"I know y'all are not cooking greens up in here, and was not going to invite me!" I shouted.

As soon as those words came out of my mouth, my sister—Teresa—poked her head around the corner to see me strolling in. "Hey sis!" she exclaimed. She greeted me with a warm hug. I walked into the kitchen to see Mama standing over a pot of greens.

"Mama I can't believe you were going to cook greens without telling me!" I complained.

"Ah hush girl, you know I was going to save you some," my mother proclaimed. Mama gave me a kiss to pacify me.

Mama's greens were legendary. Whenever friends or family came into town they always took home a Tupperware container of Mama's greens. Mama always managed to cook her greens just right. They were just spicy enough to give you that necessary kick and soft enough that they seemed to melt in your mouth. Mama had a way of making you believe you were eating a delicacy.

"What are you doing in this neck of the woods," Teresa inquired.

"What? I can't come visit my parents?" I protested.

"No, that isn't it. It's just that you live out in the boonies. Maybe, if you moved in closer to town people would visit you more often."

"All right you two," Mama interjected. Mama took off her apron and sat down at the kitchen table. "Ivy, you want some coffee?" Mama motioned like she was going to get back up.

"Yeah, but don't worry about it Mama, I got it," I told her. I took the coffeepot over to the sink to fill it with water.

"So, have you made partner yet!" Teresa yelled.

"No, my review is the Friday after next," I replied.

"As hard as you work, I would have thought you owned the place by now." Teresa paused for a moment as I put the coffee grounds into the coffee machine before asking her next question.

"So, Mama tells me you got a new man. She said he's fine too." I looked over at my mother who was trying her best to hide the smirk on her face. "So, where did you find him at?" Teresa continued.

I had hoped I could go without having to talk about Thaddeus but it appeared as if that was not going to happen. "I met him at a party I was invited to by a mutual friend. He is from Chicago and we are no longer together," I stated as I took my seat at the table.

"What?" my mother exclaimed.

"Damn! That was quick!" Teresa replied.

"Teresa, watch your mouth!" Mama scolded. "What in the world happened Ivy? I thought everything was going so good?" I could tell by the expression on my mother's face and the tone of her voice, Mama liked Thaddeus and deep down she had hoped he was the one for me.

"I thought so too," I answered.

"So, what happened?" Mama repeated, anxious to hear my answer.

"Well, a few weeks ago Thaddeus told me he needed some space so I gave it to him."

"Let me guess, as soon as you was out of the picture you catch him stepping out with someone else—probably a white girl," Teresa said, filling in the blanks.

"You guessed it," I stated.

"A white girl?" Mama yelled. Teresa simply shook her head in disgust.

Mama in turn got up from the table and went into the kitchen to check on the greens. "I just don't understand what it is our black men see in chasing behind these nasty ole white girls!" Mama took the top off the pot and began to stir the greens. "I need to turn these greens down and let them simmer. Do you want me to pour you a cup of coffee Ivy?" Mama asked, obviously disgusted.

"Please," I sighed.

"Well, if he is out there chasing white girls he was not meant for you in the first place. You're too good for him. Don't worry sis, there are plenty more men out there," Teresa stated.

I know Teresa was trying to lift my spirits but it wasn't working. "You know I keep hearing that, but I seem to be having a hard time finding them," I replied.

"Girl, they're out there. You just have to look harder," Teresa insisted.

"That's easy for you to say. You're married. You got yourself a decent man. On the other hand, I am single and there is not a whole bunch of men out there running around trying to get my phone number like they were when we were twenty. I'm thirty-six years old now, Teresa. The pickings at this age are slim. Most of the good black men are tied down, in jail or they are now damaged goods due to the fact they married the wrong woman who has left them emotionally scarred.

"It's very hard to find a man without issues of some sort, or to find a man without some kind of attachment to another woman. I compromised one of my commandments when I started dating Thaddeus. That was to never date a man with kids."

"But you did…. Why?" Mama interjected. She placed my cup of coffee on the table before me.

"Because I saw something in Thaddeus. He made me feel special," I told her.

"So, to experience that wonderful feeling you got when you were around him, you decided to forgo your rule about men with kids?" quizzed Mama.

"Yes, I did," I sighed.

"That just goes to show you that you do not choose love. Love chooses you…. You love him don't you?" Mama questioned.

"Yes, I do." The words had escaped me before I had time to think. I knew deep down that I was in love with Thaddeus, however, I had never came out and said it.

"Did you tell him that?" my mother inquired.

"No," my voice cracked as I replied. I could feel the tears swelling in my eyes. Teresa slid her chair next to mine and put her arm around me.

"Love is a funny thing. We never know when it will hit, but when it does it hits you like a Mack truck. After that we never want that feeling to go away. Ivy if you love this man you need to tell him. You need to let him know how you feel, so you can at least go on with your life without always looking back and wondering 'What if?' If the two of you do not wind up together at least you can look back with no regrets and say you gave it your all."

"But Mama he is seeing someone else. What good is me telling him 'I love him,' going to do?" I asked. Tears streamed down my face.

"Just do what your Mama tells you. I've been around the block more times than you. So your Mama knows a thing or two about love. You just might be surprised at what happens."

I sat there for a moment debating on whether I should take my mother's advice. After giving it some thought I saw no harm in it. If anything else, I would at least gain a sense of closure from the whole ordeal.

The rest of the evening my family and I sat around and ate while enjoying each other's company. It felt good to spend time with family. Due to my busy schedule I never got to see my family as much as I would've like, especially Teresa since she lived clear on the other side of town in Brooklyn Park, a northern suburb. Seeing my sister, Cynthia, was even harder since she had moved to Los Angeles. Still, when we got together there was always a lot of love amongst us. There is nothing like family. They seem to heal any wound no matter how severe. When it was time to go, I felt a lot better than I did when I arrived.

That Monday morning, I awoke once again depressed. At least this time I was able to get out of bed before noon and go to work with no problem—a significant improvement over the day before. For a week I immersed myself in my work in hopes it would keep my mind off of Thaddeus. I focused on work and avoided any contact with Thaddeus, which meant ignoring his persistent phone calls. It was difficult to do, but in the end I believe it was for the best. With my review for partner taking place at the end of the following week, it was best if I did not have any drama in my life. My review for partner had already made me a nervous wreck and I did not need Thaddeus compounding the stress.

So, I ignored him.

Erin—It's My Life

After leaving the Wild Onion, Belinda and I walked up Grand Avenue to a café for some cheesecake. People were still congregating at the local bars and eateries. Both, Belinda and I could not believe the guile of Stacy to invite Marty and John to the bar. Although Belinda had totally washed her hands of Stacy, I was not ready to totally abandon her just yet. I don't know why. Even though I should have been the one who never wanted to see Stacy again. I guess it harks back to me knowing what it was like to be naïve. In some way I hoped I could make Stacy open her eyes and see the real world rather than the one she grew up learning.

Sunday, I lounged around the apartment. Belinda had left early that morning to spend the day with her grandmother. Spending the day with her grandmother was apart of Belinda's typical Sunday routine. I spoke to Thaddeus briefly on Sunday morning. It was not as if I had anything of importance to say. I called him more so I would have something to do. Thaddeus informed me about his night out with the guys and I told him about my evening at the Wild Onion. I omitted the part about Marty and John showing up. I did not think it would be wise to confess to bumping into my ex-boyfriend's friends at the bar. I didn't think that would assure Thaddeus that I was indeed over Brian. Fortunately for me, Thaddeus did not seem interested in hearing sordid details of my night out, which was good. Our conversation was brief. We promised to call each other later that evening and that was it.

Around eight that evening, I got a call from my father informing me he was going to be in town Wednesday for a pediatrician convention at the Minneapolis Convention Center. It had been over two months since I had seen my father, so, I looked forward to spending time with him.

However I did not expect my father to say, "Bring along that new friend of yours too," that totally threw me for a loop.

I had told my father about Thaddeus in passing. I never expected for him to want to meet Thaddeus. In a lot of regards, I was not certain if my father was ready to meet Thaddeus just yet. First of all, Thaddeus and I had not been seeing each other that long to be playing meet the parents. Also, I had yet to tell my family that Thaddeus was black. In my conversations regarding Thaddeus, I had conveniently omitted that fact. I was in no way shape or form ashamed of Thaddeus. Let's just say I was uncertain of how my parents would react. I know so many times in the past, my parents told me it would not matter what color the guy was I fell in love with as long as I was happy. However, that was talk and this was reality. To say something and actually mean it are two different things.

"I don't know dad? Like I've told you, we're just friends," I told him.

"So, what? Does that mean I can't meet the guy my little girl is dating?" I was twenty-nine years old and my father still referred to me as his "little girl." Sometimes, I often wondered if my parents felt guilty for what their divorce subsequently did to my childhood growing up. At times it seemed hard for them to see me as a grown woman.

"I'll ask him, but don't be disappointed if he can't make it," I warned.

"I hear you, loud and clear."

Monday morning, Belinda called me at work and notified me that a mutual friend of ours, David, had rented a boat and was throwing a party on Lake Minnetonka that upcoming Friday. David wanted me to attend. Belinda informed me, she had asked Darius to join her. She suggested I call Thaddeus and do the same. Belinda figured if Thaddeus agreed to go then Darius would be more inclined to attend. She also reminded me that it would be a good way for Thaddeus and I to spend some quality time together. I had to agree with Belinda. Thaddeus and I really had not spent any real time together except for our date to the movies, which ended abruptly.

Inviting Thaddeus to the boat party on Friday gave me a reason to also ask him about having dinner with my father on Saturday. I had been mulling how I intended to approach Thaddeus with such a proposal. Even I was not sure if Thaddeus meeting my father was a good idea. Meeting someone's parents implied a sense of seriousness in a relationship. Now, I admit I yearned to have that commitment from Thaddeus. However, at the same time I did not want to scare him away.

I figured at least asking him about the boat party on Friday gave me enough segue into asking him about dinner with my father. Regardless if he said, "yes" or "no", I could at least meet my father with a clear conscious knowing that I did at least ask Thaddeus. Instead of never mentioning it to Thaddeus at all, which I had contemplated doing and simply lying to my father.

When I talked to Thaddeus, his reaction to the boat party was what I had expected…doubtful. I was certain he was not going to commit to the cruise without first checking with Darius. So, that was of no surprise to me. However, when I asked him about dinner with my father, I kind of took offense to the way he tried to get out of making a definite commitment to me on whether he would attend or not. I confess…. I lied to Thaddeus when I said I had indeed told my father he was black. Needless to say, that did not explain his reluctance to give me a straight answer. It annoyed me the way he fished for excuses when I pressed him on the subject. I could not help but take it personal. If he did not want to have dinner with my father and I, he should have just said it. Not lie. I was beginning to fear Thaddeus viewed me as nothing more than a plaything. Even though he eventually said "yes" to dinner with my father and the boat ride, the thought of how he possibly viewed our relationship annoyed me.

Now that Thaddeus had agreed to meet my father, I dwelled on the idea of telling my father Thaddeus was black all week. At times, I felt I was making something out of nothing. I don't know what concerned me more. The embarrassing situation that might ensue if I did not tell my father that Thaddeus was black. Or the way Thaddeus acted when I asked him to have dinner with my father and I.

My father's plane landed late Wednesday night. Since he arrived too late for us to get together, we scheduled to have dinner together on Thursday. During the course of the meal on Thursday my dad asked me if Thaddeus had agreed to join us on Saturday and I assured him he had. I should have used the opportunity to tell my dad the truth about Thaddeus, but I didn't. I simply froze. I should have thought telling him about Thaddeus would not have been that big of a deal. Yet, something stopped me from telling him. I don't know what it was…I just couldn't.

Friday got off to a bad start. Belinda had started out the day not speaking to me. She could not understand why I invited Stacy to join us on the cruise without consulting her. Although, Stacy had apologized to Belinda and I earlier in the week for the incident at the Wild Onion, Belinda still refused to associate with her. She did not understand why I continued to fraternize with Stacy after the way she behaved when we went out. She used Stacy's recent stunt at the Wild Onion as a prime example. I can't deny Belinda had a point. Still, I could not help but feel sorry for Stacy. Other than Belinda and I, Stacy really did not have any friends. So, out of pity I invited Stacy along on the boat cruise. Big mistake. When I told Belinda I had invited Stacy to join us on the cruise, she declared I was utterly stupid and Stacy sooner or later would make me regret having ever known her. I felt Belinda was over-reacting. Unfortunately, Stacy would prove Belinda right.

Since Thaddeus and Darius were coming from Minneapolis and we were traveling from St. Paul, Belinda and I decided it was best for Thaddeus and Darius to drive in a separate car rather than attempting to pack all of us into one car and trekking over to Lake Minnetonka. Thaddeus and Darius arrived at the dock soon after Belinda, Stacy and I. Stacy had driven her car to Belinda and my apartment, so we could ride together. Although Darius and Thaddeus were late, I was happy to see Thaddeus had made it. I could hear the apprehension in his voice whenever I mentioned the boat cruise to him during the course of the week. A small part of me anticipated him to not show up, so seeing him lifted my spirits.

As the cruise got under way, I introduced Thaddeus to a few people I knew attending the party. Although David was a friend of mine, I did not know most of the people on the cruise. A great majority of the people worked with Belinda and David. I could sense my unfamiliarity with some of the partygoers made Thaddeus uncomfortable. I could understand. However, Darius seemed to blend in well.

Although I understood Thaddeus' uneasiness I asked him, "Are you having a good time?"

"It's okay," Thaddeus sighed.

"Is there something bothering you?" I questioned.

"You wouldn't understand," declared Thaddeus.

"Try me," I replied.

Thaddeus glanced at me for a brief moment before saying, "I'm not use to this."

"Meaning?" I continued to press.

"I'm use to a party being a party. People talking about things other than work. I'm use to people laughing and dancing, cutting loose and being themselves. People sitting around, getting drunk, talking about work, their kids, or where they're going to take their next vacation does not appeal to me."

"Are you trying to say the party is too white?" Although he did not say those exact words, I could sense that was what Thaddeus wanted to say. My comment caught him off guard and it showed. Thaddeus paused for a moment to contemplate his response.

"You know, it just so happens that this party is mostly white. But you know it would not matter if there were boojie negros in here doing the same thing. The party would still be sorry."

"I don't know if it helps, but I'm glad that you are here. Maybe, afterwards I can make it up to you." I gave him a sly grin.

A smirk crossed Thaddeus' face. "We'll see."

I really wanted Thaddeus to have a good time that evening because I really wanted us to make more of a personal connection beyond our conversations on the telephone. I viewed that night as an opportunity for the two of us to get closer. I really liked Thaddeus and I had a good impression he was at least interested in me. So, I could not help but be bothered by the fact he was not enjoying himself. Yet, I did manage to stop feeling guilty for bringing him along when I noticed him getting along with at least one guest at the party. Belinda informed me the guy was the boyfriend of one of her coworkers. It was at that point I did not feel so bad talking him into coming.

When the cruise was over, the boat returned to the dock and I suggested the five of us head over to one of the many restaurants along the lake. Belinda already had her plans with Darius prearranged. She was ready to take Stacy and I back to the apartment, so she could get over to Darius' apartment as soon as possible. I wanted to possibly get some arrangement of a similar nature set with Thaddeus. Thaddeus had done a good job of teasing me the night we went to the movies and I very much wanted to finish what we had started. Needless to say I was a little frisky. Although, Thaddeus and Darius ultimately agreed to join us for drinks afterwards at Sunsets it was not without much pleading and begging on my part.

As I had hoped, once we were at a restaurant Thaddeus felt a little more at ease. By that time all of us were pretty drunk, and for a while the atmosphere between the five of us was festive. Then disaster struck and once again Stacy was the culprit. Now, Stacy was definitely a little farther along in the drinking department than the rest of us. However, that was no excuse for what came out of her mouth. Needless to say, when Stacy started talking about going to a tanning salon I knew the night was heading in the wrong direction.

As soon as the words, "I guess, I would not have to worry about getting a tan since I already have a natural one," came out of Thaddeus' mouth. I knew he had opened the door for Stacy to say the first idiotic thing that came to mind. By the look on Belinda's face, I was quite certain she felt the same way. Without fail, Stacy did not disappoint. She took Thaddeus' comment and ran with it.

I was utterly flabbergasted when Stacy asked Thaddeus, "But you don't get dark like a monkey, do you?" I could not believe it. When Thaddeus attempted to give Stacy a way out of the corner she had backed herself into, Stacy conveniently dug her hole even deeper. As I watched the entire situation unfold right before my eyes I could not believe the extent of Stacy's ignorance.

When Stacy replied, "You know, dark like a gorilla." I swear I thought Thaddeus was going to punch her lights out and if he didn't I was certain Darius was going to. I sort of wished one of them had slapped some sense into her for all of our sake, but that would have made a bad situation even worse. Still, we were not the only ones in shock from Stacy's comments; the people in the booths on either side of us had grown quiet. What intimate evening I had hoped to enjoy with Thaddeus was suddenly ruined.

By the time Belinda had yelled out, "God damnit Stacy!" Thaddeus and Darius were already out the door.

All I could utter as I watched them go was, "Stacy, can't you keep your foot out of your mouth for one minute!"

I tried my best to get Thaddeus to come back inside, but he was pretty pissed off. I suggested I drop by later after ridding myself of Stacy, but that did not make him more receptive to the idea of me joining him for the night. It was apparent by his response that Stacy had totally turned him off to the idea of us getting together later. So to say I was pissed is an understatement.

As Darius pulled out of the parking lot I was furious. I stormed back inside the restaurant to find Belinda berating Stacy. I think every expletive imaginable came out of Belinda's mouth. I could do nothing more than pay the tab and glare at the guys in the next booth who had found the entire incident hilarious.

"Did they leave?" shouted Belinda.

I simply nodded my head. "Darius said there was no need for you to come over tonight," I informed her.

"God damnit! I told you to leave this dumb bitch at home!" screamed Belinda. Belinda was pissed. Her plans with Darius had been ruined because of Stacy's stupidity.

"Who are you calling a dumb bitch?" exclaimed Stacy. For as long as I had known Stacy, I had never known her to stand up for herself. Yet, that night she seemed ready to take on Belinda.

Belinda turned on her ready to pounce. If I had not jumped in between the two of them Belinda probably would have slapped her. "Can we just leave?" I asked.

"I'm not riding with her. Especially after she insulted me!" stated Stacy.

"Fine with me! I don't want you in my car anyway!" Belinda responded. Belinda headed towards the door. "You can walk home for all I care! Are you coming or staying?" barked Belinda. Belinda glared at me as she stood by the door.

I glanced over at Stacy who looked bewildered. I could do nothing more than shake my head in disgust. "Are you going to be all right?"

"I'll be fine. I'll catch a cab to your place and pick up my car." Stacy then waved me away.

I never invited Stacy out again after that night. I have bumped into her on occasion and we've talked but it's not the same. Now, Stacy usually hangs out with a group of girls from her job. I see them out every so often. Since that night at the restaurant our relationship has been regulated to small talk during these few brief encounters. I doubt we will ever be friends again.

During the drive home Belinda was on the phone diligently trying to salvage her nightcap with Darius. Taking my cue from Belinda, I decided not to give up on Thaddeus. The only problem was that Thaddeus was not answering his cell or home phone. When Belinda and I had reached our apartment, Belinda had managed to salvage her plans with Darius so she promptly dropped me off. I had desperately tried to get through to Thaddeus but was having no luck. I thought about getting in my car and driving over to his condominium—the only problem was I did not know his condo number. So, I made a few more futile attempts to reach him by phone before giving up. Realizing Thaddeus was not going to answer my phone calls I went to bed.

The events of Friday night had me a little worried as to what to expect Saturday. I called Thaddeus the first thing Saturday to confirm he still intended to make our dinner date that evening. After Friday night, I could not be sure. Thaddeus assured me, he still intended on attending. We spoke briefly. I apologized profusely for Stacy's behavior. He told me not to worry about it before hurrying me off the phone. I reiterated the time of our reservations, six o'clock, at the Capital Grille. Once again he assured me he would be there.

After spending most of the day running errands, I met my dad at Capital Grille around five thirty. My father had informed me he was going to head down to the restaurant early. I felt having that extra moment alone with him before Thaddeus arrived would give me ample time to brief him on Thaddeus.

When I arrived, I found my father sitting in the bar sipping on a drink. If I knew my father it was Scotch on the rocks. "Hey you," I said giving my father a hug.

"Well, if I would have known this place came equipped with pretty women, I would have came here much sooner," my dad joked. He put his arm around me and gave me a kiss on the cheek as I took a seat next to him.

"What do you got there?" I asked, referring to his drink.

"Scotch on the rocks," my father boasted. I knew it. "What about you? What do pretty women such as my daughter drink?"

"I'll take a Merlot."

"Done." My dad called the bartender over to place my order. "So, what brings you down here early? I thought we had not planned to eat until six."

"I wanted to get down here a little early so I can spend some time with you."

"That's sweet of you."

"So, how's Chance?" I wanted to work my way into discussing Thaddeus. I thought a little small talk might help instead of diving right in.

"You know Chance, he's day to day." My father became solemn. "When he does not have enough money for heroin he scraps enough together so he can buy crank. You should see him. He has these sores on his face from scratching. A fellow pediatrician told me they're called "crank bug sores." My stepbrother, Chance, had a serious drug habit. He had been in and out of rehab for the majority of his adult life. "Plus, I've been hearing stories that he's prostituting himself for money," my father added. I could do nothing more than shake my head in disbelief.

"I can't understand why he wants to throw his life away?" my father stated. "I've tried to warn him about the dangers of sharing needles. Now he might be selling himself for drugs. I'm scared he is going to contract HIV if he does not change his lifestyle."

"Chance is a grown man, dad. You can only do so much." My father gave me a stern glare out of the corner of his eye.

"Have you told Chance how you felt?" I questioned.

"Yeah," my father sighed.

"And what does he say?" I was eager to hear his response.

"He tells me, I'm not his father so I should mind my own damn business."

"Maybe you should…. You know dad, give him some space. I'm sure he will come around." My father gave a sigh of defeat.

"The problem is Erin no one knows how long Chance has before he crosses the wrong individual or worse becomes sick. Besides, Chance is not my only problem?"

"What else is going on? Are you and Carolyn having trouble?"

"Nah, not at all…It's Martin." Martin was my other stepbrother—Carolyn's oldest son. "His wife, Becky, kicked him out of the house because she caught him masturbating to porn on the Internet." I could not resist a chuckle.

"Yeah, that is the same response I had." My father smirked. "However, the problem is he is living out of a motel and Carolyn has been bugging me to let him come and stay with us for the time being."

"And your reply?" I questioned.

"I much rather he goes home to his wife and two kids! I love the fact I live in an empty nest. I can do without his problems disrupting the harmony of my home."

"Well, you have to understand to some women catching their husband being aroused by another woman even if it is just pictures on the Internet is cheating. Now, I could careless because I find nothing wrong with pornography but some women just might." My dad gave me a strange look as if he was shocked to hear his little girl may had seen maybe one or two X-rated movies in her lifetime.

"Why it is nothing but pictures!" my father insisted.

"Once again that is a matter or opinion," I answered. "Anyway, I did not come here to talk to you about Chance or Martin. I wanted to talk to you about Thaddeus before you met him." I suddenly realized, I might soon be adding to the list of my father's gripes.

"Oh." My father was obviously curious to know why there was a sudden need to speak about Thaddeus. "That does not sound good. What's going on?"

The bartender came and placed my glass of Merlot before me, giving me the chance to collect my thoughts. "Nothing is wrong. It is just that I thought, I should tell you that he is black before you met him."

My father paused for a second, to sip his drink. "Why did you wait until now to tell me?"

"I don't know?" I stammered. "I guess I did not know how you would react."

"I see," he replied. "Do you love him?"

"I can't say 'yes' or 'no' to that question. We have not been seeing each other for that long."

"But you do like him."

"Yes, I do. I like him a lot." Once I let those words escape I invariably held my breath.

"Then that is all that matters to me," my father replied. He turned and gave me a warm hug. I felt relived. "How about we go confirm our reservations. It's almost six o'clock?"

"Sounds great to me." I could not help but smile more so out of relief than joy. Although, I was forced to see my father only part-time growing up he always had a way of easing my fears and making me feel better. And although I hated it at times, I enjoyed being daddy's little girl.

Thaddeus arrived promptly at six. At first there was the expected awkwardness between my father and Thaddeus but that wore off in time. Since my father was a doctor, he had a knack for getting people to relax.

Dinner was going great until Thaddeus mentioned his son, Thaddeus Jr. I could sense the sudden shift in my father's demeanor. "Oh, really? How old is he?" Just in case I did not pick up on the change in my father's tone, he gave me a glare to make sure I got the hint.

When dinner came, Thaddeus excused himself so he could go to the restroom. As soon as he was a safe distance away, my father could not resist tearing into me. "You did not tell me, he had kids."

"He only has one, dad. Besides, I did not think it was that big of a deal," I declared.

My father scowled to let me know he disapproved. "Are you sure he only has one?"

"Yes…. Why? What is that suppose to mean?" I insisted.

"What it means is that you are way too young to be taking care of someone else's child," my father proclaimed.

"Dad, I think I am old enough to make that decision on my own. Besides, I have not even met his son yet. Thaddeus is very particular about the women he let meet his son. Not unless he is serious about a woman does he introduce them to Thaddeus Jr. Thaddeus does not want different women coming in and out of his son's life, and I respect that."

"That is very cavalier of him," my dad stated, sarcastically. "Is there anything else you have not told me like a prison record?"

"What are you getting at?" I beckoned to know.

"Nothing." He noticed Thaddeus returning to the table. The mood at the table had definitely changed after that exchange. I'm quite sure Thaddeus picked up on it.

After dinner, I walked Thaddeus back to his car. I had envisioned an evening of the two of us hanging out with my father but due to his comments during dinner I felt that it was best Thaddeus left.

Not much was said about Thaddeus after dinner. My dad told me he "enjoyed Thaddeus' company" but I knew he did not mean it. The underlying tone in my father's voice and his body language whenever I brought up Thaddeus' name attested to his displeasure. We went back to my father's hotel and relaxed in the ambiance of the bar listening to the piano. I did not hang around too long because he had an early morning flight back to Denver. So, I simply went home and went to bed.

Sunday morning, I attempted to call Thaddeus a few times for no particular reason. I knew he usually hung out with his buddies Sunday mornings before picking up Thaddeus Jr. Still, I saw nothing wrong in trying to call him. Thaddeus refused to pick up not only his home phone but his cell phone as well. Around noon, I had figured I had left enough messages on Thaddeus' home and cell phone for him to get the hint that I wanted to talk to him.

As I had expected, I got a call from my mother around seven thirty Sunday night. I knew by that time my father had touched down in Denver and called my mother and informed her about Thaddeus. Of course, she felt it necessary to call me and give me the third degree when it came to my current love interest. Some of her questions were inappropriate, yet I expected as much.

By the time I turned in for bed Sunday, I was exhausted. My mother's persistent questioning simply wore me out. However, the one person I had wished to talk to—Thaddeus—had not called me at all.

Baby Mama Drama

Thaddeus—Not My Son

Every Sunday it is a ritual for Darius, Marcus, and I to get together and play a few pick-up games of basketball. We sort of had this unwritten rule that Sundays were dedicated to the fellas. Wives and girlfriends were not allowed to intrude. The time we spent together gave us a break from the stress of family and work. It was our time to relax and unwind. It was our day. Even Marcus adhered to our strict Sunday commitment. To appease Lisa and be allowed to hang out with the fellas, Marcus often had to attend early morning church service. During the winter months we played ball at a local gym and usually hung out and caught a football game afterwards at a sports bar. However in the summer we tended to play ball outdoors—in particular at Painter's Park in Uptown. A string of lakes were located in the vicinity, so during the hot humid days of summer we usually played a little b-ball then headed over to the lakes to check out the honeys. When we grew tired of people watching there was always a bar close by to get a bite to eat and catch a baseball game. Besides, during the summer months there were plenty of places in Uptown that offered patio dining. That way we could watch a game as well as watch the ladies if need be.

When we arrived at Painter's Park the Sunday after I met Erin's pops not enough guys had gathered to get a decent pick-up game going. While we waited for a sizable crowd to gather, Darius, Marcus and I entertained ourselves with a friendly game of HORSE.

"So, how did it go with Erin's pops?" Darius asked. Darius threw up a prayer from the top of the key that clanked hard off the lip of the rim.

I grabbed the rebound and set up in the far right corner, along the baseline and threw up my patented jumper. The ball rattled against the rim just as badly as Darius' shot. "It was cool until I mentioned Little T. After that her dad started acting funny."

"For real," Darius responded. Marcus swished a shot in from the free throw line.

"It's on you." Marcus challenged Darius.

"Give me the damn rock," Darius proclaimed. He stood at the foul line and bricked. Darius could not play a lick of basketball. We never depended upon him to score many points in a game. However, he did do a sufficient enough job of hacking the other team's best player. Darius always liked to think of himself as the "enforcer."

"That's R," Marcus teased.

"I don't need you telling me. I know how to spell," Darius protested.

"I just wanted to make sure you did." Marcus smiled. "What did I tell you guys about white people?" added Marcus. He passed me the ball so I could take the free throw.

"Yeah, I guess her pops thought I was the type of brotha who had kids scattered all over town and didn't give a damn about them." I let the ball roll off my fingertips giving it just the right amount arch, so it hit nothing but net…Swish! It never took me long to find my stroke.

"Of course, he did." Marcus missed an easy lay-up.

"Ah shit, here we go," Darius complained. "Marcus is about to preach to us about another conspiracy against brothas with his sorry, no making a lay-up, ass."

"You can say what you want but you guys know I speak the truth. Just like I said, white people are closet racists. Hell, the Grand Dragon for the Klan lives somewhere in Wisconsin," professed Marcus.

"That's bullshit!" shouted Darius.

"Who cares if it is or if it isn't? It still goes without saying that white folks harbor a feeling of superiority over everyone else. White people's way is always suppose to be the right way," Marcus argued.

"You're getting race mixed up with politics. And what the hell does that have to do with Erin's pops!" Darius challenged.

"For your information race and politics are one and the same in this country. Just look at political ad campaigns. What about the numerous politicians who with a slip of the tongue prove by their comments that race and politics are one and the same. Race is a factor in every facet of life in America. Why do you think black people are followed around in department stores or made to show three pieces of ID whenever we use a credit card? So don't tell me race does not play a part in politics. Everything in this country boils down to white people's, and in this case Erin's father's, feeling of superiority," Marcus preached.

"God damn Marcus! Why do you always have to give a sermon? Can't you hold a conversation without making it a black and white thing? I really want to know what white dude pissed you off? I mean, brotha don't ya relax every once and a while. You're up here talking all this mess about white people and their superiority complex and you're living better than the average white dude.

"You know you take life way too serious. Don't you think about anything other than some new conspiracy against brothas? Maybe, you need to go out and genetically weed out white people by sleeping with these white women, because brotha you are way too uptight."

"I'll leave the weeding out process to you," Marcus proclaimed.

"Whatever. Have you once stopped to think if brothas and sistahs were not always trying to get over, we would not have to show three pieces of ID along with our credit card?" Darius replied, sarcastically.

"Darius, you're my boy and all, but you're an Uncle Tom," Marcus shot back. Suddenly the conversation had taken on a personal tone.

"Uncle Tom! Nigga are you crazy! Do you know whom you're talking to? Marcus, I'll drop your ass without breaking a sweat!" Darius clenched his fists and took a step towards Marcus.

"You might want to watch what you say!" Darius threatened.

Marcus stood his ground. "Darius, you buy into everything that's fed to you by the media about how great this country is. Negro, just because you can fuck a few white girls does not mean there is equality. You're too damn blind to see that some of these white women just want to sleep with you so they can say they slept with a black man, like you were some kind of oddity or side show freak. Black people don't all of a sudden enjoy equal rights because a brotha can sleep with a white woman."

I immediately got in between the two of them in hopes of calming tempers. However, if Darius wanted to get at Marcus I knew there was nothing I could do to stop him. Darius was too big for me to handle. I just hoped my presence was enough to diffuse the situation.

"What? Do you think you're doing something new and improved Darius?" Marcus must of felt assured Darius was not going to do anything to him since I was there. Not a wise assumption to make.

"Negro, please! When the railroad first came through Minnesota in the early part of the twentieth century it brought with it a slew of black men that worked on the trains as porters and cooks. There weren't too many sistahs in the Twin Cities, so many of these brothas got with the first white woman that looked their way.

"What you are doing is nothing new. For decades the well-to-do black folks up here in the Twin Cities were mulatto or fair skin. Still to this day some of the brothas and sistahs up here equate complexion to a symbol of stature in the community," professed Marcus.

"Hell! It is not just here in Minnesota. It is all over. Black people in general still have issues relating to skin tone," I adlibbed.

"Tell me about it. Nevertheless, despite all these interracial couples in Minnesota it has not lead to a better understanding between the races. It also did not stop an all white mob in 1919 from stringing up three black men in Duluth, Minnesota, suspected of raping a white woman. It didn't happen in the South, Darius. It happened right here in Minnesota." Marcus became silent for a moment to let the gravity of his words sink in. That was his legal training coming out. Although I did not totally agree with him, Marcus did present a strong argument.

"If that is not enough. Prominent black men right now in this country are receiving hate mail from racists stating how they are going to castrate and kill them if they don't stop dating white women. That is the same thing they did to black men at the turn of the twentieth century. So, despite all these advancements we have so-called made some things remain the same.

"So you see Darius, even if we are able to get into white people's inner circles, even if it means we can get into white women's pants or drive a Mercedes. Black people will always be considered, second-class as well as being seen as shiftless, lazy, and whatever other negative connotation we can be labeled with. No matter, what a black person's stature is in the community, a black man or woman will always have to prove him or herself, and one step away from prison or death. Black people have always lived knowing their freedom or their life can be taken away from them at the drop of a dime.

"All it takes is an encounter with the wrong person. Believe me, I see it every day from the people who walk into my office. I see it in the color of the faces of men and women, the system exonerates off death row after DNA testing proves that a black man or woman did not commit the crime after all. After losing fifteen to twenty years of their life, all the justice system can say is, 'Ooops, we made a mistake…. We're sorry.'"

Darius fell silent for a moment before responding. "You know Marcus, it's sad for me to hear you have such a defeatist attitude towards life. I'm so tired of brothas like you who always want to blame something on 'The Man,' instead of blaming the man in the mirror," Darius contested. I was able to ease myself out from between the two. It appeared Darius was more intent on debating than beating Marcus up.

"Besides Marcus, who in the hell are you to judge how black I am simply because I sleep with white women! All the slights and wrongs you claim happen to you—happen to me too. Just because I date white women does not suddenly make me invisible!" It was plain to see that Marcus had hit a nerve.

"Maybe, you're the one with the problem Marcus…. Did you ever think about that? Have ever thought that maybe you are the one not seeing the big picture? Have it ever occurred to you that by limiting your choices you have excluded yourself from the rest of the world?" Darius questioned.

"Did you ever think by singling yourself and black women out that you were the one acting prejudice?" Darius continued. "Me…I see no reason whatsoever to limit my choices strictly to black women simply because they're black. Just because a woman's skin tone is the same as mine does not mean we are going to live happily ever after. So, if that is the case why should I limit the options available to me?"

"I am just trying to educate you, Darius" Marcus retorted.

"See, this what you fail to realize Marcus…I already went to college. I have taken all the classes I want to take. So, I don't want nor need you lecturing to me," Darius seethed.

"I'm not trying to chose sides but after Friday, I feel what you're saying Marcus," I interrupted. "What Erin and Belinda's girl, Stacy, said about brothas being black like gorillas and all was down right foul!

"What is even crazier? I don't think she thought she had said anything wrong. It makes me wonder what do white people really say about us when we aren't around," I remarked. Darius took another shot from the top of the key, this time missing everything.

"They say the same thing that girl said to your face. If you would have stuck with a good sistah like Ivy, you wouldn't have heard anything crazy like that," Marcus interjected.

"Speaking of Ivy, how is she doing," I asked.

Marcus simply smiled. "Haven't been able to reach her…have you?" I shook my head. "I really can't say. Lisa doesn't tell me anything. For some reason beyond me, she blames me for what happened between the two of you.

"I guess she believes, since you're my boy I was suppose to keep you in check. Who knows? It doesn't seem to matter how much a brotha does right by his woman, he is always wrong."

"I do know if you would have kept your mouth shut, I would not be having this problem with Ivy right now," I shoot back.

"There you go. You sound like my woman. Of all the movie theaters in the Twin Cities, you had to take that white girl to the same one me and Lisa went to and now it's my fault," Marcus replied.

My mind floated to visions of Ivy as I scooped up the basketball and dribbled to my spot in the right corner again. I thought about Ivy's caramel frame beneath me. This time when I hoisted the ball up in the air, I imagined her panting in my ear as we made love. The only problem was Erin's head was attached to Ivy's body. It was Ivy's moans of ecstasy except they were coming out of Erin's mouth. The pop of the net as the ball glided thru knocked me out of my trance.

I quickly got the vision out of my head and smiled. My jumper was a work of art. It was just like butter baby. The sound of the ball gliding effortlessly through the net sounded sweet. I stood there with my arm in the air admiring my form. It was an old habit. Basketball for me was just like riding a bike, I never forgot once I learned.

"Please. You're not George Gervin or Magic Johnson…. This is not the NBA Finals and you are not Michael Jordan," Darius proclaimed.

"Stop hating on my skills," I told Darius. Marcus took the ball and ran to my spot.

"Let me ask why do you think so many white people live out in the 'burbs'?" Marcus questioned, standing along the baseline.

"I told ya, here he goes. Thaddeus, you shouldn't have gotten this brotha started," Darius snipped at me. "Just shoot the ball Marcus."

"Because they want to get away from people like us. White folks much rather have a hour commute to work than have to live next to someone who may not look like them.

"White people don't care about nothing more than keeping as many things as possible for themselves. The inscription on the Statue of Liberty that states, 'Give me your tired, your poor, your huddled masses yearning to breathe free…. The wretched refuse of your teeming shores.' You know what? The government should also add, 'only if they're white' because that statement does not apply to the thousands of Haitians, Africans or Arabs who come to this country every year seeking refuge.

"White folks here in Minnesota are no different. The term "Minnesota Nice" is nothing more than a euphemism for "whites only." They'll smile in your face but much rather see someone who isn't white ride their ass out of town. It's the same everywhere you go, especially if white people feel you're treading on their territory," Marcus stated. Marcus heaved a shot in the air that sailed to the other side of the court.

"That's S," Darius reminded him.

"Whatever," Marcus replied. "Believe me when I tell you, white people are very happy with this country's whiteness and they want to keep it that way. They smile in your face, but silently hope black folks get on some back to Africa kick because they sure as hell is never going to pay us any reparations."

"Why don't you move back to Africa," quipped Darius.

"Don't think I have not thought about it. But why should I? My ancestors did not come over here on their own volition. They were forcibly brought to this country. This is my country too. I see no reason why I should relocate. Whether America wants me here or not, this is my country just as much as it is anybody else's—if not more so. It was on the backs of my ancestors this country was made great. So, I feel I have a right to stay here and get my just due."

"Whatever." It was obvious Darius was tired of arguing with Marcus. Darius threw up a shot from the baseline that fell way short of the basket.

I could not resist saying, "I know this is going to sound bad, but I much rather prefer white people came straight up into my face and let me know the deal like they do down South. There is none of that shinning and grinning in your face like they do up here. These so-called progressive liberals kill me. They claim to be so color blind. They are no different than the bigots I encountered down South. At least down South you know where you stand with certain people. It is made very clear to you. Here people are undercover with their prejudice. They smile in your face and talk about you behind your back."

I grabbed the ball and dribbled to the top of the key and let go another jumper that hit nothing but the bottom of the net. Like I said, basketball was like riding a bike for me. I only wished, I could have made life and romance as simple as shooting a jumper.

After hanging out at Painter's Park long enough to get in a couple of pick-up games, Marcus, Darius, and I went and hung out around the lakes for a while. I called Stephanie to schedule a time I could pick up Little T but she informed me he had a birthday party to attend, so it was not a good day to connect with him. I was furious because Stephanie could have told me that yesterday, but in the end it worked out for the best for my boy Rob was having a barbeque. I couldn't rightfully take Little T to the barbeque. Besides, Marcus had gone back home and got Lisa and she acted pretty funky towards me at Rob's house. It didn't really bother me because I was more concerned with what Ivy thought about me rather than Lisa.

Although my relationship with Ivy did not appear to be in the best of shape, I did believe it could be mended. My relationship with Erin was kind of up in the air. It was hard to judge what direction we were heading. Unfortunately, things would get worst before they got better. I think everything started to unravel right around the time I got arrested. If my memory serves me correctly that was the same time things started getting real complicated. I'm starting to get a little bit ahead of myself, so let me explain.

I tried calling Ivy on Sunday after Rob's barbeque. It had been a week, and we still had not talked. Regardless of how long it had been I still got her voice-mail. I no longer left a message. I simply hung up. I thought about calling Erin and asking her how her evening with her father went but I really did not care. Besides, I was not in the mood for idle chitchat just to pass time.

Later that Sunday my brother, James, called to inform me a friend of his—Donovan—had a director's position open at Chicago National Bank back home. James claimed he instantly thought about me so he gave me Donovan's number and told me to give him a call. I figured I had nothing to lose, so I assured James I would call him.

Monday began like any other Monday. A great mourning for the end of the weekend and a fearful dread of knowing I had to head back to work. Still like all Mondays once I was at work and got back into the groove of things, memories of the weekend passed and thoughts of the upcoming weekend consumed me. I called Donovan as promised and talked to him briefly about the position at Chicago National. He sounded relatively busy, so I assured him I would email him my resume and if he was interested we could talk later. I was getting tired of Minneapolis and Midwestern Federal, so the job at Chicago National sounded like the perfect opportunity to get back to Chicago.

I tried calling Ivy at work once again. It was apparent she wanted to have nothing to do with me. I knew Ivy was avoiding me because of Erin. I just did not understand why she did not at least want to hear what I had to say. I really wanted to talk to her. It was more like I really needed to talk to her. Ivy had not only been my lover, but she had also become my friend and I felt she should at least give me the chance to explain myself.

I don't know why, but for some weird reason when my phone rung around eleven o'clock that morning I thought it was Ivy. It wasn't. How I wish it had been. Instead of Ivy, it was the principal from my son's school wondering if it was at all possible for me to meet with her that morning. At the time I was swamped at work but I sensed something was wrong, so I agreed.

When I arrived at Little T's school Mrs. Rowland, my son's principal, Ms. Cartwell, his kindergarten teacher, and a Mr. Patterson, a social worker from the Hennepin County Child Protective Services, greeted me. The fact Mr. Patterson was even present concerned me.

"Mr. Brown, we called you here this morning because we have noticed some things about Thaddeus that have given us cause for alarm," Mrs. Rowland began.

"Such as?" I inquired. I needed her to clarify "alarm" to me.

"To be quite frank with you Mr. Brown possible signs of physical abuse," Mrs. Rowland replied.

"Abuse?" I was shocked. I had figured the way things were going for me they couldn't have gotten any worse. I couldn't have been more wrong.

"Yes, Mr. Brown…. Now in such circumstances as these we are required by state law to get Child Protective Services involved, which explains Mr. Patterson's attendance here today. Now, we know you and Thaddeus' mother are no longer together and that she is the primary care giver for your son. We are also aware thru your son that your ex-wife is seeing another gentleman."

"Is my son all right?" I was tired of Mrs. Rowland's run down of the events. I wanted to see my son. My primary concern was Little T and his well-being.

"Yes, your son is fine," Ms. Cartwell interceded.

"Then what type of abuse are we talking about here?" I demanded.

"Over the last week to week and a half, I have noticed bruises on Thaddeus' arms and around his neck as if someone had forcefully grabbed him," Ms. Cartwell explained. "When I asked him how he got the marks, he tells me he fell down. Now, I know Thaddeus is a little boy and little boys tend to be a bit more physical in their play than girls. Yet, I find it hard to believe that Thaddeus is that clumsy. On top of that I had never seen such marks on him before. So, I could not help but become concerned for his safety."

"Thank you for your concern Ms. Cartwell." Ms. Cartwell nodded her head in acknowledgment. "Where is my son? I want to see him." I tried desperately to keep my cool. It was hard for me to believe this was happening, especially to Little T.

"Thaddeus is in class right now Mr. Brown. Believe me when I tell you he is fine. However, in light of such circumstances as I said, we are required by law to hand this matter over to Child Protective Services in order to decide what must be done. With that said I will let Mr. Patterson take it from here," Mrs. Rowland informed me.

"Mr. Brown how are you doing?" Mr. Patterson extended his hand for me to shake.

"Not too good right now," I said. I gave him a quick shake, so we could get on with it. I was growing impatient waiting to hear what was my son's fate.

"That is understandable," Mr. Patterson said. He tried to play like he sympathized with my current situation.

Mr. Patterson continued, "Mr. Brown in normal instances such as these, where we suspect abuse, we take custody of the child and place him or her in foster care. The reason being it is hard to determine, which parent or if it is both parents involved in the abuse or neglect of the child. Usually, upon the completion of an investigation we decide on whether the child should become a ward of the state, placed with a relative if the child's parents are not capable of carrying on their parental duties or foster care. However, in your case we know that Thaddeus does not reside with you and after interviewing your son and discussing the matter with Principal Rowland here and Ms. Cartwell, I have decided that in the best interest of your son I grant you temporary custody upon the completion of an investigation." I could not help but breath a sigh of relief. "I have made your ex-wife aware of my decision to award you temporary custody.

"However, if you don't mind me asking, when was the last time you saw your son?"

"I saw Thaddeus Saturday. I was supposed to see him yesterday but his mother claimed he had a party to go to." The bruises on Little T's arm he claimed he got from playing tee-ball suddenly came to mind. Not only that, it was plausible that Stephanie did not let me see Little T Sunday because I might notice other marks I might have overlooked Saturday.

"Do you recall seeing any noticeable marks or bruises on your son Saturday?" My mind flashed to the bruises on Little T's arm.

"Yes, he had a bruise on his arm. He said he got it while playing tee-ball," I replied.

"Did they look like this? Mr. Patterson slid three photographs across the table for me to look at. I examined the photos and immediately recognized the bruises on Little T's arm in one photo. The markings had faded a bit, yet they were still recognizable. Now, the purplish markings on Little T's stomach and back I saw in the second and third photograph I had never seen before. If I had not known any better I would have guessed Little T had been whipped with a belt or extension cord.

"The bruises on his arm look familiar. However, I don't recall seeing the welts on my son's stomach or back." I was stunned.

"I suspect not. Those markings are fresh. If I had to summarize, I would have to say they occurred within the last twenty-four to forty-eight hours," Mr. Patterson remarked. That explained why Stephanie did not let me see Little T on Sunday.

"Just so you're aware Mr. Brown a police report has been filed regarding your son's injuries," Mr. Patterson added.

Mr. Patterson wrote feverishly on his notepad before asking his next question. "Were you aware Mr. Brown that the police had been called to your ex-wife's residence twice in the last three months to handle reports of domestic violence?"

"No, I was not." The more Mr. Patterson talked the angrier I got. "Is that it?" I needed to get out of there…. I needed some air. I wanted to see my son!

"For the time being Mr. Brown…yes. Nevertheless, I want to remind you we are conducting an investigation. I will need to see your son to ask him some more questions. Most likely I will need to videotape him during the next interview in case his testimony is required in a possible criminal case," Mr. Patterson informed me.

"I understand. When can I see my son?" I begged.

Mr. Patterson looked over at Mrs. Rowland and Ms. Cartwell before stating; "I see no reason why you can not see him now. Yet, I recommend that you wait until the end of school today. We don't want to startle him or scare him into thinking he has done something wrong. When you pick him up after school today try to make it seem as if it is like any other day.

"Also Mr. Brown, I know you want answers. If you feel your son will open up and talk to you that is fine. Just don't force it. Sometimes these things take time for a child to feel comfortable talking about. Here is my card. If your son tells you anything about those bruises on his body please give me a call."

"No problem." I took Mr. Patterson's card.

I decided to listen to Mr. Patterson and wait until school was out before seeing Little T. Despite my decision to wait, I could not help but agonize over how I could've let something like this go on right under my nose without even noticing it. In my mind I had failed Little T as a father. I had failed to do the one thing every father is supposed to do and that was protect my child. I was scared and at the same time furious. I was fearful of the repercussions such an event in Little T's life may have on him psychologically.

At first I thought that in some sick, twisted, way Stephanie was trying to get back at me for our shortcomings by taking it out on Little T. Yet, I found it hard to believe Stephanie would do such a thing. Stephanie loved Little T too much to harm him. I immediately deducted it had to be her boyfriend, Willard, but I was not positive. I was so confused at the time; I did not know what to do or think. I felt such a mix of emotions. One minute I was angry and the next minute I was afraid. I needed someone to talk to. The first person who came to mind was Ivy but I knew she was not accepting my phone calls, so I called Marcus even Darius but got their voicemails. In the end I wound up calling Erin. Erin could have easily told me she was too busy to talk but she didn't. Instead, she suggested that we meet somewhere so we could talk in private. She suggested Loring Park on the outskirts of downtown.

For an hour and a half I sat on a park bench pouring my heart out to Erin. She listened intently, occasionally offering her advice or her opinion when I asked of it. However, she mainly sat there and listened. She did not pass judgment nor did she attempt to offer solutions. For the better part of an hour and a half, Erin simply listened to what I had to say. As funny as this may sound that meant a lot to me. At that moment I simply needed to vent. By the time I had finished spilling my heart out to her, it was time to pick up Little T. Besides, Erin had gone well beyond a typical hour lunch. The sweet thing about it was that in the end, Erin assured me everything was going to be all right. I know that sounds corny but during that crisis it meant something to me. To hear her say that, somehow made me feel like I could help my son overcome the situation. Talking to Erin that afternoon really helped me gather my thoughts and sort out what I needed to do. For example, immediately upon leaving Erin I called my lawyer to begin custody proceedings so I could get full custody of my son…permanently.

When I picked up Little T, I tried my best to act like nothing was wrong. That was hard for me to do. I am the type of person who wears his emotions on his sleeve. When Little T questioned me as to why I was there to pick him up instead of allowing him to catch the school bus home, I almost let my emotions get the best of me. Yet, I kept my cool. I simply told him, he was going to stay with me for a little while. As I drove home my most immediate urge was to press my son for answers. I wanted to know who had beaten him in such a manner. I fought back my need to know because I did not want to scare him. It was difficult but I did my best to remain calm. I figured I could wait until we got to my condo before I bombarded him with questions.

When Little T and I got home, I noticed there was a call from Erin on the caller ID. I wanted to call her back and thank her for that afternoon but I was too preoccupied with Little T. I waited until Little T had gotten settled in before I decided to ask him a few questions. I had sworn to myself that if Willard was indeed responsible for my son's condition there was going to be hell to pay.

I sat down at the kitchen table next to Little T as he drew a picture and contemplated a subtle way to lead into the subject without startling him. "So, did you have fun at Grandma Lou's last weekend?"

"Huh," came his reply. It was the universal reply a child gives if they did not hear what you had said or did not wish to answer.

"I said did you have fun down at your Grandma Lou's in Chicago last weekend?" I repeated, this time louder.

"I did not go to Grandma Lou's last weekend," Little T replied. I knew by the curious look on his face he was telling the truth. After meeting with Mrs. Rowland, Mr. Patterson, and Ms. Cartwell, I had suspected as much. Stephanie had lied to me in order to keep Little T's abuse hidden from me.

"So, you did not go to Chicago last weekend?"

"Nope," my son reaffirmed. He calmly drew a big circle for his caricature's face.

"Hum, maybe I heard your mother wrong," I replied, playing along.

"Maybe," he said. He continued to draw.

"Okay, how was the birthday party yesterday?" I questioned.

"What birthday party?" Also as I had suspected. There was no birthday party either.

I sat there for a moment contemplating my next move when I decided to simply tell him. "I spoke with your teacher today…Ms. Cartwell."

I could see a look of concern spread across my son's face. "About what?"

"About those sores on your arms and back." Little T stopped drawing for a second as those words sunk in. "You want to tell me what's going on?"

My son sat there frozen for a moment as if he was caught before saying, "Nothing, I just keep falling down." I sat there silently staring at him. He knew I was watching him. I could tell by the way he fidgeted in his seat. It was a nervous reaction he demonstrated whenever he was scared or unsure of himself.

"If something was wrong you would tell me…wouldn't you T?"

"Yeah," he replied. He nervously tapped his pencil against the table.

"Then tell me the truth. Did you really get hurt by falling down?"

My son sat there for a moment silently looking for a way out of the corner I had backed him into before sadly confessing, "I'm not suppose to tell."

"And who told you that?"

"Mama."

"Your Mama told you not to tell?"

"Yeah." Once again, I was suddenly finding it difficult to contain my rage.

"Well, I am your father and I want to know how you really got those sores on your arm, around your neck, as well as on your stomach and back. I think you can tell me."

"I know, but I don't want you to get mad at Mama," my son professed.

"Look son, I know it bothers you when your Mama and I argue. I'm not going to promise you I will not be upset with your mother. But I do know that I will be even more upset if you do not tell me how you got those bruises. Do you understand what I'm saying to you?"

"Yeah."

"So, what do you think is better, telling your dad or not telling your dad?"

"Telling you."

"That's right. So, now I think you need to tell me how you got those bruises and welts."

Little T looked up at me before taking a deep breath. "Mama's boyfriend, Willard." My son had just confirmed the last of my suspicions.

"Willard hit you?" I questioned. I wanted to make sure I heard him correctly.

"Yes. He spanks and whips me sometimes when Mama is gone. Mama tells him to stop but then he hits her. So, I try not to tell Mama but she finds out anyway when she helps me put my clothes on."

"How many times has this happened?" Little T put his hand in the air and stretched out his five little fingers.

"Five times!" I shouted.

"Yeah."

I could tell that I had scared him by raising my voice. So I tried to ask my next question in a more subdued tone. "What has your mother done about it?"

"Mama kicked him out. She said he broke his promise to her that he would not put his hands on her or me ever again," he replied.

"She did huh."

"Yeah, she did. That is because no man should put his hands on a lady. Right daddy?" he said sternly. I suddenly felt a sense of pride in knowing I had at least raised my son right when it came to putting his hands on a woman.

"That's right. Still, it does not matter if your Mama kicked him out that does not excuse Willard from putting his hands on you," I stated. From that point on it was apparent to me what must be done.

Within half an hour the phone calls had been made. Marcus and Willard shared a mutual friend by the name of Carl. So, Marcus called Carl up in hopes of getting an idea of where we might find Willard that evening. It seemed as if Willard usually frequented a bar on Washington Avenue called Bunkers on Monday nights. I took Little T over to Marcus' house, Marcus had convinced Lisa that the fellas were going out for drinks and it would be helpful if she could baby sit him for a couple of hours. Lisa did not mind for she liked Little T as well as she saw him as practice for when Marcus and her had their own children…. For the time being Marcus and Lisa were in the process of trying to have a child, yet it did not seem as if Marcus' swimmers were having any luck in hitting their mark.

As for Marcus, although he acted whipped at times he was a true friend. If he had told Lisa the real reason why he had asked her to watch Little T, he risked not only his marriage but also the possibility of being disbarred. There was also the damage it could do to Lisa's reputation as a lawyer. I told him repeatedly that he did not have to ride along with me on this one, but Marcus as well as Darius insisted. Of course, their presence made me feel better just in case Willard was not alone when I confronted him.

After dropping Little T off at Marcus' house I assured Marcus I would meet him at Darius' apartment after I made one last stop. As I made my way to Stephanie's house, my old home, I realized Stephanie was just as much at fault as that asshole, Willard, for she tried to hide what Willard was doing to our son from me. Despite the fact, Little T had told me that Stephanie had kicked Willard out that did not make up for the fact she allowed Willard to remain around my son after he had placed his hands on him.

By the time I knocked on Stephanie's door I was ready to explode. I had never wanted to strike Stephanie before but at that particular moment I wanted to beat her. I wanted to beat her for her stupidity in allowing that man to remain in the same house as my son after physically abusing him. I wanted to at lease slap some sense into her. Yet, when Stephanie opened the door and I noticed her black eyes, all of that pent up rage inside of me dissipated. The sight of Stephanie in such shape bothered me. I could only assume by the rivulets of tears streaming down her face Mr. Patterson had contacted her. Despite all of this…despite the fact she had brought Willard into our lives, a piece of me still wanted to console Stephanie.

"I'm here to get Thaddeus' things," I huffed. I refused to look at her. Seeing Stephanie in such a state only angered me more.

"Come on in, I've been expecting you," Stephanie sniffled.

"I can wait right here."

"Please Thaddeus, come inside." I hesitated a moment before walking inside. As I stood there in the foyer of my old house an eerie sense of déjà vu came over me. I had come to the house plenty of times to pick up Little T, still that evening it felt like it had been ages since I had stood in that doorway. It was if I had came home, but I no longer recognized it. I stared at the couch I use to read my newspaper on. There were plenty of Sunday afternoons I would sit Little T on my lap and we would watch football games together. I could not help but feel strange standing there looking upon that furniture once again—in my mind everything in that house had suddenly been tainted by Willard.

"I already packed Thaddeus' clothes. They're sitting right there next to the sofa." Stephanie pointed towards the suitcase. I glanced over towards the couch to see the suitcase. I stormed over to the sofa and grabbed Little T's belongings.

"I packed some of his favorite books he likes read to him at bedtime." I ignored Stephanie. Instead, I headed back towards the door.

However, before I could escape Stephanie felt the urge to tell me, "Thaddeus, I want you to know I would not do anything to hurt my baby. You know that don't you?" she cried.

I turned on Stephanie so vehemently I think I scared her half to death. "How can you stand there and say that to me! You brought Willard into this house! You let him stay here after he laid his hands on our son! And it was you who tried to hide it from me! How many times did he lay his hands on Little T Stephanie? Huh? Huh?" I screamed. I wanted to hit her but the rational side of me prevented me from doing so. If I had given into that urge I would have been no better than Willard.

"Do you know we could have lost our son? Do you know Little T could have become a ward of the state and we would not be able to see him? Were any of these thoughts going through your mind when you allowed this man to remain in this house." Stephanie could do nothing but sob. I took it as an admission of guilt.

"The Stephanie, I knew didn't play that! She would have killed that nigga for laying his hands on her son!" I screamed.

"I made a mistake okay! I realize that! Everybody makes mistakes Thaddeus!" Stephanie sobbed.

I stormed down the walkway to my car. I didn't want to hear anything else Stephanie had to say. As I opened my car door Stephanie called out to me, "I know I'm not suppose to see Thaddeus until the investigation is over, however, I was wondering if I could possibly see him before then?" I could not believe Stephanie had the guile to ask me such a question

"Hell no!" I shouted. With that said I got into the car and drove off.

After leaving Stephanie's, I managed to calm down and thank rationally about what I intended on doing. I questioned if following through with my plan was really within the best interest of my son. There was already enough hurt between Little T and Stephanie to go around and there really was no need for me to instigate any more. I should have just went home and let the authorities handle the situation, but I didn't. I got caught up in my own selfish emotions. I felt the only justice for Willard was the type only I could dole out. So instead of going home, I went to Darius' where I let the talk of revenge and the taste of liquor get the best of me. By the time we left his apartment, I was once again a time bomb ticking.

We arrived at Bunkers around eleven thirty. We figured we had given Willard plenty of time to settle in if he was there. I knew there was a chance he may have not been there. For all I knew the police may have already picked him up for what he had did to Little T. Yet as Marcus' friend, Carl, had predicted Willard was there and unfortunately alone. When Darius, Marcus and I walked in Willard was trying his damnedest to get one woman's attention. Although, I should've realized how confronting Willard was only going to make matters worst. I could not see beyond my own blind rage.

I wasted no time. I walked right over to where Willard stood whispering into the woman's ear. "What's up muthafucka?"

Willard was so preoccupied with putting his mack down; he failed to notice me standing there. When Willard turned to see who had called him out of his name and he saw me standing there, I could tell by the expression on his face he knew why I was there. I think in that instant Willard's instincts took over because he tried to hit me with a punch I easily sidestepped. Before he could regain his balance and take another swing at me, I countered with a right cross flush upon his jaw. The blow sent him to the floor.

As I stood over Willard beating him to a bloody pulp, all I could envision were the bruises on my son's arms and the welts on Little T's back. Willard is lucky the bouncers pulled me off of him. I am certain I would have been charged with manslaughter that night instead of aggravated battery.

Ivy—It's Time to Get Mine

It was difficult but I managed to survive a week without Thaddeus in my life. I did not call him nor did I reply to any of his messages or emails. At first it was hard but with each passing day life became a little more bearable. I had wanted to pick up the phone on several occasions and ask Thaddeus why he drifted into the arms of another woman, but I resisted. I needed a clean break. I had to focus on work—on my job. My review for partner was fast approaching. I needed to have a clear head, free of drama. As the week progressed the numbing pain in my heart left behind by Thaddeus began to dull. Life went on and I had to go on right along with it. Dwelling in the past did nothing but leave me in the past. That was not apart of my make up. It is not the type of person I am. I have always looked forward to a new day with wide-eyed hope it brought something new my way. Don't get me wrong I still every once and awhile relapsed into bouts of self-pity, anger, and depression. For example, I experienced such a fit of anger going on my second week of avoiding Thaddeus.

I don't know what it was about seeing Judy, my admin, prancing around the office tossing her blonde hair while flirting with every delivery guy, who showed up that Monday afternoon that made me angry. I never had a problem with Judy before. Yet, seeing her wiggle her little narrow ass around the office like a dog in heat irritated me. I could not help but wonder if that was all Thaddeus' current love interest had to do to get his attention—a simple toss of her hair and a little flirtatious banter. I knew it was wrong for me to assume that was how all white women behaved but at that moment I could not help myself…. I was upset. I don't know if it was the stress from my upcoming review for partner or if it was the fact that someone who looked similar to Judy had my man that brought me to the edge.

I don't know.

I do know by the end of the day I did not want to see another white woman as long as I lived. That afternoon all white women had became my enemy. All of them simply got on my nerves. It was not like a white woman had to say anything or do something to make me upset. Just the sight of them bothered me. I know it was nothing more than my own anger towards Thaddeus and what he had done that caused me to project my anger on to all white women. Still, I was angry for I was a good woman once again left alone. I needed to relax. So, I called Lisa and talked her into having a few cocktails with me at a nearby bar.

"So, do you think you're going to make partner girl," Lisa asked. I sat next to her sipping on a Long Island Ice Tea. I was going for the hard stuff.

"I hope so. None of the associates up for partner this year has busted their butts the way I have. There is not an associate that has produced as many billable hours for Grimble & Kline or brought in as many clients over the pass seven years as I have."

"Well, I don't want you getting your hopes up. Don't get me wrong I want you to make partner and all because Lord knows you deserve it. I just want you to be prepared just in case it does not happen. You know how company politics can be," Lisa warned.

"Company politics my ass. I've been playing the partners' game and kissing their smelly butts, all the while busting my own. I brought in clients while at the same time lining their pockets. It's time now for me to enjoy some of the fruits of my labor," I proclaimed.

"Look Ivy, I know all that but I don't want you to get blind sided in case it does not happen…. Remember whom we are talking about here—Grimble & Kline. Their reputation for promoting associates of color to the ranks of partner is not the best. I mean take Warren Thomas for example. That brotha was thorough, yet he did not make partner."

"Warren was nothing more than another brotha with a white girl," I interrupted. Warren was one of those brothas I had spoken of earlier who thought sistahs were too demanding and too high maintenance to be bothered with. So to go along with his big house and Mercedes, he went out and married the first white woman he could find.

"What does that got to do with it? Oh, I get it. I see why you have this attitude. You have Thaddeus on the brain. I hear you and all but let's put that aside for the minute because I really don't want you to set yourself up for a fall come Friday. Warren worked his butt off, kissed what he thought was the right ass, mingled with the partners but still did not make partner."

"I can't just put it aside. Why is it that white people have to steal everything away from us? A white woman stole my man. And now I have to worry about a group of mostly white men stealing from me a promotion I rightfully deserve.

"Do you know I saw a white kid with his jeans sagging off his butt and wearing a do rag. Can you believe it? This little white boy had the nerve to be wearing a do rag. This boy does not have a clue as to why brothas even wear do rags. Just because he has seen rappers wearing them in the music videos, he thinks they're cool."

"Let it go Ivy," Lisa warned.

"No, I'm not going to let it go. Lisa, you know I've tried hard not to buy into the stereotypes of brothas with white women. I've tried to keep an open mind but every time I meet a white woman with a brotha, she attempts to over compensate for being white by acting out of character as if to show people she is down with black folks.

"I hate it when white women think just because a brotha puts a little black in them, they can all of a sudden act as if they have a pass to freely say and do whatever they want around black people…. I think not.

"From our culture, to our slang, to our men, they just steal everything away from us and try to sell it right back to us as if they came up with it in the first place. And we like fools buy it. We change up on them and they eventually copy that. Why should I have to be worried about making partner after working extra hard? I know I have to be two times better than the next attorney because not only am I black, but I'm also a woman. I've fashioned what little personal life I have around Grimble & Kline. I've sacrificed, now it is time for that sacrifice to pay dividends!" I exclaimed.

"I hear you girl, but what can you do. They're pulling the strings. I do not want to put what you have done down but plenty of brothas and sistahs such as Warren has sacrificed and brought big dollars into Grimble & Kline. It was not until Warren left for Henderson & Hobbs in Chicago did he make partner and from what I hear he took some of Grimble & Kline's clients with him."

"Well, that's Warren Thomas. It's not me," I assured her. I requested the bartender to bring me another Long Island.

"Look Ivy how many black lawyers has Grimble & Kline hired as associates has gone on to become partner?"

"None," I replied.

"Out of how many?"

"Maybe out of ten, since I've been there," I replied.

"Exactly. That is not counting the number of black associates that were employed by Grimble & Kline before you arrived. Not one black associate at Grimble & Kline has worked their way through the ranks to make partner. Of course, they have hired one black attorney from another firm to come in and be a rainmaker, but that is it."

"Whatever…. They are not going to deny me from making partner," I insisted. "I wont stand for it."

"I don't believe they will. I just think it might not be at Grimble & Kline," Lisa retorted.

Lisa watched in astonishment as I downed my second Long Island. "I think you need to slowdown girl because you are definitely not thinking straight." I did not want to hear Lisa dispensing advice. I came to the bar to vent.

"I'm fine," I protested. I felt lightheaded, but I did not let Lisa know it. When it came to drinking I am what you would call a lightweight.

"Sure you are. If you ask me I think you are letting Thaddeus get to you." Just then Lisa's cell phone ranged. I could decipher by the way she spoke it was Marcus. After a short conversation, she gave him an affirmative 'okay' and hung up the phone.

"Speak of the devil," Lisa muttered. She stuffed the cell phone back into her purse.

"Marcus?" I asked.

"Yeah, he calls begging me to watch your boy's son," Lisa complained.

"Who? Thaddeus' son?"

"Yeah, Marcus claims they're going out tonight for drinks and Thaddeus can't find a sitter. I was tempted to tell him 'hell no' but it is not the boy's fault who his daddy is." I sat there silent for a moment. All of a sudden it had struck me that I had met Thaddeus' son only once the entire time we dated.

"Oh, hell no! I can't believe this!" Lisa stated. Lisa's proclamation damn near knocked me out of my seat.

"What?" I said, abandoning my trance. Little did I know the answer to my question would make my day only worse.

"You see that white girl at the end of the bar?"

"Which one? There are a lot of white girls in here," I informed Lisa.

"The ones that just walked in—the woman with the blonde hair and her friend the brunette. They are just now sitting down." I had been daydreaming, so I had no clue who had just walked in or who had walked out. Nevertheless, I did notice the two ladies Lisa pointed out pulling up seats at the end of the bar.

"Yeah, so what?" I stated.

"I swear to God that is the same girl I saw Thaddeus with at the movie theater!" Lisa exclaimed.

"Which one?" I asked, this time paying closer attention.

"The blonde hair one." As I glanced down the bar a second time, this time my eyes met those of the woman in question. I could tell by the expression on her face, she was curious to know why I had taken a sudden interest in them.

"Are you sure?" I questioned, checking the blonde hair woman out.

"The more I look at her, the more certain I am," Lisa said. Lisa also stared down the bar at the two women. There was one thing you could say about the

Twin Cities; it was small. It was not uncommon for a person to accidentally bump into an ex-boyfriend's current lover, whether she was white or black.

"How can you be certain? Wasn't it dark in the theater?"

"Yeah, but they walked right by me on their way out. I got a good look at the heifer." I watched as the blonde hair woman tossed her hair as she turned to say something to her girlfriend that elicited a chorus of giggles.

"If she flips her hair like that one more time, I'm going to go down there and yank her hair out of her head by the roots," I uttered.

"That's it! You're not drinking any more." Lisa snatched my third Long Island away from me. "Besides, it's time to go. I told Marcus I was leaving in ten minutes."

"No Lisa, lets stay," I pleaded.

"Oh no girl. It's time for us to go. You are not going to cause me to lose my job because you want to beat down some white girl. What you need to do is kick Thaddeus' ass." Lisa quickly paid the tab.

I never intended of doing anything. I was doing more talking than anything else. I also knew, I had too much to lose over a brief moment of satisfaction. Besides, I knew the blonde hair woman was not the one to blame in this case. Like Lisa had said my issue was with Thaddeus. The woman appeared to have unknowingly stepped in to the middle of a situation she knew nothing about. Still at that moment, at that very instant, the thought of that woman with Thaddeus burned inside of me. So even if I was selling wolf tickets, I am glad Lisa dragged me out of that bar before I did something stupid and wound up making a complete fool of myself.

Erin—I'm Here For You

I was in the process of wooing a client away from a rival ad agency when Thaddeus called me Monday afternoon. I was tempted to tell him I was busy, but I sensed by the tone of his voice that something was wrong. Of course, by me shifting my focus from closing a deal to that of sympathetic friend, or however we defined our relationship, jeopardized me from landing the account. Still, I felt I had the client on the hook well enough to where I could lay off on my sales pitch and still manage to get them to transfer their business over to our firm. Not until I listened to Thaddeus closely did I realize the magnitude of the situation. I suggested we meet somewhere to talk over my lunch hour. That way I could speak freely without anyone eavesdropping. I suggested we meet at Loring Park.

I met Thaddeus at Loring Park, a park on the outskirts of downtown. I could tell he was really upset. In the two hours we talked, Thaddeus' emotions ran the gambit from being angry, scared for his son to out right confusion. I probably learned more about Thaddeus in those two hours than I would have learned about him in two months. To be honest with you, I was quite surprised yet honored that Thaddeus had chosen to open up to me. I was unclear as to whether this signified a shift in our relationship from being quasi friends to something more like lovers. His newfound sense of trust in me had caught me off guard and I did not know what to make of it. So as soon as I got back to the office I called Belinda in hopes she could give me some insight into what it all meant. Unfortunately, Belinda was too busy to talk so I was only able to give her juicy tidbits of my conversation with Thaddeus. Belinda and I planned to meet later at a nearby bar, so I could go into greater detail.

Still, I could not shake the thought of how gutsy it was for Thaddeus to totally expose himself to me without fear of possibly leaving himself vulnerable. It was something that had taken me years to achieve with Brian and quite honestly if the shoe was on the other foot I doubt I would have done the same. I decided to call Thaddeus and make sure everything was all right as well as make it clear I was there for him. It appeared he had yet to make it home, so I left him a message on his voicemail. The remainder of the day I went through my regular routine as usual, however, I could not stop thinking about Thaddeus and wondering if we were embarking on something a little more serious than what we had been engaged in before. When I stopped and really thought about it, such a possibility scared me.

Just the thought of possibly starting all over again with someone new made me nervous. I know that sounds strange since I wanted my relationship with Thaddeus to take on a more serious note. Yet for years I had dated only one man...Brian. If I indeed was going down the road towards commitment again, I wanted it to be right. I wanted it to be love. No more phony imitations. I had played my share of games with Brian and those that came before him. I was tired of playing the games. I wanted this time around to be for real.

I guess fate had a strange way of answering my question about Thaddeus being the one and at the most inopportune time. What were the chances of me arriving at the same bar as Ivy? Now, I see that chance encounter as an omen to what lied ahead for Thaddeus and I. No matter if it was Ivy or his ex-wife, Stephanie, there was always going to be another woman in Thaddeus' life. I did not know if I could handle another woman always lurking in the shadows.

Instead of meeting Belinda at the bar I decided to walk over to her job after work so we could walk to the bar together. As we headed over I filled Belinda in on the details of my conversation with Thaddeus. At first when we entered the bar, we did not notice Ivy and her friend sitting there. In fact, I was too busy talking to Belinda to really pay attention to anyone else. However, it was hard not to notice Ivy since she was staring directly at us the moment we sat down.

I placed our order with the bartender before asking Belinda, "Do you know them?" I pointed down the bar towards Ivy and her friend.

Belinda peered down the bar at Ivy who was still glaring at us. "I can't say I do"

"Then what is her problem," I stated. I figured if I just ignored Ivy and her friend, they would return to whatever it was they were doing before we arrived.

"Who knows? Maybe, she thinks you're cute and wants to take you home." Belinda giggled.

"That's not funny. Besides, I don't think she's my type." Both of us could not resist a chuckle.

I could not resist asking Belinda my next question, "What is it with black women anyway? Why are they always so hostile? They always treat us with so much contempt. Do you know the night Thaddeus and I went to the movies a bunch of black women acted as if they were going to beat me up."

"What's new?" Erin's revelation did not seem to faze Belinda. "Black women will bump into you on purpose and even curse at you if they see you with a black man."

"What is their problem?" I exclaimed.

"They're just jealous," Belinda replied. "They always think we're trying to steal their man. Maybe, if they stopped walking around here with a chip on their shoulder and paid less attention to us and more attention to their men they might be able to keep them.

"Besides, half the time black women don't want the guy in the first place. Yet as soon as a black guy starts dating a woman who happens to be white they get all bent out of shape."

"Why is dating a white woman such a heinous crime? Does it really matter if a black guy is dating someone who is black or white?" I stated.

"Black women really need to ask themselves why do their men leave them in the first place?" Belinda interjected. "However, I will admit it is not just black women who think a white woman dating a black man is a crime. There are plenty of white people who think the same. Take for example Stacy," Belinda reminded me.

As Ivy got up to leave, the idea she might be connected to Thaddeus crossed my mind. I did not know why the thought came over me. I guess you can say it was woman's intuition. I could not figure out any other reason why a couple of complete strangers would show such interest in Belinda and I. Thaddeus had told me that he was seeing other people. I could not help but wonder at the time if Ivy just so happened to be one of the people Thaddeus was so called "seeing." Even if Ivy was it did not matter for Thaddeus had chosen me.

Right?

Thaddeus had chosen me to pour his heart out to and trust with his secrets. That meant something..... .Didn't it?

Once Ivy and her friend left the bar, I let the thought of Ivy having something to do with Thaddeus fade. Sadly enough, my suspicions about Ivy would later be confirmed.

"So, what do you make of the whole thing?" I asked Belinda, trying to forget the incident at the bar.

"You mean with Thaddeus?"

"Yeah."

"From what you have told me and from my own personal experience, I would say the two of you are moving beyond being just friends. Take it from me, if a man bears his soul to you like Thaddeus did today, he sees you as much more than just his friend."

"I know, that's what scares me," I professed.

"Why is that? I thought you was really into this guy." Belinda had a surprised look on her face.

"I am."

"Then what's the problem?" she beckoned.

"I guess the thought of starting all over again. You know the laying your heart out there on the line for someone to trample all over it. I just don't know if I'm ready to take a chance like that again. I'm just confused."

Then Belinda said, "If you never take a chance Erin, then you will never know." Belinda was right. If I planned to move beyond Brian, I had to take a chance.

We finished our drinks and went home. For a brief while that Monday went along like any other Monday. However, all of that changed when there came a knock at the door around eight o'clock. I went to the peephole to see to my dismay Brian standing on the other side. I had expected as much. I knew after seeing Marty and John at the Wild Onion two Saturdays ago, it would be only a matter of time before Brian showed up at my door.

I let him in but not without first chastising him for not calling. "You can not just drop by my place unexpected. You need to call first," I insisted.

"Well, I can go if you got company." Despite his statement, Brian strolled on in anyway. He had no intentions of leaving.

"One of these days Brian you just might be surprised on what you may find," I informed him.

"Yeah, I've heard," he replied. Brian then gave me a shit-eating grin while he made himself comfortable on the couch. Belinda decided to give us some privacy, so she excused herself and went to her bedroom.

I turned the television off making sure Brian did not get too comfortable. "What are you doing here Brian?" I asked. I sat down on the love seat across from him.

"Marty and John told me they saw you a couple of Saturdays ago, so I thought I would just drop by to see how you were doing."

"Yes, unfortunately, I did run into your asshole friends." Brian smirked.

"Marty tells me you're seeing some black dude?" Brian tried to sound as if he was simply making conversation.

"And if I was, what does that got to do with you?"

"Nothing at all. I'm just repeating what I've heard," he stated.

"Well, for your information, I am seeing a guy who is black. What is it to you?"

Brian sighed. "Come on Erin, you're dating a black guy makes not only you look bad but me too." I knew it would not take long for the real reason behind his visit to come out.

"Excuse me? I really could care less how you look," I exclaimed. I was shocked he would even say such a thing.

"It figures...I'm the butt of all my friend's jokes. It looks bad for a guy's ex to leave him for a black guy. The only thing worse is if you were to become a dyke or something. If this was your idea of getting back at me, well it has worked. Now can we put an end to this game?" I could not resist but smile at how vain Brian was to even think my seeing Thaddeus had something to do with him.

"You would be conceited enough to think I'm dating Thaddeus to get back at you. You know if I choose to date a black guy or become a dyke for that matter it's my business. Not yours or your pea brain friends. So, don't flatter yourself. Contrary to what you may believe, this is not about you. I genuinely like him."

"Ah, come on Erin! Everybody is talking! I know you cannot be serious about this guy! For God's sake have you even checked to see if this guy has a police record or half a dozen kids around town!" Brian shouted.

"What is it with you? I cannot believe you even said that!" I was totally surprised. It was hard for me to believe my father had insinuated such a thing about Thaddeus, but to hear if coming out of Brain's mouth as well was a little bit too much for me to handle.

"Why not? It's the truth. You have to do a background check on the 'brothers.' Or is it that you like being his 'bitch.' Isn't that what they call their girlfriends? Or is the more appropriate term—hoe? I get confused on the lingo," Brian taunted.

"Fuck you! Brian, I think it is time for you to go!" I demanded. It infuriated me he would even go so far to say such a thing.

"I knew you moving in with Belinda was a bad idea," he grumbled while I showed him to the door.

"I'll just believe I did not hear that," I commented.

"Just don't come crawling back to me when he leaves you barefoot and pregnant," Brian pouted.

"You know Brian, you will not have to worry about that because you do not have to worry about ever seeing or talking to me again!" I slammed the door behind him.

I could not believe Brian had the audacity to come over to my apartment and make such a scene. If there had been even a remote chance of Brian and I ever getting back together it walked out the door that night.

Belinda and I sat up the remainder of the night talking and laughing at how much an asshole Brian turned out to be. I thought about calling Thaddeus before turning in for the night but decided I would wait until tomorrow to see how he was doing. Besides, it had been an eventful day and I was exhausted. I went to bed around ten-thirty. It was sometime around midnight that the phone started to ring off the hook.

It appeared as if my day was not over yet.

That's The Way Love Goes

Erin—Where Are We Going With This?

When the phone rung around midnight I would have never imagined it would be Thaddeus on the other end calling me from jail. I was half asleep, so it took a while before the gravity of the situation registered with me. I would have never guessed in a hundred years, Thaddeus would have taken matters into his own hands and actually gone out and beat up his ex-wife's boyfriend. Of course, when I had spoken to Thaddeus earlier in the day he seemed distraught but not to the point where I thought he was prone to violence.

Thaddeus had called slightly after midnight and Darius called soon after asking Belinda to bail him out as well. It took three hours before the paper work between the bail bonds company and the county was complete and Thaddeus was released. It was three-thirty in the morning when Thaddeus walked out of the Hennepin County jail and into my car. Yet, even then my night was not over for Thaddeus had to pick up his son at his friend's house. It was four-thirty in the morning when Thaddeus and I finally made it back to his condo and even then we had neglected to pick up his car parked outside of Darius' apartment complex. It was way too late to try and get it, not to mention it was too late for me to attempt to drive back to St. Paul. So I stayed the night at Thaddeus' place. I slept in Thaddeus' bed while he slept on the couch. It was five o'clock in the morning and both of us were thankful to just get some sleep before having to get up and head out to work.

Needless to say, I was late to work the following morning. The drive to St. Paul to change clothes and back into Minneapolis during the morning rush hour traffic was not going to allow me to make it to work on time. It also did not help that I suffered from exhaustion.

Around four o'clock that afternoon, I got a call from Thaddeus telling me he wanted to take me out to dinner to show his appreciation for me bailing him out of jail. Thaddeus claimed to have found a babysitter for his son, so he figured dinner was the best way to show his gratitude. I wanted to tell him paying me back the five hundred dollars I used to bail him out was the best way for him to show me his gratitude, since I had to dip into my savings in order to secure his release. Yet, there was no reason to make an issue of it just yet. I figured we could discuss that in due time. Besides, it was a beautiful day and I had no plans after work, so I gladly accepted the invitation.

After contacting Belinda at work and telling her not to expect me home until later that evening, I hurried home and changed out of my work clothes into something more appropriate for the weather. After that I drove back into Minneapolis and met Thaddeus at his condominium. Thaddeus had retrieved his car from Darius' place, which meant there was no need for me to drive. It was a lovely end of June day and I insisted we go eat somewhere in Uptown where we could sit outside and enjoy the weather.

In Minnesota you have to enjoy the summer months while you can. After all, summer is a natural aphrodisiac. In the Twin Cities summer takes on special meaning due to the long, cold, winters. As soon as the thermometer reaches sixty-five degrees, it is not uncommon to see people in shorts and guys prancing around town shirtless regardless if they had what one might consider a washboard stomach or a beer belly. The same can be said of the women who go out of their way to flash a little skin. Of course, all of this is done in hopes of luring a prospective mate home before the next snowfall.

Thaddeus and I ate dinner on the patio of a local restaurant, which allowed for us to enjoy the weather while taking in the Minneapolis skyline. Eating an exquisite meal and drinking a fine chardonnay while basking in the sun was bliss. The evening would have been perfect if I could've enjoyed a cigarette along with my glass of wine, but since I started dating Thaddeus I was trying to cut back on social smoking.

Dinner was great. Thaddeus' company was even more pleasurable. Thaddeus had a knack for making me feel special. It usually came in the form of a glance or the soft caress of his hand against mine. He was addictive. I quickly learned to simply shut my mouth and enjoy the time we shared together. Especially, after putting a slight damper on the evening by bringing up Stacy and the incident at Sunsets on Lake Minnetonka. I thought that was a safe topic for discussion since I had tried to talk to Thaddeus about his altercation with Willard the night before and got no response. I quickly deducted his ex-wife's boy-friend and the fight the night before was a topic best avoided.

As Thaddeus and I left the restaurant we could hear blues music emanating from a near by tavern. Both of us were curious, so we decided to go inside and sneak a peek. Inside the bar, we made complete fools of ourselves dancing about but we had so much fun. The fact we could not make a night of it sort of put a damper on the evening. That night was one of those evenings I simply wanted to last without the headache of going to work in the morning.

When we pulled up into Thaddeus' condominium parking garage, I could not help but feel sadden by the fact the night had come to an end. It had been a long time since I had such a wonderful time. I know it was selfish of me but I was not ready to go home. It had been a long, hot, humid day. The humidity made the air feel thick and heavy like a shroud. My body screamed out for air as my short-sleeved shirt and denim skirt suffocated my skin. I could not help but contemplate what a relaxing dip in a swimming pool would feel like.

So as Thaddeus walked me to my car I could not resist asking him, "Do you have a swimming pool here?"

"Yep, it's on the second floor. It's closed now. They usually close the pool and weight room around nine o'clock," Thaddeus stated.

"What time is it?" I asked.

Thaddeus glanced at his watch. "It is nine fifteen."

"I want to take a swim, don't you?" I asked. I attempted to badger him into going upstairs to see if the pool was indeed closed.

"Yeah, on a night like this a dip in the pool would be nice," he replied.

"On a night like this a dip in the pool would do a body good."

"How about I fill my bathtub up with water and let you splash around all you want." Thaddeus laughed.

"Stop being a scaredy-cat. Come on let's see if they have closed the pool yet." I grabbed Thaddeus by the hand and dragged him towards the elevators.

When we got off the elevator on the second floor I quickly noticed the door to the patio still open. I looked over at Thaddeus and smiled. "It must be our lucky night. It looks like we can take that dip after all."

As I ran out on to the deck Thaddeus called out to me. "But you don't have a swimsuit?"

I looked back at him and grinned. "Who says I need one." The bewildered look that crossed his face was comical. I admit...I was a tad bit tipsy but not enough for me to not know what I was doing.

As I slipped out of my clothes, an expression of shock spread across Thaddeus' face. I could not help but laugh. As I stood there totally nude, I slipped into the heated pool while Thaddeus stood there stunned.

"Are you just going to stand there and watch or are you going to join me?" I waded across the pool towards the deep end. An unconscious smile emerged on Thaddeus' face as he glanced around to make sure no one was watching. "What's wrong are you scared someone might see you? Believe me you have nothing to be ashamed off, trust me," I teased.

"I'm not scared," Thaddeus declared. It sounded more like he was trying to convince himself instead of me.

"Then what are you waiting for?" Thaddeus stared at me for a brief moment as if to say I was crazy before taking his shirt off. As he undressed Thaddeus kept a weary eye on the lookout for possible interlopers on what would have been a very embarrassing moment.

It took Thaddeus a few minutes before he was completely nude and had entered the water. To see him completely naked standing there before me was a treat. I swam over to him and planted a juicy kiss on his lips and said in a soft, seductive, tone, "Now was that really that bad?"

"No, not really," Thaddeus whispered. I could feel the muscles in his body begin to relax. I'm certain the kiss helped plenty in helping him reach a level of comfort.

Up until that evening, Thaddeus and I had never been intimate. However, an evening of dinner and playful banter had set the mood for a night of intimacy. We spent some time simply making out before Thaddeus slid his hand down my stomach to gently massage my erogenous zone. My moans of passion echoed throughout the courtyard as he feverishly stimulated my spot. His gentle technique quickly brought my body to an orgasmic crescendo. I could feel my spine lock as my body prepared for the rush of pleasure poised to cascade over me. Beads of sweat sprouted on my brow as Thaddeus' fingers quickened their pace. Then it hit me. I could feel wave after wave of pleasure washing over me as my muscles stiffened into place forcing my body to become rigid. Thaddeus attempted to pull back but I held him close to me so he could share in my pleasure.

Once I had relaxed, I gave Thaddeus a kiss. I refused to let that be it. Instead, I allowed the buoyancy of the water to lift my hips up high enough so I could effortlessly wrap my legs around Thaddeus' waist and gently slide down upon him. I loved the way his body felt next to mine. Judging by the way we devoured each other it was obvious we had longed for that moment.

Despite this fact Thaddeus hesitated. "Wait, we need protection," he insisted.

"Don't worry I'm on the pill," I assured him.

My assurance that I was on birth control seemed to set Thaddeus' mind at ease for he appeared to allow himself to once again relax and get caught up in the moment. Our moans of ecstasy reverberated throughout the courtyard as we gave into our carnal desires. That evening we became so engrossed in each other, neither one of us realized the summer rain that drenched our bodies.... If it was not for the innocent patter of raindrops upon the concrete I doubt we would have even noticed.

By the time we exited the pool it was ten o' clock. Thaddeus was late in picking up his son, Thaddeus Jr., and I needed to call Belinda before she blew a gasket worrying about me. Yet, while we basked in the after glow of sex those thoughts, although immediate, seemed irrelevant. All I could think about was Thaddeus as we strolled back to his condo, hand in hand.

When we entered Thaddeus' condo, I peeled myself out of my damp clothes. Thaddeus disappeared into the bathroom only to return with a towel for me to dry off. He went back into the bathroom and started the shower. I could hear the water pound against the bathtub as I dried my hair.

I had a craving for something sweet. "Do you have anything sweet to eat?"

"I don't know. You're more than willing to help yourself to whatever is in the fridge," Thaddeus replied.

"Don't you want a dessert of some sort? I all of a sudden have a sweet tooth," I stated. I watched with envy as Thaddeus' naked frame pranced back and forth between his bedroom and the bathroom.

"I thought I just had dessert." Thaddeus smirked just before slapping me on the rear end.

I couldn't help but grin. "That was just a warm up," I proclaimed.

"Before I forget, I want to give you this," Thaddeus stated. Thaddeus handed me a wad of bills. "I want you to know I appreciate everything you have done for me." I could not help but be surprised.

"Thank you."

"No, thank you."

The fact Thaddeus repaid me the bail money without me asking made me feel good. I was glad he did not try to take advantage of me. "Are you sure you don't want dessert? I make a very good banana split," I chided with a sly grin.

"I would love to, but I got to go get Little T. So, I might have to pass tonight. If you want, I think I have some ice cream in the fridge!" Thaddeus shouted as he got into the shower.

"Don't worry, I can whip you up something pretty quick," I yelled. I opened Thaddeus' refrigerator to see if he had the ingredients I needed to make an extra special banana split. Thaddeus lacked a few necessary ingredients, but I figured I could make do with what I had and what I lacked I would simply improvise.

The look of surprise on Thaddeus' face when he walked out of the bathroom was well worth the trouble I went through preparing his banana split. The sight of me lying on his dinning room table with whip cream placed meticulously on all the right parts of my body definitely caught his attention. Thaddeus stood there with a devilish grin on his face while I informed him, "I wanted to make you a banana split but you did not have all the ingredients, so, I had to improvise."

It was obvious he was pleased with my choice of dessert judging by the bulge emerging from underneath the towel wrapped around his waist. Thaddeus stood there for a moment contemplating my invitation before taking a seat in the chair resting in between my legs.

As he kissed and licked away the whip cream in between my thighs, Thaddeus sent a wave of pleasure circulating throughout my body. When he was done Thaddeus quickly proceeded to my breast where he immediately cleaned the whip topping away before continuing upward to my mouth where our lips locked in a passionate kiss. At this point Thaddeus was in position for me to easily receive him inside of me.

By the time Thaddeus had left to pick up Thaddeus Jr., it was eleven o'clock. An evening of drinks, sex and lack of sleep from the night before had left me drained. I staggered into Thaddeus' bedroom and collapsed onto his bed. I had promised myself, I was only going to take a quick nap before heading home. I had figured if I slept for too long Thaddeus would wake me when he returned. He didn't. I did not even hear him enter the room or feel him snuggle up next to me. So, once again the following morning I was rushing over to my apartment in St. Paul to change into my work clothes with the hopes of making it to work on time. I was starting to wonder if I needed to keep an extra set of clothes in my car just in case I started to make staying the night at Thaddeus' place a habit.

After work, I decided to stop by Thaddeus' condo. I had called ahead of time, so he did not think I was coming by unannounced. Despite the events of the past two days…I did not take anything for granted. Thaddeus did not seem to mind. When I arrived he was cooking dinner. Thaddeus seemed a little uneasy about me meeting his son, but after a while he seemed to relax. Of course, I had been at his home the past two nights while his son was present, however, each time Thaddeus Jr. had been asleep so we were never formally introduced. To avoid being detected by his son in the morning, Thaddeus made me sneak out before he woke him.

Thaddeus asked if I wished to join him and Thaddeus Jr. for dinner, and I gladly accepted. It was not every day I had a man cook for me. As Thaddeus prepared dinner I entertained myself by playing video games with his son. I was into my second game of auto racing when the phone ranged. Immediately, I could tell by the way Thaddeus answered the phone and the subsequent way his voice dropped almost to a whisper when he spoke that he was talking to another woman. And if that was not a big enough hint, Thaddeus took the telephone into the bedroom so I could not over hear his conversation. It was when he retreated to the bedroom that I had my fill of auto racing and contemplated simply leaving. The only reason why I stayed was because I did not want to make a scene in front of Thaddeus Jr.

"Do you want to play again?" Thaddeus Jr. asked.

"Nah, you're too good." I got up to examine the pictures on Thaddeus' bookshelf. Out of the entire two days I had stayed at Thaddeus' condominium, not once had I ever looked at the pictures that adorned his condo.

I wish I had done so a lot sooner.

Maybe then I would have found the picture of the other woman a lot sooner. At the time I did not know who Ivy was or her relation to Thaddeus. What surprised me the most about that particular picture was the striking resemblance she shared with the woman I had seen at the bar with Belinda, Monday during Happy Hour. Suddenly, that brief encounter at the bar made sense. It became clear to me as to why the women had exhibited such an interest in Belinda and I.

"Are you my dad's new girlfriend?" Thaddeus Jr. asked.

I put the picture back on the shelf. I was so disturbed by the photograph I did not reply to Thaddeus Jr.'s question right away. I immediately assumed the woman in the picture was Thaddeus' ex-wife. Yet, even if it was Thaddeus' ex-wife why was her picture on his bookshelf if they were divorced?

I stared at the photo for a moment longer before answering Thaddeus' son. "No, I'm just a friend of your father's."

I don't know why I felt my heart sink as those words came out of my mouth. Although, Thaddeus and I had one evening of intimacy we had yet to define our relationship. I could not assume after one night of sex we were suddenly a couple.

When Thaddeus returned, I noticed he avoided making eye contact with me. It was nothing more than his subconscious admitting his guilt. Instead of confronting him, I decided it was best if I waited for the appropriate time when his son was asleep.

After eating dinner and a few video games later, Thaddeus tucked his son into bed and plopped himself down on the sofa next to me. It was then when I decided to confront him.

"Where are we going with this Thaddeus?" I could tell the question had caught him off guard.

"What do you mean?" he stammered.

"I mean what are we doing? Are we building towards something here or am I some type of plaything to you?" Thaddeus sat there for a moment with a stunned look on his face. I could tell he was trying his best to figure out what was the reason behind my line of questioning. I did not care. I needed clarification and I wanted it right then and there.

"I see you as a good friend Erin," Thaddeus professed.

"A good friend you may tend to sleep with every once and a while?"

"I don't understand where this is coming from Erin?"

"I just want to know where I stand with you. I see you sneaking around into other rooms to talk on the phone. I notice the picture of you and another woman over there on your bookshelf and I cannot help but wonder if I am being taken for a fool." Thaddeus sighed as he realized he had sowed the seeds that brought forth this conversation.

"Who is she?" I asked, turning my attention to the picture.

"Ivy," he responded, reluctantly.

"What is she to you?"

"We dated before I met you." I had originally suspected the woman in the photo was his ex-wife, Stephanie. To hear it was a totally different woman was too much for me to handle.

"Do you still see her?" I continued my cross-examination.

"I did up until about a month ago," Thaddeus answered.

I quickly laid his answer against the time period Thaddeus and I began seeing each other and quickly deduced, "That coincides with about the same time we started dating. No wonder she was giving me dirty looks at the bar."

"What do you mean giving you dirty looks?" Thaddeus exclaimed.

"Belinda and I went to a bar on Monday after work. Your friend, Ivy, was there with a friend. They gave us dirty looks the entire time they were there."

"Look Erin, I apologize to you for her behavior. Yet, I told you from jump that I was seeing other people."

"Yeah, you did Thaddeus. I guess I fooled myself into believing there was nobody else. Now that I know there is someone else, I don't think I can continue to play this game."

"Like I said, we stopped seeing each other over a month ago," Thaddeus proclaimed. He tried his best to convince me there was no reason for me to be upset.

"Maybe so. Nonetheless she still means something to you or else you would not be creeping around here from room to room as you talk on the telephone or still have her picture up on your bookshelf." I paused for a moment. I could feel my emotions getting away from me. Tears had begun to stream down my face.

"I think it is time for me to go."

"Wait Erin," Thaddeus begged. Thaddeus tried to grab my hand as I tried to leave but I made sure it was out of reach. "I thought we had a good time the pass few days? I thought we made a connection?"

"I thought so too. But to be quite frank with you Thaddeus, I want to be more than someone's toy. Something they pick up and play with when it is convenient for them. I've done that before and I'm tired of playing that game."

Thaddeus was confused and it showed. I did not blame him. I knew the rules when I started seeing him and now I was changing them. I really liked Thaddeus and I did not want our relationship to be based solely on sex.

"Look, when you figure things out give me a call, okay?" I tried but I could not stop the tears. I gave Thaddeus a kiss and showed myself out. It was a hard thing to do, but it was the right thing for me to do.

Ivy—Do You Love Her?

I got the call around eleven thirty Monday night. It was Lisa and she was hysterical. She wondered if I could watch Thaddeus' son, Little T, while she went downtown and bailed Marcus out of jail. It appeared Marcus, Darius and Thaddeus had gotten into a fight at a local bar. Lisa pleaded with me to do her this favor because she had no one else to turn to. I could not turn my back on my girl, so I assured her I would be there just as long as she did not mind I stayed the night. Marcus and Lisa lived clear across town in a northern suburb. I was not going to make that trek clear across town twice in once night. The thought Thaddeus might call me seeking to get bailed out as well crossed my mind, so I made sure my cell phone was turned on.

When I arrived at Lisa and Marcus' house, Lisa was livid. She could not understand how Marcus could have been so stupid to get himself involved in a barroom brawl. She ranted on and on about how Marcus could be disbarred, if he was not able to distance himself from the incident. Lisa was quite certain it had something to do with Darius. Lisa left soon after my arrival. Little Thaddeus was asleep so it meant I was not needed unless he woke up. Since there was nothing for me to do, I made myself comfortable on the couch and went to sleep.

It was two thirty in the morning when I was awaken by the sounds of Lisa and Marcus making their way into the house. I could tell by their tone and the volume at which they were speaking, they were arguing. I checked my cell phone to see if I had missed any calls. To my surprise no one called. I called my voice mail at home to see if Thaddeus had left a message there…nothing.

Lisa walked into the house screaming my name. "Ivy!"

"Yeah," I groaned. I was still half asleep.

"Did Little Thaddeus wake up?" Lisa kicked off her shoes.

"No."

"Thanks girl."

"Sure, no problem. Is Marcus all right?"

"He's fine! This fool, so called helping his boy is going to get disbarred if he keeps it up. It's your boy's fault that he got his behind thrown in jail in the first place," Lisa snapped.

"Who? Thaddeus?" I quickly woke up hearing reference to Thaddeus.

"Yes girl. I'll let him tell you the story," Lisa seethed as Marcus entered the room.

"Did Thaddeus call you?" Marcus demanded to know.

"No not at all. I just checked my voicemail and there were no messages," I informed him.

"I was certain he was going to call you," Marcus said. Marcus appeared to talk more to himself than to me.

"Is he alright?" I asked concerned.

"Thaddeus is fine. I'm just wondering how my man is going to get bailed out. I knew Darius was going to have one of his females bail him out, but I was not certain about Thaddeus. They had him in a different holding cell than me and Darius."

"What happened?" I questioned.

"Your man went down to a bar on Washington Avenue with the intentions of beating down his ex-wife's boyfriend for placing his hands on his son," Lisa interrupted. She came down the stairs in her pajamas. "Although I commend him for it, Thaddeus shouldn't be dragging my man into his mess. How does that look? Here I am a lawyer, and my man is in jail."

"How many times do I got to tell you, Thaddeus did not drag me nowhere. I am a grown man. I go where I please. Besides, that is my boy and I would do it again if he asked me to."

"You need to be worrying about the needs you should be tending to here at home—like your job!" Lisa barked.

"You know Lisa, I'm about tired of your mouth! I'm sorry you don't understand, but Thaddeus is my boy and when he needs me I'm there for him!" Marcus proclaimed.

"Whatever," Lisa sighed.

"Excuse me, but I'm lost here. What has been going on with his son?" I interceded.

"I'll let the negro *down* for his boy tell that story," Lisa said, sarcastically.

"You know, why don't you just shut up!" Marcus shouted. I waited patiently for Marcus to tell me as him and Lisa bickered back and forth. Finally, he looked at me and said, "Here's what went down."

It was close to four in the morning when Marcus had finished telling me the entire story. It was also about the same time the doorbell ranged. Curious to see who it was at that hour of the morning I peeped out the window. I did not recognize the car, however, I did recognize the white woman sitting behind the steering wheel. She resembled the same white woman Lisa had pointed out to me earlier at the bar. My heart fell when Marcus opened the door and Thaddeus walked in.

"What's up? You all right?" Marcus peeked outside to see who was sitting behind the wheel of the BMW before shutting the door.

"Yeah, I'm fine," said Thaddeus. Thaddeus had yet to notice me standing there.

"What did they charge you with?" Marcus inquired.

"Aggravated battery," Thaddeus replied.

"They hit me and Darius with obstruction of justice," Marcus told him.

"Where is my boy?" Thaddeus asked, eager to see his son.

"He is upstairs asleep in the spare bedroom," Lisa said, prancing into the living room. Thaddeus could tell by the expression on Lisa's face she was not too pleased with him, so he wisely treaded lightly.

"Hi Lisa, I want to thank you for watching Little T for me," Thaddeus stated.

"Don't thank me. Thank Ivy. She watched him." Lisa promptly pointed in my direction. Thaddeus seemed surprised, if not shocked, to see me standing there. He had been in such a hurry to get his son; he had not even noticed me.

"Oh…tha, thank you," he stuttered. It was all Thaddeus could muster.

"Sure thing," I said just barely audible. A sense of awkwardness descended amongst us.

"You don't mind if I go get him," Thaddeus said unsure of himself.

"Go right ahead." Lisa smirked. She seemed tickled by the look of shock on Thaddeus' face when he saw me standing there. Thaddeus ran up the steps only to return a few minutes later with his son asleep in his arms.

Thaddeus looked over at Marcus and told him, "I'll call you in the morning," on his way towards the door. Thaddeus told both Lisa and I thank you once again on his way out. However, Thaddeus inadvertently choose not to make eye contact with me. I watched as he went out to the car and laid his son across the backseat of the BMW just before hopping in the front seat and speeding off.

Tuesday, and a good part of Wednesday, I wanted to call Thaddeus and tell him all the things my mother told me I should've said to him when I had the chance. However, my mother did not mention to me the part about getting up the courage to do so. It was not until Wednesday evening that I finally got the nerve to call Thaddeus.

"Hello?" Thaddeus said into the phone.

"Hi."

There was a slight pause in Thaddeus' voice before he said, "Ivy?" He brought his voice down just barely louder than a whisper. That instantly alerted me to the fact he was not alone.

"Yeah, how are you doing?" I heard a woman laugh in the background. "Did I call at a bad time?"

"No, no…not at all. A friend of mine is just playing video games with Little T." She was a friend all right. "Regardless, to answer your question I'm doing all right. How about you?" Thaddeus quickly attempted to change the subject.

I could tell he was trying to figure out the reason behind my impromptu telephone call. I would have been curious myself if after two weeks of refusing to accept my phone calls Thaddeus all of a sudden called me.

"I'm doing fine. I just called to see how you were doing and to tell you I'm real sorry to hear about your son."

"Well thank you." Then I froze. I wanted to tell him I missed him but the words just got stuck in my throat. Instead, there was this awkward moment of silence.

"Ivy, you still there?" I could tell by how quiet it had become in the background that Thaddeus had moved into another room. I seriously doubted he would have kicked his company out simply because I called.

"I'm here. I just got side tracked for a moment. So have you found a lawyer to represent you in court?" I asked, trying to make small talk.

"No, I haven't. Do you know of someone?" That was a veiled attempt to flirt.

"I'll see what I can do and let you know."

"That would be great." I could hear a smile in his voice.

"Well, I will let you get back to your company. I got to review a legal brief before I turn in tonight."

"Have you made partner yet?" I was surprised Thaddeus even remembered.

"I will find out Friday," I replied.

"Well good luck."

"Well, thank you Mr. Brown. You have a good evening."

"Your welcome Ms. Martin, and you do the same."

"Good-bye."

"Bye-bye." Although I did not say what I wanted to say, talking to Thaddeus made me feel better.

Friday came and I was feeling good about my chances of becoming Grimble & Kline's newest partner. I had been looking forward to that day for a long time. Plus, I believed there was a ray of hope for Thaddeus and I.

My review was to be conducted by a partner by the name of Richard Post. Grimble & Kline had hired him away from a cross-town rival a few years back. I had worked with him on several occasions and had a good rapport with him. I found him to be an honest and fair guy. My review was towards the end of the day, which placed me on pins and needles for most of the morning. However, when it was time, I was pretty confident I would be walking out of Richard's office as one of Grimble & Kline's newest partner.

In the beginning, the meeting went well. Richard praised my work ethic and the job I had done for the firm. It felt good to be recognized for my contributions to the law firm. I had busted my behind representing our clients. It was hard for me to believe by the way Richard started off the conversation that my review was nothing more than a formality that must be performed before bestowing the title of partner upon me.... That was until he said "but." In a review, the word "but" is not good.

The "but" in this case was the insistence by the existing partners to not take on any new partners until some of the existing partners retired. I was stunned. I could not believe I had worked my ass off to come so far only to be denied. That was a bitter pill to swallow. I challenged him on the partner's insistence of not taking on any new partners by bringing up the new attorney the firm had just hired on as partner. Richard quickly explained to me that he was the exception to the rule because he was bringing a large portion of his clients from his previous firm over with him. In other words he was a rainmaker brought in to further fill the partner's coffers.

For the remainder of that meeting I sat there in silence. I had nothing to say. What could I say? If I wanted to keep my job, it was best I kept my mouth shut. Despite Richard's assurances I would be the first person in line to be selected as partner when the moratorium was lifted. I silently wondered when that would be. Even if it was lifted the following morning there was no guarantee I would be made partner. Richard was basically telling me that after seven years of proving myself, I had to go back out there and prove myself again and hope for the best next year.

I was pissed.

After my review I went directly home. I did not hang around the office chit chatting. In my opinion there was nothing to talk about. Lisa had called and left a message at the office wondering how it went. I decided I would call her back when I felt like talking.

Instead, I went home and shut all the curtains and blinds. Despite it being a sunny summer day, I sat in the confines of my townhouse alone. I put on my pajamas and curled up into a ball on the sofa and watched television. The phone ranged constantly throughout the evening. I never bothered to get up and check the caller ID. I simply stayed under the blankets in front of the TV. I knew it had to be Gloria, Lisa or my mother calling to see if I made partner and I did not feel like talking about Grimble & Kline or hearing the word partner.

At nine thirty the annoying phone calls turned into an unexpected knock at the door. I really did not want to answer it, however, I knew if I did not my mother or Lisa would have the police pay me a visit because they would have figured out by that time I had not made partner and would've feared the worst. So, I poked along over to the door and opened it to unexpectedly find Thaddeus standing there. I had expected Gloria, Lisa or even my mother, but never Thaddeus.

"What are you doing here?" I said with much attitude.

"I tried calling, but I got no answer. When I called Marcus to find out if you made partner, Lisa told Marcus she had not talked to you all day. So, I got worried and decided to come on by and see if you were all right."

"I'm fine and no I did not make partner. So, now that you know you can go announce it to the rest of the world, okay!" I snapped.

I was ready to slam the door in Thaddeus' face when he asked, "May I come in and use your phone for a minute?"

"Don't you have a cell phone?" I barked.

"Yeah, but I left it in the car." Thaddeus suddenly sounded unsure of himself.

"If I really wanted to be a bitch, I would make you walk back to your car. But since you're here come in." I slammed the door behind him.

As Thaddeus went to use the phone, I returned my attention back to my spot on the sofa. I could over hear him talking to Marcus. When he was done he stood there staring at me.

"What negro?"

"Are you just going to sit there all night and sulk?" Thaddeus asked.

"If I choose to that is my business," I informed him. Thaddeus looked at me and smiled before heading upstairs. "Where are you going?" I shouted.

"To the bathroom," Thaddeus yelled. As Thaddeus stole away to my bathroom I could hear running water. It sounded like bath water. "What are you doing up there? I said you could use the phone not make yourself at home!" I yelled. A few minutes later the water stopped and Thaddeus came bouncing back down stairs with my baby oil in his hand.

"What were you doing up there? And what do you intend to do with my baby oil," I questioned.

"Why don't you get up and see for yourself," he teased.

"Thaddeus, I am not in the mood to play games. Don't you have to get home to your girlfriend," I quipped.

"What are you talking about?" All of a sudden Thaddeus wanted to play dumb.

"I'm talking about the white girl that drove you to Marcus' house in that BMW to pick up Little T the early Tuesday morning," I replied. I knew that would jog his suddenly selective memory.

Thaddeus hesitated a moment before responding. "It's not what you think."

"Oh yeah, then what is it? You had your son around her, and I know you don't introduce your son to no woman unless it's serious." I could not wait to hear him explain that one.

Thaddeus stood there silent for a moment knowing he was busted before saying, "It's nothing."

"Yeah, right," I sighed.

"Come on we can talk about that later, right now lets tend to you." Thaddeus yanked me off the couch.

"What are you doing Thaddeus?" I questioned as he led me to the steps.

"Don't worry about it just relax," Thaddeus replied, dragging me up the stairs.

When I entered the bathroom there was a tub full of steamy hot water equipped with moisturizing beads and scented candles placed around the tub. If there was one thing I could say about Thaddeus Brown, it was that he knew how to set the mood.

"I want you to relax," Thaddeus whispered in my ear. He then proceeded to undress me.

"Thaddeus what are you doing?" I said. I knew what he was doing and although I wanted him to stop, my body did not have the energy to resist. I was emotionally spent.

"Hush, there is not an inch of your body I have not seen or explored. Or have you forgotten?" Thaddeus whispered.

Once I stood there before him nude, Thaddeus grabbed my hand and led me to the tub. I could not help but melt as the hot water enveloped me as I slid in until the water rested just above my breast.

"I'll be back to get you in twenty minutes," Thaddeus informed me. Then he disappeared.

For twenty minutes all of my problems seemed to melt away. As I lay in the tub I could not help but smile when I heard India Aire's "Good Man" fill the house. I always thought of Thaddeus when I heard that song. It did not matter where I was or what I was doing that song always reminded me of Thaddeus. When India Aire was done serenading him I heard a husky, sultry, female voice spouting poetry amongst the music beyond the bathroom door. From the sounds of it Thaddeus had found my Ursula Rucker CD. I was surprised to know Thaddeus even knew anything about Ursula Rucker. Ursula Rucker was one of those hidden gems that I kind of stumbled upon by accident. Her poetry was always very thought provoking. I probably would have never heard of her, if I had not seen her perform during a business trip at a club in Philadelphia. Thaddeus probably thought a little insightful poetry mixed with melodic rhyme would help soothe my pain. Hearing Ursula recite her poetry somewhat eased my soul but more than anything she made me think—particularly when she crooned, "Lonely can be sweet."

Thaddeus came to retrieve me from my steamy bath exactly when my twenty minutes were up. "Thaddeus, what are you doing?" I asked as he helped me from the tub.

Thaddeus patted me dry ever so slowly, allowing for his touch to linger upon my skin. The feel of his breath upon the nape of my neck and his lasting caress upon my body sent warm currents of pleasure through me.

"I'm only trying to take care of you," Thaddeus insisted.

"It looks like to me as if you're trying to take care of something else." I watched as Thaddeus' reflection in the mirror smiled.

Once I was dry, Thaddeus led me into the bedroom where I quickly noticed the additional candles. Thaddeus placed my towel down on the bed and instructed me to lie face down. I did as I was told without a fuss. I decided to surrender myself to him. Thaddeus straddled my waist and poured warm baby oil down my spine. Before the oil could run off my back and on to the sheets, Thaddeus slowly rubbed the oil into my back. I could not help but moan in satisfaction as the warm oil moisturized my skin. As Ursula weaved her rhymes amongst the rhythm as if she was weaving a beautiful quilt, Thaddeus proceeded to massage my body to the point of titillation. When he was finished with my back, he made me roll over so he could do the same to my front side. When Thaddeus was finished he pulled the covers back and placed me ever so delicately in bed before crawling in bed next to me only to hold my greased body next to his. The baby oil from my body made grease stains upon his shirt.

Yet, he did not seem to mind. We lay there in each other's arms for some time not saying a word. At that moment, I felt as if Thaddeus needed me.

If it were any other night I would have drifted off into a deep unconscious sleep right there in his arms—thoroughly enjoying the air of security and warmth Thaddeus provided me. However, this was not any ordinary night. I could not sleep. Nor could I relax. Although the things Thaddeus had done to make me feel better were sweet, there was one burning question I needed answered. I could feel the question weighing on my heart like a huge boulder attempting to quench the life out of me. I knew it would stay there unless I got up enough courage to ask Thaddeus the question.

"Do you love her?"

"Who are you talking about?"

"Don't play dumb Thaddeus, you know who I'm talking about."

There was silence for a moment. "I can't say I do. I think love is too strong of a word to use for my feelings toward Erin."

"But you do care for her don't you?"

Once again hesitation on his part, "Yes, I do." At times I hated Thaddeus' brutal honesty. Yet, I knew he would always give it to me straight.

I laid there absorbing his response, contemplating if I should ask the next burning question knowing I feared the answer to this question even more. Still, I knew if I did not ask him it would eat away at me.

"Do you love me?" I could not help but hold my breath after those words escaped me to hang out there for him to easily crush asunder upon my heart.

There was no hesitation this time. "Yes, I do. I do love you Ivy."

I breathed a sigh of relief but I knew his admission only made it harder for me to do what I knew had to be done. I suddenly had realized in my dealings with Thaddeus that I had lost my balance. I had got so caught up in Thaddeus. I had neglected the things in life that were important to me. My routine work-out regiment had become sporadic and my butt and thighs showed it. I could not recall the last time I had simply sat at home and listened to music by myself with a glass of wine or read a good book. I had to regain my footing and get back to the things that brought me joy, inner peace, and kept me going before I met Thaddeus. I felt as if I had let Thaddeus and my situation at work cause me to lose my bearings, and I hated it. I have always been one to believe I controlled my fate. I knew as I lay there it was time for me to get back into the driver's seat…at least when it came to me.

I laid there for a moment letting his proclamation of love float out there between us on the scented vanilla fragrance of the candles. I turned to Thaddeus and said, "Thaddeus, I have to ask you to leave. I love you baby, but I cannot let you keep coming in and out of my life like this. I have to move on. I can't sit still while you sort things out. When you do get things right with yourself, feel free to give me a call. However, I cannot guarantee to you that my feelings will be the same or that I will even be here when you call." When I finished saying my piece, I turned my back on Thaddeus so I did not have to see him leave nor could he see the tears in my eyes.

Thaddeus lay there for a moment before getting up and quietly leaving the room. I could not help but sob out loud when I heard the front door slam shut behind him. Just like that it was over. It was one of the hardest things I had ever done in my life because in my heart I truly loved Thaddeus. The only problem was I could not be the only one putting forth the effort.

That following Monday I went into work to find out one associate indeed did make partner, Michael Kennard. Michael was managing partner, Thomas Grimble's "golden boy." So, despite the fact I had brought in more clients and sacrificed my personal life for Grimble & Kline, office politics won out over hard work. At that point I had enough. After having read the memo announcing Michael's promotion, I promptly got on the phone and called my headhunter.

Thaddeus—I Can't Go On Like This

Marcus' warning came to fruition.

On top of that, I now had legal problems stemming from the unresolved issue of abuse concerning my son. Did beating up Willard do me any good?

Looking back on it, I would have to say the brief gratification and the numerous legal problems I created for myself was not worth it. My ordeal with Willard only made matters worse. My lawyer quickly informed me my altercation with Willard and subsequent arrest jeopardized my chances of gaining custody of Little T. For someone who thought he had it all together, the events of that week served as a harsh reminder of how quickly things can fall apart.

I was grateful to Erin for bailing me out. I couldn't help but feel fortunate to have her there for me. Erin's unselfish behavior in helping me out of a jam made me think deeply about my insecurities pertaining to dating white women. It struck me as superficial that I refused to see the inner beauty of Erin by getting caught up by what I saw on the exterior. Erin did not appear to have inhibitions regarding being seen or even sticking her neck out for me. However, I could not say the same.

I was quite sure Erin got the same stares and glares from people as I did when we were together. Or did she? Regardless, Erin acted like it was the individuals doing the staring with the problem—not us. As I contemplated this, something Darius had said struck me. Darius had said, "If the type of woman that makes me happy just so happens to be white, so be it." Now, I knew the reasons why white women appealed to Darius were far different than those that attracted me to Erin. Still there was something about his statement that rung true. Darius did not care what other people thought about him as long as he was happy. Unfortunately, I had a complex. A part of me was hung up on what being seen with a white woman said about me. The perception people, particularly black people, would get of me if they saw me romantically linked to a white woman. I was no sell out, but the stigma of dating a white woman said you were. It explained why it was easier for me to sleep with a white woman rather than romantically date one. However, by harboring such feelings I was not giving Erin a fair chance. She deserved much more, especially after everything she had done for me. Still, I felt like I was betraying black women by even considering taking my relationship with Erin beyond the realm of friendship.

In my household growing up, my family use to congregate together and talk about white people like they had tails. Yet, there I was contemplating a relationship with a white woman. In my family that would be considered sacrilegious. Nevertheless, I realized denying myself the chance to know Erin due to her color possibly negated my chances of ever finding true love. So, I decided as I laid on the couch early Tuesday morning that I was going to open my heart and my mind and accept Erin for who she was regardless of color.

To show Erin my appreciation for bailing me out, I took her out to dinner Tuesday evening. I was hesitant about being seen with her in public but I figured it was time to challenge my insecurities. The few looks and glances we received while out annoyed me a little bit. I even noticed how some white people's demeanor towards me changed. It seemed like I was considered less of a threat since I was with a white woman. An observation that did not go unnoticed. Nonetheless, no matter how hard I tried to shake my inhibitions and focus my attention on Erin, I found a part of me still worried if someone black perceived us as being romantically linked.

Erin only further pointed out the differences between us when her topic of discussion focused on race. "I sure am glad you don't dress like that."

"Like what?"

"Like that guy the waiter just seated two tables behind you," she informed me.

I nonchalantly glanced over my shoulder trying to be inconspicuous. I noticed she was referring to a brotha, who sat two tables back. The brotha gave me the universal head nod, the customary exchange between black men. Similar to me, the brotha had chosen to enjoy his meal in the company of a white woman. Regardless of the company he had chosen for the evening I did not see anything unusual about my man's dress.

"I don't see nothing wrong with the way he is dressed." I returned my attention to my meal.

"Ah come on Thaddeus look at him. He has on baggy jeans. He has these huge diamond earrings in his ears like he is a hip hop mogul or something. I bet you they're fake. Then to top it all off he wears the brim of his baseball cap to the side. The girl he is with looks like white trash. If I was to guess…I would say he probably does not have a job." I was astonished. Erin's entire assumptions about the brotha's character and employment status were based on something as shallow as the way he dressed.

"You know what? You really got some nerve. What do you think people say seeing us sitting here together?" That comment seemed to unnerve her. Erin had not sat back and looked at it from the perspective of someone on the outside looking in.

"And by the way, I dress like that sometimes. Also, a brotha does not have to be a rapper or an athlete to wear diamond earrings. For all you know that brotha could be a vice president at a Fortune 500 company or own his own business for that matter." Erin did not say a word.

"I see now why you and Stacy get along," I blasted.

Following that exchange not much else was said during dinner. It was not until dessert did Erin brave to open her mouth again. "Can I ask you a question? This has been bothering me since the night Stacy offended you and Darius."

I hate to say this, but whenever I hear "Can I ask you a question?" come out of the mouth of a white person, particularly if they have been drinking I automatically brace myself. I had plenty of white colleagues at work on several occasions suddenly get the courage while under the influence to ask me questions pertaining to race as if I had suddenly been appointed the spokesman for Black America. Every single time without fail they began their idiotic question in the same fashion as Erin did that night.

"That depends on what you are about to ask me," I replied sternly. I really did not want any more bullshit comments or questions about race. After Erin's comment about the brotha two tables back, I had begun to drink heavily in hopes of helping me loosen up.

As soon as Erin said, "Why is race such a touchy subject with black people?" I immediately felt my buzz from the alcohol start to wear off.

Erin noticed the scowl that graced my face for she quickly added, "I'm not saying what Stacy said was appropriate. I'm just curious to know why if anyone says anything about race around black people, they're always up in arms?"

Although the answer to such a question seemed obvious to me, I realized it was not so clear to her. Not until I placed myself in Erin shoes did I realize she did not see the world from the same vantage point as I did. So, there was a possibility the desire inside Erin to comprehend was genuine. In some weird way, I was touched by her need to try and understand me.

So, I chose to put my anger in check and tried to answer her question. "The black community is constantly reminded daily of the color of our skin. When we are followed around in department stores. When we are driving our cars. Black people are constantly reminded of our color. So being constantly reminded of what we look like and at times knowing some people use the color of our skin against us has conditioned black people to be sensitive to matters of race. Do you understand?" I knew it was stupid of me to ask her if she understood. There was no way she could truly understand unless she stood in my shoes.

"I guess so." Erin paused for a moment, allowing what I said to sink in before continuing, "There is something you said that I have always been curious about."

"And what's that?"

"This 'black community.' I hear about this 'black community' all the time. From what I can see black people have thoroughly integrated into society. Yet, there is always this talk about the 'black community' from black leaders.

"Not only is there always talk about the 'black community,' but black people always act like they are trying to alienate or separate themselves from the rest of society by creating their own slang, or style of dress. I just don't understand why it is so hard for African Americans to assimilate to American culture. A good example could be the way you acted on the boat cruise Friday night. You must admit you were very stand-offish."

Erin had a point. I was not the most approachable guy on the boat. Also, her observations in regards to the term "black community" were not too far off base. However, a few things she said I did not necessarily agree with so I decided to challenge her.

"What do you mean assimilate?"

"You know assimilate; conform to the morals of the dominant culture in this country."

"What is exactly the dominant culture in America? As far as I can tell that is pretty hard to define. American society consists of so many different flavors. We have a smidgen of Italian, a dash of Irish, a pinch of Asian American, a teaspoon of African American and a cup of Latin American. So, I ask you once again.... Out of all these different cultures and ethnic groups that make up America, which one constitutes the dominant culture?" I snapped.

Once again Erin was silent.

"Hard to answer isn't it. American culture borrows something from every ethnic group or culture that has populated this land. It is hard to sit back and point at one ethnic group or race and say that's the dominant culture," I stated. "Now your observation about the so called, 'black community' is not far from the truth. The quote-unquote 'black community' no longer exists. It has become nothing more than a term used to refer to Black America. The 'black community' is just as diverse, economically and ideologically as American society itself but that might be hard for you to comprehend."

"Why do you always say that?"

"Because of such statements as 'that guy must not have a job due to the way he dresses.' Besides, there are just going to be certain things you're not going to understand. Just like there are certain things about white people I will never get."

"Maybe if you just try me, instead of assuming all the time I will not understand. You might be surprised."

"Maybe you're right. Look, I did not ask you out tonight so we could discuss race relations in America. I wanted us to enjoy a wonderful evening together."

Erin grew silent.

I sensed she was frustrated and confused. Instead of arguing her point further I assumed she decided it was best to simply change the subject. I was glad she did. I wanted to keep the evening festive and if we had continued on with the topic of race in America, I doubt the evening would have ended on a pleasant note. Although it took me a while to ease back into the groove of things, I managed to return to my level of semi-comfort I had enjoyed prior to our conversation. I realized once I let myself relax and see beyond other people's perception of Erin and I together, I found out I really enjoyed Erin's company.

After dinner Erin and I returned to my place. By that time I was late in picking Little T up from Saundra's. Saundra had a son close to Little T's age and she had been hounding me about getting the two of them together, so I took her up on her offer. I really could not ask Marcus and Lisa to watch my son again after what happened Monday night. Lisa was Ivy's friend and I had gotten the impression my arrival to Lisa and Marcus' house with Erin in the car did not sit well with Lisa. I surely was not going to let Little T spend time with his mother. Besides, I had my doubts about Stephanie and her claim she had ended her relationship with Willard.

Even though my intentions to pick Little T up at my agreed upon time was genuine I became sidetracked by Erin's insistence we take a late night dip in the pool. At first I thought she was joking until she got poolside and started to strip. Initially, I was surprised but after a while I could not help but admire her figure. Erin had nice, full, breast. She sported a navel ring and an ornamental tattoo on the small of her back. I found both items rather sexy. Her legs were long, sleek and muscular. I will not lie, her derriere was not like a sistahs', yet it was one that was distinctly all her own. However, Erin's heart shaped booty did exhibit some of it's own admirable qualities.

Now, I had no intentions of joining Erin in the pool. However, her persistent taunting played on my ego, so I could not let her challenge slide. I confess at first I was more than a little paranoid someone would see us. Yet when Erin beckoned me towards her once I was in the pool, I no longer cared who saw us. I could not help but become aroused by the way Erin pulled me in close to her and pressed her body firmly against mine. The feel of her supple lips upon my skin eased my inhibitions. When it was evident neither one of us could resist anymore, Erin wrapped her legs around my waist and gently eased me inside of her.

"Wait, we need protection," I proclaimed.

Erin reassured me she was on the pill. That was good enough for me because it would have been hard for me to stop at that point. I had gotten caught up in the moment.

After leaving the pool Erin and I went up to my condo. I had promised Saundra I would pick Thaddeus up around nine, however, I was now an hour late. When we got up to my condo I wanted to make sure I gave Erin the money she spent bailing me out. I did not want her to think I was trying to take advantage of her. After giving her a towel to dry herself off I paid Erin back the money. She seemed not only grateful but also surprised.

Once out of the shower I had planned on rushing over to Saundra's to pick up Little T, yet, it seemed Erin had plans of her own judging by her naked frame laying on my dinning room table. She enticed me to stay for dessert.

What could I do other than pull up a chair?

I remember sitting down in between Erin's legs and examining the moles that dotted the inner part of her thighs. Some of the moles were blacker than me, while others were a shade of brown or even pink. As my hand gently caressed her thigh I could not help but notice the contrast of our skin. I wondered when our bodies met did the lines between black and white blur and meld together to the point the color of our skin no longer mattered. Or even in something as intimate as love did the color of our skin stand in stark contrast. It was a perplexing thought, however, at that moment I did not let it consume me for Erin's rich, musky, aroma—beckoned me to take a taste. Just the smell of her love drove me to the point where my body yearned for her. Yet, I intended to enjoy the dessert she had so painstakingly took her time to prepare. It was only right I enjoyed my sundae.

The skinny-dipping in the pool, the navel ring and tattoo as well as the whipped cream sundae had changed my perception of Erin. I had originally thought Erin to be conservative, yet that night I saw a wild side to Erin I liked.

By the time I got to Saundra's house to pick up Little T it was eleven fifteen. I could sense Saundra was a little perturbed I did not call to inform her I was going to be late. I apologized for my tardiness before retrieving Little T and leaving.

I rushed Erin out of the condo early Wednesday morning before Little T woke up for daycare. School had adjourned for the summer, so Little T spent his summer days frolicking with other children at a nearby daycare. After getting Little T dressed and fed I realized as I drove him to daycare that an explanation was in order pertaining to my legal woes when my son asked, "Dad are you going to jail?"

"No…Why do you ask me that?" I replied. I was curious to know what made him ask such a question.

I could see the deep concern on Little T's face when he said, "I heard you talking on the phone about beating up Mama's boyfriend, Willard."

I paused for a moment. No matter how hard I tried to hide things from my son he always managed to figure it out. "Yes, son there is a possibility I could go to jail. What I did was wrong. I should not have beat up your mama's boyfriend. There are other ways to settle things instead of fighting. Since, I chose a way that is unacceptable I must take responsibility for my actions. That is what it means to be a man. A man takes responsibilities for his actions."

"That is why you beat up Willard, huh, because he was not a man. He hit a woman and no man should hit a woman…. That's what you told me," Little T exclaimed.

"That is right son but most important of all—no man should hit a child…particularly mine. I am willing to take responsibility for what I did because you are my son and it is my undying duty to protect you and make sure no harm comes to you."

"Even if it means you might go to jail?" Little T said in amazement.

"Even if it means I have to go to jail."

Little T paused for a moment. He seemed to take in what I had said before looking at me with tears in his eyes, "Dad, I don't want you to go to jail."

I put my hand on my son's head and said, "Don't worry son, I'm not going no where."

"What about Mama? Is Mama going to jail?"

I thought about what Little T was asking me and for a moment I did not know how to answer him. I don't know why but the only answer I could come up with was, "I hope not, Thaddeus. I hope not."

My response seemed to lift his spirits somewhat because he suddenly had the courage to ask his next question. "Dad who is that white woman who keeps sneaking out of the house in the morning?" When he said that I could not help but laugh.

For two days I had been trying to make sure Little T did not happen to see Erin leaving the condo. I often woke Erin up an hour before I went in Little T's room and got him ready for daycare. Yet, it was apparent my attempts at concealing Erin from him did not work.

"She is a friend of mine."

"What is her name?" he questioned.

"Her name is Erin."

"Is she going to be my new mommy?"

"No. What made you ask that question?" I should not have been surprised as to why Little T would ask such a question but I was.

"My friend, Dougie, said when people's mom and dad break up the kids get new mommies and daddies."

"That is what Dougie said?"

"Yeah." It was obvious by the look of curiosity on Little T's face he sought an answer to his question.

"Well, Dougie is right. Sometimes when kid's parents break up they do get a new mom and dad. It depends."

"On what?"

"Excuse me?"

"On what? What does it depend on?" my son clarified.

"Whether or not if that kid's mom or dad fall in love again."

Little T paused for a moment as if he was soaking in my words. "Do you love Erin?"

"I like Erin but I don't love her. Yet, who is to say I will not love her later on."

Once again, Little T appeared to be deep in thought. "Do you love Ivy?"

It took me a second to answer him. It amazed me how such tough questions could come out of the mouth of a five year old. "Yes, I do."

"Then why are you not with her?" he asked.

I could not help but ask myself the same question. Little T made it sound so simple. "I wish it was that easy, son. Just because two people love each other it does not always mean they should be together. Sometimes its hard for people to be together."

"Like you and Mama, huh?"

The ability for my son to grasp what I told him astounded me. "Yeah, just like me and your mom."

"But you still love Mama. Don't you?" My son looked at me with knowing eyes.

"I do…. I do still love your mother. However, it is a different kind of love."

Once again my son became quiet as if he was pondering what I said. "Do you think you will ever love Mama like you did before?"

"I don't know. It's possible," I stated.

"I hope so. I want you to come back home and live with us." In that instant I realized I had been so preoccupied dealing with my pain from Stephanie and my divorce that I failed to see how our separation had affected Little T. I could not help but look at my son and see the little boy hiding in his bedroom gazing out the window at the stars in search of his father.

My conversation with Little T really got me thinking. It made me think about Erin, Ivy and most importantly Stephanie. After I dropped Little T off at daycare I headed to work. Although, Stephanie and I had our problems I did not want to see Little T lose his mother due to her poor judgment in men. So I placed a call to Mr. Patterson at Child Protective Services to find out if there was a way I could help Stephanie's cause by acting on her behalf. Of course, my request caught Mr. Patterson off guard. He promptly made it clear to me that by saying or writing anything on Stephanie's behalf pretty much ended my chances of gaining full custody of my son. I understood the ramifications of writing a letter, yet I decided I had to do what was best for my son. Before hanging up the phone Mr. Patterson informed me despite my attempt to help Stephanie he would still need to interview Little T soon in order to determine if Stephanie was a willing participant in his abuse. I assured Mr. Patterson I would bring Little T by the following Thursday as promised. After hanging up the phone with Mr. Patterson I sent him an email hoping it would clear Stephanie's name.

That evening Erin came by. At first, I was a little reluctant about Little T meeting Erin, however, I saw no reason to continue to hide her from him. Fortunately their initial encounter went well, of course, that was before I got Ivy's call. Ivy's phone call caught me totally by surprise. I think I made more of the conversation than I needed to by lowering my voice and slinking between rooms, such behavior only drew attention to myself. Once I got off the phone the atmosphere between Erin and I had changed. What once had been pleasant was now subdued and tense. I could feel it as soon as I hung up the phone. I knew once I put Little T to bed I would have some explaining to do.

So, after I grudgingly put my son to bed I went into the living room fully expecting an argument. When Erin told me that she had found the picture of

Ivy and noticed my behavior on the phone there was nothing I could say. I expected her to be hurt but I did not expect her to leave. That was totally unexpected. I must have sat there for half an hour after she left trying to figure out what had just transpired.

Thursday of that week, I took Thaddeus in to see Mr. Patterson as arranged. He spent about an hour interviewing Little T while I waited. When Mr. Patterson finished, he informed me he had gotten my email regarding Stephanie and he would take it into consideration when the time came. He also informed me that I should be receiving the findings from the investigation within the following week as long as Little T did not provide him with any new information. That worked out conveniently because the custody hearing took place two weeks from that Thursday. I was quite certain if Mr. Patterson exonerated Stephanie from any wrong doing in his investigation I would be denied full custody of Little T.

For the remainder of that Thursday, I spent time with my son. I had grown accustomed to having Little T around and I knew in two weeks things between us could possibly return back to the way it had been before the whole incident with Willard took place. So, I did my best to try and soak up as much of our time together as possible.

Friday was the day of my court appearance. Of course, Marcus represented me. Who else would have my best interest at heart other than my best friend? I also hope it helped that Marcus was an acquaintance of the assistant prosecuting attorney. Marcus had gone to law school with her. Marcus was able to get the obstruction of justice charges against him and Darius dropped due to a lack of evidence. People at the bar who had witnessed the brawl between Willard and I corroborated Darius and Marcus's story that they were only trying to break up the fight. Although, I did see Marcus sneak in a kick while Willard was on the ground. Despite his ability to get his and Darius' charges dismissed, Marcus was having a tough time making my charges disappear.

Marcus attempted to get the charges against me dismissed on a self-defense plea but the prosecuting attorney did not buy that argument. The fact I had discovered Little T was being physically abused by the same gentleman I had the confrontation with at Bunkers did not lend much credibility to that argument. However, fortunately for me the woman Willard was talking to at the time I approached him in the bar confirmed to the police that Willard threw the first punch. Besides that woman's testimony...I had two other factors working in my favor—Willard's police record of violent behavior and the fact the injuries he sustained during our altercation were not serious. In the end, after negotiating with the prosecution, Marcus was able to get the aggravated battery reduced to misdemeanor battery in which case the prosecution would recommend to the judge to suspend the one-year jail sentence as long as I stayed out of trouble for a year, paid a one thousand dollar fine and serve thirty-two hours community service.

So showing up in court that Friday was nothing more than a formality. I simply showed up and pleaded guilty to the lesser charge. Of course, the thousand dollar fine set me back a bit financially and not to mention I had the threat of jail hanging over my head for a year. Still, it was a price I was willing to pay in order to maintain my freedom. Originally, I had feared pleading guilty to the battery charge would affect my chances of landing the job with Chicago National, however Marcus assured me it would not affect my employment opportunities because it was classified as a misdemeanor. Regardless of the outcome, I was glad I had a friend in the legal profession. More importantly, I was happy to have the whole ordeal behind me.

The fellas and I decided we wanted to go out and blow of some steam that Friday. It had been a stressful week for me—going to jail and appearing in court. I pleaded with Saundra to watch Little T again. This time I assured her I would pick him up on time. Saundra had began to realize her eagerness to watch Little T did not equate to the possibility of a budding romance between me and her. So in such case, she began to make her babysitting services less available to me. The last thing I needed at that time was another woman in my life.

My intentions of hanging out with Darius and Marcus got sidetracked when I called Ivy to congratulate her on making partner. When I called her home and got no response I did not think much of it. I assumed she was out celebrating with her girlfriends.

Yet, when I called Marcus to find out what time the three of us was meeting up and he asked me, "Have you talked to Ivy today?" I suspected something was wrong.

"No. Why?"

Marcus quickly informed me that Lisa had been trying to contact Ivy to no avail. Upon hanging up the phone with Marcus I immediately tried calling Ivy again. Ivy had worked real hard to become partner. I knew if she did get the promotion she would be devastated. I called Ivy's house several times but I still got no answer. Around nine o'clock I decided to hell with calling and simply drove out to her place. I was beginning to get worried.

The first thing that caught my attention when I pulled up into Ivy's driveway was the fact that all the lights were off. As I made my way to the door I noticed a glimmer of light inside that seemed to come from a television set or a lamp. The first time I rung the doorbell and got no response, I became concerned. I did not think Ivy would become suicidal if she did not get the promotion, still after calling several times to no avail and to not have her answer the door I will admit the thought began to creep into my mind. Not until I rung the doorbell a second time did Ivy finally answer the door. By the attitude she greeted me with I was assured she did not make partner. If the manner in which she answered the door was not enough, Ivy made her displeasure to my un-announced visit very clear by screaming, "What are you doing here?"

After some coaxing, Ivy allowed me inside to use the phone. I called Marcus and told him to tell Lisa that Ivy was okay. After hanging up the phone I realized I could not leave Ivy there in that state of mind. So, I decided to use a technique I used on Stephanie whenever she was depressed or stressed out. It took a little effort on my part to get Ivy to participate but eventually she succumbed. I gathered up as many candles as I could find, ran a hot steaming bath and grabbed Ivy's container of baby oil. After getting Ivy upstairs and into the tub, the last thing I needed to do was put some music on to soothe her even more. Of course, I popped in India Aire's *Voyage to India* CD and programmed in track fourteen. While India Aire's "Good Man" serenaded me I rummaged through Ivy's CD collection looking for Stevie Wonder's *Songs in the Key of Life*. Instead, I was pleasantly surprised to stumble upon Ursula Rucker's CD, *Silver or Lead*, amongst Ivy's CDs. Ursula Rucker was a spoken work artist Marcus had hipped me to. Rucker's sultry rhymes always managed to nourish the soul. She always had something deep to say.

While Ursula Rucker's luminescent voice performed her medley of rhythmic word play amongst the various rhythms, I quickly warmed up the baby oil I had taken from Ivy's bathroom on the stove. I did not let it rest on the burner for too long because I did not want the oil to be scalding hot—just lukewarm. Once the baby oil was nice and warm I gathered any remaining candles I could find and relocated them in Ivy's bedroom. When everything was in place I retrieved Ivy from her bath. Ivy's beautiful body was a sight for sore eyes. I patted her body dry, letting my hands linger upon her caramel frame. It felt good to touch Ivy again. When she was dry I lead her by the hand into the bedroom where the baby oil and candles waited.

When she had made herself comfortable on the bed I poured a little baby oil down the crease of her back and watched as it overflowed down her sides and pooled at the small of her back. I could not help but admire Ivy's beautiful body beneath me. I gently kneaded the oil into her moist skin starting my journey at the nape of her neck and moving down her back ever so slowly in a rhythmic motion. I enjoyed the silky feel of Ivy's skin against the palms of my hands as they glided effortlessly over her body. I massaged Ivy's back down to the point where those two nice round mounds of flesh rose majestically from her backside. I gently worked the oil into the ripe, fleshy, hills that made up Ivy's beautiful posterior—giving each half the special attention and adulation it rightfully deserved.

From Ivy's rear end I worked my way down her thighs, to the back of her knees and down to her feet. When I was finished with Ivy's backside I requested that she turn over so I could show the other side of her body the same amount of attention. As I had done in massaging Ivy's back I started at the base of her neck and slowly worked my way down to the cleft that separated her chest into two supple breasts. I gently accentuated each breast with the soft shimmer of baby oil before traveling down her bosoms' wayward side. I watched as goose bumps sprouted upon her skin in random rolling waves like the currents of the sea. I smiled with satisfaction as Ivy's body quivered beneath me from the heat generated from my touch.

I continued on my quest down Ivy's abdomen past her navel to the downy thicket of hair that led to her treasure cove. I took particularly extra care in oiling and massaging the inner part of her thighs, leaving behind a slick layer of baby oil. From Ivy's thighs I moved to her knees and once again to her feet.

When I was finished, I laid there next to Ivy suddenly wondering what the hell was I doing? I had taken what had started out as genuine concern for Ivy's well-being and turned it into an erotic interlude. That was not my intentions. It was not like I was sorry for what transpired between us nor was I sorry to be lying there next to her in bed. I just did not want to give Ivy the impression that was the reason I had came over in the first place. I found it hard to fathom that only three days prior I was having sex with Erin in my condominium pool and all of a sudden I was at Ivy's house oiling her down.

Everything started to get real confusing.

The fantasy of juggling two women at the same time was starting to wear thin. Everything in my life was becoming way too complicated—my relationship with Erin, Ivy and even Stephanie was becoming jumbled together. Making it hard for me to tell one relationship from the next. Then on top of all that there was the issue of abuse pertaining to Little T. I was beginning to find it hard to think clearly. I don't know if I told Ivy I loved her that night because that was how I felt or if I was simply saying the words because I knew that was what she wanted to hear. That is why; when she asked me to leave I did not argue. I simply got up and left.

I spent the remainder of that tumultuous week with my son. I avoided contact with both Ivy and Erin because I really needed time to myself to think minus the distractions. My grand scheme of just dating Erin and Ivy had blown up in my face due to the fact feelings had gotten involved—particularly mine. Once that happened it did not matter how honest I was, the emotional ties that bind were forged. When those feelings were established, it became complicated and emotionally draining to separate myself from them.

It was difficult for me to be like Darius and juggle several women at the same time and remain emotionally detached. It was because of emotions I found myself in the predicament Ivy and Erin had suddenly forced upon me. Still, being by myself was not all that bad. It allowed for me to sort out my feelings and ultimately confront the ghosts from my past and present.

The Little Things

Erin—Expect the Unexpected

When I walked out of Thaddeus' condo that night I had no intentions of being the first one to initiate contact between Thaddeus and I. I decided if Thaddeus and I were going to pursue a relationship it was going to be on my terms. I had gone almost a month and a half without talking to Thaddeus before I suddenly found myself forced to. I might have been able to go without speaking to Thaddeus ever again if I had not missed my period. I actually did not miss my cycle. It was just that it did not behave normally. Instead of a steady flow, all I got was three days of spotting. It caught my attention immediately. A woman knows her body, and I knew for me that was not normal. Still, despite this being out of the norm I did not panic nor contemplate the unthinkable. So, I let it go figuring everything would be back to normal next month. I figured maybe it was some side effect to the new medication I was taking to combat my allergies. It was three weeks after that when I started feeling ill that I realized I was not suffering from any side effect.

The possibility I was pregnant lurked in the back of my mind, yet I refused to believe that could be the case. I took the pill religiously. However, I did occasionally slack off when Brian and I split up. Still, I swore that I had taken my pill before sleeping with Thaddeus. Then it hit me. I had been in such a rush trying to get to work the morning I bailed him out of jail as well as the following Wednesday morning after having sex with him the night before in his condominium pool I forgot to take the pill on both occasions. I checked my packet of birth control pills and realized I indeed had two extra pills. Upon the realization of this oversight my heart fell to my stomach.

I sat in my room and sulked for hours before deciding I needed to make sure I was indeed pregnant. So, I drove down to the drugstore and picked up a home pregnancy test before rushing back home to lock myself in the bathroom and await the results. I practically broke down in tears when the little window on the applicator displayed a positive sign. Despite the obvious, I did not want to believe it. I was certain I did not perform the test right or else the damn thing was broke. So, I rushed back to the drugstore and bought the three other brands of home pregnancy tests they had in stock. However, in the end it did not matter who manufactured it or which test I used each pregnancy test said the same thing…positive. There was no question at that point I was pregnant.

When Belinda came home and knocked on the bathroom door I was an emotional wreck. "Erin are you okay?" she asked.

My muffled sobs were all she received in the way of a response. After calling out to me a second time and once again getting no answer Belinda decided not to wait any longer and barged into the bathroom.

"Erin are you all right?" Belinda asked. She quickly noticed the empty pregnancy boxes strewn about the bathroom floor. Once again I said nothing. I was quite sure she could put two and two together.

"Are you—," she gasped. Belinda paused long enough to notice the numerous applicators resting on the bathroom sink.

"Yes." I cried.

"Is it Thaddeus'?" she questioned. Belinda knelt down on to the floor next to me.

"Yeah." I sobbed.

The only response Belinda could muster was, "Whoa."

It took Belinda a while, but she eventually was able to get me to calm down. She had managed to get me off the bathroom floor and into my bedroom where we sat on my bed contemplating my next move.

"Well, you definitely have to tell him," insisted Belinda.

"Not yet."

"What do you mean not yet? When do you plan on telling him? When you are about to go into labor?" Belinda bellowed.

"Please Belinda, I really don't need you lecturing to me right now. I'll tell him when I'm ready. I want to go to the doctor first to make sure I am indeed pregnant."

"What…the multiple home pregnancy tests were not enough?" Belinda replied, sarcastically.

"No, they were not!" I was already emotional. Belinda's nagging questions was not helping the situation. I took a deep breath in hopes of calming myself down.

"If I'm going to go to Thaddeus and tell him he is the father of our child I want to be absolutely certain I am pregnant. The only way that is going to happen is if I go see my gynecologist," I proclaimed.

"I understand." Belinda paused for a moment before looking me in the eyes and asking, "And if she says you are…then what?"

The only response I could muster was "I'll cross that bridge when I get there."

I made an appointment with my gynecologist as planned. The only problem was that I had to wait an additional week because my gynnie informed me they did not test a person unless their menstrual cycle was at least six weeks late. That week was the most agonizing week of my life. I remember sitting at home trying to decide if I wanted to keep the child or not. Belinda was against abortion, so some times after talking with her I thought I might want to keep the baby. Yet, after thinking about how hard it would be raising a child on my own and not to mention the shock and possible shame it would bring to my family I had second thoughts. I could just see the expression on my parent's face when I told them I was pregnant with Thaddeus' baby. I knew for a fact my father would freak out. Even still, I found it hard to consider terminating the pregnancy.

By the time I went to the gynecologist, I was still unclear as to what it was I wanted to do. So when she confirmed what the home pregnancy tests had already told me, I fell further into depression not to mention confusion. My gynecologist understood my uncertainty and assured me, she would do what ever she could to recommend an excellent clinic if I chose to end my pregnancy.

I had brought Belinda to the clinic with me for moral support, which in all honesty I'm glad I did. I found Belinda's presence comforting and by her simply telling me that she would stand by me no matter what I decided to do made me feel a little bit better. Nevertheless, I still dreaded having to tell Thaddeus. Yet, now that my gynnie had confirmed my suspicions I could not put off telling Thaddeus any longer. It took plenty of coaching from Belinda, but I eventually got up the nerve to call him.

I already knew Thaddeus was going to accuse me of lying to him. In the pool that night at his complex I had swore to him I was on the pill. Yet, here I was about to tell him I was pregnant. I knew he would probably think I was attempting to trap him. Of course, none of that was true. However, regardless of what Thaddeus thought, we had a situation that we now needed to deal with in one way or another—I only prayed we could handle the matter like civil adults. I called Thaddeus when I was certain he would be home.

"Hello?" Thaddeus said into the telephone. Thaddeus was quick to answer the phone. I figured he did not want the ringing of the telephone to wake up Thaddeus Jr.

"Hi Thaddeus, it's me Erin." I was nervous.

"Oh hey! What's going on? Longtime no hear. I thought I was never going to hear from you again," Thaddeus claimed. He seemed surprised to hear from me. I knew he would soon regret I had even called.

"Yeah, I thought it was best I gave you your space."

"That doesn't mean you have to become a complete stranger." It was funny Thaddeus should say such a thing since I did not see him rushing to the phone to call me.

"Well, I thought giving us a break would be the best thing for the both of us," I stated.

"I understand," Thaddeus sighed.

"Thaddeus, I called you because we need to talk." I reluctantly got to the point.

"What about?" I could sense by the tone in his voice he was searching to find out what was so pressing it warranted a telephone conversation after more than a month of silence.

Despite the urge for me to say "oh nothing" I knew I had to tell him. There was no way I could come that far and set him up without going all the way. So, I took a deep breath and said, "I'm pregnant."

What came next was silence. I mean complete silence. I had expected some outcry of rage or confusion but what I got was nothing. It had grown so eerily quiet on the other end of the phone I wondered if Thaddeus had hung up. "Thaddeus are you still there?"

"Yep." His response was short and curt. I was certain that my announcement did not go over well.

"Is that all you have to say…simply yep?" I demanded. I wanted to know how he felt, how he thought we should handle this. Instead, all he could say was "Yep."

"What do you want me to say?" Thaddeus snapped. "I can only assume by you calling me and telling me this Erin is that you're implying it is mine."

"Do you think so?" I said, cynically. I could no longer control myself. "Who the hell else's would it be?" I yelled.

"I don't know possibly your ex-boyfriend's? You're the one who told me you guys are constantly breaking up and getting back together. Hell, I haven't seen your ass in over a month!" I could not believe Thaddeus had the audacity to say such a thing. He was being so cold.

"I can't believe you said that. I have not seen Brian since you and I started dating and you know that." There was no need to tell him Brian had dropped by the apartment. That was irrelevant.

"I don't know anything! How am I suppose to know if you've seen your ex-boyfriend or not?"

"Because I told you!" I cried.

"People say a lot of things. Just because they say them does not make them true. Take for example you telling me you was on the pill," Thaddeus quipped.

There it was, just as I had predicted. Thaddeus was throwing my words right back in my face. In all honesty he had every right to. I did tell him I was on the pill only to turn around and tell him six weeks later that in actuality I had forgotten to take the pill those two particular days I stayed at his condo.

"Whether you believe me or not I forgot to take the pill the mornings I stayed the night at your place."

"How convenient!" Thaddeus barked. I could tell by that remark that he did not believe me.

"I know you probably think I am trying to trap you and that I lied to you about taking the pill—"

"If the shoe fits, then wear it," Thaddeus interrupted.

I ignored Thaddeus' last comment. "And I know I could probably talk until I am blue in the face trying to convince you that was not the case. However, you can believe what you want to believe. So, I'm not going to try. Nonetheless, that does not negate the fact we have a situation here that needs to be addressed."

There was a brief moment of silence before Thaddeus said, "What is there to discuss? Erin, you are going to basically do what you want to do."

"What do you mean by that?" I demanded to know.

"What I mean is, if you want to keep the baby then you'll keep it. If you don't want it then you wont keep it."

"So, you don't want to have any say in this at all?"

"Why Erin? It would not matter what I had to say. No matter what I say, you're going to do what you want to do."

"Fine, if that is how you feel!" I screamed. I had heard enough so I hung up the phone. I sat in my room and cried the rest of the night. Belinda had come by my room a couple of times to check on me and I assured her I was fine. Realizing I needed time alone, she gave me my space.

For two days I did not speak to Thaddeus. For two days, I could have cared less if Thaddeus Brown was dead or alive. Within those two days I got in touch with my gynecologist and she referred me to a clinic. I would have made it through those two days without any problem if Thaddeus had not called me the evening before I was scheduled to go in and have the abortion performed. Belinda had gone out with Darius that evening so I had lost the convenience of having someone screen my phone calls.

"Hello?" I spouted into the phone.

"Hi, Erin." I knew it was Thaddeus the moment he said "hi."

"What do you want?" I was intent to be just as cold and callous with Thaddeus as he had been with me.

"I want to apologize...that was not me. I...I just do not know what to think. I want to do whatever you want to do. If you want to keep the child then lets keep it. If you choose to have an abortion then I'm there for you."

I was glad to hear from Thaddeus, not to mention happy that he had come to his senses. However, I was not going to let him off the hook that easy. "You're a little too late. I've already made an appointment to have this taken care of," I told him.

"Are you sure this is what you want to do? What about how I feel about everything?" Thaddeus questioned.

"Yes, I am sure. I gave you the chance to voice your opinion two days ago and you basically treated me like shit."

Even though I had told Thaddeus I was certain I wanted to go through with the abortion, in all honesty I wasn't so certain it was exactly what I wanted to do. However, at that point I had made up in my mind that no matter what inner turmoil I was feeling I was going through with the procedure. My inner turmoil did not matter. Deep down, I knew that it was best I aborted the child.

"Where," Thaddeus asked. He sounded resigned to let me have my way.

"The Women's Clinic in the Medical Arts Building in downtown Minneapolis. Why do you care?"

"Because I'm going with you."

"There is no need for that. Belinda is going with me." Not only was Belinda going for moral support, but also because the clinic required that I have a ride home once the procedure was complete.

"Well, I guess I will be there too."

"Thaddeus, you do not need to do anything you do not want to do. I'm touched by you calling and apologizing but you don't need to act as if you genuinely care."

"After the way I acted, I guess I deserved that. Nevertheless, I am serious Erin. I want to go. What time is your appointment tomorrow?"

"Thaddeus please," I sighed. I was not sure I really wanted Thaddeus present.

"Erin that is my baby too, and I am just as much entitled to be there as you."

I was prepared to rebut but hesitated when I realized he was right. "It's at eleven thirty. Don't let me down."

"I will meet you in front of the building at eleven fifteen," Thaddeus assured me.

"I swear Thaddeus, you better be there," I warned.

"Don't worry I'll be there." And with that said I hung up the phone.

I was already confused as to whether I truly wanted to go through with the abortion and hearing Thaddeus talk only made me more confused. I have to say that was one of the longest nights of my life. I had never been pregnant before. I had plenty of scares, but never had I been honest to God pregnant. I can remember plenty of times I gave other women "so called" advice by recommending they terminate a pregnancy since it was unexpected like there was a right time to have a child. I realized that it is a lot harder to take your own advice when the tables are turned.

Still, when I pondered bringing a child into the world without a father living in the same household I could not help but think of the hardship both the child and I would be forced to endure because I chose to go it alone. I knew no matter if I had Thaddeus' child or not, the chances of Thaddeus and I being together where slim. Besides, I had never intended nor envisioned having a child without having the ideal nuclear family—a mother, father and two kids. Besides, my parents would be extremely disappointed in me.

When I walked to the Medical Arts Building the following morning I found Thaddeus standing out front as promised. I had told Belinda that she was no longer needed since Thaddeus was coming along. Of course, Belinda thought it was stupid of me to trust Thaddeus especially after the way he treated me on the phone. Yet, deep down I knew Thaddeus would not desert me. Thaddeus tended to be a man of his word.

The first thing Thaddeus said to me the morning of the procedure when I walked up to him was "Are you sure you want to go through with this?" I simply nodded my head.

I was scared and I think it showed. Thaddeus held my hand and looked at me earnestly. I avoided his gaze for I knew if I looked into his eyes I would lose my will and never make it to the clinic. So, I held Thaddeus' hand and walked inside the Medical Arts Building.

The fact I was embarking on something I really knew nothing about really frightened me. When Thaddeus and I arrived at the clinic this uneasiness only grew. I could sense Thaddeus was uncomfortable as well. Neither one of us spoke as we sat in the waiting room. Instead, I chose to fill out the necessary paperwork in silence. Judging by the attire of many of the women whom occupied the waiting area it was clear to me that many of them worked downtown. There were expecting mothers there for their monthly checkups and other women there for the same reason as myself. This was quite transparent in the forced smiles on their faces trying to mask a look of shame and guilt. I am quite certain my facial expression was the same. I am confident the same guilt and fear stricken look that graced their faces was mirrored in mine.

When they called my name I gave Thaddeus' hand a squeeze before getting up. He attempted to ease my fears by assuring me, "I'll be here when you get back."

I could not stop the tears that streamed down my face as I made my way back towards the room. I continuously asked myself was I doing the right thing? Was I making a mistake? By the time I got to the room and saw the sanitized examination table with the stirrups I found myself tormented by what I was about to do. The sight of that table only made my indecision worse. The nurse had me take a seat while she explained to me the procedure and quizzed me on whether I was certain I wanted to go through with it. I was under the impression if I did not calm down soon the nurse was going to recommend I come back another time. I could not endure the agony of spending several more days contemplating my decision. So, I managed to assure the nurse I had thought long and hard about what I was about to do and I indeed wished to proceed. Once feeling confident I made the decision to have an abortion on my own volition, the nurse told me I needed to remove my clothes and put on a smock before she left the room.

It took a while but I ultimately calmed down long enough to take off my clothes and put on the smock as the nurse had instructed. After a while the nurse poked her head into the room to see if I was ready. Upon seeing me sitting on the examination table, she darted back out just as fast as she had darted in. Eventually the doctor arrived accompanied by the same nurse. The doctor was a female, which made me feel a little bit more comfortable. Her name was

Dr. Winter. No matter how hard I want to forget that woman's name I simply can't. Dr. Winter had a very pleasant bedside manner, which allowed me to relax a bit. When the doctor had finished telling me what to expect, she prepped me for the operation and before I knew it they had began.

There was no turning back after that point.

Throughout the course of the procedure I felt degraded. The operation was the most humiliating thing I have ever experienced in my life. No matter how much I tried, I couldn't stop the tears. I could feel my uterus cramping from the suction tube inserted inside of me, vacuuming out my womb. I tried to blank out—I tried to think of something else. I tried every tactic I could to take my mind off what the gynecologist was doing to me. Yet, no matter how hard I tried I could not deny the fact I was killing my baby. I was denying my child a life before it even had a chance to develop.

The whole procedure took about an hour. This included the time they allowed for me to rest in the recovery room afterwards. Before leaving the clinic that day, a nurse gave me instructions in order to prevent infection and remind me to schedule a follow up appointment with my gynecologist to make certain I did not suffer from complications. To be honest, I doubt I heard a word the nurse said to me. I was numb.

When I exited the room and came out into the lobby I found Thaddeus waiting patiently. I could see the look of concern on his face the moment he looked into my eyes. I am quite certain everyone could tell from my swollen eyes that I had been crying. However, I cared less about what other people thought…I was more troubled by what I thought of myself.

"Take me home please," I muttered to Thaddeus. Thaddeus obliged with no questions asked.

The ride home was quiet. Neither one of us said a word. When I got home to my apartment, I simply changed into my pajamas and got into bed. I remember Thaddeus lying in bed next to me simply holding me. He attempted to be comforting but it was not working. Thaddeus' tendency to act like a dotting mother was quite annoying. Plus, I hate to say this but the sight of Thaddeus constantly reminded me of the deed I had done. Simply looking at him made me sick to my stomach. If by chance the sight of Thaddeus did not remind me of what I had done, then the painful cramps wrecking havoc on my uterus did. Although Thaddeus' intentions were true I simply wanted to be left alone. I was baffled as to why he would even want to be around someone who had just killed his child. After a while, I think Thaddeus got the hint because he simply got up and left. He did not say a word. He simply left.

I did not blame him.

If I could've gotten up and walked out of that apartment leaving the part of me that went through with the abortion behind—I would have in a heartbeat. But I couldn't. I had to live with me. I had to wade through the guilt and remorse and I hated Thaddeus, the world and myself for that fact.

Although I began to feel better the following morning, I stayed in bed for three days. The complications I suffered from the abortion were not physical. I tried my best not to think about what I had done, but that was impossible to do. I often caught myself wondering what would have happened if I had kept the baby. I try to stop myself before my imagination gets carried away, but it is hard at times not to play "What if?" If I were ever placed in a similar situation again—God forbid—I would without a doubt keep the child.

Following my day at the clinic, it took me a while to warm back up to Thaddeus. I don't know if it was because I blamed him for what happened or if I were too scared he would want to talk about the entire ordeal. I really don't know. For a while after that incident I was really confused. To be quite honest, after finding the photo of Ivy in Thaddeus' condo and the turmoil I experienced aborting our child I no longer knew how I felt about Thaddeus. I cared for him but I did not know if attempting a relationship with him was the best thing for me mentally.

Of course, all of that changed when Thaddeus' mother experienced a heart attack.

Ivy—Different Town, Same Ole Problems, Same Ole Faces

The Monday following my review, I was on the phone with my headhunter. To be considered for partner and not achieve the distinction is not viewed favorably in the legal profession. To be an associate considered for partner and not achieve partnership twice is a death knell for an associate's legal career. After that, the only options available to a lawyer who was once on the partner track are few. An associate can still practice law as either a staff attorney or practice corporate law. A few brave souls start their own private practice, which is not a bad idea if an individual can make it through the lean months when they are trying to find reliable and paying clients. Sometimes that takes time and a helluva lot of luck. However, neither one of those options were for me. I was partner material and I knew it.

I considered filing a discrimination lawsuit against Grimble & Kline following the announcement of Michael Kennard's promotion to partner, but I decided against it. I was a lawyer so I knew all the tricks Grimble & Kline would play in order to drag my name and career through the mud. I knew because I used the same tactics when defending Grimble & Kline's clients. I would've more than likely been portrayed as the disgruntled employee, which to some degree was true. Or even be labeled the hostile, trouble-making, black woman. Ultimately, I would be blacklisted in the legal profession.

In the end I realized pursuing a lawsuit was not worth my time, the headache, or in my best interests. After all, I did not want to play the race card. I was bigger than that. I was better off looking for a job elsewhere.

As you can guess during my job search, I instructed my headhunter to concentrate his search in cities with a decent African American population such as D.C., Houston, Chicago and Atlanta. I even considered New York and LA if the offer was right. My sister Cynthia lived in LA, so I at least had family there. Despite everything that was going on I was not just going to take the first offer that came across my desk, so I could leave the Twin Cities. I was not going to let a broken heart or a battered ego run me out of town. And in regards to my broken heart, I had not spoken to Thaddeus since the night I had dismissed him. He had attempted to call me a few times, but I refused to answer his calls. So after a while he just stopped calling. I felt some guilt by just cutting him off but I could not dwell on it. My life had to continue on with or without Thaddeus Brown.

After several promising job leads and a few I could have cared less about, I finally accepted a position as a partner at Henderson & Hobbs—a black law firm in Chicago. The same law firm Warren Thomas went to upon leaving Grimble & Kline. In fact Warren played an intricate part in me landing the position at Henderson & Hobbs. We had been at an impasse in the negotiations over my insistence of being brought on as a partner. After the partners at Henderson & Hobbs conferred with Warren, knowing that he had worked with me at Grimble & Kline, my insistence on being hired as a partner was no longer a sticking point. I guess just because the brotha married a white woman he isn't all that bad. There was a black law firm in the Twin Cities that made me the exact same offer, but I decided it was best I get a change of scenery to go along with a new job.

So, after three weeks of interviewing here and there I was finally on my way. The partners at Grimble & Kline were not too happy to see me go but with all things in life I was quite certain they would get over it. They could find plenty of people willing to bust their butts in order to line their pockets in hopes of making partner.

The best thing about my move to Chicago was that I was still close to home. If I wanted to see my mom and dad or Lisa and Gloria they were an hour away by plane and six hours if I chose to drive. I found it to be the ideal situation. However, it was while I packed to relocate my last Saturday in Minneapolis, Lisa decided to drop a bomb on me.

"You know Thaddeus is trying to move back to Chicago," Lisa exclaimed, while she wrapped a cup in newspaper.

"What!" Gloria screamed. Gloria damn near dropped the bowl she was wrapping on to the floor. "I know I did not hear you right?"

"You heard me girl. I said Thaddeus is trying to move back home," Lisa repeated. She looked to me for some type of reaction.

"What are you looking at me for? It's a free country. That man can do whatever he pleases," I said. I tried to act as if I was not fazed by this little tidbit of information.

"So girl, you need to tell me why is this fool trying to get back home?" Gloria demanded to know. Gloria was not going to let the subject die.

"It appears as if Stephanie, his baby's mama, is moving back to Chicago. And since he wants to stay close to his son, he's looking for a job back home," Lisa informed Gloria.

"Even if the negro was shiftless when it came to my girl, Ivy, Thaddeus is at least serious about his son. That is more than I can say for some of the men out here." Gloria stared over at me.

"I don't know why y'all keep looking over here at me. That man is not mine," I stated.

"That's good to hear because I did not want to tell you this but I think you should know. While I was getting my perm this morning Rhonda told me she saw Thaddeus and that white girl at the Women's Clinic Thursday."

"What the hell is Rhonda doing over there," Gloria asked.

"She's pregnant," Lisa informed her.

"Damn, aint that her fifth or sixth kid? I have trouble dealing with two and here is this broad with five or six. I tell you, I don't know how some women do it," Gloria professed. "I surely hope she is doing a lot of business down there at the hair salon because her and her man do not know a damn thing about birth control. Somebody needs to show her what a diaphragm is or teach her husband how to put on a condom or something because that girl is just too fertile to be running around here practicing the rhythm method. Hell, she already has her own basketball squad."

I did not realize it until it was too late but upon hearing about Thaddeus, I had fallen deafeningly silent. I knew that any woman visiting the Women's Clinic was pregnant. Thaddeus' new girlfriend was either coming in to get a check-up or to end her pregnancy. It made no difference, which one, for it all meant the same thing—Thaddeus had gotten the woman pregnant.

The two of them must have caught on to my pain for Gloria promptly shut up about Rhonda and quickly stated, "Who cares anyway? Thaddeus is a thing of the past isn't that right girl?" When I did not answer, it became obvious to the both of them I was no longer in a talkative mood.

That following Monday, I moved to Chicago. I quickly realized that the problems I had faced in Minneapolis in regards to finding a decent brotha would plague me in Chicago as well. Mixed couples dotted the landscape of the Windy City just as they did Minneapolis—black men with white women, black women with white men, black men with Hispanic women—you name it I saw a couple that fit the bill in Chicago. I was beginning to wonder was I missing something. I began to question if I had given interracial dating a fair chance judging by the countless ethnically mixed couples I encountered.

Along with my move to Chicago, I had managed to go close to a month without thinking or interacting with Thaddeus Brown. Of course, images of him popped in my head from time to time but now since there was some distance between us I was certain those images would fade too.

At the time if you were to ask me was I over Thaddeus? I would've sworn up and down that I had moved on. That was until I received a call from Lisa.

She informed me that Thaddeus' mother had a heart attack.

Thaddeus—Changes

The Monday following Ivy's dismissal of me, I got a call from Donovan at Chicago National. Donovan informed me Chicago National was interested in meeting with me and wanted to fly me to Chicago for an interview that upcoming Friday. The timing could not have been any more perfect. It was a good time for me to go back home and escape the headaches I had created for myself in Minneapolis. It was an added plus that Little T would be able to accompany me. He very rarely got to see my side of the family. Plus, the trip would allow for me to spend some quality time with my son. Although we had more time together since the incident with Willard, the trip back home would allow for me to dedicate more one-on-one time with him. There was no telling how much time Little T and I had together before Mr. Patterson concluded his investigation and made his recommendation.

The Friday we landed in Chicago, I was bogged down in interviews with people from Chicago National all day. Little T hung out with his grandmother, my mother, while I interviewed for the director position. It appeared that Donovan wanted me to meet with as many people as possible due to my time constraints and the fact I did not reside in Chicago. Despite spending the entire day in interviews, I left Chicago National feeling good about my chances of landing the job. The group I would be tasked with supervising seemed to be a good bunch of people. I say, "seems" because looks can always be deceiving. Although I hoped to get the job I was not going to hold my breath. I learned to never get overly excited about something I had no control over.

Regardless of what become of my interview with Chicago National, I viewed my time back home amongst my family as a blessing. Being around family and friends had a calming effect upon me. Seeing my son laughing and playing with his cousins made the trip well worth the while. Very rarely did Little T get to see his cousins.

As a kid growing up I use to imagine sitting around with my brother and sister watching our kids grow up together. Rarely was it a reality for me as it was for James and Althea. Nevertheless, I enjoyed watching our children play together. I loved watching the innocence of childhood before adults managed to taint it. There were plenty of times I wished I could go back to those childhood days of naïve bliss. I often longed for the days I would walk to Russell Park or ride my bike to Rainbow Park where the "real" basketball games were played and simply hoped I got picked to play on someone's team in a pick-up game. Back then my only concern was playing basketball. It's funny how as a kid growing up I could not wait to be an adult and now I yearned for the days of childhood. Back then the only thing I worried about was if the older boys were going to steal my basketball. Life was so much simpler back then. It didn't seem so confusing or complex as it does now.

Being back home amongst family gave me a reprieve from Ivy and Erin. That weekend I focused only on my son. Little T and I went to Navy Pier, and Field's Museum. Places as a child I had imagined my father would have taken me if he had been alive. In some aspects, spending time with Little T was like a dream come true for me. In many regards that weekend in Chicago helped exorcise some of my own inner demons.

Growing up I use to walk along Lake Shore Drive and make believe my dad was there with me. I would pretend he was watching me as I tossed rocks into Lake Michigan. It pleased me to make what had always been a dream for me a reality for my son. It was satisfying to know that all the things I had dreamed my father and I doing together, I was able to do with Little T. I was actually present to see the joy on his face when he managed to skip a rock on the lake. Due to my never-ending problems with Stephanie, I very rarely got to enjoy quality moments like that with Little T.

The time I spent in Chi-town was the remedy I needed for my return to Minneapolis. There was a mess I had left behind in the Twin Cities I was now ready to clean up. Of course, all sense of calm I had achieved while in Chicago was wiped away Monday when I received Mr. Patterson's letter. Mr. Patterson stated that he had concluded his investigation and did not find Stephanie at fault for Little T's abuse. Although I was glad Stephanie was found innocent, I was saddened by what Mr. Patterson's correspondence meant for my relationship with my son. Of course, Mr. Patterson had returned primary custody of Little T back over to Stephanie. Once again, I was being forced into the role of part-time dad. I figured at least Little T would be glad to see his mother again without stipulations. Unlike Stephanie, Willard was going to be charged with a litany of offenses ranging in assault and battery related to his beating of Stephanie to aggravated child abuse when it came to Little T. After receiving Mr. Patterson's letter I dreaded the phone call from Stephanie demanding I bring Little T home, but that call never came.

The Wednesday after receiving Mr. Patterson's letter I woke up depressed. It was the day of Little T's custody hearing. It was extremely difficult for me to walk into the courtroom that morning knowing that my relationship with my son would probably revert back to the way it had been prior to the incident with Willard.

The hearing went as I had expected. My motion for full custody of Little T was denied. I had anticipated that once the judge's gavel fell Stephanie would arrange for a time when she could whisk Little T away from me, but she didn't. Instead, she surprised me. Stephanie chased me down in the corridor outside the courtroom. I thought she wanted to coordinate how and when I returned our son to her.

"Thaddeus!"

I really did not want to talk to Stephanie but I realized I had no choice, so I neglected the pleasantries and got straight to the point. "How do you want to do this Stephanie? Do you want me to drop him off or do you want to pick him up?"

Stephanie simply smiled. "Neither."

"What?"

"I said neither," she reiterated.

"What do you mean by neither?" I was confused.

"I mean I do not want you to drop Little T off and I do not want to pick him up. I wanted to simply tell you thank you."

"For what?"

"For the letter. Mr. Patterson told me that you wrote a letter on my behalf. He even let me read it and I must say it was quite touching."

"Despite all that we have been through Stephanie, you are still my son's mama. For the sake of my boy that was the least I could do."

Stephanie smiled. "If there is one thing I can say about you, Thaddeus Brown, you are always looking out for your son."

"He's all I got…. What's up with you? I thought you would have came and got Little T after receiving Mr. Patterson's letter."

"My first urge was to come and get our son but I caught myself," Stephanie stated.

"You caught yourself?"

"Yeah, I caught myself. I realized right now our son is better off with you, Thaddeus. I have to get my life back in order. I guess neither one of us has been the same since the divorce. While I get my life straight I think it's best that Little T was with his father."

"What are you saying, Stephanie?"

"What I am saying is that I want Little T to spend the summer with you. Of course, he will spend some time with me."

"But of course," I exclaimed. I could not believe what I was hearing. Of course, I should have known there was a catch.

"I'm moving back home to Chicago, Thaddeus. I think life will be a whole lot better for me if I move back home where I have some support. So, there are a few things we need to talk through. If you're up for it I would like to discuss what we're going to do about our son tonight."

"I'll be home," I assured her.

"Then I'll call you tonight," Stephanie remarked.

"Yeah, sure." With my reply Stephanie walked off.

The thought of not being able to see Little T ate away at me the entire drive home. The possibility of us living in separate cities damn near brought me to tears. I knew if trying to see him while we lived in the same city was difficult then trying to see Little T with four hundred miles in between us was going to be next to impossible.

Stephanie called me that evening as promised. She reiterated to me her plans to move back to Chicago. In the interim until she got situated she wanted Little T to stay with me. Although, I was excited to spend the summer with my son the news was bitter sweet. I knew once summer ended, the time Little T and I spent together would most likely be reduced to Thanksgiving or Christmas visits. This put a damper on the relationship that I had established with my son in the brief period of time I enjoyed sole custody. Unless I moved to Chicago, Stephanie returning home meant I would see Little T far less than I had in the past. Stephanie assured me she was willing to work on a parenting agreement that let me see my son often, however, I knew such a parenting agreement would be hard to live up to. Still, it was pleasing to know Stephanie and I could act civil and courteous towards one another when it came to the care of our son.

For two days I agonized over Stephanie's decision to move back home to Chicago. Then that Friday Donovan at Chicago National called and offered me the director position. I can't describe how relieved I felt to hear Chicago National wanted to offer me the job. After going back home to Chicago and Stephanie's talk of moving back home, I too began to long to be amongst family. So, landing the job at Chicago National became important to me. It solved the problem Stephanie presented to me when she declared she was moving back to Chicago by allowing me to continue to see Little T on a regular basis. I guess Minnesota had served its purpose and it was time for me to move on.

I missed Chicago. I missed the days I could stand on Lake Shore Drive and look out onto Lake Michigan and be unable to tell where the horizon ended and heaven began. Or the way Chicago's skyline sprouted up along Lake Shore Drive as it wound its way north. I missed the wind barreling in over Lake

Michigan and hitting me flush in the face as I rushed inside to shield myself from the bitter cold. I wanted to go home.

After a week of negotiating back and forth about salary and benefits, I accepted the position at Chicago National. It was the end of July, so I informed Donovan I would be willing to start the beginning of September. It would give me enough time to satisfy my community service hours as well as leave me enough time to get situated back home and enroll Little T into school. When I broke the news to Little T, he was ecstatic to here I was moving back to Chicago too. Even Stephanie seemed pleased to hear the news. It definitely eliminated the need to work out what would have been a messy joint custody agreement.

For two weeks I felt like things for me was turning around. I began to satisfy my community service hours at a local food bank. Hopefully putting my legal woes behind me for good. Regardless of satisfying my legal requirements resulting from my altercation with Willard, Little T still had to endure the possibility of a trial stemming from the child abuse chargers filed against Willard. Still, I felt things were starting to look up.

That was until Erin called.

Up until the first week of August I had not spoken to Erin or Ivy for roughly six weeks. Then out of nowhere Erin called to inform me she was pregnant. Just when it seemed I had gotten from underneath my women problems, Erin comes along to prove ridding myself free of the drama I had created was not going to be easy. When Erin told me she was pregnant I was stunned. I did not know how to react to such a proclamation. I simply went numb. I did not know what to think. One minute Erin tells me she is on the pill. Then in the next breath she tells me she forgot to take the pill and had missed her period. I did not know if she was playing games or what? Now Erin did not appear to be the type of woman to try and hustle a man out of his money, but you could never be foolhardy and trust anybody one hundred percent. I have ran into plenty of women who claimed to be pregnant long enough to torture a brotha to death and milk him for every penny. Immediately upon getting off the phone with Erin, I called the fellas and convened an emergency meeting.

Since Mr. Patterson's letter had exonerated Stephanie from any wrongdoing in Little T's abuse I no longer had to rely upon Lisa or Saundra to baby-sit my son. Instead, I simply called Stephanie and dropped Little T off at his mother's house before meeting up with Darius and Marcus at a local sports bar. When I explained to Darius and Marcus my predicament in regards to Erin's pregnancy, both of them expressed doubt to Erin's claim of forgetting to take the pill.

"That bitch is playing you. How can she all of a sudden forget to take the pill unless she's trying to get pregnant?" Darius exclaimed.

"I would have to agree with Darius. Lisa is habitual when it comes to taking the pill. She takes it consistently. The only time Lisa has not taken the pill is when we decided we wanted to have a baby. Other than that she did not miss a day," added Marcus.

"Look Marcus, you cannot go telling Lisa about this. I don't want this relayed back to Ivy," I advised.

"Please, you do not have to worry about this getting out," Marcus assured me.

"You might want him to swear on it," joked Darius. I simply ignored Darius. I was not in a joking mood.

As the thought of Erin not lying crossed my mind I could not help but ask, "What if she did just forget? Erin just does not strike me as the type of person who would try to play me," I said emphatically.

"Okay, what if she did? What if Erin did forget to take the pill? Are you ready to have another kid?" asked Marcus.

"I think you know the answer to that question.... Hell no!" The idea of making two child support payments instantly gave me a headache. "But that does not answer my question on what to do if Erin is pregnant?" I stated.

"You ignore her," Darius blurted out.

"I can't just ignore her," I professed.

"Like hell you can't! If you ignore the broad you will force her to play her hand. So, if Erin is playing games she'll realize you're not going to play along. I guarantee you the next time you see Erin she'll claim she had an abortion."

"And what if Erin really is pregnant?" I asked.

"You still ignore her. In that case she'll get an abortion for real. Either way you will not have a child," Darius stated. Darius finished off his rum and Coke.

I shook my head in disgust. "Darius when are you ever going to grow up. I am really getting tired of listening to your wannabe pimp shit. This is serious. I am in a real predicament here. I really need your help right now, not some bullshit," I seethed.

"Suit yourself. Don't say I did not try to tell you," Darius warned.

"Look Thaddeus, don't pay him no mind. Darius does not have a clue as to what he is talking about," Marcus interjected. Darius simply grumbled something under his breath. "What is it you want to do?"

"I don't know. But I do know I cannot ignore Erin. Whether she is telling the truth or not, that just is not my style. Besides Marcus, you know me I do not shy away from my responsibilities regardless of what Darius may say."

"Well my friend, it sounds like you have answered your own question," Marcus stated. I realized he was right.

After discussing the matter with Marcus and Darius, I really wanted the opinion of a woman. I thought about calling Ivy. I actually picked up the phone one time only to refrain from dialing her number. I knew Ivy would never answer my calls. Besides, that would be awkward talking to her about getting another woman pregnant. A call like that would do my relationship with Ivy more harm than good. Yet, I had no one else to turn to—at least I thought. Surprisingly I found advice in the most unlikely place…Stephanie.

When I went by to pick up Little T a couple of days after conferring with the fellas, I found myself telling Stephanie about my dilemma with Erin. At first Stephanie did not seem comfortable talking with me about my relationship with another woman. I didn't blame her. I am certain I would have felt weird giving her advice pertaining to a man she was interested in. Although Stephanie did not sound pleased to also hear I may be having another child, she did not judge me. Instead, she dispensed some helpful advice.

The one piece of advice that stuck with me from the conversation was when Stephanie advised me to, "Do what your heart tells you to do Thaddeus."

It pleased me to know Stephanie and I could talk to each other like adults instead of arguing and screaming. We had been arguing and yelling at each other for so long I began to think it was the only way we knew how to communicate with each other. I guess the one good thing I can say that came out of our ordeal with Willard—is it got rid of a lot of the leftover bitterness that lingered from our divorce.

Armed with Stephanie's advice, I realized I needed to come to some decision about what I was going to do in regards to Erin. The only way that was going to happen was if Erin and I sat down and talked.

Now, I did not expect Erin to be cordial to me especially after the way I had treated her. However, I did not expect her to have already made a decision on the fate of our unborn child. Although I knew I did not want another child, particularly in this manner, the thought of Erin having an abortion did not sit well with me. Yet, I knew in reality the choice was not mine to make. So, after questioning Erin as to whether she was making the right decision I insisted I join her at the clinic. I felt it was my right to be there. However, when Erin saw me standing outside the Medical Arts Building the next morning I could tell her heart was not in what she was about to do. Seeing such indecision in Erin's eyes, I wanted to be certain she had thoroughly thought it through. Although Erin sounded less confident than she did the night before on the phone, her answer was still "yes."

There has only been a few times in my life when I felt as scared as I did that day walking into that clinic with Erin. My first kiss in the sixth grade with Nicole Billings and the first varsity basketball game I played in as a freshman. Other than Stephanie and now Erin I had gotten only one other woman in my life pregnant. I was in high school at the time and her name was Tawana Freeman. I remember panicking all the way up to the moment she informed me she decided to go to Planned Parenthood and get an abortion. Neither one of our parents knew, so we could not rightfully ask our parents for money so she could have an abortion. So I begged my brother, James, for the money. I remember giving Tawana the money James had scraped together as she boarded a CTA bus on her way to Planned Parenthood. Tawana gave me a call later that night to let me know it was done and just like that I forgot all about it. I can recollect feeling so far removed from the situation that it did not even seem real to me.

As Erin and I walked into the clinic that Thursday afternoon, I wished I could once again go back to being that teenage boy in high school. All the people watching us as we entered the waiting room made me feel uncomfortable. As Erin filled out the paperwork, I expected someone to stand up and scream, "Baby killer!" Even though that did not happen, I could not help but believe the women in the room thought I was forcing Erin into having the procedure. Even if that was not the case, I could not help but feel guilty. So to pacify my guilt, I avoided making eye contact with anyone.

When the nurse called Erin into the backroom I sat there patiently doing my best to ease my conscious. When the sound of Erin crying filtered out into the waiting area, I could sense a growing anxiety amongst some of the ladies in the room. I wanted Erin to shut up in order to calm the frayed nerves of everyone in the clinic, including mine. It took Erin a while but her weeping eventually died down.

When Erin appeared with tears in her eyes an hour later, I felt terrible. I wished I had talked her out of it. I wished I had insisted she keep the baby. Yet, it was too late. The deed was done.

I drove Erin home. I stayed with her until I sensed she did not want me around. I wanted to stay more so out of guilt than any true sense of commitment, but it was obvious she did not want me there. Erin and I did not speak to one another for a while after that Thursday. When we did our conversations were brief. I do not blame her. In some respects it did not surprise me after what we had been through that she had chosen to shut me out.

I could tell things had changed between us the moment we left the clinic that afternoon. My trust in Erin had been shaken and I was quite certain her faith in me had been affected as well. I often wonder to myself what would have happened if I had been able to talk Erin out of having that abortion. I can't help but imagine what our child would have looked like. Most of the time I simply let those thoughts pass. They are often too troubling for me to contemplate.

For two weeks I grappled with a mixture of emotions stemming from what Erin and I did that eventful Thursday afternoon. I think Marcus sensed I was in a funk for he suggested the fellas get together and celebrate my accepting of the position at Chicago National with a night out on the town. Although I had accepted the position with Chicago National some time ago, my departure date was fast approaching. Darius, Marcus and I had yet to celebrate the good news properly. By that time I had already terminated my contract with Midwestern Federal and had completed the community service hours of my sentence for pleading guilty to the misdemeanor battery charge.

That Friday Little T spent the night with his mother so I could go out and celebrate with Darius and Marcus. Darius, however, had to cancel at the last minute because he had finally managed to tip toe out behind Belinda's back with Raquel, the bisexual stripper he had spoken so highly about, only to have her rob him blind while he slept. Instead of hanging out with Marcus and I, Darius had to go to the police station and file a police report. Darius claimed he would catch up with us later, however, I doubted it. His ego seemed to have taken a hit from the whole ordeal. Plus, I was quite certain Darius did not want to hear Marcus' mouth as he inevitably would if he did show up. So, Marcus and I went out on our own.

We trekked over to the Artist Quarters in St. Paul because they had an open mic for poets on Friday nights. Marcus had a poetic vibe going, so I obliged him. Marcus and I relaxed and listened to some jazz in between the poetry sets. After an hour of listening to many spoken word artists verbalize their most intimate thoughts in rhyme, Marcus decided it was his turn to bless the mic with a few of his own rhythmic insights on life. As usual Marcus brought down the house, sending a wave of applause throughout the crowd when he was done. Marcus had a gift for blending words together into beautiful poetic masterpieces. He also had great stage presence.

"You need to think about performing on a professional level. You know perfect your craft," I told Marcus as he took his seat.

"Craft? This is no craft my friend this is a love affair. Poetry is my mistress, whom I meet on those cold dark nights and make love to in a medley of word play." It was obvious by his reply that Marcus was still caught up in the moment.

"Seriously, Marcus you should think about entering in one those spoken word contests."

"Nah, no thanks," Marcus spouted. "That's not me. I got a day job that provides me with money. Besides, if I started looking at my poetry as a means to make ends meet it would become a job to me and that will sap my creative energy. It's not what my poetry is all about. It's my passion and it's my life line that keeps me afloat in troubled waters.... You know what I'm saying?"

"I feel you," I replied. Marcus was having a difficult time shaking his poetic vibe, but I did feel where he was coming from.

Marcus took a sip of his drink before telling me, "Speaking of money how much more bread are you going to be making at this new job of yours?"

"Enough." I smirked. I never let friends or family know how much money I made. When I did they always seemed to show up at my door begging.

"Yeah, I bet," exclaimed Marcus. He gave me a sly grin. Marcus then paused for a moment before saying, "You know Ivy moved to Chicago."

"Nah, I did not know." I was shocked to hear Ivy had moved. I was under the general impression that she still lived in the Cities.

"Still have not talked to her huh?" Marcus must have seen the surprised look on my face.

"Nah, I gave up long ago."

"Well, she took a job with Henderson & Hobbs. They brought her on as a partner."

"Are you serious?"

"Yes I am. She's been in Chicago close to a month now." Marcus glanced at me out of the corner of his eye.

"Wow, I'm happy for her. Tell her I said congratulations."

"Why don't you tell her yourself?"

"I would if I could but Ivy doesn't return my calls, and brotha I've given up trying."

"That has never stopped you before. If I recall you were the brotha who went over to her house when no one else could get in touch with her." Marcus reminded me.

"That was then and this is now. I am not going to chase down no one that does not want to be caught." I was starting to let my ego do the talking.

"Suit yourself, I just thought you would like to know?"

"Yeah whatever." I knew Marcus' true intentions as to why he felt compelled to share that bit of information with me. Although there was no talk of Ivy the rest of the evening, I couldn't seem to stop thinking about her. Even after I went home and crawled into bed, thoughts of Ivy transposed themselves upon my dreams.

I was awoken the next morning by the ringing of my telephone. I squinted at the red digits of my alarm clock and saw it read 6:32 AM. I picked up the receiver, groggy and somewhat agitated. I immediately recognized the voice on the other end...it was James.

"Thaddeus."

"Yeah." I was still half asleep.

"Mama's in the hospital.... She had a heart attack."

Love

Erin—Life is Too Short

When Belinda called and told me, via Darius, that Thaddeus' mother had a heart attack I was at work. It had been two weeks sense I had talked to Thaddeus. The last time we spoke was a couple of days after the abortion. Although we had not spoken for sometime, I still could not help but be concerned. When Belinda gave me the news I contemplated getting on the phone and calling Thaddeus right away. However, I did not know if that was a wise idea judging by our lack of communication over the past two weeks. After giving it a considerable amount of thought I concluded it was best I called him.

When I called Thaddeus I got no answer. I wondered if the fact I had not used Thaddeus' number in quite a while caused me to forget his phone number. So, I checked my phone book and tried calling him again…still no answer.

I tried reaching out to Thaddeus throughout the course of the day to no avail. Even his cell phone immediately rolled over into his voicemail. Not until Belinda called Darius and did a little snooping was I able to learn Thaddeus had left that morning for Chicago. Since I did not know how to reach him in Chicago, I simply was forced to wait for Thaddeus' return to Minneapolis.

Four days after receiving the initial news of Thaddeus' mother illness, Darius informed Belinda his mother had passed. Despite never having met Thaddeus' mother, the news of her untimely death bothered me. The news of her death suddenly brought my life into focus. Suddenly, it became crystal clear to me that life was too short to dwell in the past. I realized if I continued to live for what *was* I would miss experiencing what *might be*. I concluded I could not sit back and play it safe. Life was about taking risks and it was time for me to take some, especially when it came to matters of the heart.

Five days after Thaddeus' mother past away, Darius and Belinda drove to Chicago to attend the funeral. It was beautiful to see the two of them together. I could not resist but to be somewhat envious. Their blossoming relationship only made me hunger to enjoy a love affair of my own. Nevertheless, I was happy for Belinda. Belinda had endured her fair share of horrendous relationships with a myriad of men. It was pleasing to finally see her with a man who truly loved her.

Fourteen days after he originally left for Chicago and five days after laying his mother to rest Thaddeus came home. I questioned whether it was a good idea to call Thaddeus so soon after his return. I was certain he was still in the grieving process. Three days went by and I still had not contacted Thaddeus. We had not spoken for so long I wondered if I knew how to strike up a conversation with him. I also feared Thaddeus might want to discuss the abortion and I did not know if I was ready to talk about that just yet. I had conveniently pushed the entire ordeal out of my mind. I silently tried to convince myself that it never happened. Unfortunately, Darius being shot gave Thaddeus and I a reason to talk. I spoke briefly with Thaddeus at the hospital while we waited on news regarding Darius but that was it.

After Darius was released from the hospital, Belinda suggested I try calling Thaddeus. After thinking it over, I decided regardless of what happened I could at least say I tried to mend our relationship.

When I called Thaddeus, he sounded subdued—despondent. Of course, this was understandable. First his mother passes away then his best friend gets shot by a deranged stalker. Even though Thaddeus' mental health was none of my business I was concerned. So, when I asked him if he would like some company and Thaddeus did not protest I rushed over to be by his side.

When I arrived at Thaddeus' condo it looked as if a cyclone had blown through. Clothes and boxes were strewn everywhere. The brief time I had known Thaddeus he tended to do a pretty good job in keeping his condo clean. To see his place in such shambles immediately gave me cause for alarm. When I questioned him about it Thaddeus informed me he was returning to Chicago. Despite the countless clothes and boxes around his condo it never registered with me that he was returning to Chicago for good. For some reason I thought he meant for a week or weekend. I guess I did not want to fathom the thought of Thaddeus leaving after it had taken me so long to get my act together and figure out what I wanted.

I had not intentions of staying the night with Thaddeus that evening but when he asked me to stay I could not resist. His emotional pull upon my heart was strong. With Thaddeus Jr. in Chicago, Thaddeus and I were left to our thoughts with no interruptions. For a good majority of the night Thaddeus and I simply laid on his bed and said nothing. Occasionally Thaddeus would say something, however, we were simply left to wallow in our thoughts. When Thaddeus did talk a great deal of his conversation pertained to his mom.

Then out of the clear blue, without warning, Thaddeus brought up the abortion. A subject I so desperately wanted to avoid. "Erin, I want you to know I'm sorry."

I tried to play like I did not know what he was referring to, but my body language deceived me. "Sorry for what?"

"The whole thing—the abortion, not coming clean about Ivy—the whole damn thing. I know it does no good now, but I wish I had stopped you from going through with the abortion."

Although I had managed to move on and come to terms with the role Thaddeus and I played in the death of our unborn child, I was not ready to openly discuss the subject.

"Apology accepted. Can we talk about something else now?"

"No, we have to talk about this Erin. If we don't it will haunt us for the rest of our lives."

"I don't want to talk about this Thaddeus!" I sat up on the bed and prepared to leave. I did not want to talk about babies or abortions. I wanted to run as far away from the subject as humanly possible.

"Why?" Thaddeus continued to pick at my wound.

"Because it was a mistake!" I sobbed. I had been holding on to so much guilt, it was hard for me to resist my body's urge to let it go. "It was a mistake! It was a mistake I can't take back! It tears me apart every time I think about it!"

"It tears me up too." Thaddeus attempted to comfort me.

We sat there on Thaddeus' bed the remainder of the night not saying a word. We ended up falling asleep in each other's arms. That night I felt secure, protected, nestled in the cleft of his arm while he held me. I felt as if I belonged. I felt at home. I did not mind if I was going to be late to work that morning. Work did not concern me. I wanted to lie there in Thaddeus' arms.

"I need to get these clothes packed and go buy some more boxes so I can pack up the rest of my stuff," Thaddeus said over the eggs and bacon he prepared for us the following morning.

It still had not grasped the idea of Thaddeus going back home for good. I was so clueless. I even helped him pack a few items away before it dawned on me he had practically everything he owned boxed up or ready to be stowed away.

"If you ask me from the looks of it you are going back to Chicago for more than a couple of days."

"I am…I'm moving back to Chicago for good." Thaddeus paused. He must've noticed the shock on my face. "You didn't know did you? I thought you knew."

It felt like someone had reached into my chest and ripped out my heart. "No, I didn't know," I stammered. I was stunned.

"I've quit my job at Midwestern Federal and accepted a position at Chicago National in Chicago. I start the first week of September."

"Oh." What more could I say.

I could not believe it. Just when I had tossed aside my inhibitions and decided on what I wanted out of life—the thing I wanted the most had suddenly decided to move to Chicago.

"I'm going to live in my mom's house until I can find a place of my own. When I do, my sister, brother, and I are going to sell the house and invest it in some rental property. I plan on leaving tomorrow night."

"That's great. I got to get going. I can't afford to be late for work. Hopefully, I'll see you before you leave." I tried to act as if I was not taken back by Thaddeus' announcement, yet, I was certain my disappointment showed.

"That would be nice," Thaddeus replied.

I hurried out of Thaddeus' condo as fast as I could. When I got to my car I broke down in tears. Within the span of twenty-four hours I had ridden a gut wrenching roller coaster of emotions. Still, I had come too far to simply watch Thaddeus walk out of my life so easily. So, I spent the majority of my day at work searching job placement websites for ad agencies hiring in Chicago. It was not until the end of the day did I come to my senses and realize I could not follow Thaddeus to Chicago even if I wanted to. The main reason being, there was no guarantee Thaddeus and I would be together even if I relocated to Chicago. Secondly, I did not want to live in Chicago. So, just like that I had to say good-bye to Thaddeus.

I came to the conclusion it was best I did not to see Thaddeus before he left. I did not want to get a sense of finality to our relationship. I wanted to make believe that despite the distance our relationship would endure, even though, I knew it could not. Distance is tough to overcome. Despite my determination to stay away, I showed up at Thaddeus' door the next day in tears. Although I tried my best to convince Thaddeus to stay, I knew deep down his move to

Chicago was what he needed. So that evening after I left, Thaddeus got in his car and returned home to Chicago.

In the days following Thaddeus' departure, I called him constantly. Then as time passed the phone calls dwindled until ultimately they ceased. I realized in order for me to move on I had to let Thaddeus go. It was hard, but I had to. I still cared about him, yet our lives had gone in separate directions. If Thaddeus had stayed in Minnesota, I believe we could have worked out our differences and built a lasting relationship. Unfortunately, my hopes and dreams of such a relationship did not materialize.

My relationship with Thaddeus was not a total waste. Thaddeus taught me a lot about myself. Despite the fact we no longer speak to one another, I will always love Thaddeus Brown for who he is and what he taught me about life. He taught me above all else, how important it is to take care of me…both mentally and physically.

Right now, I am doing just that. I am taking care of Erin. This is the first time in my life I have gone an extended period of time without a "significant other." To be honest, it feels good. For so long I had always kept a boyfriend. It is hard for me to remember a time period I went without one. Right now, my life centers on me and I love it. I admit it has taken me some time to get use to, but I've managed. The time I have spent to myself has been a great learning experience. I have learned so much about me.

I have been able to reflect and ask myself some very serious questions pertaining to my constant desire to keep a guy in my life. I'm curious if that was a by-product of a life growing up in an environment where I bounced between parents. I questioned if I silently sought stability. Who knows? I have yet to know the answers to such questions, however, I have begun the journey in search of the explanations with the help of my psychiatrist.

Still, not until I had the chance to spend time with myself did it strike me how I never took time out for me. I had gotten so use to always having a boyfriend and making him the center of my universe I did not know what it felt like to love me. When I realized this I decided it was time to celebrate me. So in celebration of my newfound freedom, I decided to take a trip to Santorini, Greece. Belinda wanted to join me but she is too far along in her pregnancy to risk such an adventure. There is a chance Belinda could deliver her baby any day. I find it ironic that after being a bystander to my dilemma surrounding my pregnancy, Belinda found herself pregnant a month later.

Life is so weird. Still, no matter how weird it gets I intend to enjoy it.

Ivy—Love is Not Perfect

In no way, shape, or form is life perfect.

It does not matter how much I wish everything in life just fell into its proper place. Often things happen that are out of my control or far from the way I had envisioned them. Sometimes, something totally unexpected can happen that changes my entire outlook on life. Thaddeus mother's heart attack was one of those unexpected events that changed my perspective not only on life but also love. I was not close to Thaddeus' mom. However the few times I met Miss Brown, I found her to be a warm—very loving—woman.

When I heard of Miss Brown's heart attack I had been working my tail off at Henderson & Hobbs. I had been busting my behind at the law firm ever since I arrived in Chicago. I had been there a month and still had not fully unpacked. Late nights and working lunches were the norm, thus not allowing me to spend much time at my downtown loft unless it was to catch a few hours of sleep. My mother always warned me to be careful of what I wished for. I was beginning to wonder if making partner was worth the sacrifice of not having a life.

Nevertheless, I did find the time to start dating another lawyer at the firm by the name of Ronald Appier. Ronald was an older brotha who had been married once but had no kids. His desire for a rewarding career meant Ronald spent plenty of time at work as well. Of course, this made for our interaction outside of work sporadic. It was not how I had envisioned our relationship. Still, Ronald was handsome, dashing and ambitious. All the things I thought I wanted in a man. However, there was one thing Ronald was not. He was not Thaddeus. Although I tried not too, I continuously found myself constantly comparing Ronald to Thaddeus. I was attracted to Ronald, yet he did not make me feel the way Thaddeus made me feel.

I heard about Thaddeus' mother passing away from Lisa. She called and informed me of Thaddeus mother's death. Although, I was no longer with Thaddeus I wanted to send him something to express my condolences. Since I was living in Chicago, I wondered if simply showing up at his mother's funeral service was a good idea. I had not spoken to Thaddeus since the night I had asked him to leave my house. Keeping that in mind, I concluded showing up at his mama's funeral would be rather bold of me. In the end I settled on sending Thaddeus a card…. It seemed appropriate.

Marcus and Lisa drove down to Chicago from Minneapolis a day before Thaddeus mother's funeral service. Lisa came over and visited while Marcus comforted Thaddeus. Lisa informed me Darius intended to show up as well, except he was planning on arriving in Chicago the day of the funeral. Of course, Lisa told me how Thaddeus was holding up as well as his constant asking about me to Marcus. I admit that made me feel good. I really wanted to talk to Thaddeus. I wanted to tell him how sorry I was to hear of his mother dying but I also wanted to clear the air between us. I wanted to bring some sense of closure to our past.

Marcus and Lisa left town immediately following the funeral. So there really was not a lot of time for Lisa and I to catch up. A heavy caseload back at Grimble & Kline was calling her back to Minneapolis. Lisa confessed to me that life at Grimble & Kline was not the same since I had left. To hear her say I was missed made me feel good because I missed Lisa and Gloria terribly, even if they occasionally got on my nerves. Although, I could pick up the phone and talk to them it was not the same as being there with them and sharing in that sisterly bond. I missed sitting around with them gossiping over a cup of coffee.

I had met a few sistahs in Chicago, however none of them were women I could call my girls. I think a lot of it had to do with the fact every woman I met was single. Single women, no matter what color, will act cordial and friendly to each other until a man enters the picture. If a man enters the picture single women become down right catty. I guess a single black woman from out of town treading on already staked out territory did not sit too well with some of the sistahs I met. On several occasions I thought about calling Althea, but decided against it since Thaddeus and I were not together. It made for an awkward situation between her and I if we hung out together, especially if I was no longer dating her brother. Regardless of my lack of friends and my own selfish desire to see Lisa and Gloria on a regular basis Lisa and I both knew moving to Chicago and taking the job a Henderson & Hobbs was the best thing for my career. However, I was beginning to question if it was the best thing for my love life.

A week had passed since Lisa and Marcus left and I was contemplating how I could "accidentally" bump into Thaddeus. I had conferred with Lisa and Gloria about my wish to see Thaddeus once again and their advice to me was to call him. Of course, I could have done that but I was not sure if I wanted to pursue the direct route. However, I was pretty much forced to settle on such an approach when I realized my chances of happening upon Thaddeus in such a large city as Chicago were slim.

Then one late September afternoon, I decided to get out and enjoy the Indian summer Chicago was being blessed with before winter came rushing in off Lake Michigan. I remember walking by a small sub shop on Jackson Avenue when I noticed inside—amongst the lunchtime crowd—Thaddeus. It was hard for me to believe, but there he was. It is hard not to notice Thaddeus. To me, he always seemed to stand out.

It was obvious Thaddeus was there with colleagues from work, still when he saw me standing in the door way his co-workers no longer seemed to matter. He called me over to where he was waiting in line. I really had no intentions of eating at that sub shop that day but when Thaddeus insisted I join him for lunch I could not resist. After buying our hoagies, Thaddeus' colleagues took their leave while Thaddeus and I made ourselves comfortable. I told myself to treat our conversation that afternoon as nothing more than two old friends chit chatting over lunch. I did not want to place myself in a situation were my heart longed for Thaddeus again.

Thaddeus and I sat down at a small booth. It was nice to enjoy that waning day of summer with Thaddeus. Although I had warned myself not to get drawn back into this man, I could feel my heart being drawn back into the comfortable groove Thaddeus and I had shared before he abruptly put an end to our budding relationship. While I sat there eating lunch with him it felt as if we had not missed a beat. I told Thaddeus how sorry I was to hear of his mother's passing and he thanked me. I could tell the pain from his mother's death was still fresh.

I missed Thaddeus. I can't deny it. Despite this fact, despite how natural it felt being with him, my heart could not get past the pain he had caused me.

When we parted ways that afternoon Thaddeus said to me, "Maybe, I'll see you again."

I remember smiling. "Maybe."

For three days straight, I returned to Mr. Submarine during lunch in hopes of seeing Thaddeus. Just like our first night out at the pizzeria, we had forgotten to exchange phone numbers. Of course, I could of called Lisa or even Chicago National if I really wanted Thaddeus' number, however I did not want to do that…not just yet. However, I knew it would be just my luck that when I returned to the sub shop those three days in September Thaddeus would not be there. I called Lisa and asked for her opinion on how I should handle my feelings for Thaddeus without getting drawn in and possibly leaving myself vulnerable again.

What Lisa said to me really made sense. "Love is not perfect, Ivy. Take it from me love is never easy. It takes work and constant vigilance. Go to him. It's obvious you're in love with the man and from the sounds of it he is still in love with you.

"Go to him girl and work it out. I'm tired of hearing you mope around pretending as if everything is okay."

I was still in love with Thaddeus and I knew it. But I fought it with every bit of my soul. I did not want to let myself fall back in love with this man. Yet, I could not resist wanting to see him. Thaddeus made my heart sing. So, the following Friday I went down to the sub shop one last time to look for Thaddeus. To my surprise he was there…alone.

Thaddeus sat at the same table we had occupied three days before. He appeared to be waiting for someone or something. Even if that was the case, I was not going to let something else ruin the opportunity presented to me. I ordered myself a salad before nonchalantly coming to his table and asking, "May I sit down?" When he saw me standing there Thaddeus' face lit up. His smile seemed to beam. I was flattered to know I had such an affect on him. Thaddeus insisted that I join him and I did not hesitate. Once again, I could feel his tug upon my heart.

After we ate lunch that Friday, Thaddeus insisted that he walk me back to my office. When we reached the foyer of my building, Thaddeus grabbed my hand. He held my hand as if he was afraid to let go. He looked into my eyes and said, "Ivy, I know I have not always done right by you. I know I've made some mistakes and I apologize…. I also know that I love you and I want to be with you and only you. No woman makes me feel the way you do. I don't want to be with none of these women out here because I'm in love with you. I want no other woman but you…. That is if you'll have me?"

"I don't know Thaddeus."

"At least think about it…. Here this is where you can reach me…Call me." Thaddeus placed a piece of paper in my hand with his home, cell and work phone numbers scribbled on it.

"I suggest you use my cell phone if you do decide to call me. It is the best way for you to get in touch with me…Call me Ivy, because if you don't I'll be out here everyday in front of your building waiting for you to change your mind."

I could not help but smile. I took the piece of paper. "I'll have to think about it Thaddeus."

"You do that."

As we went our separate ways, a part of me wanted to call him back. A piece of me wanted to tell him that I loved him—that I had never stopped loving him. Something my mother said I should have done a long time ago. I wanted to hear him promise to me there would no longer be any more games and that I would be the sole keeper of his heart and no one else. But for some reason I did not cry out. Instead, I watched him go.

It never bothered me that Thaddeus had dated a white woman. Well, that's not totally true. It did bother me a little bit. However, to me it never mattered as much as simply having Thaddeus back in my arms. I longed for the way Thaddeus looked at me. Yet, a part of me still could not let go of the pain he had caused me the first time around.

I spent most of that Friday afternoon in my office digesting what Thaddeus had said. I daydreamed about the first time I saw him standing in my living room. I recollected the nights we danced until our feet got sore, intimate conversations, and nights filled with passionate lovemaking. I could not help but yearn to have those wonderful moments back. However with those same memories came the possibility of reliving the heartache as well.

I wanted to call Thaddeus. My heart wanted me to call Thaddeus.

Every time I felt my hand inching towards the telephone my mind told me "no." I mean I had to think realistically about this. There was a chance Thaddeus might be having another child. I had a hard enough time adjusting to the fact that Stephanie would forever be a fixture in Thaddeus' life if the two of us became serious. I did not know if I could accept another woman with some emotional tie to him. Despite all of this, I still found it hard to resist picking up the phone.

I managed to fight the urge to call Thaddeus Friday. However, Saturday was a different story. Several times, I picked up the receiver and proceeded to dial his number only to hang up the phone before it could ring. The only thing that stopped me from calling Thaddeus was that my heart had yet to clear the matter with my head. My mind was having a hard time of letting go of the past.

Besides, I had to ask myself what about Ronald? How did I handle my relationship with him now that Thaddeus beckoned to be back in my life?

I was scared. Despite that fact, I sat there Saturday next to the telephone with my hand resting uncomfortably on the receiver in thought.

Did I really want to call Thaddeus? Did I want to journey back down this road with him again? Was I ready to forgive?

Whether I was ready or not I picked up the telephone and dialed Thaddeus' number.

Thaddeus—Ready to Give Love Another Chance

Once I hung up the phone with James I woke up Little T, threw a few clothes for both of us to wear into a duffel bag, got in the car and headed to Chicago. The entire drive home I did not want to believe Mama's condition was as bad as James made it out to be. A part of me wanted to believe that James was over reacting. I had just seen my mother two weeks ago and she seemed fine. It was difficult for me to imagine the woman who had always been the tower of strength in our family had suddenly taken ill. I know everyone grows old, yet I had envisioned my mother always being there for me. Yet, listening to James it appeared as if my mother's health had deteriorated rapidly. After so many years of James, Althea and I leaning on Mama for support, we were now called upon to be there for her. Mentally this was a hard adjustment for me to make.

When I arrived in Chicago, I drove Little T directly to Stephanie parents' house in Evanston. I did not feel it was appropriate to bring Little T around Mama just yet. After dropping off Little T, I headed over to the hospital to be by my mother's side. By the number of grieving relatives and friends packed into the tiny waiting area I was glad I had decided to take Little T to his grand-parents. Even for me the circumstances relating to Mama's condition was a bit overwhelming. I could only imagine what it would have felt like for a young child to deal with such emotions.

Due to her dire condition Mama was placed in intensive care, thus limiting those who could visit her down to only immediate family. The sorrowful expression on James and Althea's face when I entered Mama's room did nothing to ease my fears. It was obvious this sudden turn of events had taken its toll on all of us. The sight of my mother laying in bed with tubes branching from her body and the annoying mechanized sound of the respirator frightened me. I became so overcome with grief I could not control my emotions. So, I sat at my mother's bedside and wept like a baby.

It had been a long time since I had cried the way I did the day I saw my mother lying in that hospital bed. I think I needed to cry for more reasons than one. I think I had kept so many emotions pent up inside of me since the day Stephanie and I decided to get a divorce. Yet, I ignored them. I tried to sup-press them. Seeing Mama in such condition broke down the wall I had built around my heart and forced me to confront my pain. The tears I spilled that day were long overdue. Following my out pouring of emotions, I was able to let go all of the emotional baggage that had been holding me back and focus my efforts on doing everything possible to see my mother through her illness.

I kept a constant vigil over my mother. Often, I was amazed at how the human condition could deteriorate virtually over night. When Little T and I had left my mother a little more than two weeks ago she appeared as healthy as can be. Yet as I sat there next to her she appeared to merely be a shell of her former self. She had become frail, a far cry from the woman I recognized. I hated to think about it but I knew a very uncomfortable but necessary conversation needed to take place between James, Althea, and I. There were plenty of decisions that needed to be made in regards to Mama's care as well as what needed to be done in case she did not make it. It was a very painful conversation neither one of us wanted to have, however, it was necessary.

For three days I practically lived at my mother's bedside. Often James, Althea, and I switched off tending to our mother while the other took a catnap or went home to wash up and put on fresh clothes. Despite monitoring Mama in platoon shifts during the day, I refused to leave her side at night. So, every night I stayed with her. On occasion James and Althea joined me throughout the night. However for the majority of those three days, I spent the night with Mama alone. The silence that engulfed the hospital after visiting hours was unnerving. I attempted to break the maddening monotony by watching T.V. but that did nothing more than delay the inevitable silence. Sometimes I found myself staring out of the window like the little boy who use to steal away to his bedroom to gaze at the countless stars in the sky in search of his father. Only in that hospital room I searched the heavens for a sign that gave me hope my mother was going to make it. Unfortunately, that sign never came.

Thursday morning, the fourth day of my mother's stay in intensive care, I was awaken from my sleep to find my mother staring at me. Actually, she appeared to be staring through me. It was like she was looking at something in the distance. The sight of her propped up in her bed gazing into space scared me. In fact, I thought I might have been dreaming. When I realized I was indeed awake I hurried to her side.

Still, groggy and fighting back tears I managed a few words. "Hi Mama?" Mama's eyes grew wide and she tried her best to smile. "You've given us quite a scare. James and Althea should be here in a little bit. They will be glad to see you awake."

My mother's cloudy, almost milky, eyes that had sunken into the recesses of their sockets appeared to look beyond me. Her lips quivered like she wanted to speak but she was too weak to say the words. So I came closer.

"I'm sorry Mama, I can't hear you."

I remember my mother swallowed hard before saying four words to me I will never forget. "I missed you Raymond."

For a brief moment I thought my mother made a simple slip of the tongue and called me by my father's name. Yet as she gazed earnestly out into space I realized she intended to utter my father's name.

"Mama, its me Thaddeus?" I knew by the glazed, distant, look in her eyes that my words did not register with her. I grew concerned. "Mama, I'm going to get the nurse. I think they need to know you are awake. I'll be right back, okay." Once again Mama tried to smile.

I hurried out to the nurse's station and promptly returned with a nurse to my mother's room. Yet, back in the room the nurse and I found my mother fast asleep. When I told the nurse of what transpired, the nurse informed me it was not uncommon for patients under sedation to hallucinate.

When James and Althea arrived that morning I informed them of Mama's episode. I did not tell them what she had said because I still did not know what to make of her remark myself. Still, we regarded Mama's moment of consciousness as a good sign. After updating James and Althea about the morning's events, I went to Mama's house to shower and change clothes. After cleaning up and grabbing a bite to eat—I detested hospital cafeteria food—I prepared to rush out the door to join James and Althea at the hospital when I noticed my parents wedding picture sitting on the mantel. I must have passed that picture a hundred times before and never really paid it much attention. Nevertheless, that day the picture caught my eye and I saw it in a different light.

In that picture I saw my mother and father embarking on a life together filled with uncertainty and only their vows of love to comfort one another. At that time they had nothing. They were flat broke, living in a one bedroom flat and expecting their first child. For some reason at that moment, on that day, my parents wedding picture spoke volumes to me. It became crystal clear to me why my mother never remarried. In my mother's young eyes staring out towards me I could see the power of love that moved inside of her like the flutter of a butterfly's wings upon her heart. Mama had pledged her heart, body and soul to one man…my father, Raymond Brown. It was within her eyes I saw she had pledged her life. I could see the same undeterred love burning within in my father's eyes. They were in love. Not even death itself would be able to extinguish their love.

A love like my parent's is eternal. Very seldom do people realize they've had such a love until it is gone. However, my parents seemed to realize what they had and decided to grab a hold of it the day they said, "I do." Despite my father being struck down, my mother's love for him never wavered and my father's love for her never abandoned her. His undying love for her lived on in James, Althea and I. She saw in our faces and the faces of her grandchildren the never-ending love my father had for her. He never stopped loving her. Despite not being able to touch her physically, my father lived on through his children and his grandchildren in spirit.

While I stared at that photograph I realized the riddle I referred to as love had allowed me to unlock a small piece of its mystery. It was up to me to do with the secret as I wished.

When I returned to the hospital, I sensed something wasn't right. I saw the hospital counselor consoling family members in the waiting room. I looked into Althea's eyes as I walked to Mama's room and I knew. Mama was gone. No one needed to tell me. Still I walked on to my mother's room, hoping to see her one last time and tell her good-bye. I wanted to tell her I understood. I wanted to tell her I knew my father had called her up to him that day. However, before I could reach my mother's hospital room James stopped me. Pain was etched on his face. While James struggled to tell me Mama had passed away a sense of relief, not grief, passed through me. Although, I shed tears that morning I was not sadden by the fact my mother had passed away. Honestly, I felt happy. My mother had found her star that morning.... She had found my father.

Five days after my mother's passing, James, Althea and I laid our mother, Mabel Brown, to rest. I was touched by the out pouring of fellowship and love for our mother from family and friends. The shear number of people our mother touched was mind blowing. I was proud to say I was her son.

Lisa and Marcus traveled from Minneapolis to attend the funeral. Even Darius and Belinda made the trip. I was shocked to see Darius bring Belinda along. Even Stephanie and her parents attended the funeral services. I think my mother would have been surprised to see how many people truly adored her.

Often I sit back and reminisce about the day my mother called out to my father. Contrary to what the nurse said, I do not believe Mama was hallucinat-ing that morning. Instead, I believe my father was there in that hospital room with us that morning, eagerly awaiting for my mother to join him. My mother was so overjoyed with the thought of rejoining my father she could not help put call out to him. The only regret I have was that I was not able to share in her vision. I've found some solace in Mama's passing by believing that she has indeed been reunited with my father.

The days following Mama's funeral I grieved and I in turn began to heal. I bought a telescope and spent my nights in the bedroom I shared with my brother growing up gazing out the window at the stars with my son. For Little T it was something new...something fascinating. He marveled at being able to see the craters on the moon and distant stars. For me it was pleasing for a totally different reason. I silently hoped I would see a fleeting glimpse of my mother and father in the flash of shooting star or the flickering of a distant sun. Despite my age, the kid in me lived on. A piece of me wanted to cling to something that assured me the pain experienced in life led to happiness.

Besides stargazing, I spent the majority of my days after Mama's death with Althea and James. Although it was difficult for us to come to grips with a world minus Mama, I got the sense we would make it through. It was going to be difficult at times but I was certain over time we would manage. The sound of laughter that still sprung forth from us whenever we got together gave me reassurance time would heal our wounds. All we had to do was believe and love each other.

The passing of my mother made me extra thankful that I had got the job at Chicago National. I seriously doubted I could've returned to Minneapolis to stay. I did not want to be away from my family anymore. I needed to be near them. So, the fifth day following my mother's funeral I decided it was time for me to head back to Minneapolis and close that chapter of my life. I left Little T in Chicago with Althea while I went back to the Twin Cities and gathered up the rest of our belongings. I knew the sooner I got to Minneapolis, the sooner I could get back home to Chicago and my family.

I had been back in the Twin Cities no longer than three hours and had just begun packing when I received a frantic call from Belinda. I was curious as to what made her call me, however that did not matter when I was able to get her to calm down and tell me what was wrong.

"Darius has been shot!" Belinda screamed. The blood in my veins seemed to curdle as she screamed those words into my ear. The last two weeks of my life had already been mentally and physically taxing. I didn't need Darius' brand of drama adding to it.

"What do you mean 'Darius has been shot'?"

"I mean exactly that Thaddeus! I was with him when some psychotic woman came up to us outside of his apartment complex and began screaming about how he was cheating on her before she took out a gun and started shooting!"

It was obvious Belinda was upset. I was not going to get a clear explanation of the events that led up to Darius being shot from her. "Where is he at?" I asked, calmly.

"Hennepin County Medical Center!"

"Okay, I'm on my way."

As soon as I hung up the phone with Belinda I called Marcus and relayed Belinda's message on to him. I could have waited for Marcus and we could have gone to the hospital together, yet the Hennepin County Medical Center was only a couple of blocks from my condo. So, I assured Marcus I would meet him there. When I arrived at the emergency ward I found Belinda being questioned by police officers. Erin was trying desperately to console Belinda while the police questioned her, however it did not seem to be working. Up until that point, I had not spoken to Erin for close to three weeks. We managed to force a brief "hello" but that was it.

It did not take long for Marcus to show up at the hospital. However, Marcus, Erin and I still had to wait until the police were done questioning Belinda before we could find out exactly how Darius ended up in the hospital. Belinda told us how the two of them, Darius and her, had gone out for dinner and was returning to Darius' apartment at the end of the night when a crazy woman came out of no where screaming that Darius was cheating on her. From Belinda's account an exchange of words between Darius, Belinda and the lady ensued just before the woman pulled out a gun and started shooting at Belinda and Darius. Belinda was fortunate to avoid being hit by taking cover behind a car, Darius on the other hand was hit twice in the behind as he ran. I know Darius being shot was no laughing matter but I could picture Darius running for his life while he left Belinda behind to fend for herself. Darius did not care about nobody except himself.

Now, the number of women that might want to take a pot shot at Darius was too many to even take a guess. Darius had dogged so many women out in his life, the question of what woman would want to shoot him and why was irrelevant. The correct question to ask was which one? Fortunately, there was no need for us to guess because the police had apprehended Raquel a few blocks away from the shooting with the gun still in her possession. Darius had mentioned to me in passing while in Chicago for my mother's funeral how he had to place a restraining order against Raquel because she had begun harassing him. However, in my state of mind at the time I really did not pay him any attention. For all that talk Darius did about how freaky bisexual women were it appeared like they were also crazy…at least in Raquel's case. I was just glad the police had Raquel in custody and Darius was all right. Raquel could have easily shot Darius in the kidneys or the spine instead of the butt and that wouldn't have been a laughing matter.

The doctor came into the waiting area and informed us Darius' wounds were superficial and that he expected Darius to have a speedy recovery. He intended to release Darius that night, however, he did inform us his behind would be tender for a few days and due to the soreness he may have some difficulty sitting. After the doctor had briefed us we were allowed to see Darius. I will never forget the sight of Darius' butt hiked up in the air when we entered his hospital room. Marcus and I had a difficult time trying to contain our laughter. Of course, Darius did not see anything funny.

Once it was apparent Darius was going to be fine, I returned home and spent the remainder of the night and most of the following morning packing. It was impossible for me to try and sell my condo in the weeks leading up to my departure. After a while I gave up trying to sell the place and simply decided to rent it out instead to a newlywed couple. Marcus had promised he would manage the condo in my absence, which made me feel better about renting it out to strangers.

The following evening when Erin called I was still in the midst of packing. Although we were cordial to each other the night before at the hospital, I did not expect to speak to her again. When Erin asked if she could come over I was surprised but did not protest. Besides, there were a few things I wanted to talk to her about before I left.

I felt a little awkward seeing Erin standing at my door. I don't know if that had anything to do with the way we left things between us the last time we saw each other. It was hard to tell. I sensed there were things both of us wanted to say, but we did not know where to start. After giving it some thought I asked Erin to stay the night. I wanted to feel close to her one last time. There was a possibility I may never see her again. It took some time but after a while I finally felt comfortable enough to talk with her about my mother. I think I rambled on and on about Mama for the majority of the night. I guess talking about Mama only gave me the courage to talk to Erin about what was really troubling me when it came to our relationship. The abortion. Although the conversation was difficult at times, discussing my feelings relating to Erin's pregnancy and subsequent abortion was necessary for me. I harbored so many feelings of guilt for the role I played. Judging by Erin's reaction to my confession, she was burdened by some of her own guilt. Even though there was plenty of pain and grief amongst the two of us, I think both of us felt a little bit better once we talked about it. We ultimately ended that night in each other's arms.

The next morning, I awoke and fixed us breakfast from the remaining food I had in my refrigerator. Immediately after eating I began stowing away my belongings into boxes. I planned on arriving in Chicago the following evening so I needed to pick up the pace. At first Erin just watched, she even helped me pack a couple of things in boxes. However, after she watched me began to crate and box more and more personal belongings she seemed confused.

"If you ask me from the looks of it you are going back to Chicago for more than a couple of days," she stated.

"I am...I'm moving back to Chicago for good." I could see the force of my words hit her so hard they almost knocked the wind out of her. "You didn't know did you? I thought you knew."

"No, I didn't know."

Erin tried to play like she was not disturbed by the news, but I could see my words stung. I watched as Erin painfully sought for an excuse to leave right away. I did not know what I could say to ease her pain. Instead, I simply watched her leave with a hurried good-bye.

Later on Marcus and Darius came over to help me finish with the packing. The movers were going to be there in the morning so I wanted to finish up packing everything away that night. Due to the fact his rear-end was still tender Darius did more standing around and talking than actual packing. Despite his inability to do much of anything other than watch I was glad Darius had came over. Just to sit around and talk shit with Marcus and Darius was all I needed to lift my spirits. I was saddened by the fact I was leaving them. It would be their camaraderie and friendship I would miss the most upon my return back home.

After we had squared everything away into boxes, we reminisced about the good times we shared together. It hurt me to imagine our trio breaking up. It hurt even more to know I was the reason for us splitting apart. Darius and Marcus were my closest friends and we had shared many memorable times together. I loved them like brothers.

Even though, that was not going to be the last time the three of us would see each other I did know the dynamics of our friendship would change once I moved to Chicago. We would not stop being friends. It was just that time and distance takes its toll on a relationship. So, that evening I soaked up our friendship and committed the love we shared for each other to memory.

The following morning the movers showed up bright and early. By the afternoon the condominium was empty, the boxes, my furniture, everything was gone. My car was jam packed with a few personal items I wanted to take with me. I was ready to hit the road. However, before I could get on the highway and head towards Chicago I received a surprise visitor.

Seeing Erin standing at my door one last time caused a rush of emotions to sweep over me. In some regards, I was glad she had come to see me off. I wanted to see her one last time as well. Yet, I did not know if it was appropriate for me to call her and tell her I wanted to see her after the night before. Talk of the abortion had really upset her. In the course of an hour, Erin tried her best to convince me to stay. Despite her attempts, I think deep down she knew my place was in Chicago. After an emotional good-bye, I got in my car and left Erin and Minneapolis behind.

I truly believe Erin and I could have worked out. Although my insecurities in the beginning made me unable to handle an interracial relationship, in the end I realized race did not matter. The only problem was that I came to this revelation too late. Not until I sat with Erin in Loring Pak did I realize that I had allowed everyone else to define what love meant to me. Because of someone else's idea of love I saw Erin as a white woman…not as a woman. She was just like any other woman searching for love. At times, I wonder what would have become of Erin and I if life had not taken me out of Minneapolis. My life could've been a whole lot different if I had stayed in Minnesota.

My first month back in Chicago, Little T and I lived in my mother's house until I could find a place of my own. Of course, I could have stayed at Mama's house as long as I wanted but being there without Mama felt strange. After a while, I eventually found a townhouse in the Wicker Park/Bucktown area. The location was perfect. I was close to the pubs, clubs and restaurants on and off Milwaukee Avenue. I was only ten minutes away from work in downtown Chicago. The only problem was I had to endure another month and a half at Mama's house before I could close on the townhouse. That wasn't good for it meant I would have to move in the dead of winter, but I could not put relocating off. I couldn't stay in Mama's house for long. There were just too many memories.

Since arriving in Chicago I worked my ass off at Chicago National. Stephanie and I had managed to get Little T enrolled in a private Catholic school close to Wicker Park and for the first time in a long time, I enjoyed my job. I was working with a good group of people, which made being at work pleasurable. Since being back in Chicago, I really did not have much time to do much of anything else but work. Occasionally, I met a lady when I was out having a drink with James but that was about it. The only true date I had was with Stephanie and that was when we got together to work out the logistics of picking up and dropping off Little T for the upcoming school year. It was nice to be back in Chicago where we had family who could assist us whenever our work schedules conflicted with Little T's school activities.

Since the incident with Willard, my relationship with Stephanie had improved dramatically. I think we wondered if the fire still burned between us because we wound up in bed one night. I think at the time, both of us were lonely and were seeking comfort in another. In the end we realized we were better at being friends rather than lovers. Too many things were done and said between us that made reconciliation difficult. After that night the two of us decided to keep our relationship strictly plutonic. Besides, my heart no longer belonged to Stephanie and I knew it. My heart belonged to Ivy.

Since returning home to Chicago I had not seen Ivy at all. Chicago is a big city, so it isn't like I expected to see her. Still a little piece of me hoped I did. Of course, thanks to Marcus I knew where she worked and I could have easily called her if I wanted. However, I did not know where I stood with Ivy. The last time we were together she kicked me out of her townhouse. So to save myself the embarrassment and pain, I decided it was best if I did not call her at all. Yet one Friday afternoon, when I had rushed out to lunch with a few co-workers I got an unexpected surprise.

I was working up against a tight deadline and I had only intended on walking down Jackson Avenue and grabbing something to eat at Mr. Submarine and heading back to the office. That was my intentions until Ivy walked through the door. When I saw Ivy walk into the sub shop everything else became secondary—work no longer mattered. I think my co-workers sensed something between Ivy and I because they left me behind with Ivy at Mr. Submarine.

After Ivy bought her lunch, I convinced her to stay and chat with me. Like the first time we met, time seemed to stand still. For me no one else existed in that restaurant that day but Ivy. It was like we were in there all alone. I was glad the conversation between us was cordial and we parted ways that afternoon on good terms. Even better the subject of Erin was not brought up. Like before it felt like I was having a conversation with an old friend. Even though, I knew I wanted it to be so much more. I could not help but recollect the evening in my apartment after we first made love how I wondered if this woman could be the one to test my faith in love. After sitting in that sub shop I no longer doubted my belief in love or the love I had for her.

After lunch, I couldn't stop thinking about Ivy. I went home that evening wondering if I should call her or back off and just leave it alone. If Ivy and I were meant to be, then fate would bring us together.

Wouldn't it?

I called Marcus to ask for his advice because I knew he would give it to me straight and not feed me a bunch of garbage, which I would most likely hear from Darius. Even though, Darius had suddenly sworn off his playa days and gotten serious about Belinda. I guess getting shot in the ass a couple of times by a deranged, psychotic, woman will help anyone—even Darius—see the light. In fact Darius and Belinda were expecting their first child. Funny, how the world turns. Nevertheless, Darius swears he is not ready for marriage. The funny thing about it...despite being pregnant, Belinda doesn't know if she wants to marry Darius. The whole incident with Raquel had caused Belinda to question Darius' ability to be faithful. No matter what becomes of Darius and Belinda, I am really looking forward to the day when the self-professed pim-pologist is confronted with fatherhood.

"Hello." Marcus said picking up the phone.

"What's up?"

"Nothing. Lisa is driving me crazy. Got me going out at all hours of the night picking up weird stuff she might be craving at the time. This pregnancy mess is for the birds. Why didn't you warn me before I signed up for this?" Marcus complained. Marcus had finally succeeded in getting Lisa pregnant.

"Guess who I saw today?" I baited.

"Let me guess...Ivy."

"Yeah, I saw her at Mr. Submarine. How do you know?" I questioned.

"Oh, just a wild guess?" Marcus replied.

"Anyway, we had lunch and everything was real cool. I don't know if I should call her or simply let it go. What do you think?" I asked.

"What do you want to do?" came Marcus' response.

"I don't need you answering my question with a question. I need your advice."

"Why? I will only be telling you what you already know," Marcus pro-claimed.

"And what might that be?"

"That you should have never messed with that white girl in the first place," Marcus declared.

"Come on Marcus, I'm serious," I said, irritated.

"So am I."

"Please can you just put that aside for a moment and help your boy out," I begged.

Marcus gave a sigh that came off heavy. "Why don't you just tell Ivy how you feel—at least then you can say you tried?"

"Are you sure?"

"What harm is it going to do?"

So, that is what I set out to do. I bought lunch from Mr. Submarine everyday that week in hopes of seeing Ivy. Although, Ivy claimed she frequented the sub shop everyday during lunch after our initial encounter as well, I never saw her. By Friday of that week I was ready to give up. That was until Ivy walked through the door. I was so excited to see Ivy that I could not stop talking. I was scared if I stopped talking she would walk out of Mr. Submarine's and out of my life. I walked Ivy back to her law firm on LaSalle and Financial just so I could spend a few more minutes with her.

While standing in the foyer of her building I decided to pour my heart out to her. "Ivy, I know I have not always done right by you. I know I've made some mistakes and I apologize…. I also know that I love you and I want to be with you and only you. No woman makes me feel the way you do. I don't want to be with none of these women out here because I'm in love with you. I want no other woman but you…. That is if you'll have me? Here is where you can reach me. Call me."

With that said I handed Ivy the piece of paper I had written my work, cell, and home phone number on. I recommended she use my cell number. It was obvious Ivy had her doubts. Nonetheless, I perceived by the tone of her voice as we parted ways that Ivy longed for me too.

As we went our separate ways, I could only hope Ivy would overcome her fears and give me a second chance. All I could do was hope. Once again, she consumed my thoughts. I remember the way she made me laugh and the nights we sat cuddled in front of the television simply enjoying each other's company. I never realized how hard it was to find someone whom I enjoyed spending time with. I had once thought I found it in Stephanie, but Ivy made me realize there was a lot more to love.

By Saturday Ivy still had not called. I know it had only been a day, but I found myself anxiously praying Ivy would call. I was jumpy every time my cell phone ranged. I wanted so desperately for it to be Ivy. I wanted to show her that despite all the drama I had taken her through I was sincere when I told her

I loved her. I knew she had no obligation to give me another chance whatsoever. Still, I hoped she did. All I could do was hope…

Then my cell phone ranged.

"Hello?"

"Hi, it's me…." It was Ivy.

"Hi."

"I was thinking maybe we get together this evening and talk?"

"I would love that."

There was a pause. "Thaddeus?"

"Yeah."

"Do you love me?"

It did not matter if I had told her once before I wanted to tell her again and again. "Yes, I do."

"Then say it Thaddeus…. Say you love me."

"I love you Ivy."

Another pause. "Thaddeus Brown, if you ever make me look like a fool again, I will beat the living shit out of you. Do ya hear me?"

"Loud and clear."

My experience with Erin and Ivy has taught me one thing—love is a gift not a right. I realized love is never easy. Love cannot be taken…it can only be given. I am fortunate to have found love in two very different women at the same time. I know it may surprise people, but I believe what I shared with Erin was love. Love takes on so many different shapes—so many different forms. There are so many people out there in this world in an endless search for what I have been so fortunate to find not once but twice. People, like myself, have been just as stupid to let it slip away never knowing what they had until it was gone…never to enjoy its warm embrace again. However, there are those who are smart enough to catch a hold of love and never let go. My mother and father were such individuals. I am fortunate to be given a second chance at grabbing a hold of love and not letting go.

I've learned…. Love is what it is—love. My mother showed me that love is special. The ties that bind one's heart to another's can endure the test of time. Love knows no boundaries. Sometimes love hurts. However, the amount of joy it brings to those in love is beyond measure. Its inability to not adhere to a preconceived notion or see the shape or color of those in love is its gift. For love is truly blind.

Simply put, love knows only one thing…love.

Group Discussion Questions

1. Does Thaddeus' past (i.e. growing up in a single family home, not having a male role model around while growing up, etc.,) have an effect on the way he approaches and handles his relationships with his son and women?

2. Does Thaddeus' relationship with Ivy and Erin reflect the current dilemmas being faced by couples today?

3. Do you think Thaddeus was justified in questioning his allegiance to black women when he found himself attracted to Erin, or was he simply blowing the situation out of proportion?

4. Why did Erin hesitate in telling her father Thaddeus was black? Why is there a stigma still associated with interracial relationships?

5. Is having a relationship with someone from a different ethnic background difficult? Or is it a misconception society has perpetuated?

6. The characters of Marcus Gowens and Stacy touch on many stereotypical misconceptions about race. Yet is there any truth to either characters summation about race in their dialogue throughout the novel?

7. Do you think Ivy was abandoning black men by contemplating a relationship with men who were not black?

8. Is Thaddeus just as much at fault for not being more inquisitive when he saw the bruises on Little T as Stephanie was for hiding it from him? Why or why not?

9. Should Thaddeus have written that email to Mr. Patterson on Stephanie's behalf? Why?

10. Should Erin have aborted her and Thaddeus' child? Would you have done the same in that given situation?

11. Do you think Thaddeus and Erin had a true chance at developing a lasting relationship?

12. Do you think Ivy should have called Thaddeus in the end? Why?

13. Often we equate love to a deep intimacy between two people. However, what other forms or expressions of love are exhibited in the novel?

About the Author

Love is Never Easy: A Love Story is the follow up novel to P. L. Hampton's debut novel *Picking Chrysanthemum.*

Originally from Seattle, P. L. Hampton currently resides in Minneapolis, where he is a professor teaching Economics and Finance.

Please, visit P. L. Hampton at www.plhampton.com for upcoming events and sneak peaks at soon to be released novels.

If you enjoyed P. L. Hampton's novel *Love is Never Easy: A Love Story*, then read the author's debut novel *Picking Chrysanthemum*.

Visit the author's website at **www.plhampton.com** for author events, excerpts from P. L. Hampton's upcoming novels as well as discussion group questions.

978-0-595-35724-6
0-595-35724-5

Printed in the United States
33008LVS00013B/72